D0401123

scarlet blush...

Blush

What he needed now, what he *craved* from Gus Featherstone was her inner warmth, her female essence. He wanted to know her baby soft skin, her mysterious heat, the curve of her body, the crazy grace of her heart. He hungered for the taste of lips that stumbled over words and sometimes couldn't get them out right. . . . But if he let himself have all of that, or any of it, he might never be able to go back to what he had now, which was nothing. If he had a taste, he would remember what he was missing.

He would die from starvation.

She glanced over her shoulder at him, clearly curious about his intentions. He was down to two choices. He could walk out now and pay the price of denying himself. Or he could stay and get to know the real Gus Featherstone. . . . Either way he would pay.

The pipes rattled above them, and water danced on her shuddering body . . . her beautiful, naked, shuddering body. Just looking at her made him want to tear the place apart.

Hell, she was making up the rules as she went.

He would, too.

Berkley Books by Suzanne Forster

SHAMELESS
COME MIDNIGHT
BLUSH

SUZANNE FORSTER

Blush

BERKLEY BOOKS, NEW YORK

BLUSH

A Berkley Book / published by arrangement with
the author

PRINTING HISTORY
Berkley edition / February 1996

ISBN: 0-425-15188-3

BERKLEY®
Berkley Books are published by The Berkley Publishing Group,
200 Madison Avenue, New York, New York 10016.
BERKLEY and the "B" design
are trademarks belonging to The Berkley Publishing Corporation.

PRINTED IN THE UNITED STATES OF AMERICA

10   9   8   7   6   5   4   3   2   1

Blush

For Terry —
Hug & happy
blushing!

Suzanne
Forster

CHAPTER
1

AN ENORMOUS .357 MAGNUM, AIMED POINT-BLANK BETWEEN her eyes—that was Gus Featherstone's first clue that something had gone awry with her plans. The second was the black ski mask the gunman wore and the terrifying glint in his dark eyes. *Apparently she should have been more specific when she arranged to have herself kidnapped.*

As it happened she'd been curled up on the chaise lounge by the pool, painting her toenails a rather rude shade of pink, when he'd crept up behind her. He must have crept because she hadn't heard a thing, not a hush and squeak of his shoe soles, not even the granular scrape of loose bricks as he crossed the terrace floor. And now the damn sun was so bright, she couldn't even make out the outline of his features. He was nothing more than a gigantic black amoeba against a sizzling white summer sky.

"I can't possibly do this today," she told him, wishing her hands weren't occupied so that she could shade her eyes. It really was exasperating trying to talk to someone you couldn't see. "I'm signing a spokesmodel contract with American Naturals Cosmetics. You have heard of American Naturals, haven't you?"

His silence baffled her. If this was Tuesday, then she most assuredly had a luncheon meeting with the company chairman, the CEO, and the legal flacks to finalize her contract. They were having lunch at Citrus on Melrose. She couldn't have confused something that important, which meant the gunman must have *his* days turned around. The abduction was scheduled for Friday.

She started to tell him that, and then it dawned on her what the problem was. No, dawned didn't begin to do the insight justice. Reality reached out, plucked her up like a child's toy and shook her silly. The kidnapper—this ominous creature in black, from his ski mask to his jumpsuit to his crepe-soled commando boots—had no idea that all of this was a ploy. He hadn't been told anything except where to take her once he'd kidnapped her and how much he'd be paid. He'd either confused the days or intentionally changed the plans, thinking to gain some advantage, and she couldn't inform him of his error without blowing months of preparation and perhaps her entire future.

"*Get up,*" he told her.

The rasped command startled Gus with a strange little thrill. Heavens, the man sounded as if he could grind glass with his teeth.

"Could you hold on just a minute?" She held up the bottle of nail polish and waggled it at him. "I need to screw the top back on." The obscene black thing he was holding to her face made her a little giddy, honestly. It reminded her of a microphone, and she wondered what he would do if she broke out in song. Clearly she'd inhaled too much toluene. Over the years the ritual acts of manicuring and pedicuring had turned her into the equivalent of a nail polish junkie. She'd actually come to love the smell of the stuff, but who knew what it was doing to her gray cells.

"Move!" he ordered. "*Now.*"

"Well, okay, but my toes aren't dry yet." She pretended to be having trouble with the polish top, which in fact, she was, although the man's surliness was beginning to unsettle her. Rob Emory, her fiancé, had made all the arrangements for the kidnapping through some clandestine underground network. He was also her manager, and since he handled other talent besides Gus, she'd wanted him to hire an actor for the job. He'd insisted the kidnapping had to look real, that the media, the law, even her family, would never believe it otherwise, and a publicity-mad actor couldn't be trusted to keep quiet about something like that. All the contracts had been made anonymously, apparently for the protection of everyone involved, much like contract killings were arranged, she imagined.

But she couldn't tell this man any of that.

The sun's brightness brought tears to her eyes. She looked away, heedless of the gun, and saw his reflection in the swimming pool. A blaze of darkness, he flared across the surface of the water like the hooded executioner of a medieval inquisition. A bright corona surrounded him, and the effect was one of a solar eclipse, but the pool's slow ripples distorted his seemingly huge frame, lending movement and fluidity to its sinister strength.

He was more than she'd expected, more than she could ever have imagined. More primitive, more terrifying, more everything. She told herself it was his macabre appearance. She could even see details, and his clothing mystified her. The ski mask was bad enough. She simply couldn't get over the fact that he was dressed in the zipper-front jumpsuit of an auto mechanic, or a fighter pilot . . . or a Mafia hitman.

A blotch of shocking pink splashed her golden brown skin.

Rob had hired a real killer.

Her fiancé had inadvertently employed a hired gun!

"Get rid of that stuff." The Magnum twitched menacingly, indicating the polish.

Gus's pulse beat went liquid and swerved to a steeper pitch. Very carefully she settled the nail polish brush back into its shocking-pink well and screwed the cap on tight, giving it an extra twist. She should have stayed on top of this and insisted on certain precautionary measures instead of yielding to Rob, who openly admitted to having seen every *Rambo* movie twice. If she'd been seeking the services of a kidnapper, she would very specifically have said no assassins, no wet work. She would have made that clear. Why hadn't Rob?

When she looked up next, her vision had adjusted to the light. She could see him now, but it might have been better if she couldn't. Because of his camouflage, the only visible feature was his eyes, which gleamed like those of a dead animal in a lightning storm.

"The gun isn't necessary," she tried to assure him. "Really, it isn't."

"Get up," he snarled. "Get the *fuck* up!"

She jumped like a startled cat, then rose warily. He was taking this job *very* seriously. She was still clutching the bottle of nail polish, but she'd also surreptitiously snatched up a tiny pair of manicure scissors that had been hidden under her leg.

She dropped the polish to distract him, and as it clattered across the bricks, she closed her hand over the scissors, concealing them. She had no other choice. The thong bikini she was wearing didn't have enough material to conceal anything, including most of her.

"Turn around." He issued the command as if he were pulverizing something under his shoe.

His hostility made Gus wonder if he knew of her reputation. The media loved to make her out as difficult, citing the Featherstone family wealth as if it were all the proof required. In the early stages of her career, they'd stuck her with labels like "beautiful brat" and "trust fund baby." Ironically the only trust money she ever saw was a meager monthly allowance, which was the primary reason she'd gone into modeling. And if she had been a smidge detail-oriented where her career was concerned, she was at a loss to understand why that should be held against her. She'd always considered herself to be among the most reasonable of women, even in a crisis.

"Couldn't we talk about this?" she asked him.

He kicked the bottle of polish into the pool, whipped her around so suddenly she lost her balance, and pressed the gun barrel between her naked shoulder blades. Fortunately her closed fist escaped his attention as he drew her hands behind her back and looped her wrists with black electrician's tape.

"Apparently not," she observed.

"One more word," he warned through clenched teeth, "and you'll be sucking cement off the bottom of the pool."

The gun barrel dug into her back, forcing her forward.

"Ouch!" she cried.

Two sharp clicks told her a bullet had been chambered.

"That wasn't a *word*," she explained frantically. "It was a cry of pain!"

Another push caught her off-guard. She fought to keep her balance on the uneven bricks, but with her hands tied behind her it was impossible. She lurched helplessly, stumbled and fell to the rough surface, landing hard on her knees. He might as well have shot her for her reaction. Pain popped and streaked like burning bullets, unleashing both her legendary temper and her tongue.

"Look what you've done!" She reared back and gasped at the oozing lacerations. "Now I've skinned my knees, and I've got a photo shoot tomorrow. For depilatory cream!"

Gus was only getting started, but the tirade died in her throat as she twisted around to glare at him. One of the security team who guarded the Featherstone estate had entered the pool area and he was coming up behind the kidnapper. He must have been hired recently by her stepbrother, Lake, because Gus had never seen the man before. A huge, hulking brute, armed with an automatic weapon, he looked positively lethal.

"I've got an M-16," the guard snarled. "Drop the gun, turn slowly, and kick it to me. *Move*, you sick bastard!"

There was a crackle of light in the kidnapper's eyes that terrified Gus. The dead animal had come to life. All of the malevolence in him seemed to come through his eyes as he lifted his ominous black head and silenced her with a savage glare. She couldn't imagine what he was going to do, but her adrenaline was geysering like shaken champagne, and she was riveted.

"Go inside, ma'am," the guard warned. "Do it now."

But Gus didn't move from the terrace or from her knees. She watched with the same horrified fascination a child would who watches two dogs suddenly turn vicious and attack each other. The kidnapper didn't respond for several seconds, and then, to Gus's complete surprise, he did just as the guard ordered.

He dropped his gun to the bricks, turned, and kicked it hard. As the weapon skipped across the terrace, Gus wondered why it didn't go off. The kidnapper's shoulders had slumped in an attitude of defeat, and she was caught somewhere between relief, disappointment, and disbelief. He hadn't struck her as a man who would give up so easily. He hadn't struck her as a man who could ever give up.

The guard scooped up the gun, all the while watching the kidnapper. A grin wreathed his fleshy face as he rose, the M-16 still trained on his target. He moved to tuck the Magnum in the waistband of his uniform, but something made him hesitate. The gun gleamed in his grip. He scrutinized it and froze. Horror replaced his grin as the weapon exploded with a blinding flash.

Both weapons clattered to the ground as he reared backward, gripping his fist. A guttural howl ripped from his throat. The kidnapper flew at him, a blinding flash of movement as he aimed a kick at the guard's midsection. The bulky man was lifted several feet off the ground. The next kick caught him under the chin and sent him careening backward into a potted palm.

He hit with an impact that cracked the massive pot in two, and then he sprawled to the ground, unconscious.

The sudden eruption of violence had locked Gus in place and left her shaking, but she hadn't moved from her knees through the whole thing. She thought about screaming as the kidnapper scooped up the M-16 and whirled on her, but that's all it was, a thought. No sound could make it through the vise grip of her throat. He slung the weapon's strap over his shoulder and strode to where she was crouched. With one hand he lifted her to her feet and spun her around. His strength was frightening.

"I have an ap-appointment," she whispered hopelessly.

His arm roped her midriff and she was hauled up against a wall of solid muscle. A hot jet of air burned the back of her neck. "You don't get it, do you," he grated. "Your appointment's been canceled. I'm taking you on a little trip."

Gus could feel the act of violence still humming through the man's body, and the raw, animalistic power of it startled her into silence. He was hot and vibrant, breathing with brute force. She'd never experienced anything quite like it, but she had no doubt that he could snap her in two with a flex of his arm if he wanted to. To her profound dismay, she began to tremble. Her own body's natural reaction to the threat of violence was to go limp and shivery. It made her think of the dominance rituals in animals, beta yielding to alpha's superior show of strength. But this wasn't the jungle, and she had to keep her wits about her, or the months of planning that had gone into this kidnapping scheme would be lost. *Everything would be lost.*

She'd always believed that people were too quick to confuse destiny with bad management, and as far as she was concerned, this mess was just one more example of the latter. Clearly there were certain contingencies she and Rob hadn't planned for, like the brute behind her, but what choice did she have other than to cooperate and get the ordeal over with? Once the kidnapper had taken her to the prearranged destination, it would only require a day or so to accomplish what she wanted and then she'd be free. It was the only sensible option.

"How little's this trip?" she wanted to know. "If we're going to be gone overnight, I'd like to pack a bag."

"Don't make me kill you," he warned in an evil whisper. "I'd like that."

"Of course you would," she said under her breath. "Killing women is probably your favorite hobby, after molesting small boys."

He pressed closer, crowding her backside with the heat of his groin. "Killing women *is* my favorite hobby. The only thing I like better is having sex with them once they're dead."

Gus quelled a sound of disgust. He was trying to frighten her! He wasn't going to kill her. He couldn't, not if he wanted to be paid for his trouble. But even so, he was dangerously caught up in this kidnapping thing. *Dangerously.* If only she could tell him that this was a ploy rather than an actual operation, simply a means to an end.

A flash of light from behind brought her head up. It was a moment before she realized what was happening, and then she saw the guard's reflection in the glass of the terrace doors. The man had reared to his feet, a glinting object in his hand.

"He's got a knife!" she cried, stumbling forward. Her wrists strained against the electrician's tape as she fought to keep her balance. The kidnapper had released her, but by the time she got herself turned around, she saw that it was already too late. There was no way to stop the nightmare that was unfolding before her eyes.

The guard lurched toward the kidnapper, brandishing a pair of pruning sheers. "You're dead!" he snarled.

"I don't think so," the other man said softly.

Gus held her breath, expecting the kidnapper to spring into action. Instead, with the icy deliberation of an assassin, he drew a gun from the cargo pocket of his jumpsuit, released what looked like a safety and took deadly aim.

"Not today, anyway," he breathed. His hand kicked slightly up as the gun fired.

"No!" Gus sank to the ground in a huddle. "Oh, God, no!"

The guard reeled backward in shock, caught his hand to his chest, and dropped. He crumpled to the ground in a heap, still clutching the shears.

Gus closed her eyes and began to rock, unable to help herself. *This couldn't be happening. It couldn't be. She had only meant to jolt the family trust officer out of his blind devotion to the status quo, to force Ward McHenry's hand, not that anyone would be hurt. Never that.*

She heard the kidnapper telling her to get up, but she

couldn't. The horror that gripped her had robbed her of all control. Her disbelief was so great she forced herself to open her eyes and look at what she'd seen, certain she must have hallucinated it. But she hadn't. The guard was sprawled on his side not twenty feet from her. The shears lay next to his hand.

"You k-killed him," she whispered, unable to tear her gaze from the fallen man. "He's dead!"

The kidnapper stowed the gun in the pocket of his jumpsuit and came for her. "He'll get over it."

"Get over being *d-dead*?" She stared up at him, horrified, and saw something change in his expression. For a second, unless she was so desperate she imagined it, she saw a flicker of humanity in his eyes, a whisper of something alive. Hope surged in her throat and a terrible weakness enveloped her.

"Please," she implored him, "don't do this. Please—"

"Come on."

He reached for her, but she shrank away. "No!"

"Come on," he repeated, something husky breathing into his tone, perhaps even a trace of concern. He lifted her to her feet, but with far less force then he'd used before. Gus wondered if he might actually be trying to reassure her, and her heart squeezed painfully. But the wild hope that had risen within her died as he turned her away from him.

A blindfold dropped over her eyes.

"What are you *doing*?" she whispered.

Her answer was two powerful arms. He hooked one under her knees, scooped her up like an accident victim, and began to carry her toward the gated entrance of the pool area. Screaming was a distant thought, but it would have taken far more concentration than she possessed. She was vibrating uncontrollably, all through her being, like a quaking, terrified newborn. She felt as if she'd been reduced to that, embryonic terror. By the time he'd settled her on the ground, she'd lost her bearings altogether.

Ignoring her muffled cries, he began to roll her up bodily in something. A rug, she realized. He was rolling her up in an area rug! No, this *couldn't* be happening! She was caught between laughter and sobs, on the ragged edges of hysteria, and that one line kept playing through her mind, a frantic attempt to deny the insanity that seemed to have overtaken her.

This can't be happening.

She felt herself being hoisted high into the air and draped over his shoulder in a fireman's carry. She was on her way to the dry cleaners apparently. Or at least that's how it would look to the neighbors! A gasp burned in her throat, and suddenly in the midst of all the chaos that was short-circuiting her mental processes, one thing made perfect sense. His jumpsuit. It was the uniform of the service industries.

She fought the urge to dissolve in laughter, a chorus of thin, hysterical sobs. She was losing it, and she had to find something to cling to, some thread of reality, no matter how slender. At least she wasn't claustrophobic. She could be thankful for that much, though it didn't make it any easier to breathe as he loaded her into the back of a vehicle she imagined was some kind of van. The weight of the carpet had rendered her completely immobile, and the summer heat made it suffocatingly hot in her mummified state. Apparently he didn't care if she smothered. She didn't even want to think about what condition her still-wet toenails were in.

Hysteria bubbled anew as she imagined the tabloids: "Fashion model found dead in bizarre sexual asphyxiation ritual. Carpet fuzz adhered to her body with shocking-pink nail polish."

She forced her thoughts to the route the van was taking as it roared away from the Featherstone enclave. They were supposed to be going east toward the freeway that would take them into the San Gabriel Mountains, but it seemed as if the kidnapper had turned the other way. She assumed it was him driving because she could hear him speaking on what must have been a car phone. He was telling someone that he didn't like the feel of things.

"Something's gone wrong," he said. "I'm not going to take the rug to the cleaners as planned. I'll be in touch."

The rug? That had to be her. Apparently he'd changed his mind about taking her to the cabin that was supposed to be their destination. He *was* on his way somewhere else. If that was the case, her fiancé might never find them! And what had he meant by that first reference: *Something's gone wrong.*

Gus fought to draw some air into her lungs, but a cold, crushing weight was pressing against her chest. The kidnapping had seemed like a brilliant idea when she'd thought of it, the perfect way to get control of what should have been rightfully hers in any event—the substantial trust fund her stepfather had left her. It wasn't the money that mattered, it had never been that. It was what she planned to do with it.

But now a man was dead or wounded, she didn't know which, and she could barely conceive of either possibility. A shudder swept her, bringing another even more immediate concern. She was going to pass out. The white dots dancing behind her eyelids and the dizzying sickness that washed over her told her she would soon be unable to defend herself in any way. Within moments she would be in the most vulnerable state possible and at the mercy of a man capable of killing without conscience.

If there was any emotion Gus loathed more than fear, it was that one, vulnerability. Her stepchild status in the Featherstone family had exposed her to some terrifying and very inventive abuse by her stepbrother and stepsister. She'd had to armor herself emotionally to survive. She hadn't been able to fight her older siblings, so she'd fought instead to get control of her crippling fears. When she finally triumphed, she'd felt the first startled animal awareness of her own power, the first glimmer of what life could be like for the unafraid. Now it felt as if she were about to be stripped of that vital control, stripped of everything.

Panic squeezed the last breath out of her. It sucked her deeper into the purple waves that were crashing over her. As the undercurrent tugged her down into its infernal funnel, her oxygen-deprived brain betrayed her totally, jumping from one grotesque image to another. Her stepbrother and stepsister were standing over her open grave, and her five-year-old stepniece was sobbing. Bridget! Gus had told the child she would be away for a few days on a photo shoot, knowing the family would shield her from news of the kidnapping. But she could hardly bear to think what would happen to the little girl if she died, the neglect, the emotional isolation. They would probably send her away to school to get her out from under foot.

Gus tried to cry out, but she didn't have the strength.

Her last thought as she went under was of him, the executioner in the black jumpsuit. If he truly was a necrophiliac, if he liked having sex with dead women, what would he do to her while she was unconscious?

CHAPTER
2

GUS STIRRED AWAKE TO THE LOW WHINE OF A POWERFUL EN-
gine and the silken glide of tires on what seemed to be a
highway paved with glass. The purring motion was hypnotic. It lulled her for a moment, but when she opened her
eyes to total darkness, the shock of it brought her hurtling
back to consciousness. A deep breath kept panic at bay
long enough for her to clear her thought processes and as-
sess her situation.

She was still blindfolded and restrained with tape, her
feet now as well as her hands, but she was no longer in the
back of the van or rolled up in a rug. She'd been propped
up on the seat of the cab, and something heavy had been
thrown over her. The blindfold forced her to rely on other
senses, but from what she could tell, the heaviness was covering all of her, including her head, and it had the feel of a
canvas tarpauline.

Her shoulder joints throbbed from the pressure of having
been forced into an unnatural position, and her wrists
burned. An icy draft swirled around her bare feet, and with

so many signals flooding her, she nearly missed the most important one. Another kind of pain was radiating up the inside of her wrist, a tiny arrow of distress, sharp yet persistent. It was different than the burning, more like a needle prick. She squeezed her fist and felt a stabbing sensation that made her gasp. The manicure scissors! She was still clutching them.

It was slow, painstaking work, but within moments, laboring under the concealment of the tarp, she had cut through one band of tape and was working on another. Her progress was hampered by the fear of giving herself away. If the kidnapper was concentrating on the road, perhaps he wouldn't notice the tarp moving. Please let him be on automatic pilot, she thought, wishing upon him that altered state of highway hypnosis that often overtakes drivers on straightaways.

Her incantation held out long enough for her to cut through the second band and discover a third. A moan welled hotly in her throat. She'd thought she was done! Worse, if she didn't hurry she'd be in a heap on the floor of the cab before she could get her wrists free. Her bound limbs had robbed her of leverage, and she was inching down the slick leatherette seat with every little scooch of movement.

She continued doggedly, electrician's tape the scourge of her very existence. He couldn't have used rope? No, he had to be cute. Exploding guns, area rugs, duct tape? This wasn't just a quest for freedom on her part, not anymore, it was a vendetta against modern criminal science. She was going to cut herself loose or die trying.

The scissors jabbed her inner wrist as the van veered to the right. Swallowing a cry of pain, she swayed toward the kidnapper, then toppled to her side as they came to a tire-shredding stop. He must have pulled onto the shoulder, she realized. She could feel the vehicle quivering beneath her and smell the stench of burnt rubber, but they weren't moving and he was strangely silent.

"When you get your hands free," he said finally, his voice low and weary. "Would you let me know?"

"Why?"

"So I can knock you cold to make sure you don't escape."

She let out a sigh that was wild with frustration and then heaved herself upward, trying to get back into some reasonable facsimile of a sitting position. Nothing worked, including pushing off from the floorboards, and finally he put a stop to her thrashing. He gripped her by the shoulders and pushed her upright, much as he would have a fallen telephone pole.

She hated having to accept his help. Worse, in all the commotion the tarp seemed to have dropped off her, leaving her exposed, and the blindfold had slipped down just enough to cover her nose and cut off her air.

She settled back with an exasperated sigh. "Could you at least take this blindfold off so I can breathe?"

"I could," he allowed, "but than I'd have to kill you."

"Oh, funny," she mumbled, but the word stuck in her throat. It was hardly an idle threat considering what he'd already done. She had been trying desperately not to think about the guard. She didn't want to get sucked back into the horror of what had happened, nor did she want to think about the fact that she might have been an unwitting accessory to murder.

He flipped the tarp up around her shoulders, covering her, then pulled the van back onto the road. The car radio blared on next, startling her as he skipped rapidly from one station to another, apparently searching for news of the kidnapping, but never stopping long enough for her to hear any details. Finally he caught a female commentator in the middle of a report.

"One badly shaken security guard was taken to the hospital," the woman was saying, "where he was treated for a dislocated jaw and severe shock. He reported to the police that the kidnapper tricked him with an exploding gun and rendered him unconscious with a tranquilizer bullet. A spokesman for the LAPD reports that the tranquilizer gun used is a highly controversial weapon. It's a brand-new device, still in the research and development stages, and not yet available, even to law enforcement. . . . "

The commentator went on, but Gus didn't hear another word.

A tranquilizer gun? He *hadn't* killed the guard? A man *wasn't* dead and she *wasn't* an accessory? The relief that swept her barely lasted long enough for her to acknowledge it. Her shock at the news was too great. She couldn't believe he'd allowed her to think he'd killed the man in cold blood. She'd been reduced to a sobbing, pleading, gibbering idiot when two words would have calmed her. *Tranquilizer gun.* That's all he would have had to say. The *bastard.*

He'd made her stammer he'd frightened her so badly! The slight speech impediment was one of the legacies of her childhood terrors. She'd had to teach herself to speak all over again in order to conceal it. It mattered little to her now that her breathy, hesitant manner had become part of her trademark style and was one of the more endearing qualities of her public personality. All she could think about was the way he'd humiliated her.

"How could you d-d-do that?" Her fury spiked when she couldn't quite master the word. She wrenched at the remaining strands of tape binding her wrists, pulled one of her hands free, and jerked down her blindfold.

It didn't occur to Gus that her question was absurdly rhetorical, not for one blinking second. It didn't even occur to her that she was taking a terrible risk. She might have her sight back, but her moral outrage and her passion for justice had blinded her to the fact that she was dealing with a killer, a man capable of almost anything.

"How could you let me think he was dead?" she demanded, struggling to untie the wretched blindfold and rid herself of it altogether. "What kind of monster are you?"

"What the hell are you doing?" The van veered into the other lane as he threw out a hand to block her from whatever she might be about to do.

Gus didn't have a chance to do anything besides grab for the dashboard to steady herself. They were all over the road! Fortunately the highway was deserted as he got control of the vehicle and pulled it to the shoulder. It was also lucky the windows were up, because the dust that swirled up from the tires enveloped them like a mushroom cloud.

Once they'd come to a complete stop, and Gus had caught her breath, she hazarded a glance at him. She found herself blinking into his slitty-eyed glare, and as the icy warning in his eyes registered, it hit her like a thunderbolt what she'd done. She had looked upon the wizard. The hostage had seen her captor's face and now he was going to kill her.

"I didn't see anything!" she cried, wrenching around the other way. She hadn't, certainly not enough to identify him. But she doubted he was going to take her word for it.

"I should have let you smother in that rug," he said, his breath rasping softly with the declaration. "Back where you were. On the seat. Facedown. *Now*."

Gus knew better than to fight him. She released an unsteady sigh as she allowed him to reclaim her shoulders and put her back where she'd been. She assumed he was going to knock her cold enough to give her a lasting case of amnesia. Instead, he produced something that must have been a knife, bent over her body and began to cut away the rest of the electrician's tape. When he was done, her hands and feet were free, she'd been relieved of the manicure scissors, and her blindfold was a thing of the past.

She rubbed her tender wrists and wiggled her bare feet to get the blood flowing. Thanking him didn't seem appropriate given that he'd tied her up in the first place and his next move might be cold-blooded murder. During the one or two minutes she'd spent at Vassar, before she'd bailed out of college to seek her fortunes elsewhere, she'd come to the conclusion that there were two kinds of male intelligence—frontal and animal. Blends were a rarity. Most guys were either computers with legs or testosterone-fueled power tools, and this guy was definitely Door Number Two. It didn't seem possible that somewhere in his primitive response system lurked a truly humanitarian impulse. But she could hope.

Gooseflesh rippled her thighs, reminding her that the tarp had fallen to the floor and she was wearing a bikini. She gathered it up and covered herself, careful not to look at him, even though she sensed he was looking at her. He was there in her periphery, a dark energy field, and she could feel the weight of his appraisal. But she didn't sense the same heated interest she was used to from the opposite sex. There was a coldness to his observation, as if he had little use for women like her, beautiful or otherwise, naked or otherwise.

Women like her? she thought. What did that mean?

His van was a black Chevy Blazer, and as he pulled it back onto the highway, she realized they were somewhere in the desert. The rolling, salmon-colored hills in the distance were surprisingly beautiful, yet there was nothing in between but miles and miles of scorched clay, studded with spiny cacti and blue-gray sagebrush. It looked like a desolate outpost on the moon.

If this was the Mojave, and she suspected it was, temperatures routinely soared to one hundred and twenty degrees Fahrenheit in the shade. She'd read somewhere that Death Valley was the hottest place on earth during the summer, and this was dead-center July. He'd chosen well, she realized with a growing sense of despair. The infernal heat and total isolation would make escape impossible.

Rippling gooseflesh prompted her to pull the tarp tighter around her. The van's air-conditioning was blowing like a gale, which explained the draft on her feet. But she couldn't blame her sudden desire to tremble on that, and she was reluctant to call it fear, simply because she loathed the emotion above all others, and she didn't want to give him that much credit.

Still, her trembling hands wouldn't let her deny that something was very wrong as the Chevy Blazer peeled down the lonely highway toward oblivion, leaving black tracks on the asphalt and civilization in the dust. It was shock, she told herself. It had to be that. She was suffering shock.

"Where are we going?" she asked him, staring out the

window. She had just discovered that the tarp was actually a man's huge raincoat, and since it was conveniently inside-out, she'd tucked her hands into the pockets, not wanting to expose her unsteadiness.

"To a spa in the desert." His monotone turned faintly sardonic as he added, "You'll love it."

As they sped down the road, a solution occurred to Gus. She might be able to buy him off by offering him more money than he'd been promised. Since everyone would think she'd been kidnapped anyway, it was possible she and Rob could still follow through with their plans. It would be risky. She was close to grabbing the brass ring and reluctant to do anything to jeopardize that, but the kidnapping scheme had already gone awry.

She curled her fingers into her palms. "If I made it worth your while, would you let me go?"

"What makes you think you've got anything worth my while?"

Subtle he wasn't. "I was talking about money."

"I know. I wasn't."

"Then what do want?" She felt a twinge of pain beneath her breast as she sank deeper into the coat. Absently she wondered if she'd sprained something or cracked a rib.

"Not that either," he assured her.

The edge in his voice made her turn, and at the very moment she did, he settled back in the seat and did the same thing. She met his eyes briefly, sharply. She'd only meant to glance at him, just a tilt of her chin to catch his expression, but something happened when he looked her way, something that so rarely happened to Gus, she couldn't remember the last time.

He blew her off!

Clearly in no hurry, he held her startled gaze with the precision of a surgical laser, freezing her alive with the wintry coldness she'd sensed. Seeming satisfied that he'd found nothing of interest, he checked out the rest of her, dismissed her with a slanted eyebrow, and turned back to the road.

She was too astonished to be insulted. Still, he'd done it

so contemptuously, she felt as if he'd cut her off at the knees and left her bleeding. *Who was this guy? No man had ever looked at her that way.*

God, if she'd thought her hands were shaking before!

She could identify him now, and with or without his mask, he was the phantom assailant of every woman's nightmares, the brutal street tough you'd least want to meet in a dark alley. He looked frighteningly jaded, yet wildly attractive. His hair was black, his features harsh, but his face was so beautifully shaded with secrets, it was all she could do not to ask him how many people he had actually murdered.

His blue-black eyes had tiny, glinting diamonds at their center. But it was his voice that had awakened her to his inner state of mind. He spoke in a monotone that was low and burnt out, as dead to life as the hostile terrain that stretched before them. It had made her think of the desert, a wilderness with everything of value scorched out of it, with nothing left but the ashes.

Her theory about two kinds of men had been shortsighted where he was concerned. She saw that immediately. This one was in another category altogether, the quiet-but-deadly type that exists on the outlaw fringes of civilization. She'd come across the term in a magazine article about movie villains, and it fit her kidnapper to perfection. He looked capable of killing, of sex with the dead . . . of anything.

Her heart was racing as fast as her thoughts, but she refused to let it rattle her this time. When she was anxious or just needed to think, she often found herself clicking her fingernails against her teeth. It was an irritating, nervous habit at best, and she resisted the impulse now, although it was a powerful one. Instead, she calmed herself with a couple of deep breaths and some mental tough talk.

She was forgetting what was at stake. Deadly or not, his looks weren't relevant. He'd released her from her bonds, and he must want the money or he wouldn't have taken the job. Therefore, he wasn't going to kill her and feed her to the vultures. And she *was* going to get through this, because everything she'd ever wanted was hanging in the balance—her independence from the Featherstones, a chance at the respect she'd long been denied.

There were only a very few people in Gus's life who had penetrated her formidable emotional barriers. One of them was her deceased stepsister, Jillian, and another was Bridget, Jillian's child, the five-year-old to whom Gus had become reluctantly and hopelessly attached. What Gus wanted as much as her own independence was the chance to pay tribute to Jillian, and more important, create a legacy for Bridget.

Yes, she thought, almost sadly. It was important, this pipedream of hers. It might be the most important thing she had ever done in her life.

The kidnapper hit the brakes and wheeled the van onto a road that headed straight into the hills. Gus propped her hand against the door, jolted out of her thoughts and acutely aware of the pain just below her breast. Once he'd straightened the car out, she delved under the coat and discovered that one of the bones of her bikini bra top was digging into her rib cage.

A quick adjustment brought some relief, along with the realization that if she could get the raincoat on her body instead of over it, she would feel much more protected. With a glance at him, she began to try to work her way into the huge thing without uncovering herself.

She was still engaged in rearranging herself moments later when she realized that he was watching her. If her heart fluttered and froze for a moment, it was a completely wasted response. She'd thought he might be getting ideas. Foolish of her. She'd even thought she might be arousing his prurient interest. After all, she had aroused lots of that in her time. Even more foolish of her. His reaction was another one of those not-if-you-were-the-last-woman-on-earth looks. And that was the most that could be said for it.

Insulted, she jerked the coat off and wrestled her way into it, not giving a damn what he saw. Once she had the voluminous thing on, she belted it loosely and sat back with a sniff. The damn bra top stabbed her again, but she was

too annoyed to care. Apparently Mr. Quiet-but-Deadly reacted to nothing but death threats. She could have stripped
down to the buff and finished painting her toenails right in
front of him and he wouldn't have blinked an eye.

Something told her she ought to be grateful for that.

Something else told her she wasn't going to be.

"Our Gus, kidnapped?" Lily Featherstone clutched the
neckline of her white satin kimono together and clapped a
hand over her mouth in astonishment. Her stepsister had
been *kidnapped*? Before she could stop herself, she was
gasping with laughter, which was very unlike her.

"Frances—" She addressed the housekeeper with the
same incredulity as she would have had Ed McMahon been
standing on her doorstep, handing her a sweepstakes check.
"You can't be serious! Who would ever be crazy enough to
kidnap Gus? Give the poor, deluded soul a day or two, and
he'll be giving *us* money to take her back."

"She's been kidnapped, all right," Frances Brightly
snapped, clearly displeased at having her news so rudely received.

The Featherstones's housekeeper was a thick, dour
woman who could not have looked more out of place in the
delicate white environs of Lily's spacious bedroom suite,
especially this morning. Sunlight poured through the terrace doors, flooding the alcove that housed Lily's writing
desk, a walnut secretary, and drenching the pansies that
adorned the desktop. Shimmering in jeweled tones of blue
and purple and potted in tiny silver timbales, the flowers
were a passion of Lily's.

"Happened about an hour ago," Frances was saying. "I
found one of those idiot security guards out by the pool
when I got here. Says he was hit by a tranquilizer dart and
knocked unconscious. Says some masked guy took Gus
right off the back terrace by the pool."

"Does Lake know about this?" Lily glanced at the clock
on the fireplace mantel. It was eleven-thirty and her twin
brother always breakfasted at the club on Tuesdays.

"Mr. Featherstone's on his way home, and I don't think

he's going to be pleased when he gets here." Frances looked a little smug now, apparently taking some enjoyment in relaying the bad news. "The guard had already notified the police by the time I arrived. Nothing I could do to stop him. They're out there now, waiting to speak to you."

Lily was no longer amused. "The police?" She *knew* her brother would not be pleased. The mansion's small security force had strict orders never to involve law enforcement without Lake's okay. There were many reasons, including the problem of leaks to the press, who fed on the misfortunes of others and particularly prominent families like the Featherstones.

"Surprised you didn't hear anything," Frances said, taking careful measure of Lily's attire. "Doesn't look like you've been out."

Lily had taken a potent sleeping pill the night before and hadn't heard anything until Frances's frantic knocking woke her. She'd quickly put on a robe, smoothed her hair, and pretended that she'd been catching up on her correspondence without having bothered to dress. It was no one's business but hers if she occasionally relied on pharmaceuticals to take the edge off. It certainly wasn't a habit, and she didn't want Frances fussing at her.

"Couldn't we put the police off until Lake arrives?" Lily wasn't at all comfortable having to ask for such a favor, mostly because she knew Frances would want to glory in her newfound power a bit before she took the moral low road. "You could make some excuse for me, couldn't you?"

"Lie to the police?" The housekeeper buried her hands in the pockets of her beige bouclé sweater and put her frown muscles to good use, clearly determined to prolong the agony. "I suppose I could tell them you were ill."

"Yes, do that." By now Lily was troubled enough to feel almost ill, but it wasn't out of any concern for Gus's welfare. She'd meant every word she'd said about her stepsister, and she wasn't at all certain that this wasn't another of Gus's stunts. If the Pope had been locked in a room with Augusta Featherstone for more than fifteen minutes, he would have come out of it requiring restraints and a bib for the drool. Gus could take care of herself. Frances was the object of Lily's concern at the moment.

Despite her last name, Frances did *nothing* brightly. The housekeeper was known for her efficiency, if not her placid temperament. A large, stoic woman with lank, graying hair that she washed daily with hand soap and bludgeoned into a thin braid, Frances ran the household with a grim countenance and an iron hand. Lily suspected the family had kept the unpleasant woman on all these years because there was no one brave enough to fire her.

Even now her expression was so sour, Lily had to mentally discipline herself not to apologize. There was little Frances didn't disapprove of, including traipsing around in one's bathrobe at all hours of the morning. Lily had to subdue a smile as she imagined the housekeeper's reeling shock should she ever discover the truth about Lily Featherstone—not the world-class fundraiser and member of the Junior Philharmonic and Junior League—the "other" Lily.

"Thank you, Frances," she said, pleased at how composed she sounded. "If you would just tell whoever wants to speak to me that I'm not well, I'd appreciate it. Explain that it will take me some time to get ready, and then let me know when Lake arrives."

As if in need of further incentives, Frances walked to a laundry basket of Lily's underwear that the housekeeper had hand-washed and left on the dresser the day before. "I don't suppose you've decided about my vacation yet?" She opened a lavender-scented drawer and fussily loaded a pile of white silk panties into it. "I asked for the first two weeks in November, in case you'd forgotten . . . with pay."

Interesting that the woman balked at white lies but not blackmail, Lily thought. "That's all right, Frances," she said, her voice sharpening. "I'll finish the folding. Please do as I asked, would you? And then start lunch? Something light?"

"Lunch?" Frances harumphed. "For how many? This place is crawling with uniforms. Besides, who's going to have an appetite after this mess?"

"Very well then . . . I'm sure you're right."

"My sister and I were going to take a cruise." Another stack of silk panties floated from the basket to the drawer. "Never done that before."

"Oh, all *right*, take the cruise!" Lily would have agreed to anything at this point. She was that anxious to have the housekeeper out of her room. "November just happens to be the opening of the fall art season in London, but Lake and I will plan around you."

As Frances shut the door behind her, Lily let out a pressured sigh and released the satin material she'd been clutching together. There was a mark on her breast, just a faint thing, really, but the shape of it was telling. Frances, with her eagle eye, would undoubtedly have recognized the purplish circle as teeth marks.

Lily touched herself there now, caressingly, and felt her fingers begin to shake. Her whole body was instantly aroused, clutching and aching as if lightning had struck her. God, how could this be happening to her? How had she let herself be reduced to this state of wanton need? She almost didn't want to look in the mirror. It was too painful to see the naked hunger flaring in her gray-green eyes, making them bright with desperation.

She walked to the laundry basket and inhaled the heavy sweetness of lavender as if it could soothe her, but she barely had the control to pick out which panties she would wear. It was frightening that the police were waiting for her, that her stepsister had just been taken at gunpoint, yet all she could think about was him, what he did to her. Even now, as her thoughts returned to the possibility that Gus had been kidnapped, her concern was with how all the turmoil might affect her own situation more than anything else.

Gus was the droplet of rancid oil floating on the crystalline surface of the Featherstone family waters. She had been an embarrassing blight on their existence ever since her disgustingly trashy mother seduced Lake and Lily's father and bludgeoned her way into their lives.

Honestly, Lily thought, threading the lacy white border

of a pair of silk panties through her fingers, they might be better off to refuse to deal with this kidnapper, whoever he was, and let him dispose of her in whatever way he chose.

Moments later, deep in thought and still caressing the panties, she heard someone enter the room and come up behind her.

"Oh, it's you," she said, glancing over her shoulder. Her voice trailed off on the flutter of her indrawn breath. He never failed to throw her into chaos, this man. He never failed.

"Did you see the police?" she asked. "Did they tell you what happened to Gus?"

"I could hardly avoid them. They said she was kidnapped, and that you were here when it happened."

With considerable reluctance Lily closed the lingerie drawer and turned to him. She was quaking inwardly, and it would be dangerous to let him know the devastating effect he had on her. He would take advantage, she had no doubt of that. He had done it before, and she had already learned to her horror that it was nearly impossible to maintain control with him.

At his urging she gave him a brief account of what she knew of the kidnapping, which was almost nothing, but even before she was done, it was obvious that he didn't believe her.

He walked to the sunny alcove where her writing desk was located and stared out at the hazy blue sky and the lion-brown foothills in the distance. From Lily's angle he looked breathtakingly masculine silhouetted by the brightness, but then she was clearly biased.

"You didn't have anything to do with this, did you, Lily?"

"No, of course not," she said, stung that he should think she would be involved in something as sordid as kidnapping her own stepsister. Not that she hadn't wanted to run the woman over with a truck on occasion. "I was asleep, and no one else was here when it happened, just as I told you."

The episode had thrown him into a strange mood, Lily

realized, though she couldn't imagine that he was any more
concerned about Gus than she was. Unfortunately, it
seemed that she was going to bear the brunt of his temper.
She was learning that he couldn't slough off his emotions.
He had to share the misery, to inflict pain if he himself was
feeling it.

"What is it?" she asked soothingly. "Surely you're not
worried about this situation with Gus. Even if there really
were a kidnapping, whoever took her isn't likely to harm
her. He just wants money."

"Money's not the problem. It's publicity. The media's
sure to go crazy."

"That's true, but you know how the press is. They'll be
bored with it in a week and on to something else." It wasn't
going to work, she knew. She was only forestalling the in-
evitable.

"This place will be a three-ring circus," he persisted.

"Can I fix you a drink?" She kept decanters of Scotch
and cognac on the console table by the doors, along with
her own favorite, Manzanilla, a pale, very dry Spanish
sherry.

He was clearly offended. "I never drink at this time of
day. You know that."

Lily walked to the decanters anyway, thinking that she
might have a glass of sherry, just enough to stop the shaking. She knew what was coming. He would not be molli-
fied, and every attempt she made would only offend him
more, until finally he felt justified in taking his anger out on
her. What would the punishment be this time? she wondered.

"Why aren't you dressed?" he asked, a trace of disdain
edging his voice as he looked her over. "What kind of
woman walks around like that, her robe hanging open, still
not dressed at eleven in the morning?"

A tramp, Lily thought, wanting to laugh hysterically. A
tramp whose conscience won't let her sleep for the sickening guilt she feels and whose libido has gone stark raving
mad. But if I am a tramp— Her breath shook with the need

to turn and fling the words at him. *If I am a tramp, it's because of you.*

She could hear him coming up behind her, and she drew back her hand and pressed it to her stomach. He wouldn't approve of her drinking. It would only anger him more. Everything she did angered him and brought censure. But one day, she vowed silently, one day he would suffer and quake the way she did. She hardly dared believe it could ever happen, but however desperate the fantasy, it gave her something to cling to, a thread.

He was silent behind her, but the connection between them was so intense, she could hear him, smell him, feel him. He might as well have controlled the switches that fed stimulation to her nervous system, that was how tuned in she was to him, how helpless to stop what was happening.

"I have to get dressed," she said. "The police want to speak to me."

"The police can have their turn, Lily . . . when I'm through with you." His voice broke slightly on her name, giving her the perverse pleasure of knowing that she had affected him, too. Something quivered and stung her jaw. The sensation brought tears to her eyes.

"Why do you do this?" he asked her. "You know how I hate it when you act this way. You know very well and still you do it. Why?"

"I haven't done anything," she said.

"Don't be insolent. You'll force me to—"

She swung around, her voice going thready as she faced him. "Force you to what?" Her pulse had quickened to the point of dizzying confusion. She wasn't afraid that he would hit her. He'd never done anything like that before, but clearly they were on the brink of something new and frightening, something beyond the mutual provocation they'd indulged in up to now.

He touched the mark above her breast and his hand trembled so violently he had to draw it back. "God, but you're a slut," he said. "Look at you."

"Yes, I am . . . for you."

"Would you do anything I asked?"

"Yes, anything." She was on the brink of tears again, quaking. She had no control with him. None.

"Good . . . that's good." He stepped away from her, his voice flaring with dark excitement. "I want you to go down and talk to the police just the way you are, looking like that."

"In my robe?" No!

"Yes, I want them to see you this way, to see what kind of woman you are, Lily, what a beautiful, *beautiful* tramp."

Lily's hands fell to her sides as he drew her robe together and tied it for her, loosely, so that the neckline gapped a bit, drawing the eye to her pale flesh, to her weak, shuddering flesh. She couldn't have done it herself. She was barely able to control the wildness within her. She was barely able to stand.

CHAPTER
3

BY EIGHT P.M. ON A TYPICAL MIDSUMMER EVENING, LONdon's famed Piccadilly Circus was overrun with a rainbow assortment of touristy types, all in pursuit of some harmless revelry. Tonight the crowds that thronged the headless Angel of Charity statue were lighter, but no less primed for excitement. Laughing and consorting, distracted by the general commotion, they barely seemed to notice the Bentley limousine purring quietly on a side street in front of the Cock 'N Bull pub.

Inside the idling silver yacht of a car, Webb Calderon was trying to end what had been a brief and ultimately unsatisfying liaison with a lithe, beautiful young Frenchwoman, who knew very well that she hadn't done her job.

"You like to be massaged, *n'est-ce pas*?" she purred, her engine as soft and shivery as the limo's. Admiring him with her eyes, she visited the myriad caressable parts of his body, including the white-gold waves that swept back from his high forehead and curled in sexy, uncontrollable wisps at his temples and nape.

He'd had comments on his eyes all his life, on their eerie, marble-gray, perforating quality, but his hair was the feature women had always seemed to love best, fortunately for him. The fact that they couldn't keep their hands out of it had saved his life once, though that was a part of his past, and his youth, that he rarely allowed himself to think about. He was sure some scorekeeper in his mind had recorded every sound, every scream.

"Celeste knows pressure points," she suggested brightly. "The one inside the ankle? It gives pleasure for hours." Honey-haired, blue-eyed Celeste drew up the schoolgirl pleats of her skirt, kicked off her Penny loafers, and showed him the tattoo on the inside of her ankle, a delicate cluster of ripe, red cherries.

"You press there," she informed him proudly. *"Oo-la-la! C'est magnifique!"*

She'd apparently been briefed that "innocence" was his thing, but he had to wonder whether her outfit had been the escort service's idea, or if she'd scoured her own closet for the short plaid skirt and blazer. It might have been more effective if she hadn't been closer to thirty-five than twelve. Still, she was flawless, as beautiful as she was skilled, and he had no desire to blame her for the hurried, pointless oral sex. He, himself, had rushed things.

"Do you know the *magique* wand?" she asked.

He stayed her hand as she produced a foot-long, ultra-slim vibrator from her bag, the soft red leather valise that all Cherries escorts carried. "I've had the pleasure," he told her. "The wand is an amazing thing, and so are you, Celeste, *completely* amazing. But I've got a . . . headache tonight."

"Mais oui, monsieur? Are you sure?" Her sigh said that what promised to be one of life's greatest rewards—pleasing him—had just been denied her. She didn't pursue it, however, as that might have resulted in an awkward situation. Instead, she began to quickly and quietly gather up her things.

She was exquisitely trained in the subtleties. Webb, himself, might not have spotted her as a professional if he hadn't known. Cherries, the escort service she worked for, maintained an elite selection of female courtesans from all over the world—arguably the most elite—and the service bristled if you referred to their lovely employees as call girls. They also provided male talent on request, but stopped short of anything kinky or zoological. At one point they had catered exclusively to royalty, opening their doors to the czars of art, culture, and commerce only as recently as a decade ago.

An international art dealer himself, Webb had discovered interesting uses for the service that had nothing to do with sex. Tonight was one of those occasions. Magic wands and prolonged pleasure were not foremost on his mind, but if he hadn't let Celeste ply her trade, she might have questioned why she'd been summoned and perhaps even become curious about the "gift" she'd been instructed to leave with him.

A faint but persistent beeping drew Webb's attention. The interior of the limo had been arranged conference style. Lush chamois-leather seats formed two semicircles that faced each other and the glass-topped console in the middle held flutes still bubbling with Cristal champagne and a wicker basket of gourmet snacks.

"Excuse me a moment," he told Celeste, opening a cabinet door in the console. As he picked up the cellular phone that was mounted inside, the escort curled her long legs beneath her and gazed out the window at the passersby. Webb caught a lingering whiff of cherry blossoms, the aromatherapy scent she'd used earlier.

"Calderon, is that you?" a man demanded as soon as Webb flipped open the mouthpiece.

Webb recognized the voice as Lake Featherstone, a southern California art collector and one of his most prominent clients. The Featherstones had made their fortune in retailing and owned a chain of more than nine hundred furniture stores around the globe, though the empire was now being run by a partner of the deceased patriarch rather than by a blood Featherstone.

Rather than by Lake, Webb added silently. He spoke softly into the phone. "Is there some problem? You sound bad."

Silence was his answer. "Jesus, Webb—" Lake's pressured sigh was audible through the static on the line. "Augusta's been kidnapped. Somebody snatched her right out from under our noses, and I don't know what the hell to do."

"When did it happen?" Webb would have skipped the compassionate friend routine and come right to the point even if Celeste hadn't been in the limo. Formalities gave away too much information, and Webb knew Lake well enough to know that his chief concern was not for his stepsister's safety. His client needed to be reassured that his insular little world wasn't going to explode in his face, though Webb had every reason to think that might be the case.

"Around ten-thirty this morning—" Lake's voice faded in and out. "I was at the club."

"Do you know who did it?"

"No idea, but it doesn't appear to have been some crazy scheme of Augusta's. One of my security people tried to intervene and nearly got himself killed for his trouble. The kidnapper tricked him with an exploding gun, all but kicked his fucking head off, and then dropped him with some kind of sci-fi tranquilizer device."

Webb smiled. Lake never used that kind of language, but that wasn't what had amused Webb. Exploding guns and sci-fi tranquilizer devices sounded suspiciously like an operative once known as The Magician. The gears had been set in motion, Webb thought, pleased that he could still wield such influence with a few phone calls, that his net was ever widening. Gus Featherstone had better tread carefully, very carefully.

"Was there a note?" he asked.

"A ransom note? No, nothing. Lily's beside herself, and I've got police all over the place. What will I do if they produce a search warrant and tear the place apart? What the hell will I do?"

Webb glanced over at Celeste and saw that she'd taken a deck of cards from the console. The thought flashed through his mind that she should not have done it. She should not have touched the cards.

"You're one of the victims, Lake," Webb reminded his client, keeping an eye on Celeste as she opened the pack. "You're not a suspect. They'll investigate the crime scene and undoubtedly Gus's room. As for the rest of the estate, it should be a superficial sweep at most."

"You smart son of a bitch!" Lake's burst of laughter had more to do with recovering his composure than with humor. "I hope you're right this time. When will you be back?"

Webb had galleries in London, New York and Beverly Hills. Out of necessity he also had a residence in or near each of those cities. But he spent about half his time at his hacienda in Santa Barbara. "I'll catch a flight out in the morning."

"Good," Lake said, seeming to calm. "The kidnapping's all over the news, Webb. The media got ahold of it."

Webb wasn't surprised. Gus Featherstone was news when she blew her nose. "Just take care of anything that needs to be taken care of, do you understand? In the event that they do turn up with a search warrant at some point, be prepared. Don't leave anything to chance."

"Yes . . . all right, I understand."

With that Webb hung up the phone and turned to Celeste. She was studying the card she'd drawn from the deck. "Do you read Tarot?" he asked her.

She glanced up, startled. "No, do you?"

"I'm more of a collector," he explained, smoothing the sleeve of his black silk jacket. To her credit she hadn't removed or wrinkled a single article of his clothing. "That particular deck is a reproduction of Amerigo Folchi's Pistoia deck. Beautiful, isn't it? There's something primal about his images."

"Yes . . . there is."

"Which card did you draw?" he asked.

She glanced down at it, a delicate shudder passing through her. Her flaxen lashes quivered, then flicked up, and she searched his eyes, her own vibrantly blue. If he hadn't seen what she was holding in her hand, he would have read her sudden intensity as passion or excitement.

"This is the Death card, isn't it?" She handed him an archetypal image of a skeletal figure, sumptuously robed, and holding a gleaming scythe. "Does it mean I'm going to die?"

Webb was quiet for a moment, studying the sinister representation. "Not at all," he told her. "It could mean the death of something that isn't working in your life, change for the better."

She busied herself with arranging her bag and smoothing her skirt. The fragrance of cherry blossoms rose from her efforts like a gentle mist. "I see," she said, and he realized with some interest that she did see—but didn't believe him.

When she was ready to leave, he reached around her and opened the limo door. "Take care," he said.

He caught a glimpse of her expression as she let herself out of the car and it struck him to the core. Her soul was in her eyes. If he thought it was possible to love anyone, he might have loved her at that moment.

Once she was gone, Webb picked up the gift she'd left. The Hermes bag contained a gleaming alligator briefcase with a combination lock. Webb touched out the number and the case clicked open. It was empty but he'd expected that. He'd been given this same gift many times.

He caught the telltale roughness immediately as he ran his fingers around the perimeter of the lining. Someone had become recklessly curious. The secret compartment had been breached. Too bad, he thought, allowing himself a moment of regret. It all came and went so quickly. It all meant so little.

As the big car pulled away from the curb and crept into the oncoming traffic, Webb heard the shriek of failing car brakes. The sound was a piercing cry for mercy, but the concussion of metal and bone that followed it was infinitely worse.

The limo came to a stop. "Sir?" the driver called back. "There's been an accident. It's the young lady we just let out."

The sweetness of cherry blossoms hung in the air.

Webb reached out his hand, unsteady. For a moment he didn't know how to answer. He'd forgotten the sanity-saving drill. He glanced around the limo, searching for something, and then, to his great relief, he found it.

The Death card was still lying on the console, emanating the arcane power and evil that so many associated with it. But Webb knew the truth. Men were the sole architects of evil. It wasn't a card that had executed his family in front of his eyes in a South American gulag when he was nine years old. It wasn't a symbolic image of death that had tortured him with water and live electric current until he was dead in every way but the physical. It was a monster, a human monster, an entire army of them.

He picked up The Reaper, slipped it back into its proper numerical place in the deck, and closed the lid. The cards didn't predict evil, they mirrored it.

"Keep going," he told the driver.

CHAPTER
4

THE MOJAVE COULD BE ONE HOT BITCH OF A SEDUCTRESS when she was so inclined. Parts of her were as erotic as a lover's sigh. Stretched naked and sun-drenched for miles on end, her ripe golden hues and curves rivaled the most luscious woman's body. But surrender to her charms and she was deadly. She could drown you in a flash flood, smother you in the tidal waves of a sandstorm, or roast you alive and pick your bones clean any day of the week, without breaking a sweat.

Jack Culhane had a love-hate thing going on with the California desert, as he did with most everything else in life. He wasn't bothered by her bent for wanton destruction. Violence of one kind or another had been his stock in trade for years, though he took no particular pleasure in it. It was the desert's capacity for wanton voluptuousness that disturbed him. The soft, sensual curves of pink and gold, the gentle drift of her dunes. She undulated before him like a woman in love, a woman in languid need. She promised something he'd lost all feeling for years ago, something he didn't seem to know how to get anymore . . . satisfaction.

Sex wasn't the problem. It wasn't about being with women. It wasn't even about satisfying them. It was him-- self he couldn't satisfy. There hadn't been any pleasure in the physical act since the carnage that had erupted five years ago, a nightmare that took the lives of his wife and child and ripped any semblance of meaning from his life. He rarely allowed himself to think about that desolation now, except to remember how savagely he wanted to find the men responsible. That much nostalgia was permitted.

His focus shortened and turned inward, blurring the horizon to a golden shimmer as he navigated the endless highway to hell. It had already occurred to him that his surly mood had something to do with her, the female stashed opposite him in the cab of the Blazer. He'd been trapped in his own getaway car for the last hour and fifteen minutes with a Barbie doll hostage who had an annoying nervous habit. She was huddled inside his huge raincoat, staring out of the side window, and absently clicking her hot-pink fingernails against her teeth. That might have been the stuff of some men's wet dreams. It wasn't his.

Celebrity gossip held about as much interest for him as mail addressed to Occupant, but he'd been researching Gus Featherstone and her family for some time now, and the way he saw it, the press had nailed her. She *was* a self-absorbed brat. As for the rest of it, she was run-of-the-mill beautiful as models went—shoulder-length dark hair à la Cindy Crawford, exotic eyes, and an undeniably sensual body. He'd even come across an old *Esquire* article where she'd been given an award for her butt—perkiest ass or something.

Fortunately, flashy stuff had never attracted him. Still, something had been eating at him for the last hundred miles. His thigh muscles were as tight as if he'd been standing, and his hands felt restless. Maybe it was the desert. Maybe he'd been staring at hillocks too long.

The rising whine of the Blazer's radiator cap pierced his thoughts. Apparently the Mojave was overheating his car engine, too. He punched a button on the dash to shut off the air-conditioning, then cranked down the window, plunging the cab into a bake oven of gritty heat. The force of it was suffocating, but at least it was a distraction.

Augusta Featherstone, the society fashion model, you know the one I mean? The beautiful brat, the conniption queen? Somebody wants her kidnapped. It's not about money, it's a grudge against the family's retailing empire— political shit. The interested party wants a pro to make the snatch, then he'll take her off your hands. You game? It's worth some real dough. . . .

That was the way the call had come in. Jack had taken the rest of the information from a liquor store phone booth in San Pedro, which was a half-hour from his normal base of operations and outside his area code. It was a precaution he'd insisted on. Everything else about the exchange had been sloppy. Dangerously sloppy. The call hadn't come through normal channels, the anonymous contact had given him more information than necessary about the mark, and he'd referred to Jack by the name Jack hadn't used in years, his real name. If the job had been about anything else, about any*one* else, Jack would have hung up on the asshole.

The coldness that stirred inside him now was gallows laughter. As it was he'd said yes immediately. He'd been waiting five years for this break. He'd planned his life around it. He would have planned his death if necessary. He'd long suspected that someone connected with the Featherstones had been involved in his five-year nightmare, and Augusta Featherstone, unwittingly or not, was going to help him solve that mystery. If she wasn't his chief suspect, at least she had the keys to the kingdom.

He'd taken what safety measures he could, including covertly changing the rules once he'd accepted the job. He'd struck on a different day, at a different time, than had been prearranged. He'd changed the hideout destination, and he'd employed terror tactics to frighten the holy hell out of his hostage and put her in a vulnerable state of mind.

He'd enjoyed that last part.

The only surprise had been her reaction. She should have

been on her knees the entire time, pleading with him not to hurt her, offering him money, her body, anything to save her life and win her freedom. She hadn't acted like a typical hostage at any point along the way, except when she'd thought he'd killed the guard. He wasn't sure what that meant, but he was going to find out.

He glanced at her now, aware that she was shifting around in the seat again. "What's the problem?"

The clicking sounds ceased and from out of the depths of his coat came a mumbled, "I have to go to the bathroom."

"Suit yourself, but I'm not stopping."

Her head popped up and she glared at him with almost as much loathing as when she'd pulled her blindfold down. "How much farther until we get wherever we're going?"

"Hours." This wasn't true, but what the hell.

"Hours? I'll wet my pants!"

"Take the raincoat off first."

Her furious sniff brought a smile. It actually surprised him when he glanced into the rearview mirror and saw himself. There was a slant to his eyebrow and a dark twist to his mouth. Hell, he felt halfway good for the first time since he'd driven into the land of endlessly rolling hips and thighs, breasts and buttocks—Nature's ode to Jack Culhane's frustration.

The speedometer needle jumped up to ninety as his foot kissed the gas pedal. A sign flashed by: BISHOP 200 MILES.

They would soon be out of the hills and into the crusty basins of the lowlands, where the eye could see nothing for miles but dry lake beds, spiny Joshua trees, and white, arid salt flats. He consoled himself with that. Beyond the flats and looming to the south was the blast furnace heat and bleached animal bones of Death Valley.

The sweat beading on his forehead had begun to trickle down his temples, but the parched air blowing in the windows dried the droplets before they reached his cheekbones. There wasn't even enough moisture in the air to send up the tangy odors of creosote bush and bur sage, but he could smell the gritty desert dust. He could even taste it.

A plastic water bottle was clamped to the side of the console by his knee. He picked up the container and drank from it deeply and thirstily. When he was done, he wiped the mouth and handed it to her, all without easing up on the gas. She wrinkled her nose and continued staring pensively out the window.

"I have a theory about people who drive at breakneck speeds," she told him, not stopping to inquire about his interest in said theory. "I've always thought they were displacing aggression. Since they couldn't act on their primitive urges, they drove like bats out of hell instead."

Could damn well be, Jack thought. In his case, the primitive urge was to break a few things, starting with her fingernails.

"Their primitive *sexual* urges," she added.

That made him look. What the hell could she possibly know about his primitive sexual urges? She refrained from returning his sidelong stare, but he detected a faintly superior air in her profile, as if she prided herself on having him all figured out, urges included. He doubted that. He seriously did. But she had him curious.

"If you really want to know what somebody's like, get in a car with him," she continued, apparently determined to share her cherished theory in its entirety. "People who won't use their turn signals are probably bad communicators, habitual lane changers have trouble with commitment, and slowpokes are secretly hostile."

"What does your theory say about men who lay rubber?"

That made *her* look. "Excuse me?"

He let up on the gas, hit the brakes, and pulled the van to the side of the road. He not only laid a little rubber, he raised plenty of dust. The powdery stuff flew as he brought the car to a shuddering stop. It swirled into the cab, catching in the sunlight, fine golden motes that sprinkled his hostage with a halo that made her look deceptively angelic.

Fighting a different urge this time—the desire to stare at her lovely, startled mouth—he reminded himself that any resemblance she bore to the angels was strictly superficial. The woman was nine parts hellcat by all accounts.

Now her much-photographed features were frozen between shock and suspicion as he produced a bandanna from the pocket of his jeans, pulled the material taut, and twirled it into a band.

"What are you going to do with that?" she asked, her voice going faint.

"Act on my primitive sexual urges?"

"You're *not* going to blindfold me again?"

"No, I'm going to gag you. Turn around."

"Gag me?" She flinched back, incredulous. "Why?"

"Turn it around," he repeated patiently. "Unless you want me to do that, too."

She made a sound of disgust and swung around, her shoulders heaving as he reached up to drop the bandanna over her head.

"I can't believe you're doing this," she snapped, looking over her shoulder at him. "Apparently I must have hit pretty close to the mark with my theory? Is that it? I threatened you?"

"Yeah—" A snort of laughter escaped him. "I'm shaking in my boots. Now stay put."

She went silent, her shoulders continuing to heave as he slipped the bandanna between her soft, taut lips and secured it with a knot. Her dark hair caressed his hands like silk as he worked, and although the scent coming off her body carried hints of sweat and dust, it was a pungent female perfume—hot and angry, fervently excited.

The tightness he'd noticed in his thighs was creeping upward, bringing the promise of deeper pleasures with it. There was a hot spark of life in his jeans, and he wanted like hell to indulge the sensation. But there was only one reason to do that and a million reasons not to. Maybe she was right. Maybe he *was* threatened. All he knew at the moment was that he wanted her petulant little mouth silent and her award-winning ass still. That way he would have the peace and quiet to plan his next move. That way he wouldn't have to hear her theories *or* her clicking fingernails.

*   *   *

"I will pee my pants!" Gus threatened. "If you don't put me down im*med*iately, I'll do it, I swear."

Her dire warning fell on deaf ears. Apparently Mr. Quiet-But-Deadly had no objection to the idea of a golden shower. He might even like it, she realized despairingly. He'd parked the van some time ago, lifted her into his arms, and now he was crushing her nearly breathless as he labored through the sand toward some destination he'd refused to disclose. In a bewildering move, he'd removed her gag, blindfolded her, and tied her wrists. If he'd done it to make sure she couldn't slow him up by struggling, it had worked. She was limited to stiffening her body like an indignant child and demanding to be released.

She had no doubt that if some gossip reporter were lurking in the sagebrush, he'd say the beautiful brat was being difficult again, making unreasonable requests of her abductor, and generally harassing the poor devil. Her every move seemed to be catnip to the tabloid press, but she didn't understand why they persisted in seeing her as a holy terror simply because she knew what she wanted in life and went after it. How often did men get faulted for that sort of thing?

"If I die out here from a burst bladder," she informed him ominously, "you'll have a wet, smelly corpse on your hands and not a penny for your trouble."

He trudged on, his silence as frustrating as her bonds. He hadn't responded to a single word she'd said so far, and though she'd never been one to beat a dead horse, she hadn't been bluffing. If he didn't let her make a pit stop, she would soon be irrigating the desert.

"Kidnapping is a capital crime in this state," she said. "Did you know that? Punishable by death—the gas chamber, if I'm not mistaken—which is not a pleasant way to go. And speaking of bladders, I've heard you lose control of your bladder *and* your bowels when they pull that switch—"

He hoisted her up in his arms, his teeth grinding savagely as he bit out the first words he'd spoken since they left the van. "Why the hell did I take off that gag?"

Gus sighed for the unreasonableness of all mankind and for this man in particular. "If you'd stop being macho, put me down, and let me walk, I'd be quiet!"

"You're barefoot, you idiot!"

He had a point. She was still wearing his coat, but there was only one pair of shoes between them, and he was using them. It probably wasn't very smart to expose the most sensitive parts of her body to the griddle-hot sand anyway, though she wasn't sure which would be more hazardous, walking or whizzing.

"Ouch," she thought aloud.

Exhausted from the heat and the bickering, she heaved a great sigh and slumped against his chest. Why wasn't *he* exhausted? she wondered. He'd been hauling her and a duffel bag full of supplies around for what seemed like hours. With the desert sun pounding down on both of them like a sledgehammer, it was difficult even to breathe.

"Aren't you getting tired?" she asked, knowing better than to expect an answer. Once she had made her heroic escape from this man—and she would—if the tabloid press should ask her to describe him, she would tell them that his most annoying trait was his refusal to communicate. "I sincerely doubt that he uses turn signals, and you know what *that* means," she would tell them.

She went quiet then, surrendering to the heat, the silence, his superior strength, the ultimate helplessness of her situation, the paternalistic society at large, and everything else that was oppressive in life. It wasn't her nature to do anything halfway, including surrendering, and to her great surprise, there was something oddly relaxing about it.

His powerful, lunging gait made her body rock gently in his arms, and he was probably holding her that much tighter to compensate for the unsteadiness. She'd never been one of those give-me-a-gorilla-with-a-vocabulary women, and being carted around the Mojave was not her idea of a fun date. But she had to admit, it was rather sweet of him to carry her in one-hundred-plus degree heat. He must be dying, she thought, he really must.

Given her profession, there'd been plenty of men in her

life who'd wanted her in one way or another, but very few of them ever made her feel, well . . . Unaccountably, the word that came to mind was *protected*, though it was a strange way to characterize the situation with him. She was probably far too independent to allow that sort of relationship with a man, but this one hadn't really given her a choice, had he?

She turned her head into his shoulders, seeking shelter. The rest of her body was covered by the overcoat, but the blindfold exposed the lower part of her face, and the sun was scorchingly direct. It did no good to wet her cracked lips, because they dried almost as soon as her tongue touched them.

The heat was starting to get to her. Her body didn't feel quite right and neither did her head. She was light and heavy at the same time, and her thoughts were straying off to places she couldn't quite follow. She laughed softly for no particular reason, and then it flitted through her thoughts that she might be suffering from sunstroke. Weren't the symptoms weakness, lassitude, delirium?

"I was just wondering what I should call you?" Pleasantly woozy, she mumbled against his damp cotton shirt. "Mr. Kidnapper, maybe?"

He didn't answer, so she went on, amusing herself with the various possibilities. "Let's see . . . how about the Masked Avenger? I always liked that one. It's from a comic book, I think. How do you feel about Snidley Whiplash? Or maybe Jack? How does that strike you?"

"Jack?"

He sounded startled. Or maybe his voice had simply cracked with the heat. At least she'd got a response out of him. She could feel his heartbeat against her shoulder. "Yeah, Jack, as in Jack the Ripper."

Laughter, she thought. Was that what she'd heard? A rustle of laughter? "Okay, Jack it is," she said, glad that was settled.

"Why don't you call me what my mother used to call me," he suggested.

"You had a mother?" She looked up at him, as if she

could see him through the blindfold. "What'd she call you?"

"Satan."

Her throat burned with smothered laughter. "Your mom and I should talk."

Suddenly her forehead felt itchy and she rubbed it against his collar bone as languidly as a cat who was angling to be stroked. The stinging sensation she felt told her the sun had struck again. She was going to have little splotches of sunburn to go with her little blotches of nail polish.

He made an odd sound, as if he were clearing his throat. She liked that sound, almost as much as she liked the hard, steady thump of his heart. She'd never been around a man who seemed so completely immune to her and preferred it that way. It intrigued her.

"About how much longer?" she asked him conversationally. "Any chance there's an oasis on the way?" She had already decided to take his silence as an affirmation. Might as well think positive under the circumstances. It was possible he was nodding.

As he forged onward, her thoughts began to stray again, creating fanciful associations with the situation. Being carried like a child drew her back to the early years of her life, the sordid years before her mother married Lake Featherstone, Sr. Oddly what she remembered most vividly were the soiled rugs—crawling across them as a toddler, playing with her dolls on them as a grade schooler. Threadbare and dirty, varying little from one fleabag apartment to another, those carpets had been one of the few constants of her young life.

Her other strongest recollection was of abject loneliness. Her mother had worked nights in a restaurant, and she'd rarely come home until dawn. Too fearful to sleep, Gus had kept the lights on and the TV running all night, but it was the picture books an elderly woman in the next apartment had given her that had held back the darkness and kept the monsters at bay. Fairy tales had been Gus's salvation.

Embarrassed as she would have been to admit it now,

she'd lost herself in fantasies of Sleeping Beauty, Snow White, and Cinderella, identifying especially with the last one. She *was* Cinderella. She was every lonely, neglected young girl who had ever dreamed of being rescued by a dashing prince.

Even after her mother's marriage, the fantasy of being rescued had sustained her through the troubled years with her stepsiblings. She'd eventually realized that no one rides to anyone's rescue unless there's something in it for them. Life had made her a hardheaded realist. But now, with the sun so hot and her thoughts so fuzzy, she could almost imagine herself being cradled in her rescuer's arms, being swept up and carried off to some glorious new existence, a fairy tale life, except that she was bound and blindfolded, and the man carrying her off was *anything* but a prince. . . .

"This is it," he announced.

The kidnapper's harsh words intruded on Gus's reveries. "This is what?" she asked.

"The spa I told you about. We're here."

He tilted her until her feet made contact with a smooth, hard, hot surface, and then he began to untie her blindfold. Gus could feel him working at the knot. When the bandanna finally fell off, she blinked to clear her vision. If the sun hadn't been blinding her, she would have sworn she was staring at a mountain of rotted wood, rusted tailings, and chicken wire. "Where is it?" she asked.

She stood on a piece of granite that apparently served as the front porch, but the heap didn't look any better up close.

"Go on in," he said.

"Does it have a door?"

He kicked a column of wood that resembled window shutters. As the thing swung forward, Gus stared into the guts of what must have been a dilapidated mining shack from a much earlier era.

"Oh, my God!" she screamed as she stepped inside. The kidnapper had crowded in behind her, and she slammed up against him in her effort to back out the door. "Lizards, look at them! Millions of them!"

The tiny creatures scuttled in every direction.

"They don't bite," he assured her mordantly.

"No, but that thing does!" Gus plowed into him again, letting out a shriek loud enough to rock the shack. There was a rattler coiled not four feet away from her, and the glare of its horrible iridescent eyes pierced her courage like an icy shaft of steel.

As the snake began to slowly unwind, Gus froze solid. She couldn't move. Her coat had fallen open, but she couldn't summon the strength to close it. All she could do was whimper. She was terrified of snakes as she was of nothing else in life. She had fought valiantly to get her childhood fears under control, but she had never been able to conquer the one she was staring at now.

Riveted by the evil creature, she pressed up against her captor. "Let me out," she whispered. "Please, *please*!"

The snake flashed into the air, and Gus shrieked again.

Its twitching tail sent up an obscenely familiar sound, the death rattle. The reptile swayed toward her with a searing hiss. Its forked tongue slithered repulsively.

"You have a gun," she cried wildly, jerking at his chambray shirt "Shoot it! *Kill* it!"

Gus closed her eyes and turned her face into his chest, steeling herself for the gun shot. When nothing happened, she reared back and looked up at him. Her fists had wadded his shirt into sodden clumps. "Shoot it," she pleaded weakly. "Why don't you shoot it?"

"If you'd stay cool," he said, "it might just slither away."

But she couldn't. Cool wasn't an option for Gus. She'd been terrorized by snakes, literally locked up in a pit with the vile creatures when she was a child, and she couldn't even think about one without shuddering in revulsion. Swaying in his arms, she felt the bile rise up in her throat. She was either going to be sick all over him or faint.

The death rattle burst into her consciousness. She turned back just as the snake lunged at her, its fangs bared. Horrified she watched the whiplike blur of motion, but could do nothing to save herself. It was a silver spear of death flying straight for her bare leg!

A silver spear of death with an exploding head!

The kick from the gun rocked up the kidnapper's arm and reverberated through Gus's body. She wrenched away from him and turned to the wall, shutting out the gruesome scene. "What kind of man are you?" she whimpered. "That thing could have killed me! If you'd missed, if you'd taken one second more to shoot, it would have been too late!"

When he didn't answer, she glanced at him over her shoulder.

He was staring at the floor in front of him with a look of barely suppressed irony. "Seems I *was* too late," he said.

There was a puddle in front of him, in exactly the place where she'd been standing. As she gazed at the wet spot and up at him, Gus realized she didn't have to go to the bathroom anymore.

CHAPTER
5

HUDDLED ON THE SHACK'S ONLY BED, A SAGGING METAL COT propped up in the corner against the front wall, Gus picked at what hot-pink polish was left on her toenails and stared fixedly at a patch of dry rot on the diseased wooden floor. She was suffering post-traumatic shock. That was the only way to explain her unnatural interest in decomposing inorganic matter. It was easier to watch the floor disintegrate than her life. Stranger still, the blight appeared to be eating away a sizable portion of the wood planks even as she watched.

Some spa, she thought. This was not in the brochure.

Lizards haunted her peripheral vision, shimmying up and down the walls, their tails twitching like tiny green whips. Flies darted through the broken side window, madly buzzing the tiny spot where she'd ignominiously wet the floor and the larger one where the snake had lain before the kidnapper removed it.

Absently Gus began to count flies as they performed their aerial acrobatics and made their precision landings.

She reached a number in the high two digits before revulsion shuddered through her. Counting insects? She really was losing it. If Frances Brightly were here, she'd be swatting and stamping with a vengeance. Everyone was terrified of the housekeeper, which was why she'd become Gus's role model in the impressionable years after Gus's mother had disappeared. Even now, when Gus forgot how to be tough, she asked herself what Frances would have done.

"Frances would have shot herself," she mumbled, surveying the horrors of her one-room cell. The shack's interior and exterior were virtually indistinguishable. The whole place was crumbling, dust to dust as the Bible said, though that process had sounded poetic, and this was anything but. There was a grimy kitchen sink of sorts, a woodstove, and a strangely decorative bistro table made of rusted wrought iron.

There was also a grand total of two chairs, one lying on its side with a broken leg, the other an ancient rocker, carved with what might have been Native American designs. The rocker had appeared to be the cleanest thing in the place, so Gus had gingerly dusted it off and draped her bikini bottom over the back to dry, after rinsing the suit out in brick-red tap water.

The side wall nearest her had no windows, but a curtained alcove Gus couldn't quite see bore some resemblance to a closet. She didn't even want to think about what might be lurking inside the rusty metal cabinet that stood against the back wall. One of its doors was ominously ajar, but nothing could have induced her to look.

Hiding her face in her drawn-up knees, she let out a groan of despair that came straight from the heart. She was trapped here, in this pigsty of a lizard farm, at the mercy of a man who preferred reptiles to humans and sex with corpses.

How would anyone ever find her?

A moan penetrated her shellshocked state. Several more followed, low-pitched and guttural but every bit as agonized. She lifted her head cautiously and looked around. What in the world? The sounds had come from nearby, from outside. If someone was hurt, it had to be him. There was no one else out here but the two of them. Gus had a mental picture of him lying in the sand, half-dead of sunstroke, or fatally bitten by something. The desert was full of poisonous creatures—tarantulas, scorpions, and the snakes he so loved.

A moment later she was peering out through broken slats of the boarded front window. There was nothing to be seen for miles, except a blazing sea of white sand studded with creosote bushes and blue-gray sage. Her first impression was one of barren emptiness, a wasteland, but that awareness gradually gave way to a sense of vastness.

The shack seemed to be situated in a huge, quiet basin that swept toward a moonscape of sand dunes in the distance. Beyond the dunes a range of velvet mountains in violet and magenta rose against the cobalt sky. There wasn't a cloud on the horizon. Not even a hint of haze to subdue the dense, vibrant tones.

The panoramic view was as startling to behold as the eerie silence was to absorb. It gave Gus the feeling of boundless space and unlimited natural power. Her modeling assignments had taken her all over the world, but only the Alps in Europe had left her with a similar sense of wonder at Nature's primacy. For a moment she allowed herself to simply stare and be transported by the scene. It was the last thing she'd expected to see.

From somewhere nearby, wood creaked plaintively, as if it were splintering. Another low groan startled Gus out of her reverie. A shadow fell across the sand in front of the shack, rippling grotesquely and bringing frightening things to mind. It looked like a body twisting in the wind.

"My God," she murmured when she saw what had created the effect.

A man was hanging by his arms from an exposed beam that jutted out beyond the roof of the shack. She couldn't see his face from her vantage point. It was hidden by his arms, but she knew who he was, who he had to be. Her jailer. Blue jeans were the only thing covering his body, and it was one of the most startling spectacles she'd ever seen. He was sheened with sweat, and it looked as if he might be trying to hoist himself up onto the roof. But just the sight of him that way—shirtless and straining—was enough to make her wonder what kind of physical activity gave a man stomach muscles of corrugated iron.

Gus had never seen such savagely etched muscle definition. It was as if every sinew had been hewn through painful effort. He was powerful by any standard, undeniably brawny and virile, yet without the bulk of a weight lifter. But that was only part of what had drawn her attention. He was also riddled with scars—bullet holes, unless she was mistaken.

She watched in silence, marveling as he strained toward the beam, then lowered himself. His stomach muscles sucked in violently and one of his legs kicked up reflexively. But it wasn't until he dropped an arm to his side and hauled himself up again that she realized what was going on. He'd apparently been at this for a good long time already, and whether he meant it to be exercise or self-torture, she didn't know, but now he was struggling to lift the weight of his body with the strength of just one arm.

His neck muscles seemed about to burst as he dragged himself upward. Gus didn't think he was going to make it, and she could barely stand to watch. Sweat poured off him, and the veins in his arm distended grotesquely. Even his leg muscles were knotted, and yet somehow his struggle was mesmerizing, as beautiful as it was horrible. The sun had turned him to gold and set him on fire. His body seemed to steam in the desert heat.

Gus wanted to shout at him to stop, but she didn't dare. This wasn't exercise. It was something else, something deeply private, a ritual that made her think of purification rites or religious absolution. But if this was penance for his sins, it frightened her to think what they might be. What could a man like him have done that he believed deserved this kind of self-inflicted punishment?

A moment later he dropped to the ground, landing heavily on his knees. His clenched fists and closed eyes spoke of his brute determination to contain whatever he was feeling—the emotion, the physical pain. The anguish carved into his features made her want to shrink away from the window.

When he looked up moments later, she ducked back, her heart zinging into her throat. He would never want her to see him this way, hurting and vulnerable, and the last thing she wanted was to embarrass him. She had no doubt that he was capable of anything, including venting his frustration on her if he was provoked enough.

By the time he came back inside the shack, Gus had reclaimed some of her legendary cool, along with her bikini bottom from the rocker, but she was far from calm. He barely seemed to notice her as he strode to the table and opened the duffel bag of supplies he'd brought from the truck. A ripped seam in his faded jeans exposed a portion of his inner thigh, and his powerful back muscles glowed with heat.

Gus counted five wounds. White and spidery, they looked like bullet wounds that had healed years ago. They ranged from his shoulder to his hip on the right side, a fourth had cut through his lower back and emerged from his side, and the fifth looked as if it might have shattered his spine. How could anyone have survived such an attack?

Her desire to know more about him was sudden and sharp. The wounds told her he wasn't invulnerable, and what she'd seen had confirmed that. He was human, he suffered the same pain and anguish as the rest of the race. And yet he wasn't the same, not at all. Her intuition told her that he was as fundamentally different from anyone she'd ever known as dawn was from dusk.

Her mother'd had a penchant for unsavory characters in the days before she married her stepfather, and Gus had always wondered what the attraction was. Dark, furtive men, losers and users, they'd lurked in the shadows of Rita Walsh's life. At a very young age Gus had already known she didn't share her mother's proclivities, and that hadn't changed. She still didn't.

This man was dark, but he wasn't unsavory. He was deadly.

Gus grew very quiet inside as she watched him sort through the bag, pulling out clothing and foodstuffs. *Deadly?* She'd used that word before but not with this understanding. Her fingers stilled and her heart slowed. Even her breathing dragged as if the hot desert air had suddenly grown thick and heavy.

But while her body went silent, her mind didn't. *Don't be fooled by what he's doing,* it cautioned. *Appearances deceive. He might look normal enough, emptying a duffel bag like any other man. He might wear ripped denim and worn leather boots, but it's an illusion. Your instincts about him are right. His heart is as cold as stone, and his mind is a trap that frees no one once it's ensnared them. Despite the pain you saw, despite the wounds that make him look human. He isn't, quite.*

Gus hugged her legs beneath the tented overcoat. Though her face was chapped and burned from the sun, a chill tingled the hairs at the base of her scalp. She refused to give in to the desire to shudder, but a tiny gasp welled in her throat. Something had jabbed her in the ribs! She reared back as the hot sensation intensified, and all thought of dark and deadly men flew right out of her head.

It was her bikini top, she discovered once she'd opened the coat to investigate. The bone was hopelessly bent, and it was digging sharply into the underside of her breast. She levered the tight elastic band and moved the bra around, searching for a more comfortable fit, but no amount of adjusting brought relief.

Knowing he could turn at any moment, she pulled the coat over her head for some privacy. The tent she created cut out most of the light, making it difficult to see, but she had to do something. The discomfort had become intolerable.

She was swearing softly and fumbling with the underwire when she heard him turn.

"What are you doing in there?" he asked.

"Nothing," she snapped, her patience fraying. By now her battle with the bikini had become a mission. It didn't matter that only moments ago a little voice had warned her to beware of him; Gus never listened to little voices anyway. Perhaps because of her childhood, fear had always motivated her differently than most. Instead of backing down when she was threatened, she went forward. Maybe it was a failing, but she couldn't help herself.

"I said what are you doing?"

"And I said nothing. Ever heard of personal privacy?"

Something hit the table with a clunk. "Fuck that," he said. "You're my hostage, and I make the rules. Whatever it is you're doing in there, do it where I can see it!"

His loudness startled her, but it would have taken a bullhorn to stop her. She twisted the offending bone this way and that, aware that it was so badly bent she might never get it back into shape. The grit and sweat on her flushed skin made the material stick to her. *Her flesh was being rubbed raw*, and she couldn't see what she was doing or get the leverage she needed because she was wearing the thing. God, would she ever get back to civilization and a hot shower?

"Goddamnit, *Gus*!"

"In a minute—" Now she was trying to take the damn bra off so she could work with it, but she couldn't even manage that. The hook seemed to be jammed.

"Now!" he barked. "Right *now*!"

A gust of air swept over her as the coat flew off her head, leaving her exposed. "Give that back!" she cried, her hands frozen at the snap of her bra.

"What the hell are you doing?" he asked, gaping at her huddled form.

"I'm trying to get this thing off, if you don't mind."

"Yeah, I *do* mind."

She gazed up at him, uncomprehending, but very aware of the dark glow of his eyes and the steel in his jaw. "Why?"

"Because if you take it off, you'll be topless."

His logic still eluded her. "The woman wants to take her bra off, and the man doesn't want her to because she'll be topless? What's wrong with this picture?"

"I'm not the man, Gus. I'm Mr. Kidnapper, remember?

Who drives too fast because he's displacing his primitive sexual urges? You don't want to risk triggering one or two of those urges, do you?"

Blame it on the heat and the sweat and the gouging pain she was in, but Gus didn't give a rat's behind about his urges at that moment. "If you don't want to be triggered, then give me back that coat," she muttered, resuming her efforts.

Her more-than-ample breasts shivered with the defiance that stiffened her entire body as she worked. Glistening with perspiration and swollen with heat, they spilled from the cups of the bra like something ripe and soft and golden, fruit of the gods. As she fiddled and fussed with the jammed hook, trying to free herself, she knew very well what it must look like to him . . . all that wanton female flesh bobbing and jiggling, all that cleavage. At least she hoped it looked that way!

Being in the modeling business, Gus had been told often that her body was phenomenal. Perhaps she'd even begun to believe it, though she knew much of what was said by photographers and such was unmitigated bull. But now, more than anything, and probably for the simple reason that he'd ordered her not to, Gus Featherstone wanted to flash a pair of phenomenal breasts at this throwback to the cave dwellers.

"Ahh, that feels better," she said as she finally got the hook undone. An angry red welt marked the underside of her breast as living proof of her discomfort. With a deep sigh of relief, she looked up at him.

Her smile wavered a little as she saw his expression.

"Christ," he breathed, glowering at her partial nudity. "Are you nuts?"

"No, but I would have been if I'd had to wear that thing a second longer."

His eyes narrowed to gleaming slits as he stared at her. "Turn around," he commanded.

"You turn." Gus wasn't quite sure what had him so upset. Considering his reaction, there were only a couple of conclusions she could draw. Either he had the sexual hangups she already suspected, or she herself was woefully out of touch with everyday mores, which was entirely possible, too. She'd long ago overcome any modesty about nudity. Modeling had cured her of that. You couldn't throw clothes on and off in front of dressers and designers and be shy about your body.

Vaguely aware that both shocking pink bra straps were slipping off her shoulders, Gus couldn't make up her mind which one of them to salvage and the moment of indecision sent them sliding down her arms. The bra cups fell away next, startling her flesh into a delicate shimmy, which sent the top itself floating to the bed. It was all completely accidental on Gus's part, but, of course, certain parts of her didn't stop shaking, even when she did.

His face heated up visibly, brightening to an interesting shade of puce. Apparently he'd figured out that she wouldn't have turned around even if he'd been the Pope, nor was she bluffing.

"I'm counting to three," he growled, shouldering around furiously to face the wall. "If you don't have yourself covered by then, I'll—"

"You'll what, Mr. Kidnapper?"

"I'll strangle you with that goddamn thing!"

By "thing" she imagined he could only have meant the bra. She gazed down at it, wondering if even an engineering student could have repaired it. "I'm not going to do it," she informed him, speaking directly to his stony shoulders and bright red neck. "And I'm not wearing that damn coat anymore, either. It's too hot."

He began to tear through the duffel bag, pulling out clothing. When he came to an oversized white T-shirt, he snapped it over his shoulder at her. "Put this on."

Gus quickly rid herself of the damp bikini bottoms and slipped the T-shirt on. It was light and cool against her damp flesh. It was heaven! Unfortunately it barely covered her behind and probably revealed quite a bit more of the loanee than the lender was bargaining on.

"These, too," he said, lobbing her some jeans, which she caught, but tossed on the bed. It was much too hot for denim. The last things to come her way were a pair of huge canvas shoes, which she left where they fell.

She crouched down a little as he turned around, hoping he wouldn't notice how short the T-shirt was. She needn't have bothered. He didn't even look.

"It's time to eat," he announced, fishing once more in the duffel bag, this time for some tin pots and utensils.

"Eat? What's that?"

"You're not hungry?"

Gus was ravenous. Weakness washed over her at the mere mention of food. Her stomach began to roll and clutch and rumble loudly, but she was reasonably sure he couldn't hear with all the noise he was making.

"What are we having for dinner?" she asked.

"You tell me. You'll be cooking it." Now he was drawing a huge leather-sheathed knife from the bag.

"Sure, fine, just point me to the fridge," she said. "I'm great with frozen Wolfgang Puck pizza and a microwave, which, for your information, is the *only* thing I know how to cook."

He walked to the door, hesitating long enough to tie the knife to his thigh with a rawhide strap. "In that case, we're having roast rattlesnake for dinner."

Gus shuddered and shook her head. "Oh, God, n-n-no."

He'd meant it about roasting the rattlesnake.

Gus nearly fainted when he brought the vile thing into the cabin to cook. One look at her chalk-white face and swaying horror, and he'd had the good sense to take it straight back outside, where he'd built a bonfire and roasted it on a spit. Even the smell of it had made her ill, but she'd managed to draw herself some rusty water from the tap for cooking, which, just to be safe, she'd boiled the hell out of before adding a packet of chicken noodle soup mix.

Rusty chicken soup, warm beer, and stale saltines. To Gus it was a banquet. Russian caviar had never tasted this good. She tucked herself in the creaky rocker and drank the steaming broth straight from the pan, not even bothering with a spoon, except to scoop up the noodles. When the crackers stuck to the roof of her mouth like flour paste, she washed them down with the can of Moosehead she'd swiped from a six-pack in his duffel bag.

This cooking stuff is a breeze, she thought, feeling rather proud of herself as she piled the dishes in the sink afterward. If he'd been around she would have told him so. But he hadn't come back inside yet, even though it was getting dark. It was also getting chilly, so she bundled herself in the canvas coat and curled up on the cot, fighting off drowsiness to plan her escape.

Somehow she had to get back to the Blazer and use the car phone to let Rob know where she was. She'd heard the kidnapper say he was changing destinations and would report back, but as far as she knew he hadn't done that, so whoever was supposed to pay him off and make the exchange was still waiting for instructions. Poor Rob, she thought, he must be as frantic as she was. . . .

She rested her head against the wall with a sigh. The breezes swirling through the broken windows smelled richly of saguaro and sage. Dusty pink light filled the shack with a lambent glow that softened the gloom and lent the place a quaintness Gus might have found charming if she hadn't known there were lizards skulking in the woodwork. Still, her stomach was pleasantly full and she was exhausted.

Closing her eyes, she began to doze. . . .

"Get *up*."

Gus started awake at the brusque command, nearly crowning herself on the window ledge as she sat up. "What is it?" she asked.

It was dark outside now, and the shack was dimly lit by a couple of hanging oil lamps, but there was enough light to see that he was standing by the sink and he wasn't happy about something. Big surprise.

"You left a mess," he said, pointing to her dirty dinner dishes.

"A mess?" She blinked at him, still groggy from her nap. "Look around you. This place is a sty. It's worse than a sty.

Pigs wouldn't live here, and you're worried about an un-washed soup pan?"

He picked up the pan in question, held it up, and let it drop, drilling her with a hard stare as it clattered to the floor. "You make a mess, you clean it up. Those are the rules. Follow them and we'll get along fine. Break them, and I'll—"

"I know, I know," she said, bored already with his death threats. Throwing off the coat, she stretched like a cat, flexing every kink in her spine before she vacated the cot.

"Might as well have been kidnapped by my mother," she said disdainfully. She walked to the pan, plucked it up, and tossed it the extra feet to the sink. It hit with a racket that made his noise sound puny. "First, you're nagging me about my clothes and now this, a couple of dirty pans?"

"I can't imagine why they call you a brat."

The soft malice in his tone seemed to ignite something frightening within him. Gus felt an impulse to clutch her arms, but resisted it. He'd already reduced her to a gibbering idiot with that snake business, and she wasn't anxious to give him another opening. On the other hand, she wasn't crazy enough to provoke him, either. At least not any more than she already had.

"I'm going to clean it up," she assured him. "Don't work yourself into a state."

She started for the sink, but she'd barely taken a step when she felt a sharp tug on the back of her T-shirt. It had to be him. Knowing that for a dead certainty, she kept moving, stretching the shirt's material as far as it would go.

"Going somewhere, Gus?"

"Yeah, maybe Paris—right after I do the dishes."

He yanked firmly, bringing her to a halt midstride.

"I said I'd clean it up!" she insisted.

"I'm afraid it's too late for that."

He reeled her in like a hooked fish, dragging insistently on the shirt until he'd hauled her all the way back to where he stood. She skidded part of the way, then lost her balance and crash-landed in his arms. A sliver from the rough wood floor stung her foot and fiery anger stung her pride.

"I'm *already* in a state," he warned her, roping his arm around her middle and pulling her close. "I'm so worked up, I may go fucking crazy, Gus."

There *was* a crazy edge to his voice, which told her this was no idle threat. He meant it this time. She could feel his hipbone nudging her backside and his hot breath riffling her hair. His heartbeat, heavy against her shoulder blade, was pumping out a message all its own.

Gooseflesh crept up the front of her thighs. An uneasy glance down there told her why. Her T-shirt had hiked up when he'd pulled her back, and now it was flashing *Hustler* magazine glimpses of her private parts. "Would you mind?" she asked.

"Probably . . . mind what?"

"Could you release my shirt? It's—"

She hesitated too long in search of a safe way to explain.

The hand he'd wrapped around her waist had already begun a reconnaissance journey of its own, patting searchingly down her belly to her thigh and grazing the dark silky thatch of pubic hair on the way. "You're not wearing anything under this shirt?" He looked over her shoulder to peer down her body.

"What the hell?" He stepped back and lifted the back of the shirt, exposing her buttocks to whichever of the myriad lizards, flies, and rattlesnakes might be interested. "Where's the rest of your bathing suit?"

"It was wet."

"Jesus," he breathed. "What are you? An exhibitionist? Somebody should paddle your bare ass!"

"I wouldn't *be* bare-assed if you'd let go of the T-shirt."

"You're cruising," he warned. He released the shirt and caught hold of her arm as she stumbled forward, ostensibly to steady her, but she could tell he had other things in mind. Evil things by the look of him. She ducked, dodged, and danced like a boxer, but before she could get clear of him, he'd scooped her up in his arms and was carrying her toward the cot.

"What are you doing?" she demanded to know. "If

you've got any crazy ideas about my bare— Oh, God, no! You *wouldn't*—"

The grim flex of his jaw told her he was getting ready to claim his pound of flesh, literally. His grip was like iron, but then so was Gus's will. And if she had anything to say about it, he wasn't going to lay a hand on her ass, bare or otherwise!

She heaved up, pushing and straining against him to get free. An elbow accidentally jammed in his ribs did the trick. It also got her unceremoniously dumped. Fortunately the cot was there to break her fall.

As soon as she hit the lumpy mattress, she reared up, fists flying. "You're the one who's cruising, mister!"

He did three things then, three simple, seemingly reflexive moves that set the stage for the showdown that followed. She would never know if they were calculated or spontaneous, but she did know one thing. *She should have listened to her little voice.* First, he infuriated her by laughing, then he blocked the punch she swung at him, and last, with an amazing economy of effort, he flipped her over on her stomach and pinned her to the mattress with an arm-lock.

"You bastard!" Her moan of pain was more for effect than anything else. She was facing the wall and couldn't see what he was doing, but she could feel his knee on her bottom, holding her down. He was also up to something further south, in the vicinity of her legs. He was trying to get them apart!

She clenched her thighs and linked her ankles, then craned around to get a look at what he was doing. The first thing she spotted was the pair of blue jeans he'd given her earlier. They'd been lying across the bottom of the bed where she'd tossed them. Now he had them clamped under his arm, and he was working furiously at the hammerlock of her crossed legs.

She might as well have been naked for all the help her T-shirt was. The damn thing was twisted up around her midriff.

"Let go of me!"

"If I did," he muttered, "I couldn't live with myself."

"I'm a grown woman, you pervert! You lay a hand on me and it qualifies as sexual assault."

"It should qualify me for sainthood."

"All right, then, go ahead, beat me! Do it!"

"Beat you?" His head snapped up and he scowled at her. "I'm trying to get you dressed, you little slut."

"*Slut?*" The word fairly shot out of her. It wasn't the first time Gus had been insulted with a pejorative like that, and it wouldn't be the last. Models were fair game, and with her reputation, she might as well have been wearing a bull's-eye on her forehead. But coming from him, it felt like an open-handed slap, and it hurt like hell.

Stung, she jackknifed around and slapped him back. Her open palm made a sharp, popping sound against his cheek and left a bright crimson handprint on his skin. Tears sprung to his eyes, and she could hardly believe she'd hit him that hard.

"Okay, you're on," he warned savagely. "You want a pervert, you got one."

Gus thrashed and kicked for all she was worth, but he hauled her up by her hips, clearly determined to wrestle her into the time-honored position of prep school corporal punishment. When at last he had her prone and bent over his lap, he clamped an arm over her shoulder blades.

"You degenerate!" she wailed, astounded by his unspeakable crudeness. "You're proving my theory about men and frontal intelligence!"

"What theory?"

"That you don't have any!" She flinched in anticipation of the first whack, but instead she felt the pressure lift from her shoulder blades. He was letting her up? She twisted around to look at him. "You're not going to do it?"

He shrugged it off. "What's the point."

But Gus was too angry to let it go that easily. In fact, she was outraged. "Oh, no—you're not getting away with that," she snapped. "You do it! You just go right ahead and do it. Give vent to all those animal urges, humiliate me! You know you want to."

"I do *not* want to."

"Of course you do! It's a power thing with men like you."

"Go on, get up," he said wearily. "The party's over."

"No way! Not until you prove exactly how primitive you are! I want to be able to remember this moment for the rest of my life—and hate you for it. You've robbed me of my dignity. You will not rob me of my anger!"

"All right, for chrissake!"

His hand arced up and Gus shrieked. "No! Don't you touch me! If you touch me, I'll—*Ouuuch*!"

Another quick crack of his palm forced a gasp out of her. God, it stung like nettles! The third stroke brought a litany of swear words so obscene even she couldn't believe she'd said them.

"You have a license to carry that mouth?" Disgust in his voice, he dropped his legs and let her slide to the floor. With a sidelong glance at her smoldering fury, he shook his head. "I'm not into cheap thrills," he said, rising from the cot. "Let somebody else teach you manners."

The man who had sex with the dead wasn't into cheap thrills?

Gus glared at his scarred back as he crossed the room and wished she had a knife. A gun would be too neat, too quick. She wanted him to suffer. She didn't care how terribly he must have suffered once, considering the wounds he already had. Yanking her stretched-out T-shirt, she pulled it into place, and when finally she'd restored herself to her former pitiful condition, she scooped up the overcoat, returned to her perch on the cot, and wrapped the coat around her.

There would be time, she told herself. *Plenty* of time to deal with this man. When her fiancé finally found them, he would exact some sweet justice. All she had to do was get to the phone in the Blazer and let him know where she was. Her darling Rob would come for her. She had boundless faith.

Shifting around to avoid the tender spot on her backside, she began to examine the damage to the soles of her feet.

There turned out to be only one sliver, but it was a nasty one. She would probably need first aid. The man was a Neanderthal, dragging women around. Fortunately or not, restraint had never been one of Gus's virtues, and as she dug out the tiny shard and winced at the pain, she couldn't resist having the last word.

"If you've got some crazy he-man notion that a spanking was what I needed," she told him, "just get it out of your head. Corporeal punishment doesn't work, you know. All the experts say that. Not even with children. All it does is enrage them and teach them that hitting is appropriate, which of course, it isn't—"

"Either you shut up and go to sleep instantly, or I'll do it for you."

"Oh, yeah . . . how?"

"With this." He whirled on her, a weapon in his hand—a big weapon. It was definitely not a tranquilizer gun.

Gus watched his thumb depress the hammer.

She heard the click of a bullet being chambered.

Suddenly it was very quiet in the Mojave Desert.

CHAPTER
6

"*Eeeeeek!*" THE FIEND IS AFTER ME! *THE EVIL, TWISTED fiend!!*"

Lake Featherstone heard the childlike shrieks just seconds before he saw a bullet of pink come barreling down the formal stairway at him. He'd been in the library, lingering over after-dinner brandy, perhaps longer than he should have, and now he was headed to his room for the evening.

"She's torturing me!" the bullet cried, whizzing down the steps past him. "The wicked kitchen Amazon is torturing me!"

Lake touched the balustrade, steadying himself as he turned to watch his five-year-old niece dart down the remaining few stairs and skate in her ballet slippers across the gleaming black and white tiles of the mansion's foyer. He'd turned thirty-seven his last birthday, but living in close quarters with such a strange little urchin often made him feel twice that old.

"Bridget! Come back here!"

Now Frances Brightly was lumbering down the stairs, a

pair of children's cotton pajamas waving in her hand, and the child had begun shrieking again.

"What's the problem, Frances?" Lake asked, straining to be heard over the racket.

"Kid needs her chops busted, that's the problem." Frances snorted indignantly as she came to a halt a few steps above him. "Can't get her out of those damn tights, not even to go to bed. She wants to eat, drink, sleep in that ballet getup."

Bridget had stopped shrieking, but she was poised at the end of the hallway, apparently prepared to run out the front door into the night in order to avoid the unthinkable violation that Frances was suggesting.

"Madame Zola says we must live the dance," Bridget piped up. "We *must* eat, sleep, and drink the dance. How can I sleep the dance if I have to wear those blecchy pajamas to bed?"

"Madame Zola needs her pointy French head examined," Frances mumbled, resuming her efforts to get down the steps. "Too many damn hours in toe shoes, if you ask me."

Another shriek rose from the child, and Lake threw up his hand to stop both of them. The noise was going to wake Lily, his twin sister, and then he'd have more shrieking women on his hands than he could possibly contend with. Lily had gone up earlier, complaining of a headache, and since she'd seemed tense lately—*brittle* was probably more apt as he thought about it—and surprisingly unpredictable, he didn't want to provoke her any further.

"Frances, why don't you let me talk to Bridget?" he said in soothing, ministerial tones. "I'm sure she'll listen to me."

"Oh, yeah, right." The housekeeper's monumental disdain said teaching pigs to fly backward would be easier. "*You* can put her to bed then." She turned herself around and started back up the steps, still grumbling. "It's my day off tomorrow. Getting my things together and going home now."

And not a moment too soon, Lake thought.

As she made her heavy, unhappy ascent and left, he

seated himself in the elegant curve of the mahogany stairs, half of a double staircase that arced up in perfect symmetry from either side of the foyer to the second floor. Hung directly between the stairs, a splendid antique Viennese chandelier dripped silvery light from tier after tier of crystal ice.

Bridget was already gazing at him with interest and hazarding an approach, her fierce blue eyes blinking. He thought about what a prickly little charmer she was, with her fair skin and hair, and how sad it was that none of them had ever been able to love her the way they should have, except perhaps Gus.

There were so many disturbing reasons, not the least of which was the lingering, tragic death of her mother, Lake and Lily's younger sister, Jillian. That had taken an indescribable toll on the family, though perhaps Bridget least of all, since she'd been an infant when it happened. Privately Lake had always felt the child, herself, was part of the problem. She was a unique and difficult creature. Gus had discovered her reading at three, and Bridget had shown other early signs of genius, including an aptitude for math and science. They'd put her in a private preschool for the gifted, and she'd seemed reasonably content with her books and her ballet, until recently.

"Frances doesn't scare me, you know," she said now, pointing the toe of each foot in turn as she walked toward him. "I just let her think so. It's important to her."

He nodded, surpressing laughter. "I'm sure it is."

"When's Gus coming back?"

The child didn't know yet, he reminded himself. She'd been at a summer school session when the kidnapping had occurred that morning, and Frances had managed to keep her away from the television since.

"Gus had to go away for a couple of days on modeling business," he explained, repeating the story they'd all agreed upon.

"Yeah, I know," she said with a careless shrug, kneeling on the bottom step and gazing up at him. "She told me yesterday she was going away, but I thought she meant the weekend. I just wondered if she was coming back soon. She said she'd bring me a Wacky Wall Walker."

"A w-what?"

She peered at him and grinned. "Oh . . . you do that, too, huh? You get stuck on words like Gus does."

"No, actually I don't. I was just wondering what a Wacky Wonker is."

"A Wacky Wall Walker?" She climbed up and sat on the step next to him. "You throw it at the wall and it walks down like a spider. My friend at school has one. They're cool!"

Now he couldn't help himself. The excitement was so unlike her, he found himself laughing softly. She was usually fairly remote toward him, though he'd often wondered if it was a reflection of his own feelings more than anything else. "I don't doubt it for a minute," he said. "And I'm sure Gus will bring one back with her. What do you say? Want to go to bed now?"

"Can I wear my leotards?" He nodded and she beamed. "Will you piggyback me, too?"

"Up the stairs?" He slipped his hand in hers and felt a shadow press his heart as they rose together. So much wreckage, he thought. So many haunting regrets. Too many. "Why don't we just walk and hold hands?"

She had him riled.

Not too many women could have accomplished that. Few would have dared try. There was a time when he wouldn't have needed much more reason than that to pull the trigger. Hell, there was a time when he wouldn't have needed *any* reason. He still harbored the impulse to do violence, but it no longer ruled him. Random bloodshed wasn't the point anymore. Finding them, the ones who executed his baby daughter and destroyed his wife's sanity, that was the point.

Jack Culhane couldn't sleep. He'd stretched out on the floor of the shack over an hour ago, thoughts of Gus Featherstone cluttering up his head. He'd grown used to hard floors *and* hard women, but she was something else, a piece of work, as they said. He couldn't make up his mind if she was fearless or bogus. He did know he'd never run into a crazier female, and he'd crossed paths with some crazy ones in his travels.

He was lying flat out on his back, his jeans undone, his shirt hanging open, even though the cool air gliding through the window gave him goosebumps. He'd rested his head on his folded arms, and his shoulders ached against the rough pine slats, but he wasn't inclined to move. The cushion of his linked hands allowed him to tilt back his head and observe her through lowered lids.

He wasn't concerned about keeping an eye on her. She wasn't going anywhere this time of night, and he'd rigged the place to go off like a five-alarm fire if she did try to escape. It was purely curiosity that had him hooked, or maybe disbelief. He wondered what the media would think of her now, bent over her own filthy feet, muttering four-letter words as she gingerly dug slivers from her soles.

The lantern that glowed next to the cot lit her up like a street urchin sitting by an alley campfire. Her dark hair was a rat's nest of tangles, and the grime that coated her face did nothing for her famous bone structure. Incandescent little blobs of hot-pink nail polish gleamed through the dirt that streaked her feet and ankles. No, the beautiful brat didn't look either beautiful or bratty tonight. She looked pathetic.

"Shit," she whispered, grimacing as she twisted this way and that, trying to squeeze a stubborn splinter from the ball of her foot. Her eyes welled with tears. "Shit, shit, fuck—shit!"

"You all right?" He was careful not to let any genuine concern soften the sardonic question.

She didn't even bother to look up. "If I didn't hate you so much, I'd be fine."

"You can hate me, just keep your clothes on while you're doing it."

That brought her head up. Her dark eyes glittered dangerously, whether with tears or anger he couldn't tell.

"What's your problem?" she asked. "Is it women in general, or is it merely the female body that bothers you?"

"I have no problem with the female body, except when *yours* happens to be in my face. Naked."

She shook back her hair. "Nakedness? That's what disturbs you? *My* nakedness? That could only mean a couple of things. Either you prefer men, which I sincerely doubt, or—"

"You're right to doubt."

"Then what . . . it's me? You don't find me attractive?"

That seemed to astound her. She *was* a piece of work. "Apparently I'm the first?" he said.

"Oh, never mind."

She went back to her grimy surgery then, and Jack realized something. He was going to have to find a way to get through to this nutsball because she had what he needed. Information. Five years ago a priceless Van Gogh still life had been stolen from a vault within a secured government warehouse, and that theft was linked directly to the tragedy with his wife and child. The theft involved black-market art smuggling on an international scale, and he had reason to think her stepfamily, or someone connected with them, was involved.

Gus Featherstone could help him with that. She might be the only one who could. There were things he needed to know about the logistics and security of the Featherstone mansion, which was where the family's art collection was housed. He didn't want to have to force the answers out of her at gunpoint. However, if that's what it took.

"That idiot security guard is lucky I didn't kill him," he said softly.

She was nearly bent over double now, working away, and she didn't seem to have heard him. He rather admired her agility and considered telling her there was a makeshift shower behind the curtain near her bed that she could use— if the well wasn't dry—but then he'd have to roust himself and pump the water. Tomorrow was soon enough, he decided. She wouldn't have gangrene by then.

"Got it!" she exclaimed with real pride, holding up a

nasty-looking shard. Her expression flashed from triumph to slow-dawning perplexity as she zoomed in on him. "What idiot security guard?"

"How many idiot security guards do we know? The one who tried to stop me from taking you, of course."

"He was only doing his job."

She was going to defend the idiot. Excellent. Jack rolled to his side and propped himself up with an elbow. "I don't think I've ever seen worse security. The guard shouldn't have let me through the gate without checking my story, and then he got suspicious and compounded his mistake by sneaking up behind me."

"What's wrong with that?"

"I had a *gun*. He had plenty of time to see it before he committed himself. One whiff of my Magnum, and he should have been on the horn to the police. But no, he had to be a hero."

He loaded his heavy sigh with contempt. "Anybody could have pulled off that kidnapping, including Beavis and Butthead."

"Hardly." She proceeded to enlighten the Philistine. "Maybe the guard was negligent," she admitted, "but the security at the mansion is excellent, leading edge. The entire kidnapping is probably on video."

Yes, exactly why he'd stayed out of range of the camera at the guard gate, and why he'd put on a ski mask once he got through. "I didn't see any cameras at the pool."

"Of course you didn't. It's all done with fiber optics. They're in the pool lights."

Bingo. This was going to be easier than he thought. Her technical expertise was questionable, but the point was to keep her talking. "If it's fiber optics, then they must have run wires into the pool lights that feed information to the cameras."

"Well, yes, I suppose that's how it's done. But that's kid stuff compared to Lake's control room. There are banks of screens, and—" She went quiet suddenly, and alert. "Why do you want to know about the mansion's security?"

He shrugged off the question. "All I said was the guard was an idiot. You're the one who brought up the rest of it."

She went back to her grooming then, wadding the hem of the T-shirt and using it to dab at dirt smudges. Finally, as her efforts led up her thigh, revealing more and more skin, she hesitated and looked up at him. Her brows knit. "So, what is it you don't like about me? Specifically. My legs?"

He looked her over. "I'm sure your legs are fine when they're not covered with scuzz."

"My breasts then?"

"I'm sure they're fine, too."

"You saw them," she reminded him.

"I could hardly miss them."

"I've been told they're incredible."

He shrugged indifferently. "Are they real?"

She sniffed at that and began to pull up her T-shirt as if another look would verify their authenticity. On the way she inadvertently gave him an eyeful that nearly took his breath away. A beaver shot, he marveled. That's what they would have called it in his horny high school days. Her legs were folded Indian-style, and her creamy white inner thighs made him fantasize how she must look on a runway. All legs, he imagined. Her inner thighs were just about the only part of her not smudged with something, except for the black satin delta that sat enticingly at their center. Christ! He'd done plenty of things outside the law, but this was his first kidnapping. It would also be his last, and she could take the credit for reforming him.

His hand shot up to stop her from exposing anything else. "Once was sufficient, thanks."

"Aren't we polite?" she told him hotly. "You're not exactly Mr. January, you know."

She corkscrewed around and kicked his blue jeans off the bed, then pulled the trench coat over her and flopped down as if to go to sleep. There was a lot of twisting and sighing involved until she got herself settled, but she finally ended up on her stomach, her face smashed into the tattered mattress.

Maybe she'll smother, he thought.

The possibility had a certain macabre appeal, and much as it pained him to admit it, so did she. It wasn't just her physical appeal, it was her style. She wasn't a woman, she was an event. Like fireworks on New Year's Eve, she was more noise and flash than gunpowder, but she was incredibly shrewd under all the pyrotechnics. And cute, too, though he loathed that word. He didn't want to think about what sex with her would be like. No, he did *not* want to think about that.

Staring up at the ceiling now, he was aware once again of the aching soreness in his shoulders and the gooseflesh on his naked skin. His body was humming with an inner expectancy, readying itself for some physical encounter. His hands had that restless, empty feeling he'd noticed while driving the car and the hot spark in his jeans was kindling into something hungry and dangerous. How long had it been since he'd been with a woman? How much longer had it been since he'd wanted to be with one?

Don't contaminate the work with personal feelings, Culhane. You did that once before and everyone you loved got killed.

The litany stormed his thoughts, warning him, reminding why he was here and what he'd been doing the last five years. It had kept him straight all that time, that and a rage for justice.

Even so, he couldn't deny what was happening to his body tonight. Hunger? Shit, he had a need that hadn't been fed in years. If he was being truthful, he was ravenous, starved for a woman's touch. He rolled over on his side, facing away from her and felt the sharp ache in his shoulders as it flared lower, in the depths of his groin. The muscles were on fire, aching to be flexed, to be used. There would be damn little sleep tonight, he realized.

Gus stirred several times during the night, and each time she opened her eyes she saw something more startling and dreamlike than the last. He was awake, or so it seemed, and doing things that didn't make sense. The first time she woke he was sitting in the rocker, cradling a can of beer in his hand. He wasn't drinking from it. The can wasn't even open. He was simply staring at it and rocking as if he were slowly dying of thirst and the beer was laced with poison.

Odd, she thought, that he would bring beer he didn't intend to drink. Odd that he wouldn't even allow himself that.

The second time she came awake, it was as if she'd never drifted off, as if she'd only been dozing fitfully. She saw him bathed in the green glow of a liquid crystal display. He was sitting at the table, caught in the eerie, electronic light of a computer screen as if it had cast a spell over him, and he couldn't break away. His fingers worked the keyboard without making a sound, and the intensity of his focus frightened her. There was something sinister about it, something she didn't understand, like his palpable obsession with the can of beer.

When she woke the last time that night, she saw him as if through a drowsy, heavy-lidded golden mist. He was still sitting at the table, but this time there was a silver knife flashing in his hand.

Whittling, she realized. He was whittling.

Gradually the strange scene came into focus. The piece he was working on was a small and delicate yet very elaborate structure made up of tiny pieces of wood, some of them not much thicker than the sliver she had extracted from her foot. It looked like a fairy tale castle. Yes, he was building a castle in miniature, but what fascinated her as much as his creation was his machetelike knife. It was the same ferocious killing tool he'd strapped to his thigh when he'd gone out that day. The huge, gleaming thing glowed yellow in the firelight from the lanterns and made her think of the raw power of the outdoorsmen in Marlboro ads. He might have been one of those men himself except that there was a quality haunting his rugged profile she'd never seen in a cigarette ad. Traces of melancholy shadowed his concentration, turning him into a stoic, a man so inured to the pain he barely recognized it as his.

She drifted off again with that thought in her mind . . . and still wondering if it could have been a dream.

*   *   *

Somehow she had to escape. That was the sole thought occupying Gus's mind when she opened her eyes the next morning. She'd been pretending to be asleep for the last half hour, watching him as he pulled on his boots and tied the sheathed machete to his jeans. The purposefulness with which he'd done it and then headed out the door made her think he must be going off in search of food, and it had surprised her that he would leave her unguarded.

One look out the window above the bed told her she wouldn't get far, even if she did attempt to escape. He was a half-mile away, but still within eyeshot. The lay of the land was such that he could have seemingly walked off the end of the earth before he would have lost sight of the shack.

This wasn't going to be easy, she realized. If all else failed, the man had to sleep some time, which meant she would have to make it a point to be awake when he wasn't. . . .

Lizards skittered in every direction when she stepped out of bed a moment later. She was getting used to the little green gargoyles by now, but couldn't hold back a shiver as she crossed the creaking, sighing floor. A gritty substance prickled the soles of her feet and worked its way into the crevices between her toes. Shavings from his whittling, she realized. The wood dust and tailings were everywhere, coating the floor and the chair with feathery gray snow.

The castle he'd made sat on the table, its graceful balustrades and spires aligned so delicately she could hardly believe it was real. On closer inspection, she saw that the only thing holding the pieces together were notches in the wood itself. How had he done it with a knife that size? The carving was fantastically intricate and detailed.

The melancholy she'd seen in his profile stirred within her as she realized there was no way to preserve the piece. Its fragility made her think of her own daydreams of magical edifices, castles spun out of light and spiraling toward the misted sun. It would be a crime to destroy anything so pristine, she realized, but the desert had little regard for perfection. It was a hostile place with its charred, barren vistas and blood-boiling heat. Or was it he who was hostile?

Her growling stomach reminded her she was starving.

His duffel bag yielded two high-protein candy bars, and she grabbed both of them, scarfing one down as she continued to search the contents of the bag. Only supreme self-control kept her from devouring the other. She would save it instead, she told herself. There might be a time when she would need it more than right now.

The bag also contained a shiny metal briefcase with a combination lock that she suspected must contain the computer she'd seen. Why a kidnapper would cart a computer around with him, she couldn't imagine, but if she hadn't dreamed the castle, she doubted that she'd dreamed the computer. Her search didn't yield any weapons, which told her that he'd hidden the Magnum somewhere else or taken it with him, but she did find a photograph hidden in a side pocket of the case. It was a tattered snapshot of a still life painting, and though she was not the art expert her stepbrother was, she recognized the style as reminiscent of Van Gogh's.

Moments later as she looked around for something to wipe her grimy hands on, it hit her that her hands were the least of it. She was grimy everywhere, hopelessly filthy. A hysterical sound gurgled up. No one would believe this! If Rob could see her now— No, if *Vogue's* West Coast Bureau Chief could see her now! They would all boggle. She lifted her head and sniffed the air, wrinkling her nose. God, what was that smell? Lizard shit? No, it was *her*. And she was worse than anything lizards could have left. Gus Featherstone smelled like an unwashed jock strap.

Choking back laughter, she began suddenly, inexplicably, to cry. "Oh, my God," she whispered as tears blinded her for a moment. This wasn't like her at all. She never cried, ever, and the uncontrollable emotion propelled her to the sink, where she cranked on the tap. Red water was better than no water.

As she scrubbed at her grimy face and arms, she told herself that the tears weren't for her. She was sad for Rob, who must be frantic wondering where she was. And for Bridget, whom she missed terribly. Emotion welled up into her throat as she thought about the towheaded moppet, who seemed to have inextricably tangled herself in Gus's heartstrings. *If you dare worry about me, Bridge, even for a moment, I'll hide your toe shoes when I get home.*

The metal storage cabinet still made her uneasy, but it was time to brave the evil thing, she decided when she'd finished washing up. Sucking it in, she headed for it, but she wasn't halfway across the room when something astonishing happened. The entire place seemed to shift and shudder like an ocean-going ship.

Being a native Californian, her first thought was of the Big One. She turned, scanning the walls, the ceiling, peering out the window before she realized it was the floor beneath her. It was giving way! She sprang back and realized she'd stepped into the trap instead of out of it.

The rotting boards sagged under her weight, toppling her forward. Pain streaked through her injured knee as she landed on it, and a flurry of snapping and crackling dropped her down another half foot. The floor was about to collapse totally and there seemed to be nothing beneath it!

"Help!" she cried, knowing no one could hear her.

Desperate, she clawed at the crumbling pine slats, breaking one fingernail after another as she struggled to get enough leverage to pull herself out. "The hell with this," she snarled as another nail snapped. Heaving furiously, she hoisted herself out with a superhuman effort.

Once she was safe, she inspected her stinging knees and stanched the fresh-flowing blood with her T-shirt. The cut had been reopened, and she cursed the foul, rotting boards that did it. First slivers, now broken fingernails and mangled body parts. The goddamn floor was out to get her.

But then again . . . maybe not.

Studying the crater she'd made, she bent over the maw and peered through the broken boards. There was a pit beneath the shack's floor. A very deep pit. Another expletive fell out of her mouth, this time more awed than obscene. Rocking up to a kneeling position, she began to work frantically, putting a plan into action even before she'd had a chance to fully think it through. This might be her only opportunity, and he could return at any time. She had to work fast.

She meshed the broken boards back together as best she could, securing them with some of the sharp little pieces of wood he'd discarded while whittling. As soon as she was done, she gathered up a handful of the sawdust and covered the broken boards with it to camouflage them. After that she dragged the rocker over to the corner by the cot. The last thing she did was put on the blue jeans he'd given her, knowing it would confuse him.

From her vantage point in the chair, she watched the door and thought through her plan, fine-tuning it. It was important that he respond swiftly and without analyzing what he was doing. She was going to have to motivate him just right.

When the door finally did swing open, the first thing she saw was the burlap sack he was carrying. He tossed it onto the table, where it landed with a soft, fleshy thunk, and then he strode in after it. The floor groaned plaintively under his heavy steps, and the smells of sage and sweat filled the room.

The hunter-gatherer had returned. He moved first to untie the sack's drawstring. Once he'd accomplished that and yanked the sack open, he drew his knife from the sheath on his thigh. The silver blade flashed blindingly, sending sunlight zinging in all directions.

What was he going to do? Clean his kill? That possibility galvanized her. "We're not alone," she announced.

"What's that?" He glanced over his shoulder at her.

"There's someone or some*thing* in that cabinet." She pointed him toward the rusting unit. "I heard it scratching."

He swung around, knife in hand.

"Wait!" The chair groaned as she left it rocking and rushed toward him. "Don't go over there. It could be dangerous."

"Don't be ridiculous." He gave her a pained grimace. "It's probably nothing, a rat."

"I heard it growl. Rats don't growl."

"There's nothing in there," he insisted, setting the knife on the table. "I opened it this morning. There were some dried-up lizards, a few dead flies. None of them looked very dangerous to me."

She forced a smile and backed away. "You're probably right. I'm just jumpy."

"Of course I'm right. Here, I'll show you."

The floorboards gave way the instant he stepped on them. There was no warning, no crackling or snapping this time. They simply opened up like a trapdoor and he disappeared.

Gus didn't see him hit bottom, but she heard a *kawhump* that shook the shack violently, and the next thing she knew, a siren was wailing in her ears. She turned in horror, compelled to the window by the deafening sound. She expected to see police cars, ambulances, maybe even fire engines, but there was nothing outside the cabin but sand and sagebrush. Nothing! That's when she realized he must have wired the shack with a motion device in case she tried to escape.

She told herself to run, to grab some supplies and make a break for the van while it was still cool enough to travel through the desert. This might be her only chance! Her heart was pounding as hard as if she were running. Her nerves jumped, anticipating flight. But instead, she turned slowly back to the pit as if she were drawn by some invisible tether and stared at the gaping hole, trying to imagine what had happened to him.

The jangling bell made it impossible to hear any noise he might be making. He could be hurt or even unconscious. She would have her head handed to her if he ever got out of there, and perhaps several other body parts as well. But she had to know. She couldn't leave without knowing.

"Are you all right?" she asked as she crept toward the edge.

He didn't answer. He probably couldn't hear her over the alarm, and she couldn't see him until she got to the very brink of her homemade deadfall. He was crouched against the dirt wall, frozen where he knelt. He glanced up at her and shook his head negatively.

"You're not all right?" she persisted.

Gus didn't understand what he meant until he mouthed a word that turned her blood to ice. *Snake.* With great difficulty she crept around to the end of the pit where he was trapped and saw the rattler coiled less than five feet away from him. Its eyes seemed to glow in the dark—glittering orbs that bulged in their sockets and looked as if they were lit by the fires of hell. The evil thing was swaying slowly, its fangs bared.

If he moved, it would strike.

"Get my gun," he told her, mouthing the words. "It's in the briefcase. Five-two-seven."

But Gus had begun to teeter so violently she couldn't walk. She couldn't even speak. Just the sight of the reptile had totally unhinged her. She felt as if something inside her were screaming as loudly as the siren, shrieking so wildly it might drive her insane.

"Gus!" he yelled over the noise of the alarm. "My *gun*! You have to get it. You have to shoot the snake."

She lurched back, soaked in sweat. "No—"

"You have to—Gus!"

She wanted to, but she couldn't. Her fears had already plummeted her into the past, into a waking nightmare that swam with slithering, crawling creatures, their eyes glittering like the snake's in the pit. Screams shook her small, rigid six-year-old body as the cold, slimy ropes coiled themselves around her arms and legs, around her throat. Their hisses burned in her ears, their fangs pierced her tender flesh . . .

She heard him calling her name as she turned and burst out the door, and knew she would never forget the horrible grip in his voice as long as she lived. It clung to her as she floundered through the sinking sand, wondering which way the van was. Which way? She had to find it. This was her chance to escape. He couldn't follow her now. She was free.

*   *   *

The van was still nowhere in sight when she dropped to her knees in the desert, dizzy with confusion and gasping under the rising sun. She was lost. Her head was buzzing, her lips painfully cracked, and her throat so dry she couldn't swallow or speak. She had no idea how long she'd been walking, but she was afraid to go any farther.

Turning in a circle, she searched the arid, wind scarred landscape and realized she had no idea how to find the van. Something that might have been the shack was still visible behind her, a black spot in the distance. The moment she saw it, a sob burned in her throat. She had to go back. She couldn't leave him that way. Death by snake venom was slow and torturous. His suffering would be unbearable.

She was nearly blinded by the time she got back. The sun had burned dazzling white spots into her retinas that couldn't be extinguished, even when she closed her eyes. It was like being forced to stare into a spotlight. The pain of her scorched vision, her sunburned face and arms, was excruciating. It felt as if someone had set her on fire!

The sun could be fatal at this time of day. Sheer terror had forced her out of the cabin, that and the chance to escape. She should never have left, and now she had no way of knowing what awaited her inside. What would she do if he'd been bitten? She didn't know how to treat snakebites. She didn't know first aid, and if it was something worse— No, she couldn't allow herself to imagine him already dead.

She was wearing his canvas shoes and they were huge and unwieldy, but even without them, the three porch steps would have been more than she could manage. She didn't realize how sick she was until she tried to climb them. The railing swayed dizzily with her weight, and the handrail wrenched up as she grasped it, exposing rusted bolts and nails. By the time she'd pulled herself up to the landing, she was rocking on her feet like a drunk person and swallowing back the sour taste of nausea.

The alarm was still ringing, but she could barely hear it now, as if it were coming from a tunnel. This *was* heatstroke, she realized. Her internal temperature must be dangerously high. Even her tongue felt thickened and unmanageable. Her vision was spotty now, washing in and out, but she could see that the door was hanging open, just as she'd left it.

The interior of the shack looked cool and dark, but Gus's dread was so great that the vaultlike gloom only intensified it. She didn't want to go inside. She wanted to run back into the raging inferno called Mojave and vanish without a trace, evaporate instantly like raindrops. It would be easier than facing this nightmare. Anything would be.

But she couldn't run away. She'd been through this before, years before, when she was hardly older than Bridget, only then she was the one trapped in the pit. It was a freezing February morning, just one week after her mother walked out. Lake and Lily had caught her crying and locked her in the abandoned root cellar in the basement of the family mansion. It had been their idea of a good joke, and to be fair, perhaps neither could have foreseen what would happen.

Gus had pleaded to be let out, but no one came. And when the snakes began to crawl inside her clothing, when they pierced her flesh with their fangs, she shrieked so long and loud that her voice gave out. A doctor later diagnosed her vocal cords as permanently scarred, but that was only the physical damage. The emotional trauma left her unable to speak and quaking in terror, even after the doctor had pronounced her well.

No one understood her fears or why she couldn't control them. Lake and Lily teased her cruelly, and the housekeeper punished her for malingering. Her stepfather seemed barely able to stand the sight of her, probably because she reminded him of her mother. The fact that he'd done the honorable thing and lived up to his obligation as her adoptive parent, despite his personal feelings, was clearly all that he felt was required of him.

Gus saw only one way out of the nightmare. Her shame was so great that her desire to escape her tormentors, which included her own paralyzing fears, became an obsession. There were train tracks along the perimeter of the Featherstone property and a Southern Pacific freight train rumbled by every morning like clockwork. She stole out at dawn one day, liberated by her decision and free of her fears for the first time. But as she sat hunched on the wooden ties, absorbing their deadly vibrations and waiting with a stoic heart for her deliverance, waiting to be forever at peace, she realized she didn't want to die.

She wanted to live. She wanted to fight.

That was the day the brat was born.

His gun was somewhere in the briefcase. What was the combination? She remembered a five, a two, and a seven.

Moments later, hunched over in front of the case, her hands shaking uncontrollably, she tried several combinations before the lid flew open. In the green glow of the screen she saw the words SATLINK above a menu of choices that were too technical to decipher. The rest of the screen was a grid of the shack and the surrounding desert with two flashing sensors that must have been the intrusion devices. A message blinking across it all said SECURITY BREACHED! ALARM ACTIVATED! PRESS EXIT TO TERMINATE!

Gus searched the keyboard, hit the exit key, and the shack was plunged into silence. A sob welled in her throat, and she shuddered with relief. Now she had to find the gun! He'd said it was in the briefcase, and as she tried various buttons and dials, the keyboard lifted, revealing a compartment underneath.

The Magnum was there, as cold and clumsy as a boulder as she lifted the gun into her hands. She didn't know how to use it, but he would tell her. He would tell her what to do.

Sickness washed over her as she walked to the mouth of the pit, the gun cradled gingerly in her hands. He was still there, crouched just as she'd left him, only the light from the window had shifted. It illuminated his eyes now, and Gus could see their flat, dead stare. He had given up on people, not today, but a very long time ago. Today she had proved him right in doing so.

The rattlesnake was frozen like a porcelain sculpture, its head and neck forming the perfect *S* curve of a swan. Gus had never seen anything so graceful . . . or so evil.

She swayed over the broken boards, waiting for him to

tell her what to do. When he said nothing, when he wouldn't even look at her, she grasped the gun in both hands and pointed it at the snake.

The rattler's head flicked up. Its marble eyes gleamed at her, and a horrible, hollow rattle filled the air.

Terror slammed into Gus's body like an oncoming freight train, like the death she had narrowly avoided as a child. She stepped back from the side of the pit, her hands shaking. The only way to get through this thing was to keep moving forward, she told herself, to do the next thing that had to be done. Point the gun and pull the trigger, that was the next thing! Pull the trigger!

Her forefinger jerked back to the sound of an empty click. No! Oh, God, no! She let out a silent and terrible cry of disbelief. The gun hadn't gone off!

"Cock it, Gus. Pull back the hammer!"

Dizziness made her stagger farther back. Oh, Christ, of course! She hadn't done it right. She had to pull back the hammer first. Which was the hammer? She only knew about guns from the movies. *Which was the hammer?*

The rattling noises grew louder and louder, battering at her nerves. Someone was laughing, she realized. No, they were screaming, the terrible high-pitched screams that only she could hear. *Her hands were frozen!* She couldn't do this. She couldn't!

"Cock the gun, goddammit!"

Her thumb spasmed, dragging the hammer back with it. Pain streaked up her arm, and the gun went off with a flash of light and a deafening explosion. The stench of burnt gunpowder seared her nostrils.

"Jesus Christ! Don't shoot *me*!" The kidnapper sprang up, flattening himself against the wall.

Gus let out a cry of sheer, wretched agony. She'd missed the snake and nearly hit him!

The snake flashed into the air, a much deadlier weapon than the gun. It struck so quickly all Gus could see was a blur.

The kidnapper moaned. "It got me."

Gus began to sob. She closed her eyes and squeezed the

trigger savagely. This time the weapon's kick felt ferocious. It rocked through her, snapping her head back and dropping her to her knees.

She threw the gun away and fell to the floor, rolling up like someone under attack, splaying her hands over her head and refusing to open her eyes. The blast of the gun reverberated in her ears.

CHAPTER
7

JACK HAD LOST COUNT OF HOW MANY TIMES HIS LIFE PASSED before his bleary eyes, but he did know the rattler had struck him at least twice before Gus shot it. The impact of the attacks had spun him off balance and thrown him out of her line of fire, fortunately for him. How she actually hit the snake was anybody's guess. It took more than dumb luck to hit a flying object with your eyes closed. It took a Ringling Brothers Circus act.

Disbelief fizzed up like cold, burning laughter. She was that, he conceded, squinting up at the bright circle of light above him. All three rings, even if her timing did stink. Apparently she'd followed her sharpshooting exhibition with another disappearing act. Where the hell was she?

He slumped against the wall and bent over dizzily, running his hand down the leg of his jeans to check for puncture wounds. He'd felt the pressure when the snake bit him, but not the pain. That meant nothing, of course. He'd taken five hollow point bullets in the gut, chest, and face once, and he'd felt zip then. Adrenaline had overridden any response that didn't ensure immediate survival, including the pain. Shock had done the rest. He hoped he had enough of both now to get himself out of this sinkhole. It wouldn't have surprised him if she'd dug it herself.

The tiny remote device that controlled his security sensors had dropped out of his shirt pocket during the fall, and he hadn't been able to retrieve it because of the snake. He found it now, near the rattler's carcass, scooped it up, and hit the button to rearm the devices before dropping it back in his pocket. Now to get out of the pit.

Foot and handholds gouged out of the dirt wall got him high enough to grab hold of a floorboard that would bear his weight. The rest took gut-busting strength. His jawbone felt as if it had been ground to near powder by the time he'd hauled himself up and swung a leg over the edge. Once he was that far, it was a matter of alternately heaving and hitching his way out. He still couldn't feel the pain— any pain, anywhere—but a gash on his wrist was bleeding freely, thanks to the broken boards. There were splinters and jagged edges everywhere.

Sweat poured off him, and more than once he thought about the way his laboring heart was pumping deadly snake venom through his system. His only satisfaction came from imagining her in excruciating technicolor detail as he forced her to slice open his wounds and suck out the venom. He wanted to live long enough to see that.

What he did see once he was on solid ground again was a crazed, mumbling woman, curled up on the floor like a third grader in an earthquake drill, her arms clamped over her head. An occasional shudder racked her, and she was rocking back and forth as if the movement could somehow ease her horror at what had happened. He couldn't quite make out her choked utterances at first, partly because of his own heaving weakness, but as he listened they became more intelligible.

"I sh-shot him," she sobbed. "Oh, God, he's dead, and I ki-killed him. I have a man's blood on my hands—"

Maybe he should have been touched. He wasn't.

Apparently she'd been making so much noise she hadn't

heard him fighting to drag himself out of the pit. "I'm alive," he said, trying not to topple over as he yanked up the leg of his pants, "at least for the moment."

Dizziness swamped him, muddying his concentration as he searched for the snakebite wounds. It wasn't until a moment later, when he glanced over his shoulder, that he realized she hadn't heard him. She was still hiding her head and rocking like a demented soul. And he still wasn't touched. Where had that damn snake bit him? And why the hell didn't she snap out of it so she could be of some help? He couldn't find the fang marks, but his head was buzzing like a chain saw, and his vision was going pale and spotty. With gritted teeth and a few choice words, he pulled off his boot to inspect his foot and ankle.

"Blood on my hands," she moaned. "A man's blood—"

"Gus! I'm alive, for chrissake!" Disgusted, he tossed the boot away and hauled himself over to where she was huddled. The effort made his head swim and submerged the shack under a sea of undulating water. The castle he'd been fooling with the night before was floating a foot off the table, and for an instant he thought he was going to be sick.

Sheer effort of will got him through it, but then he was left with the problem of getting through to her. He couldn't figure out where to touch her, so he gave her shoulder a shake. He used very little force, but that had nothing to do with wanting to be gentle, he told himself. He was too weak to give her a good shake.

She went completely silent at his touch, as if afraid to move. Apparently she thought he'd risen from the dead.

"You shot the snake," he told her. *Come on, Gus, baby, don't wig out on me now. I need you.*

Another shudder racked her, but still she didn't untuck. "I did?"

"Yeah, but it got me before you got it."

Now she peeked up, looking at him through the narrow opening of her clamped arms. "The snake bit you?"

"Twice, I think."

Her arms fell away and her head whipped up as if

mounted on a spring. "Are you all right?" She searched his bloodless face.

Another wave of dizziness rocked him. Swaying back on his elbow, he realized he was going to pass out. "Swell," he mumbled thickly. "I'm just swell."

The next thing he knew he was sprawled on his back on the floor and she was all over him, seemingly everywhere at once, caressing his face, her hands fluttering over his torso, unbuttoning his shirt and unzipping his pants. He could feel her inspecting his stomach, his pelvic basin, and lower. God, it felt wonderful, all of it, only she was messing with the wrong stuff.

"My leg," he croaked. "It's my leg."

There was a flurry of movement in the area of his groin and thighs, and he realized she was pulling his jeans off. Christ, what was she doing? Playing doctor? His vision washed to pale, then faded to gray. It terrified him to think that his life was in her hands, in the hands of a flaky super-model with a trust fund. Jesus!

"Get my knife," he told her. "Sterilize it with the matches in the duffel bag—"

"Oh, my God!" she cried. "I found it!"

He tried to sit up, to see what she was doing, but he was overcome with a sickening wooziness. He broke out in a film of cold sweat and dropped back to the floor, his head clunking against the boards. *Suck out the venom.*

He gasped the words, or thought he did, wondering if she could hear him, wondering if she was paying any damn attention. In a matter of seconds it was a moot question. He was whirling in a gray fog again, spiraling down into a liquid darkness. And there with him was Gus Featherstone with a huge knife and a wicked grin. Her eyes gleamed as she surveyed his nakedness. Was he having a nightmare or did she look frighteningly like Lorena Bobbitt?

It's my leg, he tried to tell her. It's my leg!

Some time later—it could have been hours or even days—he began to float back to the surface. When he finally awakened, he was sporting a major headache and not much else. Even before he'd opened his eyes, the hot breeze skimming over his body told him he was missing something, namely his clothes.

He could feel the air riffling the dark fleece that covered his pecs, as well as the small crop much farther down. His head throbbed so fiercely he could barely bring the ceiling into focus, and when he did he saw tiny green things whipping back and forth through his field of vision.

Lizards. Great.

He closed one eye and concentrated on Gus. At least she wasn't green. Sitting cross-legged on the floor next to him and still gowned in his T-shirt, she was observing him with an expression that was more expectant than fearful. In fact, if she looked concerned about him at all it was in a motherly feeling-better-now? sort of way. But there was something else about her he found even more bemusing. A spark lurked deep in her eyes, and it flared brighter when he squinted at her suspiciously. What had she done to him? He was still alive, unless this lizard was from hell, so apparently she hadn't killed him with his own knife.

In fact, Gus had done nothing to him at all. Oh, she'd undressed him, yes, and tried everything she could think of to save his incredibly sexy butt. But as it turned out, none of her efforts were necessary for reasons she would soon explain to him. She wasn't even staring at him now for any particular reason. She just loved it when he squinted at her as if she was the woman he'd least like to be stranded with on a desert island.

She was also rather intrigued at the quite lascivious spectacle he made, lying there in glorious abandon, his shirt hanging open, his jeans bunched down around his ankles, and nothing in between except muscle after muscle of strong and sunburned masculine pride.

She'd seen her share of nude male models, flashing their hard bodies as they tore off their designer clothes between runs, but this display of raw might was nothing to sneeze at, either. He was barbed-wire lean, not an extra kilogram on him anywhere, yet he was all brawn around the shoulders and chest. His arms looked like solid muscle, even relaxed.

He was hung, too.

She caught a little corner of her lip between her teeth to keep from smiling. Rather nicely, she had to admit, though she'd been trying to keep her gaze from drifting too conspicuously to that very conspicuous part of him. The springy dark curls looked crisp, yet soft, and the other prominent feature seemed surprisingly tensile considering the man's weakened condition.

Actually, it was tensile. She knew because she'd lifted it to look underneath. She had to check him for snakebites, didn't she?

He forced himself up, resting on his elbows as he peered down the length of his body. "What did you do?" He gaped with disbelief at his exposed organs, then up at her. "Molest me?"

Nothing you haven't already done to yourself, I imagine, she thought, smiling at the wickedness of the image that brought. In truth, the jeans around his ankles did give rather the impression of a rodeo romeo caught with his pants down. "Don't be silly," she told him. "I was looking for the snakebite you kept screaming about."

He squinted at her again. "Where is it?"

"It *isn't*. There isn't one. Anywhere. Believe me, if there was, I would have found it. I even rolled you over and checked your cheeks."

Watching him turn as hot pink as her erstwhile nail polish, Gus realized she'd embarrassed him. It struck her as rather charming that someone like him could be sensitive about such things. And it gave more credence to her theory that he had hang-ups. Poor sweet boy, she thought. He was blushing. Maybe she ought to see what she could do about his problem.

"But you said you found something," he insisted. "I heard you."

"I found some cuts on your legs, and one of them was red and swollen." She pointed to an enflamed area on his shin, trailing her fingers around it lightly and watching him stiffen up. What a responsive fellow he was.

"Here, this is it," she said, fluttering her fingers over the wound again just to see his reaction. "I thought it was a snakebite, but when I cleaned it up, I saw it was only a scrape. You must have done it yourself when you fell through the floor."

"The rattler got me," he said stubbornly. "I felt it."

"It got your boot, twice. I can show you if you want," she offered, pointing to his footwear. The mangled boots were neatly aligned next to the table as if waiting for him to get up in the morning, slip them on, kiss the little wife, and trot off to work. She'd done some housekeeping while he'd been in dreamland.

"Then why did I black out?" he wanted to know.

"You probably hit your head when you fell in the pit and got yourself a small concussion."

"A small concussion? Aren't we the doctor? *What are you doing?*"

He tried to ward her off as she raised up on her haunches and bent over his head as if to groom him, but she was determined. "I want to see if I'm right. If you've got a concussion, I should feel a knot somewhere."

"Aren't you supposed to check my eyes?"

"Your eyes?"

"To see if they're dilated."

Her brows knit. "I'll do that right after I find the knot."

Jack glowered up at her with enough heat to torch the shack, for what little good it did him. She was totally into her Mother Teresa, save-the-unworthy-kidnapper thing. She soothed his hot, damp forehead with the heels of her hands, her fingers feathering lightly into his hair as she worked.

"Hmmm," she murmured softly, purling her way along the contours of his scalp with movements so light and gentle they rippled his spine and sent a pleasant chill racing down his arms.

He wanted to close his eyes. He wanted to let go of the breath he was holding in reserve. *Gus, baby, why are you doing this to me? Why are you tying me in knots?* "So?" he grumbled. "Is there a knot?"

"Oh, I'm sure there is, somewhere around here. My, but

you have a wonderful lot of dark hair . . . and very little gray. I guess we don't worry much, do we?"

She'd just love to know what he was worried about now.

It felt great, what she was doing. It could have felt annoying or distracting. But no, it had to feel great, which was the last thing he needed under the circumstances. Some other guy might even have thought it was better than great. That other guy might have thought it was damn near irresistible the way she was stroking and petting and purring all over him. Especially if the guy's shoulders and arms were turning to butter . . . if his lids had begun to droop . . . and if his spine were going limp.

Jack's droopy lids flicked open. His spine might be going limp, but he could feel nerves quickening and heat stirring in dangerous places.

"Oh, here's a little bump . . . ahhh, yes, feel that?"

All he could feel above the neck were her fingers playing hide-and-seek in his hair. Maybe he did have a concussion. That would explain why he was losing control of his bodily functions. His rational brain had short-circuited and his animal urges had commandeered the control panel.

"Maybe if I try a little lower . . . ?"

"No, I don't think—" Like he could stop her. Like a Mack truck could stop her. Her fingers were sifting and drifting down the sides of his head, running amuck in his military brush cut. She traced the outline of his ears with flirty little sensations that tickled like crazy when she got to his earlobes. And then one of her fingers slipped just inside the sensitive orifice and stroked the tender membranes. Jack felt as if lightning had struck him.

"Ouch!" he said.

She swung back to look at him. "Am I hurting you?"

More than you know, he thought.

He claimed her wrists and held her back so that he could glower at her from arm's length. Not a swift move, he realized immediately. His instinct had been to avoid eye contact with her, in fact, to avoid looking at her at all. His instincts had been right. She had the kind of eyes that a century ago might have gazed at you from behind a harem veil of exotic, Oriental silk. There wasn't a word for the color. The closest he could come was violet, but that didn't even touch the vibrance. Her lids were smoky, her lashes thick and onyx black.

Harem eyes set in a sullen, slender tomboy face.

If the word pouty had been in his vocabulary, which it wasn't and wouldn't be, *ever*, he might have used it to describe her mouth—pouty, succulent, plump. He was beginning to see what everyone was talking about. Even as disheveled as she was right now, she was still sultry enough to melt icecaps. There was one thing working against her though. She stunk.

"Go take a shower," he said.

"Beg your pardon?"

"See that curtain over there?" He jerked his head toward the alcove. "There's a shower stall inside. I got the pump going this morning."

"Why . . . thank you."

She was obviously puzzled until she glanced down at his physical condition. Sparks flared in the violet depths of her irises, painting them a deeper blue color as she looked back up at him. "Seems like you could use a shower yourself, a cold one."

He warned her with his eyes. "There's only enough water for one, cold or otherwise." She'd been warned.

"That's fine . . . I'll share."

Jack could feel himself heating up again. Christ, this woman was making him blush like an idiot kid! He ought to put her in the pit and leave her there. "Take the damn shower before I change my mind," he growled, releasing her and reaching for his jeans.

He had his butt covered by the time he'd sprung to his feet and whipped around, but getting his pants zipped would have involved an act of ritual tribal mutilation. Instead he yanked his shirt together and turned just in time to see her peeling off hers. "Undress in the shower," he bit out.

"Okay, okay!" She held the cotton material to her

breasts, which exposed her behind as she prissed across the room, taking care to avoid the abyss she'd created.

Whoever had said her breasts were incredible had missed the boat, Jack thought. Her breasts were fine. But her ass, now that *was* incredible, worthy of whatever award it had won. She whipped the curtain aside but couldn't get the corroded shower door open. Watching her struggle to unjam it made him feel as if his neck had been caught in a noose, only the tension was considerably farther south.

"Here, let me do that," he said, anxious to have her and her hot little bottom out of eyeshot.

Jack Culhane to the rescue.

The door came unstuck with one blow of his shoulder. He waved her inside with a dark look, heaved a sigh of relief as she disappeared, and turned his back on the entire situation.

The rusty groans and squeaks of knobs being forced told him she'd figured out how to release the valves. Her little gasp of surprise told him the water was cold. He swiped an arm over the dampness on his forehead and walked to the window. The breeze felt hot and gritty, choked with dust. His whole body was filmed with sweat and the aroma rising off him was ripe enough to ferment fruit. And he'd been complaining about her?

He walked over to the table and stood there, having a look at the miniature kingdom he'd whittled and aware of the physical tension in his body as he hadn't been in years. His chest tightened with each breath he took. Even the soles of his bare feet felt rigid against the rough wood planks.

Behind him the shower door swung open and the T-shirt sailed into the room. He could hear her splashing gaily, water sloshing down the drain. Little silvery droplets flew like stars.

"Sure you won't join me?" she burbled. "It's fabulous, so cool and wet! And the water's hardly even red, more like amber."

He broke out in a hot sweat. It beaded on his temples and trickled down toward his ears. As he blotted the warm rivulets with the hem of his shirt, he remembered the play of her hands in his hair and the feathery caress of her fingertips along his earlobes.

Join her? Ignoring the treacherous throb in his groin, he stared at the can of beer he'd been fondling the night before, fondling like it was a warm, soft, healing woman, a woman he could lose his mind with. Jesus, he wanted a drink. How long had it been? Far too long the way he felt. The physical craving was still strong, still urgent, almost as urgent as his need to strip down and get naked in the goddamn shower.

His body wanted what he couldn't give it, what it had been denied for so long—sexual satisfaction with a woman.

He wiped the sweat from his eyes and raked his hair back. The heat was weighing him down, making it hard to breathe. What would happen if he did it? Suppose he gave in to this insane urge to join her, what then? He knew the answer without even thinking about it. He had to be crazy. What he needed from this woman was information, not *sex*. But tell that to his dick.

"Is there something wrong?" she called out.

He spun around and yelled at the partially open door, "Not a goddamn thing, Gus. It's just hot enough to bake pottery in here, that's all."

"Brrrrrr," she trilled as if shivering from the cold. "It's freezing in here."

"Smart ass," he said under his breath.

"What is it you don't like this time? Women or showers?" Her head popped out and she looked him up and down, grinning. "I guess it must be showers. Or is that a pistol in your pocket?"

"Cocked and locked," he assured her grimly, but she'd already popped back inside and pulled the door shut with her.

He reached over and grabbed up the beer, gripping it so tightly his fingers dented the can. His thumb began to work the crease, and with every stroke, he could feel an echoing quiver inside him. Maybe they both had a death wish, he and Gus Featherstone. Joining her would make him as insane as she was, especially knowing what the repercussions could be. As he set the can down, an awareness hit him like the bullets that had perforated his body. He was going to do it anyway. Christ, he was!

Don't contaminate the work! Don't contamin—

He brought his fist down hard, causing the castle to quake mightily. Contaminate, my ass, he thought. He was in the middle of the Mojave, sweating like a pig. He had a shower, a woman, a hard-on, and what was he doing? He was equivocating like a kid in the candy store. What was missing from this picture?

"Balls," he muttered. "Mine."

A moment later, stripped down to the hard-on in question, he opened the shower door.

CHAPTER
8

THEY CALLED HER BLUSH.

Webb Calderon had understood why the moment he set eyes on her. She was kissing her own reflection in a baroque, gilt-edged mirror, shyly touching her rosebud lips to the glass and gazing at herself from beneath the lovesick droop of heavily lashed lids. Her cheeks held a feverish flush and one of her delicate hands caressed the ornate frame as if it were a man's shoulders. The other hand clutched a hat with huge red roses. Her hot, moist breath misted the mirror in a teardrop pattern, but it wasn't herself she so admired or desired. This was kissing practice for some phantom lover, some man who had yet to touch her . . . perhaps even to notice her.

Webb knew this with the same metaphysical certainty that he knew she would lose her innocence the moment she *was* touched. The imagined was pure and perfect. Her lover wouldn't be. He might fulfill her physical longings, but he could never meet the needs of a dreamer's heart. They were pristine, like dewdrops clinging to a leaf. The sun's glory made them radiant, but only for an instant before it destroyed them. Webb knew all about that kind of destruction. He specialized in it.

A doorbell sounded somewhere in his Beverly Hills gallery. He barely registered the sound, knowing it was probably a delivery and his assistant would handle it. He hadn't finished inspecting the oil painting for damage . . . or studying the young woman's intoxication. He couldn't help but wonder who had inspired such a fever of longing in her, what sort of man? A tiny, whiplike nerve stung deep in his jaw as he surrendered control of his objectivity for a moment and let himself imagine that very first touch of her trembling lips, the sweet taste of her innocence.

He breathed with the feeling, his head lifting. It had been so long since he'd felt anything, anything at all, that he wasn't willing to let go of it immediately, even the sensation of pain. It was interesting that this particular work stirred something inside him when little else could. Technique-wise it was one of the least exceptional of Mary Goddard's *oeuvre*. The American painter specialized in portraits of women and girls, and she'd done many that were more technically adept. Still, Webb could hardly take his eyes off this one. The subject's innocence was the draw, perhaps because he'd lost his in such an early, violent way.

The oil painting was two feet by three, but it looked smaller in the packing crate. Force of habit brought him to one knee, his finger glistening from a touch of his tongue. Very gently he rubbed a small portion of the canvas, cleaning it to better see the detail of the artist's work.

The art world called her Blush, but she was listed as *Girl in the Mirror* in the *Benezit's Dictionary of Painters and Sculptors*. Webb had purchased her at Sotheby's main summer auction just before leaving London, but not on his own behalf, sadly. He'd acted as the buying agent for Lake Featherstone.

An intercom buzzed down the hallway in his office.

Irritation flared as he rose to his feet. He didn't like having his concentration broken when he was working in the warehouse, but his assistant knew that, so it must be important.

The cinder-block room was huge and climate-controlled to a chilly fifty-five degrees, but Webb didn't mind the coolness. It kept him alert. Since most of the area was devoted to storing the art he bought and sold, the lighting was indirect fluorescent tubes and the humidity carefully regulated. For convenience, he'd arranged his workspace in a corner alcove that was lit by large windows and a skylight.

Paintings were propped up against walls, mounted on viewing easels, and spread over trestles, and the faint smell of rubbing alcohol was ever-present. The phone and intercom were mounted on the wall opposite his worktable, and the one hospitable touch in the austere surroundings was a black walnut Renaissance cabinet, where a decanter of malt Scotch sat on a gleaming Jean Couzo tray.

The intercom sounded again. Webb walked to the brass panel and pressed the blinking button. "What is it, Marge?"

"Mr. Featherstone would like to see you," his assistant said, clearly apologetic. "Can I send him in?"

That explained the interruption. Marge knew Lake Featherstone was one of the gallery's best clients and a personal friend. She was also aware that Lake's stepsister had been kidnapped—as was the entire planet by now—but beyond that she knew nothing of Webb and Lake's dealings or of Webb's connections beyond the legitimate world of art trading, which was exactly the way Webb wanted it. "Yes, send him in," he said. "I have something for him here."

Webb was never quite prepared for how much Lake looked like his twin, Lily, though Lake wasn't effeminate any more than she was masculine. They simply looked like the boy and girl version of the same set of genes. Webb had always privately thought of them as Donny and Marie in shades of ash blond, though, at thirty-seven, the Featherstone twins' features were more sharply planed and their bodies angular to the point of boniness.

Now, as Lake appeared in the doorway, Webb registered his wan nod of greeting and the signs of strain around his hazy jade eyes. The mauve hues of his polo shirt and the light linen slacks he wore washed him out even further. It would have been natural to assume that he was concerned about his stepsister, but this was the Featherstone family, and in the half-dozen years he'd known them, Webb had come to realize that life inside the mansion was as complicated as a French court.

It was more likely that Lake's lack of color was due to the time he spent in his war room, the security nerve center he'd had installed in the mansion when he had the house and grounds wired with video cameras. If he had to guess, Webb would have said that Lake Featherstone was developing the prison pallor of a voyeur.

"Your timing is perfect." Webb indicated the opened crate in which the painting was still packed. "The Goddard arrived this morning."

"Really? Let's have a look." Lake peered down his nose as he approached the crate. He hesitated, staring at the painting for a moment, then bent closer, as if to study the details. Finally he knelt, just as Webb had done and wet his finger. He rubbed a bit of her ivory white dress, shifted back, and let out a swift, appreciative sound. "What an exquisite thing," he said.

Webb caught the shake in his voice and knew that this was more than just another purchase of fine art for Lake. It was another *obsession*. The Featherstones were old money as those things went in California. Their retailing empire had been passed down through several generations, and besides being well-known in art circles for their enviable collection of old and modern masters, they were continual grist for the gossip mill. Their stepsister, Gus, accounted for most of it, but artsy insiders loved to speculate on the sex lives of the unmarried twins and rumor had it that they'd formed some kind of narcissistic attachment to each other. It was also widely believed that Lake's passion for art and Lily's penchant for horses were sublimations for what they really wanted, which was each other. But no one actually knew where the gossip ended and the truth began, including Webb.

"Exquisite," Webb agreed. "And expensive. Do you want to know how much she cost you?"

"I don't care." There was such low, tremulous passion in Lake's voice that he seemed to startle even himself. He laughed and brushed the lapse aside with a wave of his hand. But when he glanced up, Webb saw traces of the same uncontrollable yearning in his expression that emanated from the painting.

Webb knew little about Lake's early years except that the Featherstone children had been raised by the family housekeeper. Their own mother had gone into severe postpartum depression after Jillian's birth and was rumored to have drowned herself when she swam out into the Pacific, fully clothed, one frigid winter morning. Lake Senior's second wife, Gus's mother, had ditched the old man after less than a year, primarily because of his stinginess, it was said. It happened in the best of families, children so profoundly deprived of love and emotional nourishment that they turned hungrily to other things to fill their needs, usually material things.

Fortunately or not, the Featherstones had the money to indulge themselves. "Tell me about the kidnapping," Webb said, conscious of Lake's rising discomfort. His client's color was much healthier now. "What's the status?"

Lake seemed to be avoiding the painting as he stood and shook down his pant legs. "Nothing's changed, except that the FBI is involved now. I spent the morning being *interviewed*. Interesting, that word they use." He laughed, but was still clearly rattled. "You'd think *I* did it the way they grilled me. They had Lily on the rack when I left."

"Cooperate with them," Webb advised as he went to the small bar where he kept the Scotch. "Cooperate to the fullest. Offer the agents good brandy and sympathy. Make it cognac if you have to." He tapped the decanter. "Drink?"

Lake's good manners failed him again. He didn't seem to have heard the offer. "I doubt anyone would believe it," he said, staring past Webb and out the window that faced the hazy blue Santa Monica mountains. "But I'm genuinely concerned about Gus. These terrorists—or whatever they are—who took her are far more likely to harm her for the good of their crazy cause than if they'd been after our money."

Webb did believe his concern, and felt a flash of sympathy for the man. But that's all it was, a flash. Still, a reassuring tone seemed to be called for. "The Bureau has specialists," he reminded Lake. "They handle nothing but kidnappings, and they're surprisingly good at it."

In fact, the FBI was good at most of what fell under its jurisdiction. The CIA, however, was another matter. Webb had reason to be familiar with the competency of the various companies in the international intelligence community, especially the National Security Agency. It was widely believed that the NSA had trained and activated The Magician.

A stack of color photographs sat on Webb's worktable. They were snapshots of old masters of varying degrees of importance that he'd collected during the summer season in London. "Have a look," he told Lake. "There might be something there that interests you. The Dughet landscape appears to be from his mature period, circa 1657."

Lake sorted through the pictures without much enthusiasm, spending most of his time studying the landscape. "You're certain this is Dughet? Do you have documentation?"

"The seller's from Antwerp. He tells me he can get whatever certificates of authenticity we require." Webb joined him at the table and handed him a magnifying glass. "Check the figures in the foreground, the trees, even the clouds. It's authentic."

Lake used the glass, but only briefly. "I'd have to see the actual painting," he said, clearly distracted by whatever else was weighing on him. "If it's still available when I'm in London next month, I'll make a side trip."

He glanced over at the decanter of Scotch. "I think I'd like that drink. May I help myself?"

Webb nodded, remaining quiet.

Lake spotted the deck of art Tarot cards laying next to the mirrored tray as he reached for one of the tumblers. He picked up the pack instead, and his startled reflection was caught in the brass intercom panel.

"God, these are frightening, Webb," he said, opening the pack and drawing out the deck. He fanned the cards, seeming mesmerized by the macabre designs of demons and magicians, succubi, and incubi. "I've never seen anything so fiendish. Where did you get them?"

Webb slipped his hands into the pockets of his brushed cotton khaki slacks. "They were sent to me by someone who knows I'm a collector. I haven't had time to research them, but he thinks they're Romanian, and probably at least a century old. They're call The Devil's Tarot."

"They're in remarkable good shape if they're actually that old." Lake turned to him. "Are you ever going to do a reading for me?"

"Do you really want me to, Lake, especially with that deck?"

The other man shuddered and slipped the cards back in the pack. "No, I don't think so."

"Wise choice," Webb said, and smiled as Lake poured himself a stiff drink. He very much doubted his visitor would welcome what the Tarot had in store.

Gus Featherstone had grievously miscalculated. She hadn't thought her jailer, as she now referred to him, would rise to the bait. How wrong she'd been. Not only was he naked, he was currently *tensile* enough to cut diamonds. And that was just his jaw. She didn't want to know about the rest of him.

"I heard someone was throwing a shower," he said.

"Check your weapons at the door." She meant it as a retort, but her voice was so soft she could barely hear it over the noisy patter of water. Her heart was adding to the general clamor with some violent little reports of its own. If it had been her goal to shock him before, it wasn't anymore. Her strongest impulse was to cover something, only she couldn't decide which—her breasts or her eyes.

Gus Featherstone, suddenly shy? Must be a sign of the apocalypse, she thought.

"Got room for one more in there?" he asked.

"Just one? Looks like you brought a friend." She managed to smile *and* speak, doing both without glancing down at said friend for more than a heartbeat. She shouldn't have, not even for that long. Her stolen look sparked a dizzying rush of vertigo.

He was six feet tall and then some of magnificently clenched muscle, sheened in perspiration from head to toe, and he was looking directly at her . . . just standing there in the altogether, cocked and locked, as he'd so succinctly put it, and gazing at her as if she ought to be pleased to see him.

"Who is it you don't like?" he said. "Me or my friend?"

She ducked her head. "Your friend can stay, but you've got to go."

To her great relief he laughed. Her retorts were automatic, but only because they were the modus operandi for her entire life: When in doubt, fake it. She'd learned that early. She was the original zing'em-though-your-heart-is-breaking girl. And the way her heart was pounding now it could break at any time.

"What is it?" she asked, uneasy with his interest.

"You look frightened."

"Me? No—" She scoffed, making a face. *"Frightened?"*

The faintest of smiles relaxed his jaw a little, but had no visible effect on the rest of him. His dark eyes glinted, lending extraordinary energy to his features. He would have made one hell of a male underwear model, she had to admit. With those body scars and his . . . well, his build, he could have made Calvin Klein even more millions.

"Yeah, you are," he persisted. "This frightens you, doesn't it? Me in pursuit? Me making the moves? You like to set things up so that you can do all the pushing, so you can call the shots. This way you have to wait and see what I'll do next, *if* I'll touch you, *how* I'll touch you. Not knowing makes you jumpy, isn't that right, Gus?"

He stepped into the room, crowding her a little.

If the wooden floor hadn't been so slippery, she might have been able to give way more gracefully. As it was she had to hang on to one of the exposed, crud-encrusted plumbing pipes that fed into the faucets and flatten herself against the wall to avoid coming into bodily contact with him. And somehow that seemed very important, everything considered.

The shower was tiny, but he wasn't.

Sunlight filtered through the cracks in the walls and ceiling, ghosting over the two of them like iridescent ribbons. Sharply aware of him, Gus barely noticed that she'd moved outside the flow of water. Sparkling droplets were beginning to bead on her body and trickle into crevices in very suggestive ways.

He had noticed, though.

He feathered the hollow formed by her collarbone as if he meant to check her pulse, which she knew to be wild. It was impossible to fake nonchalance when someone was monitoring your vital signs. He might as well have had a stethoscope.

"Not knowing makes your heart beat harder, too," he said.

"I nearly slipped," she informed him. "The floor is slick."

"So are you, Gus. Very slick."

Not slick enough to fool him, however. His expression assured her of that. Much as she would have liked to shrug his observations off, she *was* wondering what he might do next. In fact, it was the only thing on her mind at the moment. That and her body. She was suddenly very aware of her body—how pink and golden it looked in this tiny sunlight-sprinkled room, how alert and flushed and eager, like a sparkling wine, glowing in the glass, ready to be drunk. Unfortunately, she also felt as if she were the one who'd been doing the drinking, and much too fast. Her head was aglitter with effervescent sensations. Her breasts felt bubbly and full, her belly tight. Even her lips were tingly and unmanageable.

"Am I crazy?" she asked him softly. "Or has something changed? Yesterday you tried to force-dress me because my nakedness was an abomination in the eyes of God.

Today you're in the shower with me, we're both naked, and you're telling me I'm slick."

"Yes . . . " He absently continued his flirtation with her pulse.

"Yes, something's changed?"

"Yes, we're both naked."

A single water droplet spilled over the dam of her collarbone and quivered on the lush bell curve of her breast. After a moment of indecision, it began to plummet recklessly, clinging to the outside swell of her breast as it sluiced its way downward. Her shower mate followed its precarious path, first with his eyes, and then lightly with the backside of his thumb.

Gus's skin was blue-veined and especially sensitive there. Even light pressure was exquisitely sharp. The glide of his thumbnail was as startling to her nerves as if a tiny knife were being drawn teasingly up the sole of her foot. It was unbearable! She shuddered and the sensation shot through her, bringing a startled sound to her lips. The tiny room flashed with rainbow colors as she blinked open her eyes, unaware that she'd closed them.

How far could she let this go?

How far was he going to take it?

Those two questions encouraged her to sober up swiftly and take inventory of the situation. She didn't have a theory that covered both sex and kidnapping, but she did have one about seduction. She'd always believed if you could be seduced, you would be. Flashing her breasts at him was one thing. Having him fondle them as if they came with the price of dinner was quite another. She wasn't quite sure who was calling whose bluff, but there was some pride involved.

"Are you having fun?" she asked sardonically.

Sunlight iced his dark hair and danced in his eyes. "Compared to what?"

"I dunno . . . a sharp stick in the eye?"

"Compared to that, yes."

His palm curved itself to her ribs, and he brushed his thumb to and fro, fanning moisture in an arc that made the underswell of her breast glisten like marble. She was momentarily entranced by the light as well as the motion, despite the awareness that she probably shouldn't be, given her theory. Her flesh danced like a mirrored surface, and the stroke of his thumb was as rhythmic as the steady tick of a windshield wiper in a bright, gentle rain. The effect was hypnotic, yet terribly stimulating.

And then he bent as if to kiss the wet spot.

She stiffened as his lips met her flesh. Her heart went still, but her skin leapt, electrified by the feathery caress. It tingled and tightened, drawing back until her breast shivered with chills of anticipation, and her nipple puckered hotly in response. The sensations were wild, delicious. Another theory proven true, she thought. *She could be seduced.* Her lids fluttered as if to close. . . .

She waited for more, but more didn't come.

Instead, his husky voice penetrated her anticipation. "I don't know about you," she heard him whisper, "but I'm here to get clean. Scrub my back?"

She opened her eyes to a bar of castile soap and a dark eyebrow, tilted expectantly. He was holding the soap out to her, seemingly sincere, but it took her a moment to reorient. He'd just been kissing her bare breast and now he wanted her to wash his back? Okay . . .

Anything to distract him, she rationalized. And herself. Still, she felt the weight of an unreleased sigh in her throat.

He turned around as she took the soap, presenting her with a backside that made her want to do something silly, like clutch her face and scream, teenage-girl style. Better than a stick in the eye, she decided. Definitely. Other than the gunshot wounds she'd already taken into account, he looked as if he'd been specially designed and built for physical action. He had big, beautiful, sinewy muscles everywhere it mattered, and narrow, lean, sexy ones everywhere else. His shoulders could have justified a wide-load warning, and his butt looked as squeezable as Charmin.

The toilet paper comparison triggered an idiotic grin. Fortunately he couldn't see her back here, losing her marbles at the mere sight of him. Maybe it was the desert air.

After all those years in the city, her nervous system had probably acclimated itself to noxious smog and exhaust fumes, and she was suffering withdrawal. Could be nail polish fumes for that matter. She'd been twenty-four hours now without a manicure. She was overdue for a facial, too. Her pores would be oozing effluvia. By the time she got back they could probably lube a car with the oil from her pores!

"Anything wrong back there?" he asked.

"Just checking for cellulite. You're fine."

He glanced over his shoulder at her, and she held up the soap as proof of her serious intent. Cradling the bar under the spray, she began to work it between her palms, building a mountainous pyramid of bubbles. Her earnest smile assured him she was doing his bidding and being a good little geisha. And the silly sap, he bought it!

He frowned and reassumed the position.

His neck and shoulders seemed the likely place to start, and to Gus's surprise they were far less granitelike than they appeared. She found herself responding to the suppleness instinctively and increasing the pressure as she lathered his skin. Her thumbs dug into the crevice between his shoulder blades and her fingertips swirled in firm semicircles.

"God, that feels good," he said, arching his back.

Latent power rippled up and down his spine in a frightening chain reaction. Some muscles tightened while others relaxed, but the way everything flowed in a stream under her hands made her feel odd inside, loose and hollow. Other than the bullet holes, he was close to perfect, she had to admit, and she'd seen enough perfection to know. His torturous encounters with roof beams might be painful, but they had paid off in raw-boned brawn.

She soaped to her heart's content, creating bubbly patterns across the width and down the length of him, hesitating only when she reached the small of his back where the dip in his spine flared out to the high, taut curves of his buttocks and a dimple-like groove in his right cheek.

"Don't stop now," he said. "I'm dirty down there, too."

"I'll bet you are," she murmured.

On a slow breath she let her hands slide out to his hips, impressed with how lean and narrowly set they were, yet buttressed with bone. His muscles had a springy resilience that her massage couldn't penetrate. Tight asses, she thought with some resentment. Men were born with them, lucky dogs.

As her hands crept down gingerly, flirting with his derriere, her stomach clinched tighter and tighter. Deep muscles shivered, sending her an odd little thrill. She almost pulled back. If she hadn't wanted to attract his attention, she would have.

The intimate contact set off another chain reaction. This one was mental, but no less uncontrollable. She was flooded with questions about him. What was happening front and center? she wondered. She was getting rather aroused. Was he? Could he get more aroused than he already was? And more to the point, what was Mr. Quiet-but-Deadly like in bed?

The mere thought made her feel fuzzy and light-headed, especially since it triggered fantasies that were astonishingly graphic. Given the way he drove a car, she would have guessed him to be swift, rough, and passionate. She was sure he was very capable of some incredibly primitive sex, but he didn't seem in any hurry now.

She stopped soaping long enough to let the spray do its work. Water streamed over his back in a gentle rush, carrying the suds away and leaving him gleaming and gorgeous. Sheened by sunlight, his flanks appeared to ripple like an animal's. God, he was so delicious she wanted to bite him. Her sudden desire to do that was sharp and visceral. She could almost taste him in her mouth. Her jaw went slack. Her heart began to clang frantically, and she bent toward him, salivating.

Gus! Be serious. You can't!

She caught herself and swayed dizzily, wanting to laugh. A sound slipped out. Quiet and choked, it was the groan of a woman overcome by an outrageous impulse, an impossible urge, a woman bent on something suicidal. Perspiration chilled the back of her neck, and her tongue darted to the corner or her mouth. Her throat felt full and hot, like a vampire's. No, she couldn't—

She couldn't!

The shower head began to sputter, apparently choked with air bubbles. Somewhere along the roof, pipes rattled and sneezed.

Jack propped his hand against the wall in front of him, wondering why she'd stopped. Water streamed over him, rinsing him clean. "Gus?"

The only answer he got was a strangled gurgle.

He was about to turn when a sharp stab of pain caught him from the rear. "*Ouch!*" He clamped a hand to his butt and twisted around. What the hell had she done? Pinched him?

She looked as shocked as he undoubtedly did, her eyes wide and sparkling, her hand pressed to her mouth. If he didn't know better, he might have thought she—

He lifted his hand and saw the hot, red circle on his abused flesh. Teeth marks? "You *bit* me?"

"No! I know that's what it looks like, but—" She began to laugh helplessly and shake her head, her whole body quivering with some trembling inner ecstasy. "It was just a tiny little thing, a nip. I couldn't help myself."

"Holy— You bit me!"

She gasped and sighed, falling against the wall for support. "I don't know what came over me. I—"

She was totally out of control, and it was the sexiest damn thing Jack had ever seen. He rubbed his butt and stared at her, trying to figure out what the hell to do with her—besides muzzle her, lower her into the pit, and leave her there for the rattlers. The woman was completely whacked out and totally deserving of her reputation. He should get hazard pay for this detail.

"Fair's fair," she got out between shudders. She turned to the wall and offered him her pink, water-slicked derriere. "Bite me back."

Jack found it difficult to breathe, his gut was so fucking tight. He wanted to oblige her so badly his jaws ached. Between that and his stinging backside, he was ready to eat her alive. "Don't move, I'm sharpening my teeth."

Truth was he'd been regretting the decision to get naked with Gus Featherstone from the moment he stepped into the shower. If he'd had to fall off the wagon, he should have done it with the six-pack instead of the woman. A beer would have been safe compared to this, because his need to drink was simple. His need for her was unbelievably complex. It was sexual, but it wasn't just physical. He couldn't get that kind of satisfaction with her. He hadn't come with a woman in years, not since the tragedy with his wife and kid. He'd had sex, lots of it before he began to question the point, but all he'd contributed to each furtive encounter was the thrusting and the sucking and the sweating. He'd withheld even the release a woman could give him because he couldn't give up the control, not even that much. It was holding him together, the control. It was his armor.

Eventually he'd begun to realize that he didn't have the choice anymore. His body had taken over. It would let him fuck, but that was it, no release, no relief, nothing unless he did it himself. It was the ultimate protection against vulnerability, he supposed. But it was damn empty.

What he needed now, what he *craved* from Gus Featherstone was her inner warmth, her female essence. He wanted to know her baby soft skin, her mysterious heat, the curve of her body, the crazy grace of her heart. He hungered for the taste of lips that stumbled over words and sometimes couldn't get them out right. He wanted to know what frightened her, besides his "friend." And yes, he wanted to bite her delicious ass. Christ! Even just to cup her in his palms would give him such unbelievable pleasure. But if he let himself have all of that, or any of it, he might never be able to go back to what he had now, which was nothing. If he had a taste, he would remember what he was missing.

He would die from the starvation.

She glanced over her shoulder at him, clearly curious about his intentions. He was down to two choices. He could walk out now and pay the price of denying himself. Or he could stay and get to know the real Gus Featherstone, the woman who'd won awards for her butt and was probably as terrified of intimacy as she was of snakes. Either way he would pay.

The pipes rattled above them, and water danced on her shuddering body . . . her beautiful, naked, shuddering body. Just looking at her made him want to tear the place apart.

Hell, she was making up the rules as she went along.

He would, too.

CHAPTER
9

GUS DIDN'T KNOW ANYTHING ABOUT RULES. SHE ONLY KNEW that desire was flaring up inside her at the mere sight of him. The moment he'd turned, the moment she'd seen the stab of need in his eyes she'd been reduced to a single violent heartbeat. Now her heart was storming in her ears, drowning out every other concern. She'd sensed something hidden and hurt in him from the first, but her intuition had told her not to trust it. She had to now. Even if the diamond-hard glint she saw was what made him dangerous, she still couldn't deny its impact. That was the part of him that spoke to her . . . needed her.

Her sigh was anguished. *What was happening to her?*

The weakness struck first at the back of her knees. It felt as if all the cartilage in her legs, all the glue that held her together, was dissolving. The feeling that fluttered up and down her body was sweet, utter helplessness. It was one of the most riveting things she'd ever experienced, and she hated it. Vulnerability was her enemy. She had fought against it her whole life, and if this was what she had to look forward to—this swooning, sickening weakness—she would pass, thank you.

He must have seen it too, the craziness that had taken possession of her, because as he approached her, he reached out and caressed her cheek. She tried to turn, but there was nowhere to go, and he wouldn't have let her anyway. His hand closed on her face, and he held her there, gazing at her, at the strange, wild energy that must be lighting her eyes.

"Have you lost your mind?" he said.

She nodded. "It's gone, without a trace."

"Yeah . . . me too."

He swallowed tightly, and Gus felt as if her stomach had left her body and was tumbling headlong into the pit beneath the floor of the shack. She had run out of theories. She was trapped in a mine shack with the man who'd kidnapped her—a hard, hungry, naked man who so clearly—so thrillingly—wanted her. And weak-kneed or not, she wanted him, too. She could ponder that until the desert turned into a swamp, but she couldn't change it. It was the only reality she had.

"Go ahead," she said softly, struggling a little with the rest of it. "T-take me."

"Take you?" He sounded surprised, if not bemused.

"Well, of course." She didn't know quite what else needed to be said. It was so obvious what was happening between them. They were both aroused. His body was testimony to that. "You *know* you want to," she added, her voice going warm and throaty.

His brow knit quizzically. "How's that?"

"Well, you—you're excited." She lifted her shoulders. "You're giving me one of those hot, narrow-eyed stares, and you're breathing through your nostrils, so you m-must want to."

"Take you?"

"Yes, you do. You *want* to."

"Like I wanted to spank you?"

"Well, yes . . . like . . . that." Damn, why couldn't she talk? And why was he beginning to annoy her when a moment ago she'd been ready to throw herself in front of a thundering herd for him?

"Apparently you know a lot about what I want. I wonder how much."

He brushed his thumb over her lips with a lightness that made her want to do something embarrassing, like sigh or squirm. And suddenly it felt as if they'd slipped back in time, as if they were playing out a bedroom scene from an old Hollywood movie. His brows were still knit in puzzlement, and he was frowning at her like she was some haywire dame out of a forties musical that he didn't know quite what to do with. What was more, he was perfect for the part! He just looked so goddamn tough with those bullet holes all over his body. He reminded her of all the old movie tough guys rolled into one, men who were as deadly as the weapons they carried and yet incapable of handling one seemingly harmless female. It was corny. It was adorable! She wanted to melt.

"Geez, you're cute," she said impulsively, laughter bubbling in her throat. Her fingers feathered the dark thicket of his two-day beard, reveling in its roughness. "I can hardly stand it you're so cute."

"Cute?" It was all he could do to manage the word.

There wasn't any time for an explanation on Gus's part. She'd meant it as a compliment, but he didn't seem to take it that way. He backed her to the wall and held her fast, his hands sliding into her hair, his elbows splayed against the wood slats for leverage. With a searching purpose, he lifted her dark tresses high off her neck and probed the depths of her eyes as if he were looking for something he'd lost. "Cute?" he breathed.

"I didn't mean—" She accidentally brushed her leg against his and he released a harsh breath, lifting her up the wall.

"Let's see what you know about me," he whispered.

The diamonds in his eyes had gone dark with desire, and the latent sexual power that flared through his hardened body truly put the fear of God in Gus. He'd turned her heart into a triphammer, and if she'd thought her legs were weak before, she'd been wrong. *This* was weak. Her bones were melting like a gelatin dessert at room temperature.

"But I—" She was still trying to explain when his lips touched her and put an end to whatever silly thing she'd been planning to say. His hips came up against hers with hot, thrilling force. She could feel the hardness she'd been fantasizing about. She could feel it *where* she'd been fantasizing about it, and it spoke to her in ways that words never could have.

He kissed her swiftly, his hands in her hair, his tongue stealing into her mouth, raping it sweetly. He kissed her roughly and passionately, just as she had predicted. And he was going to make love to her that way too, like a car bearing down on a blazing stretch of desert road, thrusting itself into higher and higher gears, speeding faster and faster until it spontaneously combusted in flames. She could believe that his mother had named him Satan. He was going to take her straight to hell.

She broke the kiss, a breathless gasp on her lips, a sudden realization in her heart. "What's your name?"

"What?"

"I don't even know your name! I've never seen you before yesterday."

"So what?"

"So I'm about to have sex with a man I don't *know*."

"Has that ever stopped you before?"

"Of course! What are you saying, that I'm promiscuous?"

"What are *you* saying?" He laughed at her. "That we haven't been properly introduced. This isn't a date, Gus. I kidnapped you. They don't cover that in the etiquette books. Possession is nine-tenths of the law, and even if it weren't, there isn't any law out here but me. I'm the sole proprietor of this desert oasis, this palatial shack, *and* Gus Featherstone. I hold uncontested title. I'm the man, you dig?—and until somebody takes you away from me, you're mine, scraped knees, incredible breasts and all."

"Just what I always dreamed of, being kidnapped by a

rap singer." She'd wanted to be contemptuous, but that was the best she could manage.

"You don't want to hear me sing, trust me." He reached down and scooped up the bar of soap she dropped. "In the meantime, no hostage situation is complete without a little torture, and I think I can speak for everyone here, including the lizards, when I say that I do want this to be a complete experience for you."

Soap suds sluiced into her cleavage as he drew the bar across the shivering swells of her breasts. "Prepare to be tortured," he informed her softly.

"I won't cooperate with this," she said. "You'll have to use force."

"In that case—" He took her by the shoulders and turned her around before she could protest. "Prepare to be forced."

"Excuse me?"

"I'm going to scrub your back whether you like it or not. It's your turn." He began to soap her lightly, his huge hands nearly engulfing her shoulder blades.

Gus held on to the plumbing pipe and shivered involuntarily as he worked his way down her back, purling the delicate linkage of her spine. Silly man. He was undoubtedly acting out some adolescent male fantasy, and well, all right, she'd have to play along with it for a while. Let him amuse himself, let him imagine some helpless, nubile love slave to his heart's content. She was totally in control of the situation. She even knew what was coming next . . .

A breath bubbled in her throat and she closed her eyes for a moment. He was going to touch her the way she'd touched him, and the anticipation building inside her was surprisingly strong. Secretly, it was rather delicious. She could feel that same glittery sparkle of fear and exhilaration. It was like the diamonds dancing in the shower spray, like the diamonds burning in his eyes. The facets were so bright, so sharp, they hurt.

"I'll let you know when I've had enough," she said.

"Ummm . . . you do that."

The pipes were rattling and the shower stream had fallen off to a drizzle, which meant the holding tank must be

nearly empty, but Gus was oblivious for the most part. She
had his hands to think about. His palms sluiced into the
small of her back, flowing like warm water, and then his
fingers spilled onto the soft curves of her bottom. He
cupped her, squeezing gently and the pressure sent out
streaming ripples of surprise and shocked delight. "Whoop-
sie," she murmured.

"What did you say?" His voice was irresistibly husky.
"Had enough?"

"Well—" Excitement deepened the natural arch of her
spine.

His lips found her nape, hot and steamy. He was murmuring how good she felt, how perfect in his hands. His
light, illicit touchings stirred her into a sweet frenzy, and
her flesh grew uncomfortably heated. The way he'd taken
control made her feel taut and urgent, as if this were her
first sexual experience, and she were being tenderly initi-
ated in the pleasures of the forbidden. A questing fingertip
played about the cleft of her buttocks, tickling and feathering, tantalizing her for a flurry of seconds before it dipped
into the sensitive space.

"I think—"

"Enough?" he asked.

"Yes . . . ahh, almost."

Gus sucked in a breath, swaying on her tiptoes as he rode
the crest of that tight, lush place. It was torture, all right.
His caresses were almost unbearably stimulating. They had
her twitching and tingling with pleasure. She honestly didn't
know how much more backscrubbing she could take, but
she wasn't quite ready to cry the E word yet.

Tension bowed the curve of her spine. Tilting madly, she
leaned into him, her shoulders nestling into the hollows of
his, her neck deeply arched. It was all so exquisitely precarious, she wanted to moan. Her feelings were soaring to an
intensity that should have warned her to resist them, but she
couldn't, even when he slipped a hand between her braced
legs and fingered the dark, damp curls of her pubis, even
when he found her tiny, engorged center and began to trace

languid circles around it. Waves of pleasure throbbed and pulsated. A flick of his thumb made her convulse.

"Enough?"

"*Enough!*"

She let out a throaty moan and tried to pull away from him, but the bar of soap had fallen to the floor, and the wood was slick with sudsy water. Her feet began to slide, and the next thing she knew she was careening forward, heading for the decks.

"Oh, my God!" she cried as she caught herself with her hands. It was a perfect four-point landing, her hands and feet on the floor, her fanny in the air. Her palms stung from the impact, but she was too stunned to think about awkwardness or vulnerability or any of that until he brushed up against her.

The sound he made held as much anguish as desire.

They both heard it and froze.

Gus wondered why she wasn't moving, why she *couldn't* move.

Jack wondered if the gods were laughing at him or with him. He'd tried to catch her, but the soapy surface was like skating on ice. It had all happened too fast. Now she was kissing the shower floor, and his erection was pressed up against her buttocks. Or vice versa. It didn't really matter which, because unless she stopped him, the animal in him was aroused beyond any possibility of backing off.

He could see the pale petals, the deep, alluring pinks and magentas of her female garden. He could see everything he'd been touching, and how thoroughly he'd aroused her. She was moist and flushed, her lips plump with desire. His mouth watered as he thought about kissing her there. His cock shuddered savagely.

He began to caress her with his hands.

Gus let out a long, tight, earth-shaking sigh. He was rocking against her, and her body craved the physical motion, craved the deep pleasure he could give her. He felt huge in comparison to her, much too large for *any* of her natural orifices, including the one he was caressing. But instead of frightening her, his size aroused something wild in her.

She moved against him and felt him grasp her hips. A moment later she cried out with pleasure as he thrust into her tight, clutching body, gently forcing his way in, yet fiercely taking possession. He would not be denied, and within seconds his powerful thrusting became her only anchor. While her hands sought purchase in the warm sudsy water, his deep penetration held her hostage to pleasure that was as sharp as anything she'd ever known.

A cry slipped out of her, setting off a chain reaction that reverberated madly between them. He began to rock her powerfully and tenderly, the passion in his body radiating into hers and sending shockwaves all through her. As each sweet jolt freed something wild within her, it seemed to release an even deeper hunger in him. Bending over her, he cupped her swaying breasts in the heat of his palms and nuzzled her nape like a male animal. She'd asked to be taken, and he was doing it, taking her with all the wild, primal joy of a spring mating.

She felt him so deeply she could almost taste him in her throat. She couldn't possibly take any more of him, and the pressure was glorious! It built the tension in her body to an aching pitch. The tiny, throbbing inferno between her legs was hot enough to bring tears to her eyes.

It was more ecstasy than Gus could stand. She would have dropped to the floor if he hadn't been holding her. And when the first blinding tremors shook through her, when the first real, soul-deep orgasm took hold, her arms gave out, and she sagged forward helplessly.

He lifted her to him, an arm locked around her waist as he continued to make love to her. The power of it sent her body into a rippling chain of aftershocks, but she had no more strength, and her limp weight seemed to throw him off balance. The wooden floor was badly warped and the bar of soap had slid into the recess beneath them. In his struggle to get his footing, he stepped on it and pitched forward.

She cried out, startled to feel the heat of him gone.

"Watch out!" His legs buckled and he nearly came down on top of her before he caught himself against the wall. The shower creaked and groaned with his weight. "I've got you," he said, holding her tight with one powerful arm while he fought to brace them both.

Gus shuddered at the abruptness with which he'd withdrawn. Before she quite knew what was happening, he'd eased her to the floor and released her. She collapsed in a heap, shivering as he knelt next to her.

"Are you all right?" he asked. "Did I hurt you?"

"It's okay," she said, unable to stop trembling. She wasn't hurt, but she did feel cold and confused and abandoned. It was only as she was trying to understand why he'd ended their lovemaking that she realized he was the one she should be concerned about. He hadn't finished.

"Come on," he coaxed, "I'll help you up."

"No, we'll worry about me later. What about you?" She uncurled and held her arms out to him. "Please, come make love to me," she urged. "You're not done. You didn't—"

She hesitated, aware that something was wrong, very wrong. "What is it?"

Jack shook his head and brushed her hand away. "It's all right," he tried to explain. He didn't know what to say to her now. He didn't know how to tell her it was all over, that this was as good as it got for him. "It's all right."

He'd meant to ward her off, but she wouldn't let him.

"No, it's *not* all right." She sprang up, taking him in her hands. Her mouth was wet and sweet, all over him, giving him so much pleasure, so much pain. He'd had a taste, but he couldn't have any more, not even with her. He'd thought it might be different this time. He'd wanted it to be, and now she was stroking him like an angel, making his need so intense.

"For chrissake, Gus, stop it!" He took her by the shoulder, handling her more roughly this time. With a quick, warning glare, he thrust her away from him.

She huddled in the corner of the shower, bewildered, tears welling in her lower lashes. And suddenly he could see the real Gus Featherstone so clearly. It was right there in her violet eyes, all the things she didn't want the world to see—that she was vulnerable, that she didn't believe anyone could ever love her, and she would damn well prove it to anyone who tried. He saw all that in her tears, and this time he was touched.

Jack couldn't quite remember the line, but he knew the concept. It was something about beating your head against a wall because it felt so damn good when you stopped. It was a grim comment on the condition he was in that head-beating sounded vastly preferable to the low, deep, interminable throb in his groin.

He was stretched out on the floor in his usual pose, head cradled in his arms, his body engulfed in blue and gray as the last of the day's sunlight faded from the room. Across from him on the cot, Gus slept soundly, oblivious to his presence, but that hadn't been the case earlier. She'd been compressed like an accordion folder when he came out of the shower, her arms hugging her drawn-up legs, her chin resting on her knees.

He'd thought it was safe until she looked up at him, questions burning through the hurt in her eyes. Without a word he'd thrown some clothes on his back, jammed the Magnum in the waistband of his jeans, and left the cabin, determined not to give her any openings. Better the kiln furnace than a grilling on his sex life by Gus Featherstone. She would have badgered him mercilessly until she had the answers she *thought* she wanted.

She'd probably taken it personally that he'd thrown her out of the shower. He might have tried to reassure her on that score if she'd been a little less singleminded about things. He had a natural antenna for detecting drive in others. It was part and parcel of surviving in the jungle. A determined enemy was a deadly weapon. Since meeting Gus he'd added another coefficient to the equation. There were the tenacious types, who hung in there quietly, biding their time; there were the pit bulls, who went right for the throat; and then there was Gus, who'd undoubtedly trained under Margaret Thatcher. The woman could turn it on.

When he'd left the shack, he'd headed straight for the Blazer to use the car phone and to hear the status of the kidnapping on the news. But all he'd managed to do was get a message through to his contact about the change in destination before everything had gone dead, the car phone, the radio, and the car itself. He had no way of knowing whether the information had been relayed to the anonymous party who set up the kidnapping. The car battery had dried up like a raisin in the sun, and the closest source of water had been back where he'd come from, the shack.

He used the return trip to plan his next move, and it took him all of five minutes to figure out that he had to get rid of Gus Featherstone as soon as possible. She'd already given him all the information he was going to get without alerting her to his plans, but that was only one reason to move quickly. In less than twenty-four hours she'd undermined five years of effort and a lifetime of training with one incredible pair of breasts. If somebody didn't show up to take her off his hands—and goddamn soon—she was going to subvert his entire mission.

Those who operated in covert circles, whether legal or not, lived by several axiomatic laws of survival. The first was a code of emotional detachment. Emotion made you sloppy. It got you killed. Every spook knew that, even the bad ones. The good ones followed a precise set of rules designed to keep them alert and alive: *Don't get involved, don't make any exceptions to your normal procedures, give away nothing, and always let your opponents think they have the advantage.*

It wasn't written anywhere in the Annals of Correct Espionage, but Jack was about to add another one: For fuck's sake, *never* have sex with a hostage who clicks her fingernails against her teeth.

When he'd returned to the shack, he'd found her sound asleep in nearly the position he'd left her. She was lying on her side, all tucked up, as if she'd simply fallen asleep that way and tipped over. It pleased him that he hadn't been bothered by how forlorn and miserable she looked. It pleased him a lot.

He'd been told someone would show up with the money within twenty-four hours. It was getting closer to thirty-six hours now, and the longer he waited the more wary he got. Whoever said crime didn't pay was either criminally stupid or a politician, which was pretty much the same thing these days. It did pay, but Jack had spent enough time on both sides of the law to know the hazards. Any deviation from the game plan was dangerous, and there had been two already. The odds were mounting against him.

He closed his eyes and the throb in his jeans intensified. Each aching pulse squeezed like a heartbeat. He could have counted them. There was no wind tonight, no relief, and the air was so heavy with heat it felt like a second layer of clothing on his body. It was quiet, too. He could hear the rustle of displaced gravel outside the window as some night stalker, probably a kit fox, honed in on its dinner, its huge satellite-disk ears tuned up for sound.

He rolled to his side and cradled his head in his arm—not a good position for defending himself, but it was the only way he was going to get any sleep. At least the shack was secure. The sensors had been rearmed, so he'd be alerted when someone arrived, *if* they arrived. If they didn't, he would have to come up with an alternative plan. His chest tightened as he realized how extreme that plan might have to be. He hadn't done anything that involved wet work in years, but that could change very soon. She could ID him. Christ, she'd not only seen his face, she'd left teeth marks on his butt!

His stomach jerked, but it wasn't with laughter. The sound that hissed through his clenched jaw was cold. For her sake he hoped the party that wanted her kidnapped showed up. The laws of survival said she was too great a liability to set loose. He'd already made two exceptions. He couldn't make a third.

Jack fell asleep to the deep silence of the desert night.

He awoke to the thunder of a gun being cocked.

His gun? No, the barrel of the Magnum was still pressed tightly against his gut. Whoever he'd been waiting for had arrived, and somehow they'd breached his security measures, which was damn near impossible.

Jack didn't move. He didn't even allow the rhythm of his breathing to change as he tried to gauge the person's whereabouts. He was dealing with a pro.

"*Freeze,*" a male voice whispered from just in front of him. "If you fucking breathe, there'll be a bloodbath."

Jack opened his eyes to the blinding spot of a flashlight. To do anything else would have invited a blow or a bullet.

"Roll over on your back and spread-eagle," the intruder ordered. "Do it!"

Again, Jack complied. The object was to get to look at his assailant, mentally voiceprint him, not to take him down. *The object was to know what you were up against.* Jack's gut jerked as he was relieved of his weapon. The flashlight bobbed, but not enough for him to see anything clearly.

"Why in hell didn't you take her where you were told to?" the intruder demanded, cold fury in his voice.

Inexplicably the flashlight clicked off. Moonlight glinted against the gun barrel, and Jack realized it was gleaming in his face, not six inches from the bridge of his nose. He acknowledged two things immediately. The man was enraged, which was sloppy, but he knew the most effective place to put a bullet, which wasn't. Right through the brain.

Jack shifted slightly, preparing to use the only weapon he had under the circumstances, his legs.

"Don't move!"

The gun barrel struck out, slamming into Jack's forehead. Pain streaked through his eyes, blinding them for an instant as he fought to bring his assailant into focus. He'd come close enough for Jack to get a look at him. He was masked, and there wasn't enough light to see hair or eye color, but Jack had seen a dark spot alongside his eyebrow. A mole? A scar?

"I'd love to kill you," the intruder breathed harshly. "Give me a reason. Blink."

Something landed on the table. It clinked like a sack of money, like heavy metal coins.

"That's your payoff," he informed Jack. "In gold bullion, just the way you wanted it. Now, let me leave you with a word of advice. If you talk to anyone about this gig, if you even breathe Gus Featherstone's name, to anyone, especially the scumbag who contacted you, you're as good as dead. And I'll do it myself, do you hear me? I'll *fucking* kill you myself."

The intruder squeezed off a round and blasted a hole through the floor next to Jack's ear. The report slammed through Jack's head, jarring the delicate bones of his eardrum and rattling his teeth. The flaring pain sparked an impulse as savage as anything he'd ever felt. He wanted to annihilate the bastard, tear him limb from limb.

Rage shook through him, but he quickly squelched it as the intruder backed to the door, his gun still trained on Jack's skull. Jack glanced around the shack and saw that she was already gone. Gus was gone. They'd taken her.

An engine was running out front. He heard it for the first time, but it must have been idling there all along, the getaway car. As the intruder disappeared through the door, Jack sprang to his feet and sprinted after him. He reached the door just in time to see an off-the-road vehicle pull away, spewing out sand in a huge, choking roostertail.

He spun around, knowing there was nothing he could do, nothing he should do. He'd been paid to kidnap her and keep her hidden until someone showed up to take her. They'd taken her. It was all over. He'd been hired to do a job, and he'd done it, even if they didn't like the way he'd done it.

His duffel bag lay on the floor next to the table.

He knelt and fished out the briefcase. He wanted to know how the hell the intruder had gotten past his safeguards, and he had his answer the moment he lifted the computer lid. The system was turned off. He'd rearmed it with the remote after she'd silenced the alarms, so there was only one explanation. The remote must have been broken in the fall.

He slammed the lid in a rage of frustration.

The soft leather satchel the intruder had tossed on the table had nearly displaced the castle Jack whittled. His creation was teetering on the rim, ready to fall, but Jack was barely aware of it. He rose and opened the satchel, wondering how badly they'd ripped him off. To his surprise, there was nearly double the amount he'd been promised. Clearly he was being paid to keep his mouth shut, which was almost funny. What did they think he was going to do, go to the cops and report that someone had abducted the woman he'd kidnapped?

He stepped away from the table, resisting the impulse to upend the damn thing. He ought to have been down on his knees praising God that it was over, he told himself. He had enough information to move to the next step in his plan, he had the money, and he had Gus Featherstone out of his hair. That was a reason to celebrate right there.

He spun around again, searching the empty shack, anger steaming through him. Who the fuck was the asshole who'd come after her? And why did he care?

The castle glowed like an ivory shrine in the moonlight. It was breathtakingly beautiful, breathtakingly fragile, every sliver of wood so painstakingly placed. With two swift steps Jack bore down on the thing and smashed it to pieces with his fist.

CHAPTER
10

JACK CULHANE WAS BLESSED WITH A DARK TALENT FOR PRE-cision and timing. He came by it naturally. From as early as he could remember he'd been handy with things mechanical and electrical. While in grade school he'd designed his own voice-controlled robot and wired his bedroom against intruders, nearly electrocuting his unsuspecting mother on more than one occasion.

His parents were people of simple means and dreams. His father, a plant custodian of barely average intelligence, couldn't begin to fathom how he'd spawned an electronic prodigy. His mother, a housewife with an unabated lust for playing bingo in the neighborhood church's basement, grew more distant and confused as her only offspring spoke increasingly in computerese and other technical languages that were gibberish to her. They weren't bad parents, they were simply in over their heads with the boy. If they didn't understand him, they did understand that.

Unfortunately Jack also had a dark talent for trouble. By the age of twelve he'd already done time in the California

Youth Authority for assault, vandalism, and wanton destruction of personal property. A quiet, cerebral loner in a rough neighborhood, he was constantly beset by packs of young toughs who challenged his courage and savaged his male pride. When he finally lashed out, it was with full force of his genius. He struck at the toughs' most prized possessions, their cars, blowing them sky-high one-by-one with a touch of his remote, and then he took their ringleader hostage, holding him until he'd brought the entire pack to their knees.

He did two years for his acts of retribution, but Jack's prodigious talent did not go unnoticed, even in stir. The standard AM/FM radio receiver he modified to pick up secret military satellite signals quickly brought him to the attention of the school officials. That summer he was whisked away to a special camp for the technologically gifted in the Blue Ridge Mountains of Virginia.

When he said his good-byes to his mother and father and rode away in the black sedan that came for him, it was the last time he was to see his parents or step foot in their home, except as a somewhat reticent visitor during the Christmas holidays and for two-week breaks during the summer. Having been assured that Jack would receive the best and most progressive curricula available, the family had given their consent and were secretly relieved that the federal government had taken over responsibility for their bewildering son's education and upbringing.

The Feds did just that, including the full complement of intelligence training and several years of Hisradut, the formidable Israeli philosophy of self-defense. Jack was exposed to anything and everything that would stimulate his impressive mental and physical gifts, and when finally he'd graduated from one intensive program after another, and his maturing body cried out for another kind of stimulation, they conspired to provide him with the perfect cover—a home in the suburbs, complete with a lovely wheat-haired, blue-eyed helpmate named Maggie.

Maggie didn't actually come with the real estate, but she was hired to care for it, and for him, and their relationship quickly progressed from business to personal. They were quietly married, and their baby girl, Haley, who was conceived on their honeymoon, arrived exactly nine months later.

Marriage and fatherhood were the closest Jack had ever come to a normal existence, and if he didn't fully understand how to love a wife and child, at least he loved the feeling of being with them, at least he knew the profound pleasure of making his baby daughter smile. And finally he had some inkling of his own parents' simple pleasures.

All might have been well if not for his increasingly disturbing awareness that his life was not his own. The hardwiring in his brain was too valuable to be left to its own devices, according to his employers, and the classified nature of his work forced him into an existence totally apart from his family. Maggie had no idea that her systems-analyst husband was actually a high-tech counterespionage specialist who designed security for the Pentagon and other secret agencies within the industrial-military complex. She knew nothing of the man they called The Magician.

The marriage convinced Jack that he had to extricate himself from covert government service. Pressure was put on him to stay, but he left the agency and took a "civilian" job with U.S. Customs and Excise Investigations Unit, designing security for the safe transport and storage of art and antiquities.

His life took a turn toward normalcy, but it was then that disaster struck. He was approached by thugs who'd heard of the "magic" he could do, which told Jack his cover had been blown. They tried to bribe him to conspire in the theft of a priceless Van Gogh still life. When he refused, they abducted his baby daughter.

Maggie was contacted by the thugs and told that Haley wouldn't be killed if she could convince her husband to cooperate. She begged Jack, she pleaded, breaking down in sobs, but he was convinced he could trap the men without giving in to their demands. With the help of the Customs Department, he set up an elaborate sting operation . . . which failed tragically.

"Fucking fools!" the thugs had shrieked over the phone.

They'd not only sidestepped the trap, they'd sought revenge.

Jack could still hear his baby daughter's screams. The thugs hadn't sent the obscene audiotape of her death to him. The police found it on the seat next to Maggie's dead body when they pulled the car out of the ravine she'd plummeted into. They'd called her death an accident, but Jack knew the kidnappers' bloodlust hadn't been satisfied. He believed they'd tampered with the car's brakes. He needed to believe that because then he knew who to hate. And he knew what to do. But in his heart he feared Maggie had committed suicide, and that the entire tragedy was his responsibility.

Either way the guilt crushed him. Black rage drove him to alcohol, but ultimately it was his need for justice that drove him underground. He had no idea who'd compromised him, and he trusted no one, least of all law enforcement. To catch the thugs, he became one of them, haunting the streets, the bars, and one night, in a blur of booze and despair, he beat a man nearly to death that he'd mistaken for one of the kidnappers.

"Guilty as charged on all accounts," the judge had pronounced during sentencing. "The prisoner is sentenced to a period of not less than twelve months on each count and remanded to the custody of the federal marshall."

Three counts. Aggravated assault and battery, malicious mischief, and resisting arrest. Thirty-six months. It was a death sentence. Jack barely got out of Folsom alive. Someone was determined to kill him, and the last attempt left him savagely scarred. With a gun smuggled in by a bribed guard, the assassin pumped five bullets into Jack, shattering his face as well as his body. Later Jack learned the inmate, who was doing time for art smuggling, had been a driver for the wealthy Featherstone family before his arrest.

Reconstructive surgery did more than just repair the damage to Jack's face, it allowed him to take on an entirely new identity. The Magician did a vanishing act. He lived and worked in the shadows, operating from a garage-apartment in Venice with a narrow, back-alley entrance and a lack of neighbors to notice his comings and goings. To finance his search for the thugs, he designed security systems for shady types with legitimate business fronts—import-export dealers, art brokers, and gallery owners who traded in black-market goods, and who had no idea what they were dealing with in him.

But his primary focus was elsewhere. If prison had done nothing else, it had given him new direction. He'd been involved in deep background research on the Featherstone family when the kidnapping job came along. It had seemed like a sign at the time, his first break.

Now he knew what it was—a death knell for his mission.

He'd been back from the desert for twenty-four hours, and he had exactly zip to show for it. He'd slept away twelve of those hours and screwed away the other twelve. The furor about Gus had made it impossible to move ahead with his plans. The Featherstone mansion was swarming with media and law enforcement types, and until the place cooled off, he had no choice but to lay low. But that wasn't the only reason he was stalled out.

Sweat dropped from his forehead and splashed against the newsprint at his feet as he rammed his fist one last time into the punching bag he'd hung from a beam in the garage ceiling. The workouts were his outlet. They had kept him sane, but now they were getting increasingly brutal, as if some part of his nervous system had sniffed blood and gone on the attack.

TERRORISTS KIDNAP RETAILING HEIRESS!

The newspaper lying on the garage floor trumpeted the news of Gus's abduction. The frenzy hadn't surprised him. What had was the media's claim that she'd been snatched by a group of Panamanian rebels protesting Western capitalistic exploitation. The Featherstone family ran a retailing empire that used dirt-cheap Third-World labor, and the terrorists were claiming the family had made their fortune off the backs of the poor.

Jack pulled off his T-shirt, mopped his dripping face, then sent the shirt flying with a flick of his wrist. It landed on his blinking computer screen, nearly covering the grid that displayed a simulated floorplan of the Featherstone mansion. The worktables that flanked his computer were weighed down with his electronic equipment, all very precisely arranged. Despite everything, he had retained that much of his legendary discipline, the need for meticulous order.

"Terrorists?" He stooped to pick up the paper.

He couldn't get what had happened the night before out of his head—the way he'd been ambushed, the bastard who'd done it, his face, his voice. It had been preying on his mind all day. He wanted to kill a smarmy reporter on the news that morning for describing the kidnapping and then doing a retrospective of Gus's modeling career as if she were already dead. The woman had ended ominously, reporting how often the hostages of these particular terrorists were sacrificed.

Sacrificed? Panamanian terrorists?

The guy who'd come to the cabin hadn't sounded His-panic.

He dropped the paper and rose, hating the helpless feeling that had lodged in his throat. Several of his hand-carved castles decorated the stack of empty equipment crates he'd piled against the back wall of the garage. They were the only aesthetic touch in drab surroundings that consisted mostly of worn vinyl furniture and card tables of equipment. Now he had to fight the urge to go destroy them. He wanted to smash them to dust. Every minute of the day he had to fight that urge.

This wasn't about her, he told himself. It was about him screwing up. Again. Magician, my ass, he thought. Circus clown was more like it. The last time he'd let himself be ambushed, the two people in the world he cared about most had ended up dead. He'd promised himself that would never happen again. That's what was bothering him now.

It wasn't about her.

The TV was flickering silently across the room. An old

Sylvania console with rabbit ears, it had come with the place, and it was the only piece of furniture Jack wouldn't have wanted to part with. He'd replaced the guts, wired it for cable, and rigged a remote, but the reception was still lousy. Now as he glanced at it, he saw Gus's face flash onto the screen. He'd been seeing her with regularity since he got back, but this wasn't her image. It was her.

He picked up the remote and hit the Mute Button.

"I'm just so g-grateful to be free," she said brokenly. Lightbulbs flashed around her as she spoke into a cluster of microphones. She looked as if she'd been through hell. Her face was gaunt and filthy, with scratches raking her jaw. Her lip was split as if someone had hit her, and her hair was dull and tangled. Her fingers shook visibly as she touched the mikes.

Jack's hand fisted over the remote as he watched her struggle to answer the questions the reporters were hurling at her. The bastard that took her must have beaten her up. Rage surged inside Jack, making it hard for him to breathe. There was nothing he loathed more than sadistic psychos who terrorized their victims and used them for bait.

"I was b-blindfolded most of the time," she explained. "I never saw any of them, but they threatened me constantly. They said they'd kill me if my family didn't stop exploiting the labor in Latin American plants. They said they were going to ask a ransom to compensate workers who were being taken advantage of."

The reporters began to shove and shout again. "Is your family guilty of exploiting workers?" one of them yelled over the din.

"Are you employing illegals here in this country?" another called out.

Gus gripped the sides of the podium as if for support. She stared out at the crowd, seeming bewildered by their questions and the possibility that they were somehow turning against her. "I don't know the answer to those questions," she tried to explain. "But I'm going to find out."

A man next to her gripped her arm protectively, and Gus shot him a quick glance, her chin trembling with emotion.

Jack moved closer to the set, studying the man through the fuzzy reception. His face was familiar, but Jack couldn't place him. Jack had researched the Featherstones, and he would have recognized one of the immediate family members. This man was probably a family friend. Maybe an attorney or a doctor.

"Ms. Featherstone! Oh, *Gusss*!" someone bellowed. "How did you escape the terrorists?"

She seemed relieved by the question and even managed a faint smile. "If I hadn't been doing my nails when the kidnapper surprised me, I wouldn't be here today. It's true," she said at the scattered laughter. "I had a pair of manicure scissors hidden in my hand when he taped my wrists. He covered me with a tarp, but I cut my wrists free and threw the tarp over their heads—there were two of them, the kidnapper and a driver—"

"Didn't they hold you for thirty-six hours?" a woman reporter interrupted. "And is it true you jumped off a freeway overpass to escape them?"

Gus closed her eyes briefly and nodded, as if summoning strength. "The second night they decided to move me to another hideout," she said. "That's when I escaped. The driver was blinded by the tarp, and I got out the back of the van. We were on a freeway overpass, and I knew I couldn't outrun them, so I jumped. Luckily I landed in an ice plant bed."

"You're a hero, Gus!" the woman trumpeted. "How does it feel?"

The camera panned in for a close-up of Gus as she reacted to that question. Her soft violet eyes glittered with sudden tears and even more bewilderment. "I wasn't thinking about being a hero," she told them. Her voice cracked and she could barely talk for the hoarseness. "I just wanted to s-survive."

The crowd began to applaud, a smattering here and there until finally everyone was clapping. Gus hardly seemed to know what to do, but the man next to her was visibly pleased. He leaned toward Gus and whispered something in her ear.

He was almost smug, Jack thought.

Jack knelt in front of the set, searching the man's features. He was probably in his mid-thirties and handsome in a trendy, men's magazine sort of way—the Armani jacket and T-shirt look of the Hollywood ad-man. But it was the movement of his mouth as he spoke to Gus that caught Jack's interest, his profile, his thick, dark hair and eyes.

The remote slipped from Jack's hand and hit the cement floor with a *thunk*. He sprang up and stepped back, getting his bearings. He knew who Gus Featherstone's protector was. The camera's close-up on her had included him, too, and when he'd turned toward her and whispered in her ear, the birthmark hidden in the thick of his eyebrow had been visible.

He was the man who'd taken her from the shack.

Jack peered at the set, sorting out what he knew and didn't know, mentally searching for all possible scenarios just as he'd programmed his computer to do. The man who'd taken her was also the one who'd set up the kidnapping. He'd been furious that Jack hadn't followed directions and had threatened to kill him if he told anyone what had happened.

Gus's image vanished from the screen and a reporter appeared. The woman gushed with genuine excitement about Gus's "miraculous and courageous escape." She threw out statistics, expounding on how few hostages ever escaped captivity on their own, including POWs who'd been specially trained in the military.

She made an impressive case for Gus's heroism, even to Jack, who'd become somewhat cynical about such concepts. But Jack was beginning to smell a scam. In fact, the whole thing stunk out loud, and so did her story. There were too many inconsistencies. She was kidnapped by two men who held her for thirty-six hours before moving her to another hideout? She'd been with *him* for that thirty-six hours.

He didn't like what he was thinking, but he didn't know what else *to* think. Gus Featherstone had faked her own kidnapping. It wasn't that preposterous. He could imagine

several payoffs. It would be an interesting publicity stunt to
further her modeling career, if that's what she wanted. Collecting her own ransom would have been an ingenious way
to get access to her trust fund money. Either motive would
explain why she had no real fear of him, certainly nothing
close to the terror a kidnap victim would normally have
felt. She'd been more frightened of the rattler than of him.

"We're told there's a celebration in the works," the female reporter confided, breaking into Jack's concentration
as she shared some gossipy tidbits about Gus's personal
life.

"A gala party and fundraiser will be thrown this weekend
at the Ritz-Carlton to celebrate Ms. Featherstone's courageous escape and safe return. The tickets will be pricey, but
proceeds will go to the WomenPride Fashion Show, a charity event to raise funds to retrain disenfranchised women."

Another shot of Gus and her male friend flashed onto the
screen. The man had slipped an arm around Gus's waist
and was leading her away from the microphones. They
were whispering together, and Gus was smiling, but it was
the telltale sparkle in her eyes as she inadvertently glanced
at the camera that made Jack suck in a breath.

Jesus! She'd done it. The whole thing was a scam.

"But the best news about Gus Featherstone," the reporter
continued, "is that wedding bells may be in her near future.
Sources tell us she'll make an announcement at the party
that will reveal the mystery man in her life." The woman
laughed delightedly. "Let's see, how much were those tickets? I just might have to go to this party."

You and me both, lady, Jack thought grimly. But Jack
had no intention of buying tickets. He was going to crash.

CHAPTER
11

"IT WAS THE HIPPEST, HOTTEST CHARITY EVENT OF THE SEA-son, but the crowd panted for Gus Featherstone!" The *L.A. Times* society page columnist hurriedly scribbled notes for her review of the star studded charity fashion show on a cocktail napkin so as not to miss a moment of the action.

Seated at tables nearer the runway, the West Coast corre-spondent for *Elle* magazine called in her raves on a cellular phone not much larger than the palm of her hand, while a fledgling *Vogue* reporter gave a giddily breathless inter-view to one of several network camera crews who were sta-tioned around the room, covering the splashy event.

Even a grunge-garbed MTV video jockey was on hand.

"The tunes are huge!" she could be heard to squeal, turn-ing her back to the camera as live music by Nine Inch Nails rocked the Grand Ballroom of the Beverly Regent Hotel. "Don't you *love* Trent Reznor? Wait till he whips out his penis!"

Her enthusiasm was genuine enough, but no one else seemed much interested in the rock star's storied "johnson." All eyes were riveted on the laser-lit runway. The usual throng of paparazzi were stationed around it, snapping madly at anything that moved. The fiery crackle of their exploding flashbulbs and the machine gun chatter of their camera shutters rose to a crescendo with the appearance of each new model.

Every entrance became a minor media event in itself as the laughing, leggy beauties, dolled up in the latest from Chanel, Donna Karan, and Isaac Mizrahi, strutted their stuff down a luminous ramp that lit up the stately ballroom like a futuristic road to Oz. Supermodels from the New York and Paris scene shared the limelight with movie stars and society mavens, all of them donating their time and their svelteness to WomenPride.

The night's theme was inspirational women, and illuminated posters of historical and modern heroines glowed from the periphery of the room. Even more luminous was the news announced by one of the show's sponsors, super designer Donna Karan herself, when she made her opening bows. "Our first annual WomenPride fashion show is a smash sellout, ladies and gentlemen," she told them. "The demand for tickets exceeded our expectations by two hundred percent. I'm thrilled to say that people had to be turned away!"

Karan didn't have to announce what everyone already knew. The record numbers who'd flocked to the Beverly Regent were there for more than fashion and philanthropy. They'd come to see the cause célèbre, the WomenPride Foundation's guest of honor.

The crowd was affluent, artsy, and mostly black tie, with the exception of some rather dramatically costumed cross-dressers and a few dedicated grungers. The younger set rocked in their seats to the headbanger music, while their elders tapped their spoons. All waited expectantly, and the show's master of ceremonies, Christine Takamura, a local television anchorwoman, played on their anticipation for all she was worth. When it was time for the honoree's grand entrance, Christine brought the charity fashion show to a dead halt.

"Let's have an old-fashioned drumroll!" she cued the band.

Inspired, the band pounded away, hammering the crowd with drums, cymbals, and everything else they had. The result could have shattered stoneware, much less crystal.

Gus stood in the wings, exhilarated by the fanfare, yet quaking inside. All her life she'd felt like an outsider, loitering at the edges of the playground, waiting for someone to welcome her into the fold and embrace her with open arms. It had never happened, and by now she was realistic enough to know it never would. This was not her world, either. She was not a bona fide member of the fashion elite. They were happy to use her looks and her name as long as both were strong currency, but she wasn't one of them any more than she was a Featherstone.

She was too headstrong for most people, too pretty and privileged for others, and too low-born for her own family. Rarely had anyone bothered to look past the beautiful brat image, but perhaps that was because she'd been afraid to let them, afraid they would discover what she'd always believed to be true about herself—that she wasn't worthy.

She would never have the acceptance she craved, the love.

Somehow she knew that.

But tonight, this seminal night, she would come close. She had been introduced to society at sixteen and to modeling at seventeen, but this was her real debut. Tonight she was more than a beautiful mannequin, gowned and coiffed by the pillars of haute couture. She was a heroine. She had done something meaningful, something the world considered courageous. And because of that they would open their arms to her. Her dreams would be their dreams, made worthwhile because she was worthwhile. Let them withhold their love. She could live without that. But her so-called acts of bravery had ensured that they could not withhold what she wanted from them now, what she must have—their admiration and respect. That was what she needed to finish this quest she'd started. The public's acknowledgment, their allegiance. And she was willing to do anything to get it, even pretend to be an escaped hostage.

"Get out there," her dresser whispered, tugging at the backless silk and chiffon jumpsuit that had been designed especially for her. "They're waiting for you."

Gus drew in a breath that seemed to ripple up from the soles of her feet. She closed her eyes, tipped back her head, and released the air through her nostrils in a steamy rush. Her hands were suddenly dripping. Her throat was as parched as when she'd been stranded in the desert.

Please let me pull this off, she thought. Let me give them the new Gus Featherstone, survivor par excellence. A changed woman. Everything depends on my being able to do this. Everything! But she was still quaking and perhaps as frightened as she'd ever been in her adult life. She didn't know how to be anything *but* the beautiful brat. It was the role that had saved her from letting anyone get close. If you didn't care what people thought of you, you couldn't get hurt. If you defied people to love you, it was no surprise when they didn't.

"Get going!" the dresser hissed, pushing Gus out onto the proscenium.

She fumbled the first step or two, awkward in her delicate silvery sandals and her newfound terror. Had her reception been anything but welcoming, she would have backed off the stage and prayed to vanish in a mortal shudder of humiliation. But thank God for applause and spotlights. Yes, thank God, she thought, squinting into the blinding kliegs.

Almost the instant the latter enveloped her, she was transformed. White hot and radiant, the lights burned through her confusion like a surgical laser, transfusing her with energy. The raucous music, the sudden swell of clapping, seemed to lift and carry her toward the glowing ramp. The charge in the air, the excitement, was her fix of self-esteem.

Her jumpsuit sparkled around her like an iridescent mist, picking up every color of the rainbow from the lights that sheened and gathered like water in its silky folds. The halter-style bodice dropped from her throat to her waist, where it was cut away from the pants in an arc that revealed her slender, golden midriff. She'd lost weight in the desert, but the outfit was designed to cling to her curves. Transparent chiffon shimmering with silvery threads hugged her from full breasts to hips, then flared in palazzo pants that sparkled around her ankles.

Adversity breeds champions.

It didn't matter that Gus hadn't embraced that philosophy; the American culture had, and the rapt expressions of the audience, their wide smiles, told her that this crowd believed it fervently. For perhaps the first time in her life, everyone was cheering her on. They wanted her to shine, all of them. She was living proof of the triumph of the human spirit over adversity, and she wasn't that much different from them. If they could believe in her, they could believe in themselves.

Even Trent Reznor was waving something at her, but it wasn't his hand. Gus let out a soft hoot of laughter. She couldn't believe it. She just couldn't. This was fabulous. The beautiful brat would have lifted her chiffon front and flashed her breasts at the rock star. The changed woman merely shot him an encouraging wink and sauntered on by, off to see the wizard.

She was just hitting her stride as she reached the end of the ramp and spun around. The crowd roared with approval when they got a look at the back of her jumpsuit. It was cut down to her "other" dimples and came very close to revealing cleavage that was as creamy as her breasts. The flirty hint of décolletage was accentuated with every graceful swing of her hips, and the effect struck more libidinal sparks than a nudie shot in a men's magazine could have done. It was breathtakingly sexy, not to mention the perfect exposure for a woman who'd won awards for her derriere.

Christine Takamura summoned Gus to the podium.

"Come on over here, Gus, and say a few words. Everybody wants to know how you're doing. Don't we, folks?"

The response nearly blew the ballroom roof off.

It's going to work, Gus thought. It's going to work. Oh, God. let it work. Please do.

"Augusta Featherstone was taken hostage by terrorists," Christine told the audience as Gus joined her. "The world already knows her story, but for those of you who might have been off visiting another planet, this is the woman who defied death by leaping from a freeway overpass to escape the desperate and dangerous men who kidnapped her."

Scattered laughter erupted in applause. Christine waited for it to subside. "Tonight," she said, "the WomenPride Foundation takes pleasure in giving her special recognition for that amazing feat of bravery. She's a singular example of great courage in the face of grave danger, and because of her extraordinary mettle, spirit, and nerve, the foundation would like to extend to Gus an honorary seat on its board of directors. They would also like to give her this beautiful plaque commemorating her appearance here tonight as guest of honor."

Gus could hardly see through the teary blur that assaulted her vision. She accepted the gleaming plaque, glancing over the words as she cradled it in her arms. The engraved tribute to her bravery struck home as nothing else had since she began this ordeal. She wanted badly to be worthy of the honor, which made it all the more painful that she wasn't. She was a fraud. She was lying to them, to everyone. This wasn't a prank, though it had sometimes felt like one. It was a deception of monumental proportions.

Her conflicted expression shone back at her from the gold mirror, and her unsteady fingers left marks all over the face of the plaque, smudging her reflection. I had to do this, she rationalized. It's not for me, not entirely. It's for every woman who has ever felt that she wasn't enough. It's for Bridget, who will be a woman soon. It's for Jill, because I couldn't help her when she needed me.

"The mike is all yours, Gus." Christine smiled and stepped back, waving Gus to the podium.

"I don't know how to thank you for this—" Gus's voice

was as shaky as her hands, and she prayed she would be able to say what she needed to without stumbling. "I certainly don't deserve it," she told the crowd, "but if what I did inspires any of you to take a stand of conscience against the victimization of innocent citizens and the use of terror tactics as a means to a political end, then maybe I have contributed something."

Applause swelled again, but Gus raised her hand. "There's more," she said. "I've personally looked into the charges that workers are being exploited by the Latin American manufacturers who make our products, and the chairman of Featherstone, Inc., assures me that more than half of our products are American-made." At least that much was true, Gus told herself, and what she was about to say might force some corrective action. "He also assured me that he will vigorously investigate the conditions of the foreign plants we use with an eye to relocating if health and safety standards are not being met."

Someone shouted, "Brava!" and Gus's hand flew to her mouth in surprise. The applause was so passionate, she had to blink madly to stop from crying, and even then she couldn't quite manage it. Tears began to flow, and the thought of breaking down in front of all these people, the cream of her industry, was horrifying to her. She wanted only to escape, but as she moved to leave, she felt Christine's hand, staying her.

"Didn't you have something to announce tonight, Gus?" the anchorwoman asked.

Gus had almost forgotten that she was supposed to announce her engagement to Rob. That was the brainchild of the publicist for this event, but Rob had thought it a perfect way to personalize her fifteen minutes of fame. "A human moment," he'd called it.

"Oh, yes! I do!" She mopped the dampness from her cheeks with her fingers and laughed, aware that she was hopelessly flustered, which was probably just as well, since it wasn't at all like her. "How could I have forgotten the most important thing in my life? There's someone I want you all to meet—"

Rob was scheduled to enter from the other side of the stage. Gus glanced over and saw him in the wings, lurking in the shadows like the very phantom, himself. She smiled. She'd had a hand in choosing his midnight-blue tux. The rich indigo satin of its shawl collar brought out the blue in his slate-gray eyes.

"I'm a very lucky woman," she said, turning back to the crowd. "Lucky to be alive, lucky to be free, and lucky to be here. But I'm even more blessed because I have a wonderful man in my life. We've kept our personal relationship under wraps until now because we wanted to be sure it was right."

She felt herself flushing with pleasure. "Well, it is right, and now I'd like you to meet *Mr.* Right, my future husband." She threw out her hand.

The rock band served up another drumroll, and her fiancé emerged from the wings. As the crowd began to applaud, Gus's smile froze on her face. The man walking toward her across the stage was wearing a midnight-blue tux with a satin shawl collar. But he was *not* Rob Emory! Recognition sluiced over her like an icy shower as she realized who he was.

She scanned the crowd frantically, looking for some sign of her fiancé and despairing that he wasn't anywhere in sight. Where was Rob? What had happened? Her heart was pounding wildly, but it was too late to call Security. By this time the impostor was halfway across the stage, and the paparazzi were going mad. The fireworks display had begun again, shutters chattering, strobelights flashing.

A diamond glint of malice lit the man's eyes. Gus could see it clearly, even through the blinding lights. She knew exactly who he was, but as he walked up and stood before her, a barely discernible question slipped through her lips. "W-who are you?"

"I'm your future husband," Jack Culhane informed her. The smile on his face was as dark, as obscenely menacing as his eyes.

Satan, she thought. He *is* Satan.

Even if Gus could have managed the words to summon

help, he wouldn't have let her do it. She wanted to shout at him, to say that this was crazy, that he was outrageous! But she couldn't get any of that out, not even as he took hold of her arms and drew her close to him. She nearly dropped the plaque she was holding.

Suddenly his mouth was so near her ear she could almost taste the crisp, bubbly champagne on his breath. His shampooed hair gave off rich traces of lanolin. At least his grooming had improved, she thought, somewhat hysterically.

"Play along," he warned. "Or I'll blow this thing wide open. The whole world will know you faked your own kidnapping."

Gus laughed as if it were all a clever joke, part of the entertainment. What choice did she have *but* to play along? He was threatening to destroy everything. It was only for the moment, she promised herself. She would find a way out of this as soon as she had time to breathe.

"Introduce me," he said under his breath. "Tell them my name."

"Satan?"

"Jack Culhane . . . tell them how much you want to be Mrs. Culhane. *Do it*."

Gus did what he demanded, but with great difficulty. Her stammer had returned full force, and she could barely control it. While she struggled to tell the hushed and curious crowd that this was the man she would marry, she scanned the ballroom for her real fiancé. What had he done with Rob? An image flashed through her mind of her fiancé tied up somewhere, naked.

"When's the wedding?" someone called out.

"Tonight," Jack told them all. "We're flying to Rio de Janeiro. There's a limo outside right now, waiting to take us to the airport."

That was the first moment Gus realized he was truly serious. He was kidnapping her again, and this time he was doing it on national television. She had to believe that he was bluffing about the rest of it. It was too far-fetched even for him, but the mere announcement was a hideously clever way to wreck her credibility and her plans. The bastard, she thought, as he took her arm and hustled her toward the wings. He had no idea now much damage he'd done with his asinine stunt.

CHAPTER
12

"DO YOU TEK THES MAN TO BE YOUR LAWFULLY WEDDED hossban?" The young Mexican priest nodded hopefully at Gus and Jack, his eyes so huge and sad and fudgy brown that Gus wanted to say yes just to please him. She flushed the urge as she might have a wad of soiled toilet paper.

"*Hell* wouldn't take this man," she enunciated slowly, making sure he caught her meaning.

The padre consulted the holy book that lay open in his hands, apparently looking for where it said anything about hell in the sacred marriage ceremony.

"She's *dying* to marry me," Jack assured him. "Carry on."

Cold steel nudged Gus's bare backbone, reminding her that she was being married at gunpoint in an ancient Spanish mission somewhere in the wilds of Baja California. Not a shotgun wedding, a *handgun* wedding. The .357 Magnum was concealed beneath a coat draped over Jack Culhane's arm, but the weapon was hardly necessary. He had far more effective ammo than bullets. He could ruin her life with a few words, the same words he'd whispered in her ear at the WomanPride Fashion Show.

Doubtless the priest had picked up on her "reluctance." She was as rigid as one of the plaster saints that adorned the altar behind him, her posture ramrod stiff, her arms clenched about her middle. He couldn't have missed the gun, either, since Jack was doing a conspicuously lousy job of concealing it.

What the man lacked in subtlety, he made up for in sheer, clanking brass balls. The only thing Jack Culhane had been bluffing about was the trip to Brazil. Instead of a limo purring out in front of the Beverly Regent, there'd been a battle-scarred taxi, which had sped them to the Ontario Airport and a creaky Cessna charter. That's when Gus had stubbornly refused to get out of the taxi, and the .357 Magnum had become part of the scenario.

It was also when she'd realized Jack Culhane would stop at nothing. He'd blackmailed her in front of a television audience of millions, kidnapped her at gunpoint, and then skyjacked her to this isolated outpost on the Baja Peninsula. He'd also slipped her real fiancé a mickey, stolen the designer tux off his back, and left him semi-naked in a stall in a men's room at the Beverly Regent. Culhane was clearly determined—she just didn't know what about. Whenever she demanded an explanation, she got the business end of a gun barrel for her trouble. Safe to say he had a communication problem.

"So . . ." the priest queried Gus carefully. "Do you take heem? Or don you?"

Gus dragged on a section of her lower lip with her teeth, sucking the entire thing into her mouth. Not terribly attractive, she imagined. But then neither was this place. The tiers of votive candles were a nice touch, and the nave was misty blue with sandalwood incense, but other than that it was the mission that time forgot. The mudstone and stucco walls were crumbling to brown silt, and the wooden pews looked like a heavy breeze would have turned them into firewood.

Gus had always thought flies didn't buzz at night. And

lizards! There was one peeking at her from behind the brass baptismal font right now. She couldn't seem to escape the crawly things, which made her wonder if they were to be symbolic of her relationship with him.

It wasn't a relationship, she reminded herself, more like a series of fiery car crashes. And if lizards were symbolic of anything it was something perversely, disgustingly sexual. Why had she had sex with him? Why had she done that? The man was a necrophiliac, a kidnapper, and a blackmailer. And those were just the atrocities she knew about.

"The priest is waiting, Gus."

The gun barrel made its hateful presence known again.

As motivating as cold steel and bullets were, Gus was almost as compelled by the priest's plight. He seemed so desperate. She lifted her shoulders apologetically, wondering if this was his first wedding ceremony. Of course, it *was* three in the morning and he *had* been wrested out of his tiny cot in his tiny cell in the tiny mission by an American psycho, armed and demanding to be joined in holy matrimony with a hysterical woman.

"All right." She sighed, comforting herself with the thought that she would have the marriage—and her husband—annulled the moment she was stateside, *if* the ceremony was even legal, which it couldn't possibly be.

"The señorita, she say yes?"

"Yes," Gus snapped.

"Quiero dar gracias a Dos de rodillas!" the priest whispered.

Gus had just enough Spanish to know that he was thanking God on bended knee. At least someone was happy. A broad smile revealed his dazzling white teeth and healthy pink gums as he gazed at the two of them beatifically. The near-tragedy averted, he turned a page of the Bible and swung to Jack eagerly.

"Count me in," Jack said, checking the luminous dial of his diver's watch, a fashion faux pas with a tux. "Are we about done here?"

Ten minutes later the pronouncements were over, the papers were signed, and the priest, who had just been paid handsomely for his efforts by Jack, was mumbling another prayer of thanksgiving.

"There's one little fact you both seem to have missed." Gus let her would-be husband *and* the padre have it with a death-be-to-anyone-who-screws-with-me stare. "I'm not Catholic."

She swung around to leave, her silvery jumpsuit flying in its own breezes as she double-timed it to the mission's massive portals. The click of her high heels against the uneven stone floor ricocheted like drumfire. She wanted out of this den of blue incense. She wanted to run screaming into the night never to be seen or heard from again. That thought relieved some of the terrible frustration building inside her, even though she knew it was only a fantasy.

Lizards fled her path as she advanced on the wooden doors. The way her luck was running, she'd get picked up by a gang of bandidos, stripped of her clothing and jewelry, and sold into white slavery. Either that or they'd kill her and broker her vital organs to some unsavory, unlicensed medical clinic. She had no identification. No one would know who she was, what she'd risked to accomplish everything, or more important, that she was the guardian and sworn protector of a five-year-old who needed her. And no one would care if they did know, she suspected. It was the dead of night, and decent, law-abiding folks were asleep in their beds. The priest had been her best bet, but he'd wisely resorted to prayer instead of heroics.

The rusty iron bar that secured the mission's doors didn't seem to care what Gus wanted, either. It was stuck fast, and she couldn't budge it.

"Slow down," Jack said, right behind her. He slipped an arm around her waist, his fingers splaying against her bare skin.

Gus blanched at the contact, then realized he was simply moving her out of the way so he could open the door. He dislodged the bar effortlessly, but the jammed doors wouldn't give, she noted with some satisfaction. They had come in through a side entrance, a small stone courtyard, and she should have slipped out that way, too.

The huge doors groaned with Jack's weight as he rammed them with his shoulder. A second hit popped them wide open. The sudden rush of chilly night air was fragrant with the rich, almond scent of virgin's bower, a flowering vine, and the lingering residue of fried fish, probably caught fresh and cooked earlier in some neighboring sea shanty. It was dark outside, so dark Gus could only make out the swaying hovels of the oceanside village by the lonely glow of candlefire still burning in a window or two. She shivered, wishing she had something more to wear than a skimpy, translucent jumpsuit.

"Don't make any more sudden moves," he warned her, ushering her toward the battered Jeep he'd had to buy at the airstrip because there had been no rentals and no taxis. "I'm not anxious to have somebody knock me over the head again and run off with you."

Gus sliced him a disdainful look, which he probably couldn't see because it was so dark. "Why don't you just bind, gag, and handcuff me?"

"I'm saving that for the honeymoon."

"Oh, *charming*," she said through barely moving lips. "I can always count on you for a good time."

"Ask me nice, and I might let you use the toilet."

Gus made sure he saw her disdain this time. The car was parked in a sizzling patch of moonlight. As he opened the passenger door for her, she shot him a look that was designed to wither all forms of biological life down to the lowest order of toad. It was a sample of the runway attitude she'd been perfecting her whole career, apparently just for this moment. She'd used it on mashers, paparazzi and Ward McHenry, the Featherstone's trust officer. Roughly translated it meant eat dirt and die.

Unwithered, he gazed upon her scorn as if she'd just issued a challenge that might hold some interest for him. *Apparently no one told you to play with people your own size*, his dark smile seemed to be saying. *So let's see what you've got, babe.*

His call slid over her like hot syrup over fluffy egg waffles, climbing ridges and pooling in crevices. By the time its liquid heat began to concentrate on the dimpled curves of her mostly bare behind, he'd left her little in the way of illusions about what was on his mind.

She turned her back on him and slid into the car, scooping her silvery remnants after her with a sniff, and not a moment too soon. The door slammed as she gathered in the fluttering hem of her palazzo pants. Moments later as they drove away from the mission, jolting over every bump and pothole on the donkey trail that passed for a dirt road, she brought up her concerns again, speaking loudly to be heard over the rusty creak of the springs.

"Why are you doing this?" she asked him. "If it's more money you want, something can be arranged—"

"It's not money."

"Then what *do* you want?" That look again. As if he were going to have her for breakfast, with or without syrup.

"What have you got?" he asked.

"A burning desire to rip out your heart and stomp on it?"

He smiled. "Not what I had in mind."

The Jeep lurched into a rut, its rickety suspension giving up shrieks of pain. The jolt forced Jack's attention back to the road, and Gus was just as glad. She'd had more satisfying conversations with her stepsister's horses. He had nothing to say that she wanted to hear anyway, but she had noticed something interesting about her interaction with him. She didn't seem to stammer as much—or at least she couldn't predict when she would—which fascinated and disturbed her since she'd struggled for the greater part of her life to control the hesitation in her speech. It was probably because she was either in a state of rage or terror around him, she reminded herself. She was too busy surviving to be self-conscious, which didn't say all that much for his salutary effect on her.

As they drove on through the dark, traversing the rugged, desertlike terrain, she had plenty of time to shiver in the cool early-morning breezes and contemplate her situation. He'd mentioned a honeymoon, but surely he wasn't serious about consummating this marriage of monumental inconvenience, not after the way he'd forced her out of the shower in the shack. She'd never had the chance to ask why he had done that incomprehensible thing, why he sent her away. His ferocity probably wouldn't have permitted her to anyway, but she wouldn't quickly forget it.

Something persuaded her to look at him now as they drove through the oil-black night. What little light there was in the cab flickered gingerly over his strong features as if it, too, were searching for the man inside. His hair was as dark as his eyes, and the military cut lent him the kind of tough guy glamour that made screen action heroes so appealing, but that was where the resemblance ended.

Everything else about him took her right back to the day he kidnapped her. He'd nearly terrified her that morning with the dead glare of his eyes and the low, burnt-out shudder in his voice. She had never questioned that he was capable of killing her, or anyone, for that matter. It was only after she'd seen the scars on his body and the anguish in his face as he worked out that she realized he was vulnerable, human.

Now, shadowed by moonlight, he was that stranger again, that deadly stranger. His eyes were icy and remote as he glanced at her, his expression unreadable, even faintly cruel in its intent. Instantly she began to question what he had in mind and where he was taking her. The murky, mountainous terrain they were driving through warned her that they probably weren't heading back toward the airstrip. They seemed to be on a cross-country route, headed toward the opposite shore, the Pacific. They also seemed to be going south rather than north, which would take them even deeper into Baja.

"We are going back to Los Angeles, aren't we?" she asked. Then, a little less confidently, "We are . . . aren't we?"

"And skip our honeymoon?"

"You can't be serious!"

"There's a villa waiting for us in Scorpion Bay that's the equal of any honeymoon suite at a four-star hotel. It should take us another hour to get there by car. Sound serious to you?" He didn't take his eyes off the road as he spoke.

"Really?" Fear made her lace the words with a lethal dose of sarcasm. "A four-star villa? At least I'll get to endure my human bondage in first-class surroundings."

"Oh, yeah." He laughed evilly. "First class all the way. I'm going to see that you get it all, Mrs. Culhane, everything you so richly deserve."

The car hit a rut and Gus skidded forward, stopping herself with a hand propped against the dash. The Jeep had no seatbelts, and a silk jumpsuit on slick vinyl upholstery didn't provide much traction, but the moment she got herself squared away, she spun around to confront him.

"So *that's* what this is about?" She wasn't shouting only because she didn't want him to pull a gun and shoot her, but Lord, how she longed to give vent to all the terrible frustration she felt! "Revenge? You got caught napping, and now you're desperate to find some way to soothe your injured male ego? I can't believe—"

"Believe it," he said, switching on the radio as if to tune her out. His fingers drummed the console in time to a mariachi band. "My injured male ego wants plenty of soothing. It wants you, in bed."

She switched the radio off. "You've already had me, in the shower!"

"It wasn't the same. You weren't my wife."

"Are you crazy? Do you know what you're doing to my life? Do you know what you're doing to my plans?"

"Putting a little kink in them, apparently. What are your plans anyway? I'm curious what drives an already-wealthy woman to have herself kidnapped."

"Never mind." Already wealthy? She was on the upper-class equivalent of welfare. If it hadn't been for her modeling, her personal income would have been at the poverty level, which was one of the reasons she'd continued to live at the mansion—that and her niece. All-too-familiar concerns flooded her at the mere thought of Bridget. That was another reason she had to get free of this man and get back home. The little girl would be worried. They would all be worried and with good reason.

"Must have been some grand scam you were cooking up," he said, clearly curious as he looked her way.

"*Never mind.*"

She went smolderingly silent, aware of the angry jolt and creak of the car springs as she busied herself with what she should have been doing before, making plans to escape. Surely there would be some way to ditch him when they got to the villa. He could hardly keep her captive with help a telephone call away. But then there was the little problem of blackmail. One phone call to the media and he could ruin everything he hadn't already ruined. It wasn't a question of getting away from him, she realized. This was a question of *doing* away with him.

She stared out the front windshield, still outraged, and unable to keep quiet about it. "I can't believe you would destroy someone's life, their future—their dreams!—just to prove you can still get it up."

"I can get it up fine, Gus. I just can't get it off."

"Don't!" she said, raising her hand. "Don't remind me."

"I thought maybe we'd work on that problem on our honeymoon. I thought maybe you'd want to be the one to make a whole man of me again."

She clapped her hands over her ears and began to hum something, anything!—"The Battle Hymn of the Republic"—whatever it took to block him out.

"Can you hear me, Gus?"

"No!"

"Did it ever occur to you," he persisted, "that I might be doing this for the same reason that men over the centuries have been marrying women?"

"And what reason is that? So they can own the cow?"

"Go ahead, make fun of the institution, but I'm serious. A man marries a woman because he wants a wife, a companion for life, and a mate with whom to have children."

He actually sounded serious, and Gus thought she must truly be losing her mind. She removed her hands from her ears just in time to hear his voice go faintly husky, and if she wasn't mistaken, suspiciously ironic.

"A man marries a woman because he loves her." He

geared the Jeep down, sending the creaky car into shuddering fits as they began to descend a steep, rocky incline to a shimmering bay below. "Did any of that ever occur to you?"

"No," she said, perfectly horrified at the thought. She had thought necrophilia was his most disgusting personality trait, but it wasn't. He also had a sick sense of humor. "No, it didn't! Not for one second."

"There's a law against what you're planning to do."

"What am I planning to do?"

"It starts with *R* and it rhymes with *ape*. And there's a law against it. I don't care if we *are* married."

Jack Culhane's dark smile bounced at Gus from the panel of mirrors that lined the opposite wall of the villa's bedroom. One of his eyebrows was slanted at about forty-five degrees of wry interest as he gazed beyond his own reflection at hers. He'd just undone the cuffs and collar of his dress shirt. Now he was working on the bone buttons that were embedded in two rows of narrow pleats running down the front. To be fair he hadn't actually winked or leered—yet.

"Maybe I was going to take another shower," he said.

"Probably the best idea you've ever had. Go ahead." Gus mimed a pushing gesture. "I'll wait for you."

"And dig a pit in the floor? I'm not letting you out of my sight unless it's to lock you in a closet."

Gus left him to his unbuttoning ritual and took visual inventory of her surroundings. The Scorpion Bay villa he'd reserved made her think of a millionaire's hideaway in Portofino or the south of France. The spacious, sweeping affair overlooked moonlit water, with several sumptuously decorated rooms. The main salon was filled with dramatically striped couches and chairs, marble tables, and ceramic vases of freshly cut flowers. A patio that ran the entire length of the suite had a terraced pool and a short flight of tiled steps leading to a private beach.

The decor was lavish, but Gus had had little chance to enjoy any of it. The moment they'd arrived, he'd uncorked the magnum of Dom Perignon that was chilling in a silver ice bucket, grabbed the two champagne flutes that flanked the bucket, and led her into the spacious bedroom.

She'd passed on the champagne and wandered over to the French doors that opened onto the terrace, where the honeyed heaviness of frangipani floated in on balmy trade winds. She'd been lingering there ever since—to avoid him more than anything else—watching the luminous full moon roll out a carpet of silver across the mysteriously becalmed Pacific Ocean. The shimmering path of light ran from ivory shore to cherry-black horizon, and its forbidding beauty had sparked an idea. It had suggested a way to evade this man—her new "husband"—and his apparent obsession with the marriage bed.

Now he was standing by the carved Spanish four-poster, undoing the waistband of his pants, his shirt hanging open. His silk tie and tux jacket were draped on the finial of the foot post nearest him, much the way a cowboy would hang his holster and six-shooter. Symbols of ownership, Gus thought. *I claim this bed as mine. I claim this woman as mine.*

Uncomfortable with the way her pulse had quickened, she glanced down at her hands. Dazzlingly red nails, freshly manicured for the fashion show, were reminiscent of tiny, blood-tipped daggers. Men and women, she thought. It was all so damn primitive still. Twentieth century or not, the male of the species had failed to evolve when it came to territorial pursuits like war and sex. They too often reverted to cave and club.

And women? She could only speak for herself, but this particular male had stirred something uncontrollably sexual in her during their stay in the desert. Not at all like the pleasant little flutters she felt with Rob. This was deeper. Worlds deeper. It was true physical longing. It had drawn on her stores of vital energy, depleting her. It had tugged at her until she ached. She wasn't proud of it, but there it was, the bare, libidinal truth. Other men had piqued her curiosity, but none had ever made her feel as if she might languish and die if she didn't have sex with them. He had done that to her.

She couldn't let him do it again.

The bed and a few feet of space separated them. His legs braced, his hands poised near the open waistband of his tux pants, he was watching her as expectantly as she was watching him. As thirstily. The energy that came off him had a palpable quality. She could almost imagine it running all over her, enveloping her again like warm, bubbly, effervescent wine, the way it had in the desert.

He couldn't seem to keep his gaze off her unsteady mouth, and she couldn't keep hers from drifting to the dark body hair that was visible through the opening of his shirt. It swept his pectorals, and the narrow triangle that crept up from his undone pants fascinated her, too. And his irises—God, they glinted. Diamonds, black ones, if such a thing existed.

His gaze drifted to her bare midriff, as if he were savoring the thought of touching it. Her gaze drifted to his mouth.

They were having sex with their eyes, she realized.

Soon—momentarily—it would be the real thing if she didn't do something. *Stop stroking your bare skin, Featherstone.* Her arms were clamped just beneath her breasts and her thumbnails were leaving tiny white creases on her tanned midriff.

"Are you going to tell me what all this is really about?" she asked. She'd intended umbrage, but somehow a plea for reason slipped into her question.

"I'd rather show you."

His mouth actually tilted as if he might smile. How odd that she'd never thought of that as possible, him smiling, no—him happy. That's what she'd never thought of. Some people seemed fated for tragedy. Jillian had been one of those, and so was Jack Culhane. She'd realized that in the car. Something dark was driving him, and if she'd had to predict his future, she would have said that whatever he was obsessed with would ultimately destroy him. There would never have been any doubt of that in her mind, even his wood carving had seemed too fragile to survive the elements. But now, this frisson of life in his burnt-out eyes, it made her wonder.

"I'm not talking about sex," she was quick to explain. "I meant this, *us*, this sham of a marriage. Your claim that you"—her throat tightened, but she got the word out—"love me."

He glanced at her mouth again. "Maybe I do."

"That's ridiculous." It actually hurt her that he could be so casual about it, and yet she was pushing him to explain himself. Why? What was she hoping to see as she searched his darkly handsome features? Some sign of the man she was intimate with in the desert, some sign of the vulnerability she remembered?

He shrugged. "A man has to settle down sometime."

"Oh, I see, even serial killers get the nesting instinct? I suppose Charlie Manson will be announcing his engagement next?"

"As long as we're playing twenty questions with each other, tell me why you faked your own kidnapping. Hell of a publicity stunt for a fading modeling career. Or maybe we want to be an actress now?"

"My modeling career has *not* faded, and even if it had, I'd hardly give a damn. It's never been anything more than a means to an end."

"Exactly my point, but what end are we talking about?"

"We're not." She crossed the *T* with a figurative snap of her tongue, putting a stop to the conversation.

Bathed in the room's recessed lighting, the silver ice bucket gleamed on the dark mahogany secretary. Jack walked over to it and pulled out the dripping bottle of Dom Perignon. Not bothering with a flute, he gripped the magnum by its neck and hoisted it to his mouth as if he were going to drink from it that way. Just as swiftly he changed his mind. Champagne spumed out, wetting his face, and he twisted away from the alcohol savagely, wiping his mouth on his sleeve.

More than anything he resembled a barroom brawler as he dropped the bottle to his side and glared at her. With his shirt hanging off one shoulder, his dark hair in disarray and his mouth wet with expensive booze, he looked as if he'd just invented a new meaning for the word *trouble*.

"You are one hell of an actress by the way," he told her.

"Thank you." His mood was turning ugly, and she'd apparently said or done something to trigger it. Get on with it, Gus, she told herself. Get your prizewinning butt out of here.

There was a shiny black spider crawling across the floor in front of him. She noticed it at almost the same time he did. It was the size of a quarter, probably not large as Scorpion Bay spiders went, but plenty big enough to make her uneasy.

Jack watched its approach with all the dispassion of a scientist observing lab rats in a maze. The creature was quick, but hesitant, sensing danger. When it crept into range, Jack glanced up at Gus. His eyes darkened with curiosity, but the faint smile he seemed to be contemplating never materialized. She thought he was going to let the spider finish its odyssey across the enormous tundra of the bedroom. Instead he reached out one glossy black dress shoe and crushed it beneath his toe.

Gus spun around to the doors. It was only an insect, for God's sake. She might have squashed it herself. But that wasn't the problem. That wasn't it. He killed things. He could snuff the breath out of a living thing, even another human, without guilt or remorse. That should have disgusted her, and it did. So then why did she respond to him? Why did she shudder in the deepest parts of her when he looked at her? *And why had he looked at her now as if it were really she he wanted to crush in some perverse and thrilling sexual way?*

A strange, discordant hum of excitement swept through her. An invisible maestro plucked at the fibers of her being as if they were bowstrings. Her nerves shivered and tightened. The muscles in her belly coiled, crying out for something she didn't understand.

"It's hot in here," she said, kicking off her sandals. "I'm going out for a swim."

"You don't have a suit."

"I'll improvise." As she turned to escape through the terrace doors, she glanced over her shoulder at him and unbuttoned one of the side tabs that connected the bodice of her jumpsuit to the palazzo pants. "I'm good at that," she said.

Silver swirled around her, icy cold and iridescent as she waded out to her thighs and dived in. The shock of it, particularly against the skin of her breasts and buttocks, made her gasp. Plunging headlong into blackness, she penetrated the shallow depths of the bay like a porpoise and began to stroke underwater. She was a strong swimmer. Her stepsister, Jillian, had been obsessed with diet and exercise. She'd had one of the rooms at the Featherstone mansion outfitted with expensive weight equipment, but Gus had always preferred the pool for exercise.

Nearly out of air, she burst to the surface, glanced behind her at the shore, and kept going, swimming rapidly for deeper waters. There would be very little time. She hadn't seen any sign of him, but underestimating a man like him would be a costly mistake if she ever hoped to escape this place and reclaim control of her life.

Moonlight sheened the surface of the water just ahead of her, concentrating its brightness in a dazzling oval. With a few more strokes she was swimming in the midst of the magical display and glowing with its brilliance. Certain that he couldn't miss seeing her, she began to tread water, her arms and legs working rhythmically. The water temperature felt almost comfortable now, she noticed. Her system had completely acclimated and was pouring heat through her naked body, which she was sure must be a deep, rosy pink.

A moment later she felt currents stirring in the depths beneath her. Something tugged on her ankles, pulling her down. Her first inclination was to kick the shackles away, to fight the undertow. Instead, she let the warm water envelop her, creating its own silky friction as she slipped and slid down the length of a naked man's body. It was him. Dragged into the depths by Jack's weight, she felt as if she were coming into contact with every inch of his muscled frame.

In the weightless environment of deep water, even his ridged flesh was as slick as satin. His shoulders and chest, his thighs, all felt as gleaming hard as marble drenched by rain, a Grecian koros. The power was there; he was totally in control, but every move he made was slowed and accentuated by the counteracting force of the water.

She could feel the heat of him gliding over her, glancing her thighs and belly, caressing her breasts and buttocks. She couldn't always tell what part of his body was touching her, and then she realized it was his hands. They were all over her, curious and possessively male. He ought to have had his face slapped for the way he was touching her, but she made no outward attempt to stop him, even when she began to run out of air.

Her chest tightened, but the wooziness that invaded her senses was warm and pleasant. She would have loved to give in to it, but within seconds the lethargy seeping through her made her realize what was happening. He was a strong swimmer, too, and with far more lung capacity. He could hold her under until she was nearly unconscious, weakening her to the point where she couldn't fight.

Intuition told her that the only way to regain control was to give it up, to surrender completely and trust that he wouldn't let her drown. She allowed herself to go limp, and his response was immediate. Curling her loosely in his arms, he dived, and she spiraled madly, helpless as he arced into a graceful somersault and they glided back to the surface.

By the time they broke through the glassy barrier, she ached for breath. "My God!" she gasped, sucking in every ounce of air she could. But he didn't let her fill her lungs completely. His mouth covered hers before she could sate herself or regain her strength. She gripped his biceps, her chest heaving against him, her breasts shuddering with urgency. It was a desperate kiss, ignited by the panic that was running through her. She was certain she would faint if he let go of her; she might even die. What she didn't know was whether it was from lack of air . . . or lack of him.

As if he understood her hysteria, he cupped her buttocks firmly anchoring her and blew gently into her mouth, exhaling the warm, moist air she so desperately needed into her aching throat. She drew in deeply, taking everything he gave her, allowing him to be her source of oxygen, of life itself. Gulping and shuddering, she clung to him, tears squeezing through her closed lids. He was her lifeline, her deliverance, but it wasn't until she finally calmed a little that he truly took control.

As she moved to break the kiss, he released her, and they submerged again. It was over in a matter of seconds, but she was plummeting like a rock when he caught her under the arms and brought her with him to the surface. This time his grip was deliberate and possessive, driven by some male need to master whatever was ungovernable in the situation, in the woman. His breath was trembling, his mouth hungry as it touched hers.

"Be my wife," he said.

The throaty need in his voice touched something raw and needful in Gus, too. He wasn't a man given to displays of tenderness, but his lips were gentle, and yet so firebrand hot that she nearly succumbed to a melting surge of desire. She had intended to surrender, but she hadn't meant it to be unconditional. This was no longer a controlled descent. She was truly losing it.

His strong kicks kept them afloat. Gus wouldn't have cared if they'd gone under again if it would have quenched the fire that razed her insides. He was holding her under the arms, and his palms had pressed into the sides of her breasts, molding and lifting them. She gave out a hoarse moan as he raised her up and took one of her tingling nipples into his mouth. Her flesh felt so full and urgent she nearly cried.

Desire flashed, streaking a path to the heat between her legs. "Touch me," she begged him. "Deeply . . . taste me with your mouth."

He sank into the silver pool and disappeared. She closed

her eyes, praying for the strength to do what she had to. She
so wanted the pleasure he could give her that she let him
splay his hands across her bottom and press his mouth to
the dark curls that hid her throbbing center. His tongue
darted over her, bringing her unbelievably sharp sensations.
But when it touched her clitoris, she gave out a throttled
cry. Confusion and conflict flooded her. She couldn't do
this. She couldn't let him do it. She had to act.

Now, she told herself. *You'll never get another chance!*
With a sudden surge of resolve, she lifted her knee and
caught him squarely beneath the chin, sending him spuming
backward in a geyser of flashing limbs and bubbles.
Her whole body trembled with the violence of it, trembled
with the shockwave of unrelieved desire that flared through
her.

She kicked off with all the power she could muster and
began to swim frantically. They had drifted in toward
shore, which was now less than a hundred feet away. She
didn't look back until she was on the beach, and then only
long enough to see that he wasn't coming after her. He didn't
even seem to have surfaced. The flash of horror she felt reminded her of the snakepit in the desert shack. She hadn't
been able to leave him there either. She'd returned for him,
saved him.

*She wouldn't do that now. She would never be free of
him. Never. He wouldn't allow her to be.*

His tux pants were lying on the beach, next to her jumpsuit. She scooped both articles of clothing up and ran for
the suite. When she reached the top of the steps, she
glanced over her shoulder again. The bay still looked quiet,
frighteningly placid. Had he drowned? Or was it a trick?
He'd been able to swim out to her without a sound, not
even a ripple. He could be hidden in the shadows of the bay
right now, or swimming back to shore underwater.

With a choked sound, she turned and ran for the room.

CHAPTER
13

THIS TIME SHE REALLY *HAD* KILLED HIM.

Gus cupped with both hands the Bloody Mary the stewardess had brought her, chilled by the glass's icy coldness. Her palms were wet, whether with condensation or perspiration she couldn't tell, but she was unwilling to let go of the drink. It was all she could do to raise the glass to her lips.

Dead. He was dead. It didn't matter any more that the marriage had taken place at gunpoint or that the ceremony was a complete sham, based on spite, acrimony, and revenge. All Gus could think about was what she'd done. Her husband of less than a day was floating naked at the bottom of Scorpion Bay in the gulf off Baja. Jack Culhane had sunk like a stone. She had drowned him on the first night of their honeymoon, and now she was fleeing the scene of the crime.

The enormity of her predicament brought a violent shudder.

"Cold, dear?" asked the bright-eyed stewardess who bent

to tidy up the puddle of Snappy Tom and vodka that Gus's inner earthquake had created. "Need a blanket?"

"No, thanks," Gus said, quite certain that a stack of blankets wouldn't have helped. She would never be warm again. Small wonder that she'd seen a tragic aura around him. She was the tragedy. She'd sensed that his ship was headed for the rocks, but not that she was going to *be* those rocks. It was true she'd wanted to be rid of him, but she hadn't really meant for him to die . . . had she?

She lifted the shaking Bloody Mary to her lips, realized she wasn't going to make it, and passed the glass off to the stewardess, who was still hovering as if Gus needed her own personal attendant. She did. She'd been trying since the beverage service, but hadn't managed to take a single sip of the thing. So much for a relaxing drink.

"White-knuckle flier?" the stewardess asked.

No, murderess, Gus wanted to say. She nodded instead.

By the time the airport taxi reached the Flintridge neighborhood where the Featherstone compound was located, Gus had accomplished something of a miracle. She'd convinced herself that she had done the right thing in drowning Jack Culhane, perhaps even the noble thing. The way she saw it, the man had hardly left her any choice. He'd kidnapped her, blackmailed her, and compromised her future dreams. Poor, misguided soul that he was, he'd virtually forced her into the desperate act. His tragedy was that he'd picked the wrong woman to mess with, because Gus Featherstone's dreams were bigger than both of them.

This was no easy rationalization, even for Gus, who was used to defending her actions and her opinions. She'd had to work her conscience until it was as pliable as a piece of Bridget's Play-Doh before she could get it into the shape she wanted it. Fortunately, she was motivated. She had, after all, broken the Fifth Commandment. But she hadn't meant to kill him, she told herself, at least not in any calculated, premeditated way. The drowning was more an unfortunate by-product of her desperate need to escape him. She certainly regretted it now. Deeply. She felt almost sick when she thought of him that way . . . lying at the bottom of the sea, all the dark, thrilling magnetism and tortured strength gone out of him. But what else could she have done?

It was one of those "greater good" situations, an impossible moral dilemma. A bad apple had to be thrown out to save the barrel. And in this case, the apple was a man who stood in the way of everything she was trying to accomplish, a dream that could touch millions.

She'd tried to get help for him. Admittedly, it was an afterthought, but she had tried. She'd thrown on her clothes, rushed out of the villa to the Jeep, thinking to drive herself to the airstrip, and then, in a fit of conscience, she'd run to the caretaker's cottage and alerted him to the disaster. "There's a man drowning in the bay," she'd told him, hoping there might still be time to save him. But by then it was too late. The caretaker hadn't found any sign of him.

Now the taxi driver's voice broke into Gus's thoughts as he drove up to the Featherstone guard gate and spoke with the man on duty. "I'll get out here," she told the driver.

Her travels around the world had taught her to keep an American Express card sewn into a little compartment in the band of her panties, but she had no cash on her at all, so she arranged with the guard to pay the taxi driver, then waited until the cab was gone.

"Everything okay, Ms. Featherstone?" the guard asked Gus as the car pulled away. "We weren't expecting you back so soon."

"Good morning, Howard." She was grateful it was him on duty. Howard was an easygoing sort, the most congenial of the security staff, and by far her favorite. "Everything's fine, but I need a little favor," she told him conspiratorially. "Don't mention to anyone that I'm back, okay? I want it to be a surprise."

Howard tipped his hat. "Sure, ma'am, anything you say."

Gus smiled wearily as she turned and walked up the bricked road that led to the house. Fortunately it was still early. No one would be up yet, and Frances would be busy in the kitchen with breakfast, so Gus wasn't worried about being seen.

Howard had tipped his hat. Wasn't that sweet?

She was actually glad to see the spires and towers of the Featherstone mansion through the massive oaks that lined the road. The neighbor kids called the soaring Queen Anne Victorian Dracula's Castle, and Gus had always been frightened of the place when she was a kid. She'd been told by Frances that the mansion had secret rooms and passageways, but she herself had never found them, and she'd privately suspected the housekeeper of trying to frighten her. It wouldn't have been the first time.

Now she just wanted to escape inside its hoary edifice to her cozy room on the third floor and hide out for a while. She couldn't deal with anyone yet, not even Rob. She knew he must be worried sick about her, but she was going to need more time to sort things through before she saw anyone.

It was little Bridget she was aching to get ahold of. She wanted to tousle her niece's blond curls and bear-hug her until they were both breathless, but even that would have to wait. Her first step would be a ritual of mental, physical, and emotional restoration. She was going to take a scalding shower, a tiny lavender pill, and sleep around the clock. When she woke up and was sane again, she would deal with all of this.

Gus's favorite "hang" outfit was a pair of men's boxer shorts and a white ribbed cotton tank with the words AMERICAN MADE printed across the chest. And that was what she was wearing when she awoke the next morning and discovered that she'd drifted off in one of the overstuffed chairs that flanked the fireplace. According to the clock on the mantel, she'd slept nearly twenty-four hours, but despite her restoration ritual, a persistent tickle of fear remained in the pit of her stomach. Or was it dread?

She had resolved not to let herself think about what happened in Scorpion Bay, though it was still weighing on her terribly. She couldn't change what had happened, no matter how much she might want to, and it was vitally important that she go ahead with her plans. But would her family and the media take her seriously when she tried to explain the situation? Only Rob knew what had actually happened at the WomenPride fashion show, and even he didn't know it all.

"Bridget must be up by now," she thought aloud, rolling her shoulders and neck to work out the stiffness. She wasn't ready to spring herself on the family quite yet, but she did want to see her niece. Nothing could restore sanity to her life the way a visit with Bridget could. The five-year-old had more chutzpah than a deli clerk at Canter's.

Moments later in the shower Gus planned her morning. The rich, coconutty smell of her piña colada bath gel saturated the stall as she soaped herself. She was sure her stepsister, Lily, would have found it vulgar and overpowering. Lily was delicate that way, preferring to accessorize her life with subtle scents and herringbone prints. But Gus found it invigorating, especially since it had been a birthday gift from Rob.

Once she'd seen her niece, she would call Rob at his home in the Hollywood hills, tell him what happened, and the two of them would put their heads together and figure out their next move. Rob had been acting as her manager and handling all her booking and public relations for nearly two years. She could never have managed the kidnapping scheme without his help. He was also an expert at damage control, which was exactly what she needed right now. The Jack Culhane "problem" could make or break her credibility with the public, and the way it was handled was crucial.

Moments later, toweled off and wrapped in a huge, fluffy carnation-pink bath sheet, she crossed her impossibly ruffly bedroom, headed for her white diary chest. The entire room was done in the flounces and swirls of a Barbie dollhouse. Gus loved and hated it. She'd chosen the cabbage rose chintz pattern herself, years ago when she was only a few years older than Bridget was now, and in all that time, she'd never been able to bring herself to change it.

"Someone will have to wrestle me to the ground and

hold me down while they ransack the place," she vowed, riffling through her underwear drawer in search of fresh panties. Frilly sachets scented with lilac and rose flew this way and that, their competing perfumes making her sneeze. "That's the only way it will ever get redecorated."

To make matters worse, she was an obsessive collector of froo-froo girly stuff. Antique dolls, teddy bears, and fringed pillows were piled on the bed, chairs, and floor, but the most precious bit of paraphernalia was her Cinderella music box. The much-adored, much-abused ceramic box had the fairy-tale heroine perched atop it, twirling rapturously to the tune of "Some Day My Prince Will Come." Gus had been six when she'd found the kitschy treasure at a white elephant sale at her school, and she'd pleaded with her mother until Rita had bought it for her.

If a room could be a haven, this one was. But it was also an embarrassment to her now, at twenty-seven. She'd been profiled by *Marie Claire* last year, and they'd wanted to shoot her at home in the mansion. She'd accommodated them in every way, except granting them access to this room. She took some pride in her bratdom, and this decor contradicted it profoundly. Even her few friends from the modeling agency were not admitted to Gus Featherstone's frilly sanctum sanctorum.

She'd gone to a shrink once, determined to get over her fear of snakes, as well as the stammer that lay ever in wait. The good doctor had told her the ruffles and chintz represented tender parts of herself that even her tough exterior couldn't protect. If that was true, her insides were mush.

Irony tilted her smile as she picked a pair of panties whose chintz pattern matched the room's decor. She'd be ruined if people ever found out the truth about her, that her bedroom was a shrine to the sweetest, *wimpiest* heroine of all time. Still, it had been her salvation, that fairy tale. It had kept her company when she was alone at night, and it had given her something to dream about when she was huddled on dirty carpets in dingy efficiency apartments, playing with her paper dolls and creating endless scenarios of romance to the rescue. It had also helped her to survive the ghastly situation right here in this house with her two stepsiblings. That was why this was Cindy's room. And why Gus couldn't change it.

"I do not look like Rita." She told herself that firmly as she sat at her vanity moments later. Frowning at her reflection, she applied a light application of mascara to thick soot-black eyelashes. But she did look like Rita. She had the same exotic coloring and angular bones, the same smoky violet eyes, which never failed to draw compliments, but which had never impressed her, because they weren't blue like Cindy's.

Her mother had met Lake Featherstone, Sr., while waitressing a catered affair at the manse. Rita Walsh had spilled champagne in the great man's lap, then breathlessly attempted to blot it up with her apron, taking a great deal more time than necessary. It was lust at first touch.

The aging patriarch had married Rita not six weeks later, over the family's vehement protests, of course. From that point on, Gus's life had become a darkness that could not be lightened by romantic fairy tales, or by anything else that she knew of, except her own ferocious will to prevail. Nevertheless, those stories had been her only real comfort, and when she and her mother moved into the mansion, she begged Rita for a canopy bed and a room worthy of a fairytale princess. Money was no object, and Rita had eventually hired it done. But her mother hadn't stuck around to see the finished room. She'd been too preoccupied with her own goal—stealing her new husband blind and running off to the West Indies with her deep muscle massage therapist.

Pain welled as Gus thought about how hard she'd tried to please her mother all those years ago, how desperate she'd been, and how certain she was that Rita couldn't stand the sight of her own overeager, fumbling klutz of a kid. Did mothers find their own children repugnant? Gus was bone-certain that hers had.

She slapped down the mascara, sighed heavily, and plucked a lipstick from the row of tubes in her makeup tray. She really would have to grow up one of these days. Turning your bedroom into a security blanket was worse than

embarrassing when you were an adult woman. It was pathetic. Maybe she would call a decorator today and get it
over with, she thought, glowering at the blush-pink lipstick
color she'd chosen. The first thing to go would be that silly
music box.

The hallway was empty when at last Gus let herself out
of the room, wearing a fresh pair of boxers and a gray
cropped-top workout Tee. She and Bridget were at opposite
ends of the mansion from each other, Gus's room being on
the top floor of the east wing in one of the house's many
turrets, and Bridget's being in the west wing, overlooking
the tea garden, and next to Frances's. Gus would have preferred the little girl nearer her, but Gus's modeling career
had demanded a great deal of travel until recently, and it
had made more sense to have Bridget where Frances could
keep an eye on her.

The huge house was unusually quiet as Gus stole down
the mahogany staircase that descended to the Grand Hall.
Rather a lofty name for a foyer, Gus had always thought,
but the room was lovely with its mirrorlike black and white
floor tiles and elegant chandelier. If Gus hadn't known that
both Lake and Lily were in town, she would have guessed
they were away somewhere, and quite likely together. The
bond they shared as twins included their love of traveling,
opera, and fine art. They regularly went to London for the
summer and fall seasons, when Sotheby's and Christie's
held their masters auctions.

No one had been more surprised than Gus when they'd
shown up for her charity fashion show. Of course, it would
have looked tacky in the society pages if they hadn't, considering their younger stepsibling was being feted for her
heroism. Ward McHenry, the Featherstone's trust officer,
had also attended, which boded extremely well for what
Gus was trying to accomplish. More than anyone else's, it
was McHenry's confidence and support she needed to win.

Faint sounds of conversation came to her as she hesitated
on the steps. There was a small television in the kitchen,
and Frances sometimes kept it on, but the noise seemed to
be drifting up from the gallery, an enormous ballroom at

the end of the hall that the Featherstones had converted into
a showroom for their art collection.

As Gus crept closer, she heard snippets of an exchange
between two men, but all she could make out was the occasional word. They seemed to be talking about security systems, which wasn't that unusual given the value of the
collection. She heard references to microwave intrusion detectors, proximity sensors, and silent alarm systems.

As their voices grew more distinct, she realized they
were moving around the room as they talked, nearing the
gallery doorway. "You must have thirty or forty million
dollars' worth of art in this room alone," one of them said.

Gus grasped the balustrade to steady herself. She was
afraid her heart might knock her over. She knew that voice,
knew it as surely as she knew the bogeymen of her childhood nightmares. *Dead to life, a wilderness with everything
of value scorched out of it, with nothing left but the ashes.*
Oh, yes, she knew that voice. It belonged to the man she'd
thought she'd left at the bottom of Scorpion Bay.

He'd survived. He was not only alive, he was here in her
home, talking to . . . who? Who *was* he talking to?

Clinging to the railing, Gus made her way down the
stairs and crept through the foyer to the gallery at the far
end. The double doors of the room stood ajar, and she
could make out Lake, her stepbrother, near the Renoir, but
the man Lake was talking to had his back to her. She scrutinized his indigo shawl-collared jacket and khaki pants, his
powerful shoulders and the black hair, custom-cut like a
fighter pilot's. "Oh, my God," she breathed, her darkest
fears confirmed.

Her first reaction was to call the guards and have him
thrown out, but she didn't dare. He could gut her plans with
a casual inquiry: Lake, did you know your sister faked her
own kidnapping?

"I'm surprised Gus didn't mention that I'm a specialist in
security systems," Culhane was telling Lake. "Much as I
hate to be the bearer of bad news, your collection is vulnerable. Even your guards are lax. I told them I was with the
FBI, and they practically led me here by the hand."

Lake seemed surprised at that, and amused. "You never mentioned you were a family member? Augusta's new husband?"

Jack laughed. "I didn't think they'd believe me since Gus wasn't with me. What was I supposed to tell them? That we got separated at the airport, and I missed the flight back? I doubted they'd buy that story, especially since it was true."

Jack rubbed his neck, all very affable. "Besides I wanted to conduct a little test of my own. Gus had told me about the priceless family art collection, and I admit to being curious about how well secured it was."

"Perhaps the guards were negligent," Lake conceded. "But this gallery is protected by a state-of-the art system."

"State-of-the-art doesn't mean flawless."

A Rodin statue in a glass display case stood in the center of the room, the showpiece of the collection. Jack turned to it as if to make a point, and then he saw her in the doorway. His eyes lit with an energy that was as sensual as it was challenging. The message they transmitted was *I'm alive and well, baby . . . and I'm coming to get you.*

His mouth curved, but he said nothing. And though his nod to her was barely perceptible, the dark amusement in it made Gus's stomach twist. It was almost as if he'd known she was there all along, listening to his every word. Cold fear stole through her as she wondered if he'd been one step ahead of her the entire time, including her pathetic attempt to get rid of him in Baja. Was she the one being set up?

She ducked out of sight before Lake noticed her, but her heart was still wild. She had to concentrate to keep her balance as she made her way back up the stairway, and she had no idea what she was going to do next. She hadn't even had a chance to talk to Rob, but the thudding chaos in her chest told her two things. Culhane was more of a threat than ever, and she was still dangerously susceptible to him. The sneaky bastard could do more damage with those coal-black eyes of his than most men could with their hands, lips, and tongue combined.

As she hurried back to her room, she made herself one

fervent promise. She was not going to let him wreck her life because he had nothing better to do than assuage his male ego. Her futile attempts to stop him had turned this into a deadly game, and she had no choice but to play it out. If she couldn't come to terms with him in some way, then the solution would have to be more extreme. Rob had arranged for a kidnapper; perhaps he could arrange for a hitman.

Gus was dizzy with fear and trepidation. She could hardly navigate as she opened the door to the blinding sunshine that flooded her bedroom, but what unnerved her even more was her own resolve. She had never been more serious in her life.

Well, well, well, look what the *brat* dragged in.

Sitting before a bank of video screens, Lake Featherstone folded his arms and settled back in the ergonomic desk chair to watch Jack Culhane step out of the shower and towel off. He admitted to being curious about the attraction this man held for his tempestuous stepsister, but he hadn't expected to get a urologist's eye view of the reason. Still, if Augusta had married Culhane for his spectacular plumbing, then why did she relegate him to Siberia, which was what the family called this particular guest bedroom?

It was one of several rooms in the house that were monitored by an elaborate video system, and though Lake had intended the system for security purposes, he felt completely justified in using it now. The recent kidnapping and breach of the mansion's external security had forced him to be more vigilant. If he couldn't trust the guards to keep tabs on their guests, he would have to do it himself. And why should the guards have all the fun anyway?

He smiled faintly at the irony, but the stirring of guilt he felt robbed him of any lasting pleasure. He'd never reconciled his need to invade the privacy of others, but he'd never been able to control it, either, and eventually, he'd stopped trying to suppress the urge. Something dormant came to life in this room, something powerful, a wild desire to know life's darkest secrets. Art was the only other outlet that had ever brought him this kind of excitement—an exquisite, irresistible work of art.

Unfortunately, the guilt was powerful, too. It stemmed from his having been caught spying on his parents' marital bed as a child. In his moral outrage the senior Featherstone had devised a punishment befitting the "perverted" crime, a corrective action that had humiliated Lake as much as it had disgusted him, and from that day forward Lake had secretly loathed his father with a frozen rage that had never thawed. His father had confused the issue by doting on Lake even more afterward, as if some new bond existed between father and son. That was when Lake had realized they were all perverted. Not *just* the Featherstone family—everyone—and that's when he'd given himself tacit permission to indulge his guilty pleasures.

Not that there'd been much of interest to watch until today.

Frances Brightly, the middle-aged minx, had an interesting way of pleasuring herself with a Waterpick appliance. But Augusta, well, she was a profound disappointment to him. He would have expected the bratwoman to provide endless hours of viewing entertainment, but she tended to turn pensive and childlike when she was in that silly, frilly room of hers. She did have an astonishingly great ass, though. That had given him a moment or two of gratification . . . before the guilt ruined it for him.

His twin sister, Lily, was off-limits. He'd never had a camera installed in her room. That would have been too—Another smile flickered before he could control it. Too what? *Incestuous* wasn't quite the right word where he and Lily concerned. His sister could be prim and fastidious to the point of annoyance, and yet at times so unexpectedly heedless, she shocked him. The Featherstones had always maintained a small stable of Morgans on the property for riding purposes, and Lily was very proprietary about the horses. She was an expert equestrian, but he'd once seen her nearly attack a recalcitrant animal with her riding crop. He could only imagine what her reaction to Jack Culhane would be.

Several things about Culhane intrigued Lake, not the least of which was his build. The man had a physique as twisted and tortured as one of Rodin's muscular statues. Lake had even noticed scars that looked like bullet holes, all of which gave the impression that Culhane was in some kind of magnificent agony. His facial features mirrored the torment, but not nearly as prominently as his body. Perhaps he'd learned to hide it behind those Loch Ness eyes. Augusta had married a frightening man. But why?

It was a question Lake intended to have answered.

Lake was also duly impressed by the man's technical knowledge. And he was aware of something disturbingly familiar about Culhane, although he didn't remember ever having met him. But most intriguing was the relationship between Augusta and her new husband. It wasn't a love match. They barely spoke, they weren't sharing the same room or bed. They weren't even in the same wing.

He hit a button on the control panel in front of him, activating the camera's zoom lens for a close-up of Culhane's face as he dressed. Dinner promised to be interesting. He'd decided to make it a celebration of Gus's marriage, and he planned to watch every move the newlyweds made and ask a few pertinent questions. Lake had assumed that the man in Gus's life was her manager, Rob Emory. Their relationship had never appeared to be a romantic one, but they did spend inordinate amounts of time together, and well, what else could anyone have thought? Instead, Gus pops up with this mystery man, who though admittedly handsome, gave a decidedly scruffy impression with his coal-black gaze, unshaven jaw, and barbed-wire hair. He looked rather like a thug in all honesty.

A flash of movement drew Lake's attention. Culhane had moved out of range, he realized. He hit another button on the console, which brought the lens back to wide angle and then he began to pan the room to see where the man had gone.

Interesting, Lake thought as several sweeps of the room failed to locate Culhane. It didn't look as if he'd left, because he wasn't showing up on the camera that monitored the hall-

way or any of the other screens. Lake returned to the bedroom, intrigued by something he'd seen in one of the
sweeps.

There was a duffel bag lying on the bed, but a shiny object half-hidden beneath it had caught his eye. It looked like
a photograph, a little worse for the wear, but with the white
edges and glossy finish of a snapshot. Curious, he zoomed
in, expecting to see a picture of someone in Culhane's life.
Instead, he discerned the frame of a painting, along with
some of the elements of a typical still life—table and cloth,
fruit and bowl—Jesus!

He rose abruptly, his legs locking up as the chair flew
backward. Shock rippled up his spine, burning a path to the
base of his skull. It couldn't be. It *couldn't*.

He jammed the zoom control with his finger, but couldn't
get close enough to see any more detail, and there wasn't
enough of the picture visible to tell him if he was right in
his suspicions. Still lifes were commonplace. Any amateur
could paint one, but that didn't explain why Culhane was
carrying around a photograph of one. Perhaps it was a
painting he'd been hired to provide security for, but Lake
wasn't satisfied with that explanation. It didn't ease the
roaring in his ears or his chest.

All of his questions about Culhane took on a glaring im-
mediacy. If he'd been curious about where the hell Gus had
found him and what she wanted with him, he was burning
now. More important, what was Culhane's agenda? What
did he want with Gus? What did he want with the Featherstone family?

Lake glanced down at his watch and realized two things.
It was time to dress, and yes, indeed, dinner was going to
be very interesting.

CHAPTER
14

THE DRUMFIRE OF CLICKING FINGERNAILS STARTLED GUS OUT of her simmering panic. She glanced up, stared at her pensive reflection in the vanity mirror, and had to fight the urge to slap herself into action. It was six P.M., time to make an appearance at dinner, and what was she doing? She was sitting at her dressing table in a blue silk Betty Crocker wraparound, clicking her fingernails against her teeth!

She rose from the bench and began to toy with her dress. She'd wanted to look conservative, but something about the neckline bothered her. It didn't fall right. It gapped.

The *coup de grâce*, she thought as she undid the dress's fabric belt and refastened it. That was what awaited her downstairs. The deathblow to her dreams. Lake had decided a celebratory dinner was in order to introduce Gus's new husband to the family, and he'd invited several members of the Featherstone Board, including the chairman, Ward McHenry, to join them.

They might as well put her under a microscope with Jack

Culhane! Their every move would be observed by the people who held the fate of Gus's brainchild in their hands. As trust officer, McHenry controlled the pursestrings, but the others could—and did—influence his decisions.

One false step, one false word, and it was all over.

"Something's *wrong* with this skirt." Anxiety wrung a sigh out of her. "What is it? The cut? The length?" She turned, catching her reflection from the side, then drew up the hem and sighed again. "I look like Lily!"

Perhaps she'd made a mistake in not going to Culhane and confronting him herself. At least then she would have known what she was up against. But the look on his face had warned her that he had something evil in mind, *something that would remind her why his mother had named him Satan.* She'd actually thought she might be safer with the family around, but that was before she'd known it was going to be a command performance.

She was also waiting to hear from Rob, but he hadn't returned her calls. God, she needed him now more than ever.

"It's the wraparound," she declared, peering hard at her reflection and wondering why she hadn't seen it immediately. She was dressed to bake cookies! All she needed was an apron.

When she'd declared war against the bogeyman in her life, she'd adopted a persona, her own emotional armor, and a large part of that persona was *attitude*. It was time to bring the brat out of retirement, she decided. Nobody would have believed the Betty Crocker imitation anyway. Fortunately, her years on the runway circuit had made her a quick-change artist. All she needed now was the perfect kick-butt outfit.

Moments later the transformation was complete. The closet's full-length mirror assured her that she had the look she wanted. The sleek red off-the-shoulder sheath she'd slipped into was definitely vixenesque. She'd picked out pointy red pumps to match, accessorized herself with feathery earrings that tickled her throat, and as a final bit of insouciance, she released the combs with which she'd swept her dark hair away from her face and let it fall forward, playing peekaboo with her eyes. The finishing touch was a sprinkle of Hot Peppermint perfume oil, one of the products made by American Naturals, the company she would soon be representing.

"Salute when you look at me, soldier," she said, a smile curving her shiny red lips. This was the Gus Featherstone the world knew and loved to hate, and it was the person she longed to be, inside and out. No one could hurt this woman.

She was on her way out the door when a shrill ring turned her around. Gus had never moved so quickly. She was across the room and had the receiver in her hand by the second ring. "Hello? Rob? Is that you?"

Her fiancé's voice burst through the static of what sounded like a bad connection. "Gus!" he yelled. "I'm in Baja. I put a detective on Culhane, and he tracked the two of you to a villa in Scorpion Bay. I flew down this morning."

"You're too late, Rob. I ditched Culhane yesterday, but he followed me here. Somehow he got past the guards and he's in the house. I need you to come back as soon as possible."

"He's there with you? Call the police, Gus!"

"I can't, Rob. He's blackmailing me—us. He'll tell the family what we did. He'll tell *everyone*. I have to go along with him until I can figure out what he wants."

"Hang tight, Gus. I'm on the next plane back."

The phone went dead, but Gus held on to the receiver for a few moments before she hung it up. The solidness of it in her hands felt like a talisman she could draw strength from, though she was reluctant to think that it was totally the result of Rob's call. Hearing his voice and knowing he was all right had reassured her, but something else was taking shape within her, a gathering of her own forces. She'd never allowed herself to be dependent on anyone, especially emotionally. Rob wasn't here, and even if he had been, she couldn't rely on him to deal with Jack Culhane. She would have to do it herself.

Fortunately, a plan was coming to her, and this time she

wouldn't bungle it. There was more than one way to deal with an unwanted houseguest.

Secluded on several miles of wooded acreage in the hills of Flintridge, the Featherstone mansion was nearly as famous as the families who'd lived there, among them an original Hollywood movie mogul and an agricultural baron who made his fortune in oranges with a few packets of seeds he brought from Florida.

The main house of twenty-four rooms was already a quarter century old when Lake Junior's great-great-grandfather acquired it from the then-governor of California for fifty thousand dollars, a steal even in those days. For a few months of the governor's term one year, when the mansion in Sacramento was under construction, "Dracula's Castle" had even served as the official summer residence.

The Featherstones had added a wing and a spectacular two-story glass atrium, as well as redecorating several times since taking ownership, but they'd been careful to preserve the architectural integrity of the original Queen Anne Victorian design and the turn-of-the-century ambience of the interior.

In a recent spread called "West Coast Grandeur," *Architectural Digest* had called the house a historical landmark. Their photographic plates had featured the converted ballroom, where the family art collection was now displayed, and the Grand Hall, an elegant foyer decorated with Louis Quinze antiques and Empire urns.

Plates of the main salon captured the dulcet brilliance of golden candelabra and crystal chandeliers, the baroque pageantry of a ceiling mural by Descat, but pictures couldn't convey the room's true scope. The scene had to be apprehended all at once to experience its subtle majesty, and the effect was most impressive when contrasted by the *intime* atmosphere of a Featherstone dinner party.

This evening the salon was lit once again with the brilliance of crystal icicles and candle flame, light shattering light, as the family gathered to receive their dinner guests. Lake was the congenial host and quasi-bartender, making sure everyone was well watered. Lily urged hors d'oeuvres on the small, fashionable crowd and fluttered about, seeing to their every need while the catering crew hovered in various corners of the room, not sure what its purpose was.

Jack, having already been introduced around by Lake, had taken up a post by the fireplace, where he could observe the comings and goings. While he waited for one "coming" in particular, he tilted his highball glass of liquor this way and that, listening to the melodious clink of ice cubes as the golden ripples flashed in the firelight.

Not that he wasn't impressed by his surroundings. He would have been the first to concede that the Featherstone mansion had its grace notes as well as it grandeur. But then so did many things, including fifty-year-old malt Scotch. The liquor drew his gaze deeply into its seductive depths, hypnotizing him like a glowing whirlpool. His jaw tightened, his mouth watered.

He still craved the sweet oblivion that alcohol could bring, and he could still remember the time when that had been its only purpose. Somewhere in his thoughts, there'd been the awareness that if he were lucky, one day, the oblivion would be total. He wouldn't wake up, ever. At least it would have been a painless way to check out.

Apparently his need to see justice was stronger than his need to self-destruct. Even so, every once in a while he liked to hold a glass in his hand, to inhale the potent perfume and feel the deep, aching urge . . . tempting himself, tempting Fate.

Tonight the double doors to the main salon were thrown open in an expansive welcome, but the dinner guests were too busy visiting to notice the lithe, sensual figure in carmine red who appeared on the threshold. She hesitated as if to survey her domain, apparently determined to be noticed. Jack was amazed that anyone could miss the spectacle of her blazing red dress and dark hair. He couldn't take his eyes off her.

Her head tilted, her lips slightly pursed, she looked around the room as if the party held about as much interest for her as an afternoon of grocery shopping. Her eyes flickered over the guests, faintly wary, faintly bored. As her gaze caught and connected with his, her chin came up, almost defiantly. His jaw twitched, aching deeply, as if something had just jabbed him there. If she'd had any doubt about attracting attention, she needn't have. One by one the guests were turning to look at whoever that new man by the fireplace was staring at so fixedly.

"I see my d-darling husband's already met everyone." Gus's voice caught ever so slightly on the endearment, then breathed it out as smoothly as he might have exhaled the Scotch fumes, if he'd taken a drink. "How convenient," she added, strolling across the carpet to where he stood.

Darling husband? She was really heaping it on with a shovel. Secretly amused, Jack reached out for her hand as she came up to him. Not only did she ignore his overture, she flashed him a look that said she would scratch his eyes out if he so much as breathed on her.

"We have a great deal to talk about," she informed him, *sotto voce*. "Later."

"I'll look forward to it." He gazed into her hot violet eyes and felt his heart jerk to a stop. Everyone in the place was watching them, but she just didn't seem to give a damn. She was an amazing piece of work, an ultrasonic alarm system, wired to go off if you blinked. Her hair had picked up highlights from the fire, or perhaps from her vampire red dress.

Somehow he caught traces of peppermint, sharp and sweet.

"I'm so glad you made it back, darling," she said. "I was distraught when the plane took off without you. I just—" She fluttered her hands as if searching for the right word. "Well, I just screamed."

"Screamed? And I had to miss that?"

She caught a drop of condensation that was about to roll off the bottom of his glass. "I see you have a drink already." She brought her fingers to her lips and sucked up the water. "Would you get me one, *darling*?"

He shook his head.

She tilted hers. "You won't? Why not?"

"Because I'm your husband, not the butler."

Something odd happened to her eyes then. Their flaring anger revealed a hint of desperation. She raked him up and down with a toss of her head, taking in his ill-fitting dark blazer, the one he'd found in the guest room closet. "The butler's better dressed," she said, her voice dropping to a sibilant hiss. "Where'd you get the jacket? Steal it off a lounge singer?"

He ran his thumb along the rim of the highball glass, wanting very much to take a drink. "I'm not a *GQ* model, Gus. Just a guy with simple tastes."

"Just a guy who can't *finish* what he starts."

He could give her credit for one thing. She brought out the beast in him the way no other woman could. He'd never had exhibitionistic tendencies that he was aware of, or the desire to publically humiliate women, but she inspired both. He wanted to do exactly what he'd been too evolved to do in the desert. He wanted to bend her over his knee and paddle her ass until she wailed. Yeah, he wanted to hear her wail, and he wanted to do it right here in front of this bunch of society windbags.

Fortunately he was a man with remarkable control. Fortunately for her. "You got yours," he reminded her.

She mouthed a rejoinder that sounded like "Next time, give at the office," tucked her hand close to her breasts, where no one could see it, and flipped him off.

With that she went off in search of fresh prey.

She crossed the long, shimmering room as if she were strolling down a catwalk for an audience of adoring eyes. The sway of her hips was enough to give Jack sea legs. It was easy to forget that she suffered from a stammer, was terrified of snakes, and yet had shot the hell out of one to save his life. It was easy to forget she was anything but a provocative little bitch. His gut tightened with as much pleasure as anger. Jesus, what the hell was happening to him? He craved her almost as much as he craved a drink. And he'd never thought he could want anything that bad. He could taste her like she was Scotch rolling around in his mouth, hot, sweet . . . poison.

The glass in his hand was beginning to feel uncomfortably heavy. He set it on the marble mantel of the fireplace, then opened the buttons of his suit jacket and slipped his hands in his pockets.

Gus seemed to be headed for a bar set up by the caterers near the terrace doors, but she only got as far as the grand piano, where a hired pianist was playing softly. Lake stopped her to introduce her to a couple that Jack vaguely remembered as repertory theater directors. The Featherstones were bona fide patrons of the arts, after all. The pianist had already played everything from Chopin to Schubert. Now, unfortunately, he was working on what sounded like one of Bach's organ fugues in a minor key. Jack's education had been very thorough. He was familiar with it all. He just preferred Van Halen.

He was also wired in to the tension in the room—a human strain gauge—and very aware that he, himself, had pushed the needle over the top when he entered the room. Lake Featherstone in particular had been watching him with more than brotherly interest. In more ways than one, Jack thought. He'd discovered a tiny aperture near the ceiling of his room when he'd swept the area for surveillance devices. Next time Lake tuned in "The Jack Culhane Show," he would think he'd been submerged. Jack had sprayed the opening with a can of pressurized water.

The needle had just jumped again, Jack realized. A new guest had arrived since Gus, and the man was causing almost as much of a stir as she had. Tall and patrician, yet just raw-boned enough to be rugged, his Teutonic looks alone could inspire fear, Jack imagined, particularly in women.

There was something casually cruel about the glint in Webb Calderon's marbled gray eyes, a quality that was reflected in his powerful jawline, and even in the naturally wavy, dark blond hair that was combed straight back from his forehead. The weight of it made several sun-whitened locks droop forward, which would have turned another man, even one with his disturbing features, into a choirboy. Not Calderon.

He was one of the reasons Jack was here. The prominent international art dealer was known to have supplied Lake with many of the more valuable pieces in his collection, but Jack was also aware that the Treasury Department had long suspected him of masterminding several brilliant art thefts. Elaborate traps had been set for the dealer, but no one had ever caught him at anything. There were no witnesses, no evidence, nothing to associate him with the crimes beyond the fact that they were insider operations, and most of the pieces had been traced as passing through his hands at some point.

Jack himself had once been involved in a sting operation that put him face to face with the art dealer. He wondered if Calderon would recognize him now. The circumstances of their meeting were very different then. For one thing, Jack had another identity.

Apparently tonight he was going to get to test it.

Now Jack watched to see which of the Featherstones noticed the dealer first. He was surprised when it was Lily who rushed over to greet him, her white chiffon dress ghosting around her slender frame like veils. Tendrils strayed from a chignon that strained to contain her heavy chestnut-blond hair. Once she'd gracefully subdued the wisps, she made quite a point of hooking her arm in Webb's and escorting him around to meet the others. They made a slow circle of the room and finally ended up at the grand piano, where a small crowd had gathered, including Lake and Gus.

Calderon's conversation with Lake appeared cordial, but not exceptional in any way. Jack noticed that Gus whisked a flute of champagne off the tray of a passing waiter and presented it to Calderon with a little flourish. The art dealer's nod was lingering and appreciative, but then, what normal male's wouldn't have been. It was possible his relationship with the family amounted to nothing more than the legitimate business of art collecting, but Jack wouldn't have bet on it. At the very least Lake could be a buyer for the priceless contraband Calderon was thought to be dealing in, and it wasn't impossible that one or both were involved in the heist of the stolen Van Gogh Jack was searching for.

Jack had just decided to wander over and crash the party when Ward McHenry, the Featherstone's trust officer, rose from the couch where he'd been sitting and pointedly cleared his throat. According to Jack's research, the distinguished head of Featherstone, Inc., was in his fifties, but McHenry's bristly Kennedyesque copper hair, arresting blue eyes, and ruddy complexion made him look ten years younger.

"Dear friends," he said congenially, "might I have your attention for a moment? I was planning to save my news until dinner, but I find that I can't wait to share it. A moment? Please?"

The crowd obliged, and the pianist stopped playing as well.

McHenry picked up his martini glass as if to make a toast. "You all know about the recent ordeal one of the members of this family had to endure. Our own Augusta—Gus, as she prefers—was kidnapped and held hostage by radicals hoping to further their misguided cause. But let's not dwell on the negative. A tragedy was averted, and that's part of the reason we're here tonight—to celebrate Gus's safe return."

He acknowledged Gus with a quick nod, though his interest clearly lay in regaling the larger audience. "I must tell you all that my eyes have been opened by this—Gus's—ordeal. If any good can be said to come of such a thing, it's in how our perceptions are altered, how our thinking is expanded. It was both frightening and sobering for me to discover firsthand that this could happen to any of us, that we are all vulnerable to the political agenda of any terrorist group whose radical cause is currently in fashion. That's why Gus's heroism must not go unremarked upon. By foiling the terrorists with her courageous escape, she has struck a blow for personal freedom."

He paused, letting them all absorb this. "Some of us are charged with overseeing the industry that feeds and clothes and houses this country of ours. Gus has sent a message that we will not be used. We will not be victimized. And tonight we thank her for that, because we are all safer for it."

The guests' reactions were subdued. Gus was not a big favorite among them, Jack realized; however, she had prevailed against the avowed enemies of big business, or so they thought, and that alone would predispose them to be gracious.

"Life," McHenry went on, "devises many ways to test us while we're here, and Gus has triumphed in that regard. That's why, as trust officer for the Featherstone estate, I'm delighted to be able to say that the purposes for which the trust was created have all been fulfilled, and I am hereby exercising my discretionary power as trustee to authorize distribution of the entire trust estate to her at any time she decrees—for a business venture that is dear to her heart, I might add."

Jack stole a glance at Gus and saw that she'd gone pale. She stared at McHenry, breathless, bloodless, rapt, while the flute tilting in her hands sprinkled champagne on her red shoes.

Oblivious, McHenry droned on. "My dear friend and business partner, the late Lake, Sr., insisted that the purpose of the trust could be considered fulfilled only if his children demonstrated the vision, courage, and moral fiber to carry through on a business venture. Gus has done all that, in my opinion."

He held up his glass. "A woman of her mettle deserves a chance to make every success of herself, and we—the family and I—are pleased to be able to give her that opportunity."

"Hear, hear!" someone called out.

Everyone raised their glasses but Jack. Somewhere in the course of McHenry's rambling discourse, he had begun to understand what was going on. He almost laughed aloud. This was what the kidnapping scheme had been about. There'd been some nebulous special condition governing Gus's trust fund, and to shake the money loose from McHenry's clutches, she'd had to do something extreme, something so spectacular and so public he couldn't ignore it. He'd been right that she wanted publicity, but wrong about the reasons for it.

Gus had recovered from her shock, but she was still clearly astonished at the announcement. And delighted. Her smile was bright enough to outsparkle the chandeliers as she accepted the good wishes of those around her.

The rest of the Featherstones reacted with ambivalence, Jack noted. Lily, in particular, seemed disconcerted. Lake gamely held forth as jovial host, but Jack had noticed that he was particularly solicitous of his natural sister during McHenry's announcement. He'd gone quietly to stand by Lily's side, and they had exchanged a glance that told Jack the Featherstones were not exempt when it came to family secrets.

Webb Calderon raised his champagne glass. "Tell us more about that business venture, Gus. What are you going to do, start your own modeling agency?"

Gus laughed, clearly startled. "No, quite the opposite. My goals are twofold, really, and one of them I'd intended to pursue with as little fanfare as possible, because it involves a very sensitive issue, my late stepsister's death."

A quick glance at Lake and Lily apparently warned Gus that she should follow her instincts. The twins weren't pleased. Lily's hand had flown to an ornate, jeweled broach at her throat, and Lake had stepped forward as if he might intervene.

Gus stumbled over the next few words and then began again. "Let me just say that I'm planning to start a foundation in my late stepsister's name to fund research on the insidious disease that killed her. No one should have to die as Jillian did, and as thousands of other women do every year—young women, teenagers, mere girls."

She whisked up her champagne flute with a hint of bravado, and her smile returned, as potent as the wine. "The project I *can* talk about is a magazine I'm planning to launch. But it won't be a fashion magazine, at least not like anything you've ever seen before. The focus will be personal style. I want women everywhere to know that we don't have to let Madison Avenue enslave us with their concept of the perfect woman. We can define that for ourselves, each of us, individually, in terms of what's perfect for us."

The glass shot high in the air, a salute. "I want women to discover their own look, even if it's boxer shorts—"

A pale pink streak of light stopped Gus short.

"Aunt Gus!" the streak squealed, slowing only long enough to let Gus set down her glass before she bounded into her surprised arms. The last of the Featherstones had arrived, Jack realized. This must be five-year-old Bridget.

As he watched Gus and the little girl together, he became aware of his deepening respiration. It seemed to take forever to fill his lungs. Bridget was about the age that his daughter would have been if she'd lived.

"Where is he?" the child was demanding to know. She was wearing what looked like pink ballet leotards and matching satin slippers on her feet. Her blond curls bounced as she twisted in Gus's arms. "Where is he, Gus? Show me!"

"Who?" Gus asked.

"The man you married, of course! He's my uncle, right?"

"I'm right here," Jack said. His laughter had traces of sadness that even he could hear as he walked over to Bridget.

The little girl wrinkled her nose, scrutinizing him as he approached her. Even at five there was a slightly imperious quality about her that told Jack she was already taking her cues from Gus, a brat-in-training, but an incredibly cute one. His arm almost ached to tousle her blond curls so badly.

Bridget stared up at him, her eyes as intensely blue as her aunt's were violet. "Are you mean?" she asked.

"Very."

She barely cracked a smile. "I don't believe you."

"Believe him," Gus murmured.

"I think I should have dinner with you," she announced to Jack. "Then you can get to know me better."

"Darling, no," Lily intervened, speaking to Bridget from across the room. "This is a dinner party for adults."

Lake spoke up as he joined Gus and Jack. "No, Lily, I think Bridget's right. Bridget should join us." With a reassuring smile all around, he assumed the role of family peacemaker. "After all, it's a celebration of Gus's return . . . and her marriage."

Bridget beamed and gave Lake a thumbs-up sign. But Gus didn't seem to know how to respond, which intrigued Jack.

"Very well." Lily sighed nervously, clearly reluctant about something. She turned to the housekeeper, who didn't seem to like the idea, either, and was glaring at Jack quite pointedly, as if he were the cause of all the confusion.

"Frances," Lily said, "would you see that Bridget tidies up a bit. Perhaps you could persuade her to change from those leotards she wears night and day into some real clothes? Then you can bring her in to join us."

"Leotards *are* real clothes," Bridget was quick to inform Lily. "And if I can't wear them, then I want to wear my Swan Lake outfit. Can I, Gus? Can I, please? I'm going to be Odette, the white swan, in the recital."

Gus set her charge down. "You can wear the tutu, but leave all that headgear off, okay? Or there won't be room for you at the table."

As Bridget scampered off with Frances, and the others filed off to the dining room, Jack noticed that Gus was smoothing her clingy red sheath and lingering as if she might want to speak to him alone.

"Cute kid," he said. "She's heavily into ballet?"

"Lives and breathes it." Her tone was droll. "I indulge her because I know she's lonely. She has friends at school, but none around here, and the modeling has kept me away so much."

"I guess that will all change now, with the magazine?"

"Yes . . . yes, it will."

They had begun to walk toward the double doors, and Jack was again aware of the hot peppermint waves rolling off her and the sway of her slender hips. He had a vivid flashback of her exposed bottom as she pranced into their desert shower stall, and the image sent a hard jolt of desire through him. It almost made him weak.

"Congratulations by the way," he said. "I guess the trust fund money should set you up nicely?"

"Yes, thanks." She nodded, clearly not anxious to talk about the business venture of her heart. "By the way, do you ride?"

He grinned and poked a tongue in his cheek. "You know I do." The snap in her eyes told him she didn't appreciate his attempt at kinky humor, and that he had just squandered whatever good will had been established because of Bridget.

"Horses," she said tersely.

"Oh . . . horses. Sure, them too."

"Tomorrow then?" she said. "Eight o'clock. Bring your training wheels."

She returned his nod with a brisk one of her own and strode off ahead without waiting for him to answer. She didn't seem to care in the slightest that she was leaving her new husband in the dust.

The wilder the pony, the finer the horse, Jack thought, remembering the adage as he watched her sashay down the Grand Hall, a sexy red chess piece against the black-and-white checkered floor. "I'll bring my riding crop, too," he murmured, "just in case the need arises."

CHAPTER
15

IN HER DREAM SHE WAS READY FOR HIM . . . ACHING, QUIVER-
ing, ready. He had come up behind her, and he was touching her, running his hands lightly over her flanks as if she
were a trembling animal, a skittish horse he was preparing
to mount. He wasn't the kind of man who would use a saddle. He would want nothing between his flesh and the
horse's. He would ride bareback with his weight bearing
down on her spine, his powerful thighs holding her captive.

His murmurs were dulcet, meant to gentle her. His hands
felt like heaven on her sensitive, shuddering skin. Heaven
with a little bit of hell mixed in. She caught the scent of
him as he bent over her. It was a warm male smell, like
brandy laced with spices. Delicious. She breathed him in
like air. And then suddenly he was mounting her, riding
her, and she could feel his hand resting on her rump, his
fingers a lightning rod to the nerves in her rippling skin.

She shivered and her legs grew languid. A sensation of
pleasure fanned through her, filling her with such flowing
warmth she couldn't seem to move as he wanted her to. His

hand fluttered caressingly, urging her on, but she couldn't run . . . she couldn't. It was too wonderful. She was too weak.

Suddenly his mouth was at her nape, and his spicy breath was washing her skin as well as her senses. "Take me," he was murmuring. "Take me for a ride, beautiful animal, let me sit here astride you, let me ride you a little longer, just a little longer, don't stop now."

The pressure of his hand deepened, sending an odd thrill through the sparkling nerves in its path. Her legs didn't want to hold her. They wanted to fold and let her drop to the soft, welcoming ground. Her muscles yearned to give way, but her heart was wild, such an angry, clamorous thing, it drove her on. Her aching, surging heart.

She wanted him . . . oh, how she did want him. But not this way. If he would only let her drop, if he would only take her in his arms, take her away, take her to heaven—or hell—she didn't care which any longer.

"Just a little farther," he urged, an odd shake in his voice. "Don't stop now." His breath was tremulous, but his hand grew firm against her shuddering flanks, warm as it lifted and came back down, hot as it coaxed her to go on. The heat of his fingers startled her tingling skin and brought each fiber alive, quiveringly alive. The soft crack of the next stroke, gentle as it was, made her gasp.

She could feel the pressure of four long fingers, the imprint of an open palm. God, how it startled her, what he was doing, the way he was touching her, the sharpness and sweetness of it. The wild excitement!

She braced herself for another stroke, and perhaps she even wanted it, but instead he began to caress her again, lightly caress her. The feathery touches on her vibrating skin left her dizzy with confusion and crazy with desire.

"Take me, beautiful animal . . ." he whispered.

Her spine jerked into a deep arch, her hips sought his, grinding out the heavy, urgent rhythms of mating. She was ready, shockingly ready for whatever he wanted. She was ready to turn to him and open her legs, ready to have him hook his arms under her knees and lift her hips in the air as he entered her, as he slowly plunged and plunged and plunged, a man lazily riding a woman . . .

A guilty thrill shot through Gus, piercing her languid dream state with a laser of reality. Oh, so it was going to be *that* kind of dream, she realized as she came floating back to consciousness. A lustful, lurid dream. It must have something to do with him, she thought drowsily, the subliminal effect he was having on her. Her subconscious had reached threshold and the excess was spilling over.

She would have turned to him now, except that she'd decided she loved having him behind her, too, pressing into her, one hand caressing her hips and derriere, the other nestling around to cup her breasts. His hands belonged exactly where they were, fondling her intimately. They were as familiar as someone else's hands . . . As familiar as . . . ?

Somewhere in the deep switch centers of her brain, the place where sensory information was processed and routed to its ultimate destination, a tiny little alarm sounded. She knew these hands. She could feel their palpable warmth on her skin, she could almost discern their detail. His male cologne was familiar, also . . . it had the rich, spiced heaviness of Brandy. She loved that cologne . . . it was . . . ?

Brandy was Rob's scent.

The relay station went into full alert. The switchboard automatically began to reprocess the data and reroute its circuitry. She wasn't in the stable, her brain was telling her. She was in bed. Her bed. This man who was cupping her breasts and touching her quivering flanks. This man who wanted to ride her was . . . not Jack.

"Baby, it's me. Gus! We've got to talk."

Gus roused herself, all neurons firing now and hitting their targets. It was Rob! She opened her eyes to a room flooded with moonlight, Brandy cologne and feverish, undissipated heat.

"It's you? Rob?" She rolled over in a rush. In her haste she sideswiped him with her elbow, bumping his nose. "Oh, I'm sorry!"

Even in the moonlight she could see his features narrow and grow suspicious. That was Rob's one flaw, she'd always thought. He harbored a jealous streak. Still, it was a relief to have him back. Apparently he'd impetuously crawled into bed with her, fully dressed, and she loved the way his jaw muscle danced when he was tense. His deep brown eyes, dark hair, and cleft chin gave him a boyish look that had always appealed to her, except when he was angry, like now, and then the charm seemed more immature than boyish.

"Of course it's me," he said. "Who did you think it was?"

When she didn't answer immediately, he began to glower. "Are you sleeping with that guy, Gus? Did you have sex with him in Mexico?"

"No, of course not!" It was the truth, she told herself. She and Jack hadn't slept together, not in Mexico. "Let's not talk about sex, okay? We have more important things to discuss."

He propped himself up, rested his head against his fist, and gazed at her searchingly. "Right, like getting the marriage annulled—"

Gus grabbed for the coverlet he'd pulled off her, suddenly uncomfortable about her nakedness. "Don't worry about the marriage right now," she countered. "I don't even think it's legal. I've got something else in mind."

"Gus, if he touches you, I'll kill him. I swear, I'll kill him. In fact, that's a damn good idea, why *don't* I kill him?"

"I've already thought of that, and I've come up with something, a plan—"

"A plan to kill him? You'd do it yourself? No, that's much too dangerous."

"It's not what you're thinking," she assured him, shrewdly deciding not to reveal what she had in mind. "I'm just going to get to know my new husband a little better, spend some time with him, that's all."

"No sex? No murder? I don't want you doing either of those things without me."

She laughed softly, feeling almost giddy at the craziness of her situation. She was in bed with her fiancé, talking about killing her husband, who was sleeping on the other side of the house in the guest room. "I wouldn't dream of doing either without you, okay, Rob? Now let me get some sleep, *please*. It's late, and I've got a big day tomorrow."

Suddenly it hit her that she hadn't told him the news. "I almost forgot!" she gasped out. "They're giving me the money. Ward made the announcement tonight, in front of Lake and Lily and everyone. I've got the startup money for my magazine."

A surge of joy made her light-headed, and she dropped back on the pillows, staring up at the frills and flounces of her cabbage rose canopy bed. Rob was one of the few people who could appreciate what the funding truly meant. He'd been operating as her business partner for the magazine, and he knew the tens of millions that were involved in a national launch of the scope they were planning. She wanted to reach people with this magazine. She wanted to touch them.

"Jesus, Gus—" He seemed too stunned to assimilate the information. "That's fabulous. That means our brainchild worked. It if weren't for Culhane, it would have worked perfectly. Let's celebrate," he said, pulling her into his arms.

Gus felt herself stiffen as his hand slid down to her hip, and he drew her against him. When men wanted to celebrate, it always meant sex, but she couldn't do that. She wasn't sure why. She just couldn't. "Not tonight, I—"

"Have a headache?"

She sighed deeply and turned serious. "Rob, it was always your idea to keep our romantic relationship a secret, not mine. You're the one who felt it might damage your credibility as a publicist—and as my manager. We can't let people find out about us now. That would be a disaster."

She went on at length, convincing him that they had to be completely circumspect or everything they'd worked so hard to accomplish would be lost. "If something goes wrong now, if I'm f-found out—" The hoarseness that crept into her voice, the hesitation, spoke for itself apparently. He was one of the few people she'd ever told about her incident with the snakes and the resulting stammer, and now, hearing it seemed to defuse him.

He nodded reluctantly and released her. "You're right, of course. We'll have to be very careful until this is resolved."

Moments later when he'd gone and Gus was alone once more, she threw off the bedcovers and flattened herself against the sheets, pressing her naked limbs to their coolness and staring at the ceiling. She had lied to Rob, about so many things, the least of which was the fact that she wasn't tired at all. She was wide awake and thinking about tomorrow, but it wasn't murder on her mind, it was . . . riding. Riding wild horses.

"You know what they're doing, don't you? They're out there having sex on my horses!"

Lily Featherstone banged down the sterling silver coffee urn without having poured herself any coffee. She left the bone china cup and saucer rattling on the mahogany sideboard as she advanced on the dining room window and peered out.

The pale, sun-misted light of early morning crept over the rolling, wooded hills of the estate grounds and flooded the mullioned panes of the bay window, bathing her in a brightness that made her eyes teary. But Lily had no interest in the beauty of nature this morning. She was scathingly angry at her stepsister for sneaking off to ride without permission. According to Daniel, the stable hand, Gus and that primitive male friend of hers had left on Sapphire, Lily's own mount, and one of the other dozen horses they kept for guests to ride.

Husband, Lily corrected. Gus had married some lowlife security person whom no one had ever heard of! Her sigh held genuine distress. "What's happening to this family?" she asked plaintively.

"They're not having sex on the horses, I can assure you of that."

Lily swung on her brother, furious with him for being so cavalier about the latest disaster Gus had brought down on their heads. Their younger stepsister had been a constant source of humiliation since the day she and her mother arrived, with their cheap Kmart clothes packed in cardboard boxes and their drugstore cosmetics. Why couldn't the trashy woman have taken Gus with her when she ran off?

"How could you possibly think that?" she asked Lake. She tweaked the collar of her crisp white cotton blouse, unhappy with the way the placket was lying. "Did you see the way those two were looking at each other? I thought they were going to strip off in the drawing room and have at it right there."

"Would have been an improvement on the pianist."

Lake's wry smile did little to mollify Lily. Her twin brother was still sitting at the dining room table, an unfinished plate of scrambled eggs and one of Frances's apple-bran muffins in front of him. They were alike in so many ways, including their disinterest in food before noon. Lily could barely stand the smell of cooked eggs. But there was a child in the house, as Gus so often reminded them, and children's growing bodies had to be nourished. What disturbed Lily was Lake's stubborn insistence on underestimating Gus. He persisted in seeing her as a rather charming nuisance as opposed to what she actually was—an insidious threat to the Featherstone family and everything they represented.

"How can you say they're not having sex?" she wanted to know. "I'm quite sure they're having it on the horses, *with* the horses, and every other way they can think of."

Lake's expression was infuriatingly tolerant of his sister's pique. "They're not even sleeping together, Lily. They don't share a bedroom."

She made an impatient gesture and began to fuss with her blouse again. The Liz Claiborne slacks and matching vest she'd picked for her day of running errands were wrong, simply wrong. The western cut did nothing for her at all. With a growing sense of frustration, she scrutinized her reflection in the huge antique mirror that ran the length of the wall behind Lake. At thirty-seven she was already beginning to look droopy and pinched. Sad, she thought. She really looked quite sad. Time, like *everything* else in their lives, had clearly picked Lake to favor. It didn't seem to matter that they were twins. He looked ten years younger.

"What does that mean—they're not sleeping together?" she wanted to know. "Lots of married couples don't sleep together. That doesn't stop them from having sex in the bathroom sink."

"And if they were?" He threw down his napkin and rose from the table, then picked up his cup and walked to the sideboard for more coffee. The dazzling white light from the window sheened his hair and stole what little color there was from his handsome, angular features. "Their sex lives are the least of it. We don't know who this man is. We don't know what he wants."

"Yes, exactly," she chimed in, relieved they agreed on that much. "I think we can assume money's a large part of the attraction, don't you?"

"For him? Probably, but I'm not convinced that's all there is to it." He poured himself some coffee and joined her at the window, as if to help her spot the marauding couple.

"I suppose we could hire a detective," Lily ventured.

Lake said nothing for a moment. "I've already taken care of that."

"You've hired a detective?"

"Not exactly."

Lily was astonished. Glancing at him, she wondered if she were imagining the grim set of his profile as he gazed at the hills of the Angeles Crest Forest in the distance. The sprawling state park bordered the northern border of the estate and conveniently provided Lily and her guests with myriad trails for riding. He *was* concerned, she realized. "Do you think Culhane is dangerous in some way?"

"Just being cautious," he said with a quick shake of his head. His easy smile returned.

Lily had the distinct feeling he was keeping something from her, though that hardly seemed possible given their relationship. The rich aroma of his fresh, hot coffee drifted to her, and she reached for his cup with a smile, reassured when he relinquished it as if he'd read her intentions. They did understand each other. They'd always been able to communicate without words.

She sipped the coffee slowly, savoring the hint of cinnamon that Frances often added. "One of your security guards—Howard, I think it was—told me he caught two tabloid reporters trying to climb the walls yesterday. There's tremendous curiosity about Gus's mystery man, as they're calling him. I'm just afraid they'll come after us, the family, I mean, and try to find something scandalous to expose."

"The Featherstone family secrets? Our own private can of nightcrawlers, you mean?" Lake tapped the windowpane as a sparrow landed on the sill in pursuit of the muffin crumbs that Frances sprinkled around after breakfast every morning.

He was in a mood today. Lily couldn't decide if he was being mysterious or obtuse. Nightcrawlers? The analogy was so apt it made her want to shudder! "How can you be so casual about something like that? It would be a *disaster* if the media began probing into our lives. You know that as well as I."

He was suddenly contrite. "They're not interested in us, Lily," he assured her. "It will take a few days, maybe even a few weeks, but the furor will die down. Something else even more sensational will distract them."

"If Gus will let it die. You know how she is, Lake. And she's going to want all the publicity she can get for this magazine of hers." Lily could hardly contain her scorn. "She's already taken it upon herself to announce that ridiculous foundation. Can a press conference be far off? I swear, if she does *one* more thing to embarrass us, if she uses Jillian's name again to further her glory-seeking, I'll—"

Lake stepped back from the window, took the cup from her hand, and set it down. With a knowing smile he turned her away from him and began to massage her neck and shoulders. "Everything's under control, Lily," he crooned softly. "I'll take care of things. Haven't I always?"

That wasn't entirely true. Lily could have mentioned a

failing or two, including the vast sums he spent on art—
squandered, in her opinion. But the mere touch of his hands
brought a sigh to her lips. Her body was tight, especially
there, and the pressure felt wonderful. As he began to
knead more deeply, she rolled her head back and caught a
glimpse of someone standing in the arched doorway. A soft
exclamation slipped through her lips. "Who's there?"

"Good morning to both of you."

Lake's hands dropped away as Ward McHenry entered
the room. "Ward," he said, clearly startled. "I didn't hear
you come in."

McHenry looked a bit disconcerted himself. His ruddy
features were rosier than ever, and his coppery hair seemed
to be ablaze in the morning sunshine. He was carrying his
suit jacket over his arm and his shirt collar was unbuttoned
at the neck.

Lily moved quickly to get their guest some coffee and
put an end to the awkwardness. "Oh, didn't I tell you,
Lake?" she explained as she went to the sideboard. "I invited Ward to spend the night. It seemed silly for him to
make the drive back to Malibu at that time of night."

"Silly, yes," Lake agreed.

But Lily could tell by the tone of her brother's voice that
he didn't like having been taken by surprise. Ward had
practically become a member of the family since their father died, but he'd also assumed the position of leadership
in Featherstone, Inc., that would have gone to Lake had
their father believed his son capable of running the family
dynasty. Ward was chairman of the board and trust officer,
which gave the older man nearly total control over the business. Lake's only power came from the majority shares of
voting stock he'd been left by his father. He'd rarely exer-
cised that power against McHenry, but Lily knew there was
tension between them.

"Did you sleep well?" Lily searched for any indication of
Ward's reaction to what he'd seen as she approached him
with the coffee.

"Too well," he said, returning her scrutiny as he took the
cup she offered. "Apparently I missed breakfast?"

"Not at all! I'm sure the eggs are still warm." She turned away from him, flushing from his inquisitive stare and feeling very much like a kitchen maid in her own home. Secretly Lily was angry with the man. He had confided his decision to release Gus's funds, but when Lily had pleaded with him to reconsider, he'd dismissed her arguments, claiming he had no choice. That was when Lily had begun to feel the true frustration of her situation. She had always been the weakest link in the Featherstone power structure, if not content to let the men run things, then resigned to it. Only recently had she become aware of her own wellspring of power, her inner resources, and the discovery felt good. It felt right. Was it possible that despite everything, she had more guts, more nerve, than all of them?

The thunderous clatter of four pounding hooves beneath her and the rising heat of the horse's lunging body filled Gus's senses with excitement. A breeze from the west whipped the dark hair from her ponytail and stung her face with rushing blood. She hadn't ridden in years. She'd forgotten how rigorous and exhilarating it could be.

When she drew back on the reins, Sapphire snorted wildly, resisting her, and Gus was struck by the shuddering strength that was hers to control. It reverberated upward to the roots of her hair. Horsepower, someone must have called it once, before that standard of measurement was used for cars.

"Come on, girl!" Gus shouted, turning the restless horse toward the stream that ran through the Featherstone property. The glen, as the family had always called the wooded acreage on the northwestern border of the property, was still verdant and leafy green in July, its meadowlike clearings carpeted with summer wildflowers and tasseled, willowy grasses.

Shouldering around as the horses slowed, Gus saw Jack bobbing along like a proverbial jack-in-the-box on the roan mare that Daniel had recommended as one of the gentler mounts in their stable. He was still some distance behind her, and she was glad he couldn't hear her laughter.

By the time he arrived at the bank of the stream, she had already tied Sapphire to a post alongside the sparkling water, and she was standing in the shade of a large, bushy California oak, chewing on a blade of grass. She tried not to smile at his struggle to get his horse under control.

"I thought you said you could ride," she called to him over the noisy splash and gurgle of the stream. The glen was a veritable Eden this year, she'd decided, enchanted by all the growth and greenery. Summer showers had kept the streambed overflowing with clear, sparkling water, even though it was usually close to dry by now. Laced delicately through the tree branches overhead, emerald vines, heavy with summer's last honeysuckle blooms, perfumed the air with sweetness.

"I thought you were talking about a trot through the meadow, not a goddamn rodeo event," he called back. He whipped his leg over the horse's back and slid off the saddle like a pro. "Every time you goosed your horse, mine took off, too."

"It's all about controlling your animal, Jack," she said, laughing as Ruby, his mare, began to wander off behind him toward something that had attracted her attention. "For example, right now she's heading for the greener pastures, and you may never get her back."

"Shit!" Jack swung around and shot off after the beast. Ruby was apparently heading for a tasty patch of clover in the next county, but fortunately, he caught her before his outburst frightened her into flight. There was another little tussle as man and animal battled for ascendance, but to his credit, Jack quickly mastered the art of sweet talk. Crooning softly, he led her to a tree by the streambed, wrapped her reins around a low-hanging branch, and scratched her muzzle gently, making kissy noises. She seemed thoroughly charmed by the time he left her to cool her heels near a pool of water and a patch of grass. Staring after him with yearning in her big brown eyes, she nickered softly.

Swell, Gus thought despairingly. Even female animals loved him. Bridget had clearly been smitten with him at dinner, though she'd hidden it by acting like a perfect little fiend and insisting on knowing everything about his relationship with Gus, including whether or not they planned to have children. Frances had saved the evening by scooping up the tiny white swan and carrying her off, with Bridget complaining all the way that she hadn't had her Ben & Jerry's Wavy Gravy ice cream for dessert.

As Jack walked toward her now, Gus was not unaware of how sexy he looked with his long legs encased in faded denim. For a big man, he moved well in cowboy boots, too, effecting a rolling gait and an easy, unhurried air. He brushed absently at the sleeve of his denim jacket and then shook his head as if wanting to feel the breezes in his springy black hair.

It actually gave her a little thrill watching him approach. She could feel a shiver of energy gathering in the pit of her stomach, and the vibrations built with each step he took. Perhaps it was nothing more than her trained eye, but she couldn't seem to stop herself from observing him as if he were a male candidate for the catwalk and assessing the physical details.

The white T-shirt was a nice touch, too, she allowed, a striking contrast to the earth tones of his skin. So was his strong, rugged face and wide, sensitive mouth. She'd never noticed that about his mouth before, that it was sensitive.

As he neared, the thrill grew stronger, tighter . . . lower.

Okay, he was beautiful, dammit, she admitted reluctantly. Right out of one of those dusty, horsey, two-page Marlboro ads. Tall, dark, and lonesome. Too bad he couldn't ride worth a damn.

"By the way," she said when he'd climbed the small hillock and reached the shade tree where she stood, "we call it spurring the horse, not goosing, though I don't actually use spurs."

"We? Who's we? You and the Cowgirl Debutantes?"

She laughed and tossed the blade of grass away, glad she had him going. "Don't be cynical, Jack. It doesn't become you."

He looked her over now, checking out her snug jeans and cropped blouse. She'd tied the madras plaid material in a knot at her midriff, exposing an inch or two of golden skin, and he seemed very interested in the secret doings of that knot. "What would you know about being cynical?"

"Plenty, I'd know plenty."

"What's that mean? Are you telling me your life hasn't always been modeling assignments and mansions?"

"I'm not telling you anything, Jack." Her voice softened, and for a moment she was afraid she might stammer if she said anything more.

He stooped and plucked himself a piece of grass, still crouching as he peeled off the sheath and began to nibble on the tender white shoot.

The air above her was so sweet with honeysuckle, and the man below her looked so irresistibly male, hunkered down the way he was, that Gus was reluctant to break the mood. She'd brought him out here, where no one could eavesdrop, to ask the question she'd raised in Baja, the one that had gotten her into a great deal of trouble. This time she would word it differently.

"What would it take to buy your silence?" Her voice broke off, going faintly hoarse as she added, "And your absence?"

He raised his head enough so that she could see his eyes—black diamond eyes that bore into hers and always seemed to touch deeper than anyone else had ever reached.

"I'll go when I have what I came for," he said.

"And . . . what is that?"

"Information."

"Fine," she said quickly. "Ask me anything. If I know the answer, I'll tell you."

"Well, you could start by telling me this." He popped the rest of the shoot in his mouth, his jaw flexing as he chewed. "Whose kid is Bridget?"

Gus made no attempt to hide her startlement. "Why do you want to know?"

He rose to his feet. "I ask. You answer."

"All right, it's no secret. Bridget is the daughter of my stepsister, Jillian, who was Lake and Lily's younger sister.

Jillian died when Bridget was a baby, and she made me the child's guardian."

She was surprised when he didn't ask her why. Everyone else did, including Lake and Lily. They had even threatened to fight Jillian's wishes in court until Ward McHenry convinced them not to. No one seemed to understand that Jillian had cared about her, that someone could actually *care* about Gus Featherstone.

"You treat her like she was your own," Jack observed.

"I love her like she was my own."

"Then maybe you ought to take a look at what you're doing to her."

Gus stiffened defensively. "I'm not doing anything except being the best aunt I know how to be. I wish I could be with her more, but she does have Frances, and things are going to change now, with the magazine."

"I'm not talking about how much time you spend with her, I'm talking about what you do—"

"If this is a lecture about quality time," she said sharply, "please, spare me."

He gazed at her as if he were studying her. "She's just like you, Gus. The kid's adorable, but she's only five and she's already got a chip on her shoulder the size of one of these oaks. She doesn't ask questions, she interrogates and demands answers. She throws fits to get her way."

"Well, so do all kids." But Gus felt a ping of alarm. Was that true? Was she Bridget's role model and a terrible one at that? All she'd ever wanted was for Bridget to be happy and to thrive. She'd hoped to spare the little girl the heartaches she'd been through, which meant you had to be tough. She wasn't trying to turn her niece into a smart ass—she just wanted her to be brave and strong.

She met his eyes and saw pity there. *Pity.* If there was anything Gus loathed more, she hadn't run into it. Just as quickly as the alarm had sounded, it was gone, swept away by indignation. "What's so bad about me?" she snapped at him. "I'm doing okay. I'm doing just fine!"

She stepped away as if to leave, but he caught her arm and brought her back. "Yeah, you're doing just fine."

"So, why *shouldn't* she be like me?" Glaring at him, she dared him to tell her why she wasn't good enough to raise a child, dared him to tell her why she wasn't good enough period. She knew the reasons and there were plenty of them, but who had set him up as Guidance Counselor for the Masses?

"Because you're a bitch."

"You bastard—" She couldn't push him away! He'd made that impossible by gripping both her arms as if she were about to haul off and slap him. How had he known?

"Relax, Gus, I just paid you a compliment, okay? You work hard at being a bitch, and you're good at it, a rousing success. But is that what you want for Bridget? Do you want her to be as hard as you are? Think about it."

Hard? He truly was a bastard! A filthy scumbag bastard. One good whack would show him exactly how hard she could be! She struggled to get free so she *could* haul off and slap him. She wanted to pommel him with her fists until he was bloody. But a terrible pain was welling up in her throat, a terrible, burning pain that threatened to choke her.

She ducked her head as the tears brimmed. Oh, God, no! This was so utterly childish. How could she be crying when she was furious? She would rather die than let him see what he'd done to her, but the flaring pain was so sharp she could barely breathe, and she didn't understand why. It wasn't possible he could have devastated her this way with a few words. She'd been called hard before. She'd been called far worse.

"Why are you d-doing this?" she asked him hoarsely. "You said you wanted information. You said you'd let me go if I answered your questions."

"No, I never said that."

"Then what *do* you want?" She glanced up at him and spat out the question before realizing it was the very thing she'd been trying to avoid saying. "Forget it—"

"Gus—" His voice had gentled.

"Forget it!"

"There is something I want."

"Ask me if I care!"

He released her, and the pressure of his grip left hot pink bands on her arms. She shoved her hands in her jeans pockets and stepped back, refusing to look at him. The powerful scents of man and horse and leather were whirling around in her head, mingling with the honeysuckle, making her dizzy. "I want to go back now."

"Okay, sure . . . but give me a minute first? I want to carve our initials in this oak tree."

"Our . . . what?" She couldn't help herself. She had to look up to see his expression. What in the world was he talking about? His dark eyes sparkled with some kind of energy that she couldn't read, so she assumed the worst. He was making fun of her. There was a part of her that truly hated him for making her feel this way, like an aching adolescent! Why did she care what he did? She must look like a red-nosed wreck.

"Right," he said, pulling a pocketknife from his jacket. "Our initials, you know . . . your name, my name, and a heart. Jack loves Gus. Is that okay with you?"

Gus couldn't respond. She simply stared at him in disbelief as he opened his knife, stepped around her, and began to chip pieces out of the bark. His quick, expert moves reminded her that he'd carved a castle in the desert, and that he really was going to do this. He was going to carve their names in the tree.

Why . . . ?

Don't ask, she told herself. Get on your horse and ride out of Dodge. He's making a fool out of you right in front of your eyes, and you're letting him do it! He might as well be carving those names in your heart. Besides that, she realized, no one had ever carved her name in a tree before, and if that were ever going to happen, she wanted it to be real. She wanted it to *mean* something.

As the moments spun by she kept telling herself to leave, but she couldn't. Her pulse was pounding fearfully. It riveted her to the spot. "Why are you doing this?" she asked him. "You don't love me. You said yourself I was a bitch."

He continued to work, etching out both their names first,

and then putting the final touches on the last letter of hers. "Maybe I like bitchy women."

"Oh, please, you can barely stand the sight of me. You didn't want anything to do with me in the desert. You couldn't even let yourself . . . finish when we made love."

He had just started to carve the *L* word, but he stopped midstroke and looked over his shoulder at her. His expression said that she'd caught him by surprise, that he didn't believe what he'd heard. The sounds of the creek below them, of swift water swirling and gurgling through rocks, accentuated his silence. They were almost sad, those sounds.

"Ah, Gus," he said softly. "Is that what you thought?" He stuck the knife in the tree and turned to her. "Is that really what you thought? That I couldn't *let* myself?"

His voice was rough with regret, and the catch in it made her throat tighten. He was shaking his head as he walked toward her, and Gus prayed that he wouldn't touch her, or that she would be strong enough to stop him if he did. But there was little point in even trying, she knew. She *wasn't* strong enough, or perhaps she didn't want to. Whatever it was, when he reached out and caressed her face, she shuddered and her arms dropped to her sides.

She looked down, painfully aware of him as he moved up very close to her. His thumb glided along her face, whispering to her aching heart. His fingers slipped into the dark tangle of hair that had fallen free from her ponytail. "If you're thinking I didn't want you," he said, stroking her, murmuring to her, "you couldn't be more wrong. If anything, I wanted you too much."

Gus breathed in deeply, causing her senses to swim with honeysuckle and the soft thunder of the rushing stream. Or was that her heart? He was making her *want* to believe him. God, how she wanted to. It was madness. He was a diabolical man, yet in many ways he was everything she'd ever imagined a man could be, and now he was carving hearts that said he loved her when no one had ever loved her that way. It was almost perfect, or it would have been . . . except that nothing was perfect. There was no such thing.

Her heart twisted bitterly. He was lying through his gorgeous white teeth. He had to be. He had some perverse reason for trying to soften her up and make her susceptible to him. Any second she would realize what it was. Nobody ever loved you *just* because they loved you.

"Only one of those things you said about me is true," he was telling her. His fingers flirted with her lowered eyelashes.

"Which one?"

"I didn't finish what I started. I didn't get to finish making love to you. I want to do that, Gus. Right here under this tree with our names."

His smile was rough and sensual. It was tender, but his eyes weren't. They were crystallizing at the center, growing diamond hard with desire. He began to work with the knot of her blouse, undoing it, and Gus knew she had to stop him. His hands were warm on her skin, his knuckles tantalizing as they brushed the underswells of her breasts. Pleasure shuddered through her. If she didn't put a halt to this soon, she wouldn't be able to.

"We're married, and I want to make love to my wife. Is that so hard to understand?"

She closed her eyes and heard his words echoing in her head. But instead of fading, with each repetition the volume increased, haunting, like an echo in reverse. *"We're married, and I want to make love to my wife—"*

"I'm getting hard for you, Gus," he murmured. "I want to do all those things men and women do—couple and consummate and come. I want to do all of that with you." His lips touched her temple, and he whispered the rest as if his intention was to arouse rather than shock her. "You know what I want," he said, his breath warm against the delicate scrollwork of her ear. "I want to fuck my wife."

Gus felt as if something had struck her. But it wasn't the four-letter word he'd used, it was a much longer one. Consummate?

He cupped her face, and her eyes flew open just as he bent to kiss her. Was that what this was all about? He was carving hearts in trees and vowing his desire to have sex with his wife, but not out of love. That idea was ludicrous. He wanted to consummate their relationship, to make it official. He was trying to block her from having it annulled.

"I'm going back," she said, astonished at the fresh pain that welled within her. She had to get away from him, to escape the feelings that he kept triggering. God, she was nearly helpless against those feelings. He made her long for things he had no intention of giving her. It was cruel what he was doing.

"Wait—"

"No!" She broke away with such ferocious determination that he let her go. Her eyes were wet with angry tears as she ran for the horse. Stupid, stupid tears.

She was atop Sapphire and galloping away before he'd moved from the tree where the names were carved. Afraid he would follow her, she headed for the canyon, for the gorge she knew his horse couldn't jump. She couldn't think of any other way to free herself, and she desperately had to get free of him. She hadn't jumped a horse in almost as many years as she'd been on one, and she wasn't at all sure she could do it. But Sapphire could. Lily had trained her as a hunter-jumper. Sapphire could clear mountains.

Moments later as she crested the ridge that led to the ravine on the other side, she glanced behind her and saw him coming up the hill. His riding had improved greatly in one morning. He was moving up on her! She urged Sapphire down the incline at a gallop, crouching down and hanging on. The force of gravity and the horse's jolting power sent shockwaves through her, jarring her senses.

The gorge came careening toward them at breakneck speed, and Gus held her breath, hardly believing what she was going to do. If Sapphire stopped, if she refused to jump, Gus was dead. She would catapult over the horse and into the gorge.

She tucked her body into the horse's and tried not to cry out. Her face was buried in Sapphire's mane. The leap when it came was explosive. She could feel the coiling power beneath her, the muscles gathering, the massive discharge of action, and the next thing she knew they were flying.

CHAPTER
16

JACK PULLED UP ON THE REINS, TRYING TO SLOW HIS GALLOP-ing mount, but Ruby snorted and surged ahead. Gus was out in front of him by a couple hundred feet, and she was heading for what looked like a ravine. A latticework of towering California oaks crisscrossed the horizon just beyond her, making it difficult to track her as she shot through a clearing in the trees. But her horse was galloping at breakneck speed, and the way she was hunched over the animal, it looked as if they were going for it. Christ, she was. She was going to try and jump the gorge!

She had to be *crazy*. It must be twenty feet across.

Jack bent forward to lessen the wind resistance as he urged Ruby on. Gus's horse may have run away with her, and there was still a slight chance he could get to her and cut them off before they hit the ravine. The animal beneath him was fighting to catch her stride. Ruby lunged awk-wardly, sending jolts up his spine, but as her gait finally flattened and stretched into a full, rolling gallop, he felt himself melting into her surging momentum. He was getting a crash course in riding.

He'd already closed half the distance between him and Gus, but by now she had nearly reached the gorge, and she showed no signs of turning out. There was no way she would ever make it across, and a fall to the bottom could kill both her and the horse. Jack felt as if Ruby's hooves were thundering inside his chest. He virtually had no chance of overtaking her now, but he had to try. Leaning in deeper, he urged the snorting animal on.

As Gus reached the edge of the ravine, her horse recoiled with massive force and sprang like a trained jumper. "*Jesus,*" Jack breathed, watching them arc through the air and come down safely on the other side. The animal might as well have sprouted wings! Its hooves barely raised any dust when they touched. How had Gus done that? Crouching forward, he gripped the reins, hugged Ruby with his body and prepared himself for takeoff. An explosion of pain told him the horse had other ideas.

As the depth of the ravine came into view, Ruby stiffened her forelegs and put on the brakes. Jack slammed into the brick wall of her neck like a speeding car, agony jarring down his spine. The horse skidded to a stop inches from the edge, propelling him forward like a human rocket. His hand was tangled in the reins, but his body lifted out of the saddle as if he'd been launched. The last thing he saw was the hard, sunbaked ground coming up at him as he did a full twisting half-gainer over the horse's shoulder. His last thought was that horses should come with seat belts.

When Gus summoned the courage to look up, all she could see was an enormous cloud of dust where the man and horse had been.

"Oh, my God," she breathed. Dread nearly burned away the lining of her mouth as she eased Sapphire closer to the edge of the ravine. The gully was heavily overgrown, which made a visual search difficult, but as she craned around, she could see nothing that looked like a fallen man and horse.

By the time she'd convinced herself he wasn't there, the dust cloud across the gorge had settled into a sparkling golden haze, and the man she'd expected to see broken and bleeding at the bottom of the ravine had miraculously materialized. He hadn't gone over the side! He was sitting on the ground, facing away from her, shaking his head as if there were something rattling inside. Ruby stood beside him, calmly munching a patch of crabgrass.

Astonished, Gus rose up in the saddle, straining for a better look. He was facing away from her, and she couldn't see any evidence of serious injuries, no grotesquely twisted limbs or blood, though she wasn't close enough to be absolutely certain he wasn't hurt. She was still shaking inside, still horrified by what had happened. No one had ever triggered such confused, impassioned responses from her, and she couldn't begin to make sense of them. If she was desperately relieved that he was all right, she also still wanted him out of her life. Desperately!

Sapphire moved beneath her, and Gus stroked the horse's neck, giving her a congratulatory pat for having made the jump. A musty smell rose off the restless, pawing horse. It was heat and dampness from the hard ride, but the pungency of it swept Gus back to another time. It was the caustic odor of her own clawing fear when she was locked in the root cellar.

A bird called from one of the oaks across the gorge.

Ruby looked up, but Jack didn't move.

Finally, unable to stand the suspense any longer, Gus cupped her hands to her mouth. "Are you all right?" she shouted.

The last word echoed sharply through the ravine. There was no chance he hadn't heard her, but he didn't respond. It had always made her nervous when people didn't answer her. Her mother had ignored nearly everything she'd ever said, fueling Gus's ever-present fears of abandonment. Even now when people went silent on her, she was stricken with the same sense of unworthiness.

Sweat broke out on her forehead and dampened her scalp.

She could feel the unsteadiness in her lips and knew she wouldn't be able to get the words out right if she spoke again. Fortunately she didn't have to. He reached around and rubbed the back of his neck, tilting his head back and forth.

"Culhane?" She thought she'd whispered his name, but it rebounded back at her as if she'd yelled it.

He glanced over his shoulder at her, and Gus had a bizarre reaction. She was tempted to wave. The only thing that stopped her was the malevolent expression in his dark eyes. The terrifying glint reminded her of the day he kidnapped her. Only this time he had murder on his mind. Cold-blooded murder. He would have broken her neck if he could have gotten his hands on her, she was sure of that . . . and one other thing. There was no point trying to convince him it was an accident. She might as well have had a smoking gun in her hand. He believed she'd led him to the cliffs on purpose.

"Pssst . . . Bridget." Gus peeked around the doorjamb into the sunlit kitchen, careful to keep her voice low and conceal herself as she tried to get her niece's attention.

Bridget was polishing off the last of a chocolate cupcake and a glass of milk, but her attention was riveted on *Poopzie Pomerantz, Pick Up Your Feet*, a children's novel about ballet that Gus had brought back from a recent trip to New York. The precocious little thing had been reading since she was three, and once Gus had found her poring over an autobiography of the prima ballerina, Gelsey Kirkland, from the mansion's library.

"Did you know Gelsey and Misha fought all the time?" she'd asked Gus that day. "She screeched at him a lot, maybe even threw things. I didn't get that far."

She had been talking about the very turbulent, very public affair between Kirkland and Baryshnikov. Gus had known Bridget could read, but not *that* well. Since then she'd been supplying her charge with plenty of children's books.

Now Frances was also sitting at the table, absorbed in a

cup of hot mint tea by the smell of the wafting steam—and a midmorning scap opera—but Gus was being careful to stay out of the housekeeper's eyeshot as she waved at Bridget and made little *psssst* noises.

She was trying to get Bridget's attention to take her to a ballet lesson, but she didn't want to be discovered by anyone else in the house, particularly Lily, who she knew was furious because she'd borrowed Sapphire. Daniel, their twentyish stable hand—who Gus had long ago realized was Lily's personal errand boy—had been very huffy with her when she'd returned the sweat-soaked horse to him. Worse, Gus was terrified that Jack might show up at any time and confirm her worst fears, that he was going to kill her with his bare hands.

Gus hesitated as Bridget looked up from the book. Blissfully unaware that she was being hailed, the child popped the last piece of cupcake in her mouth and began to blot up every last crumb from the plate. The ones she couldn't nab with her fingertip she went after with her tongue, a little pink arrow that reminded Gus uncomfortably of the lizards in the desert. Some day she would have to tell Bridget about her stay at the health spa in Death Valley. She had no doubt the child would have loved the grisly place.

Dressed in her leotards, with her wispy blond hair swept up in a tiny knot on top of her head, Bridget looked like one of the dimpled figures on the front of a Mary Engelbreit greeting card. Gus felt a surge of love just watching her. She would have laid down her life for this child. Gus had not only been instrumental in raising her, she'd protected her like a mother lion, and from the cradle on had coached her on how to protect herself. But perhaps at the same time, she'd been overly indulgent. Bridget could be headstrong at times. Those dimples of hers camoflauged a will of iron.

Frances, who had risen from the table and gone to the refrigerator, was now hovering nearby with the carton of milk. "More?" she asked. But when she attempted to top off Bridget's brimming glass, the little girl clapped her tiny hand over the rim.

"I have plenty," she told the housekeeper matter-offactly. "Can't you see?" If the intelligence of some adults was in question in the five-year-old's mind, Frances was clearly one of them.

Frances mumbled something unintelligible and returned the milk to the refrigerator. But Gus winced at Bridget's tone. Much as she hated admitting that Culhane might be right, she did find Bridget just a touch imperious this morning. She'd never wanted the child to be rude, just tough, a survivor.

Gus glanced at her watch and realized she was going to have to make her presence known. She stepped into the doorway and waved. "Hi, Bridge Over Troubled Waters."

"Gus-buster!" In Bridget's haste to scramble out of the chair, she sent it flying. She sprinted toward her aunt, arms thrown wide, preparing to fling herself. Gus steeled herself for the impact. It had become their ritual, this exuberant body-slam hello.

"Ooooophhh!" Gus said as the little girl hit her like a pint-size linebacker, then clamored into her arms. Much grunting, groaning, and general noisiness ensued as Gus hoisted Bridge in the air, pretending that she was too heavy to lift.

"Too much cake, Bridgemeister. We're going to put you on a diet." But even as she laughed at that prospect, Gus thought of Jillian's emaciated body and was sad.

Bridget rolled her sparkling blue eyes. "Yeah, right," she said with all the mordant air of a stand-up comic. "Bite me."

"Hey, you, I just might." Gus squeezed her and nuzzled her neck ravenously, as if she were going to chew her up, which threw Bridget into a fit of shrieks and giggles. The child had picked the expression up on the *Roseanne* show and used it regularly, even though Frances was strongly disapproving.

"Let's go, Bridge," Gus urged, setting her down. Not only was she concerned about getting out of the house, but she had an important luncheon appointment right after she dropped Bridget off. "You'll be late for your lesson. Put your dishes in the sink, quick! Then grab your practice bag, and we're outta here."

A pink canvas bag stuffed with ballet paraphernalia— dance belts, ballet slippers, leg warmers, a sweater, and Band-Aids—sat on the floor next to Bridget's chair. The child looked sincerely perplexed as she reached to pick it up.

"Why do *I* have to put the dishes in the sink?" she asked. "Frances will get them, won't she? Isn't that what we pay her for?"

Gus's attempt to look stern failed miserably. "The dishes," she said. "The sink. Now."

The little girl complied, but with a look of perplexity that said it didn't make sense not to let Frances do her job, and Gus realized that a heart-to-heart about the concept of pulling one's own weight and sharing responsibilities was overdue.

Moments later, as she and Bridget were rushing out the back door to the guest garage, where Gus kept her car, she heard someone summoning her, loudly.

"Gus! I'd like a word with you."

The shout had come from behind her, and it stopped her in her tracks on the white gravel driveway. Mr. Quiet-but-Deadly was back from his ride. She was reluctant to turn and look, but Bridget harbored no such fears. Her hand in Gus's, she twisted around and breathed out a soft "Wow."

Gus turned on her heel and pulled Bridget to her protectively, thinking she might have to defend them both. Culhane was coming from the stables, and he was striding toward her with the intent of mayhem. Gus could see it by the thunderbolts in his expression.

"Boy, he looks ticked," Bridget whispered.

You don't know the half of it, Gus thought. She was wearing the equivalent of a power suit for a business luncheon later that day, and little white pebbles crunched beneath her high heels as she anchored herself. She'd never been more aware of his size in relation to hers—and the child's. He was a big man, and he looked like an angry god descending on them. His jaw was set with granite, and his focus was honed on her to the exclusion of all other life-forms.

He was clearly ticked, but at the same time Gus detected the signs of arousal she'd seen at the stream. Diamonds still glittered in the darkness of his pupils, hot with desire. Primitive, Gus thought. She'd seen language on his computer screen too technical for her limited capacity, but on a physical level, he was utterly primitive.

"Gus, what the hell were you trying to—"

Bridget stopped his question by hugging herself to Gus's waist. "If you hurt my aunt, I'll . . . cry."

Gus squelched a smile. Apparently Bridget had quickly thought through the more effective strategy with this man, screams or sobs, and she'd decided on the latter. That would have been Gus's move, under the circumstances.

Culhane hesitated, confused. It seemed to have dawned on him for the first time that there was an impressionable child involved. "No, hey, don't do that," he said brusquely, obviously alarmed at the possibility. "I'm not going to hurt anybody. I just wanted a word with your aunt."

His gaze shot to Gus. "One word? *Now*."

"No can do," she told him brightly. "Bridget has to be at her ballet lesson, and I've got a . . . date."

"A *what?*"

"Lunch," she said, waggling her fingers at him as she steered Bridget around and hustled her off at a brisk clip. Gravel crackled and flew. Gus could feel his eyes drilling holes in her back as she beat a path to the garage, and knew she shouldn't have told him her meeting was a date. Still, the flare of dark emotion that had swept through him had been something to witness. What had she seen? Jealousy? Possessiveness?

The image was still vibrant in her mind a short time later as she pulled her classic red Mercedes SL onto the freeway. Distracted by it, she forced herself to concentrate on the road. The little convertible had been her one indulgence from her modeling income, and she loved it. Every other cent had been stashed away in mutual funds to help with the capital outlay for her magazine. The start-up costs alone for a national launch were staggering. They could run into the tens of millions, which was why she'd needed her trust-fund money. Now that she had it she could do all those things she'd been dreaming about, including pouring whatever profits the magazine made into Jillian's foundation. New magazines were rarely in the black for the first few years, but Gus was optimistic.

As she merged with the oncoming traffic, Gus was aware that Bridget was observing her curiously. She'd already reassured the child that it was only a little misunderstanding between her and Jack. Nothing serious. "What's up?" she asked now.

"I thought maybe you'd like to know why Gelsey picked fights with Misha all the time. Do you? Wanna know?"

"Not really, Bridge," Gus said, quite sincerely. "But you're going to tell me anyway, aren't you?"

"She didn't think Misha loved her, and she was testing him."

"Fascinating." Gus resorted to a time-honored distraction. With one eye on the road, she wet her thumb with her tongue and rubbed a smudge of chocolate off Bridget's chin.

"Blecch!" Bridget said, grimacing. "You used spit! I hate it when you use spit."

"Bite me." Gus grinned.

Bridget scrubbed at her chin, but her focus was unwavering. "Is that the way it is with you and Culhane? Are you really in love with him, and you fight all the time because you don't want him to think you care?"

Gus's heart jerked out a slowed, stubborn beat. "Honey, his name is Jack, and he and I don't fight *all* the time. Couples go through a period of adjustment when they're first married, that's all. We're adjusting."

"How long will it last?"

"The marriage?"

"The period of adjustment?"

"Long enough for you to start calling him Uncle Jack."

Bridget wrinkled her nose. "I like Culhane better."

Gus was just as glad Bridget had shrugged off the Uncle

Jack reference, since she was already regretting having said it.

They were right on time for the little ballerina's lesson when Gus pulled into the parking lot of the small insurance building fifteen minutes later. Knowing she would be late for her appointment with Rob, Gus nevertheless walked with Bridget to class, which was in the building's basement, and stayed to watch her for a while, her heart aching pleasantly as she watched fifteen cherubic totlets doing their warm-up exercises.

Bridget was standing at the barre, concentrating fiercely as she did a series of demi pliés in the second position. One of her hands rested lightly on the bar, the other was extended out languidly to her side, and her back was gracefully straight as she dipped down again and again, with, surprisingly, only a minor wobble here and there. It was a lovely sight.

For Gus it was a wondrous thing to see such poise and accomplishment in a child she still regarded in her heart as "my baby." The kid's got my sense of timing, she thought proudly, even though she knew that was impossible. Bridget wasn't a blood relation, and she was as fair as any one of the Featherstones. But Gus claimed her anyway, claimed her fiercely. Bridget was hers, not theirs.

An *un*natural disaster. Gus didn't know how else to describe her first official lunch as the publisher of *ATTITUDE*. A cloud of hostile silence hung over the corner table at Lucene's where she picked at her black-pepper roasted tuna, and Rob stared glumly at his empty glass of chardonnay. The intimate Continental restaurant was still busy with the hangover lunch crowd, even though it was approaching two o'clock. Everyone hung out there, including the Hollywood contingent, and today was no exception.

Gus was secretly fascinated with what was going on at a prime window table where the British actor, Ralph Fiennes, was being discreetly hustled by a prominent female studio head, who was apparently trying to sell him more than her movie. At another table not far away, two of the famous

Baldwin brothers were doing stupid food tricks with their eating utensils and what was left of a heaping plate of squid pasta.

Lucene's had been Rob's choice. He'd convinced Gus of the importance of "looking successful" as they mapped out plans for the magazine. He'd made a point of introducing her to several powerful producers and studio people, and he'd taken calls all through their meal, apparently to make it look as if advertisers and publicists were clamoring to track them down for space.

Gus wasn't particularly comfortable with Rob's image-making efforts, especially since she was launching a magazine that would encourage people to shuck their facades and reach inside to discover who they really were. Still, she so badly wanted the project to succeed that she probably would have gone along with anything he'd suggested. Ironic that she would have to compromise herself in order to publish a magazine about being uncompromising.

But they had seemed to be making quite an impression, even on the jaded Lucene's crowd. They'd barely been seated when a hot young Hollywood ingenue had come up and said she'd heard the buzz about the magazine. She'd then teasingly hinted that she, herself, would make a good profile, "having done battle with the toilet seat and won," she'd said, *sotto voce*. Gus had assumed she'd meant a bout with an eating disorder and had promised to contact her as soon as the magazine was up and running.

Today's lunch was intended as a planning session. Rob had brought the media kit and dummy magazine issue he'd had his people make up from Gus's ideas, and later this week Gus would be signing the lease agreement for the top two floors of a high-rise bank building on Wilshire. After that she would start outfitting the rooms and hiring the rest of the magazine's staff. She'd already lined up most of the top editorial and administrative positions. Fortunately, her managing editor was considered one of the best. Gus had stolen the thirtyish wunderkind right out from under *Harper's Bazaar* by offering him a limited partnership.

He'd seen her idea as new and hot, a way to make a bundle, but to Gus it was far more. She was looking for financial independence and a way out of haute couture, but she also saw the magazine as a forum to encourage women of all ages, types, and sizes to throw aside their fears and live their lives boldly and audaciously. For personal reasons she'd long worried about the pervasive body image crises that stalked American women and the part she, herself, might have played in that problem as a model. To that end she particularly wanted to reach younger females whose sense of self might be undermined by the double messages from Madison Avenue and the fashion industry . . . young women like Jillian.

Gus was staking everything she had on *ATTITUDE,* but if today's meeting with Rob was any indication of her odds, she was in trouble. Everything had gone swimmingly until she'd made the mistake of telling Rob about the horseback riding fiasco. "You jumped the ravine?" he'd said, his voice so sharp and hushed that heads began to turn at tables in the vicinity. "Who were you trying to kill? Him or yourself?"

Gus had been startled at the change in him, especially in so public a place. Rob Emory, spin doctor extraordinaire, didn't seem to care that people were staring and that he was acting like a jealous husband.

"We were arguing," she'd explained. "I was upset. Sapphire headed straight for the gorge, and you know how she loves to jump. I assumed Culhane wouldn't be able to follow me, which was all I was thinking about at the moment. I just wanted to get rid of him—"

Rob's expression had darkened as he gazed at her, and she'd begun to flake pieces of tuna with her fork, aware that she was dealing in half-truths and not at all sure what the whole truth was. "What did he say that could have upset you that badly?" he'd asked, and she'd made the mistake of flushing.

"He implied I was a bad role model for Bridget."

"Oh, *well,*" he'd huffed mockingly, "no wonder you tried to kill the son of a bitch. You should sue him for defaming your maternal instincts."

"Would you *stop* that!" Gus hissed the words under her breath. "Would you please stop saying I tried to kill him."

At that point Rob had made another futile attempt to get the waiter's attention, and then he'd gone silent. Now he was ignoring what was left of the meal, the waiter, and her. The whole ordeal made Gus feel inexplicably guilty, perhaps because of what had happened between her and Culhane *beyond* their conversation about Bridget.

"Can't we save this for another time?" she suggested, her voice softening with encouragement as she touched his arm. "I thought we were here to talk about the magazine. The media kit looks fabulous by the way." She touched the brilliantly designed folder, wanting him to know how pleased she was with the way he'd brought her ideas to life.

"Yeah, fabulous." He shifted the knife he'd laid across his plate, then ran his tongue over his teeth as if trying to rid himself of a bad taste in his mouth. When finally he did acknowledge her, the look of distaste still lingered.

She was vaguely aware that a busboy had appeared and was refilling their goblets, splashing water over the melting ice, but nothing could have distracted her from the chill of recognition she felt. It was so much an echo of the reactions she remembered from her childhood that she couldn't help but wonder what Rob really thought of her. Did the man even like her? It didn't help that she was the one who'd capitulated. She'd broken the silence and tried to smooth things over, which made her feel all the more vulnerable.

"I'm putting a detective on him, Gus," he said in a voice that brooked no argument. "Once I have something on Culhane, we can back him off. Until then I want *you* to back off, is that clear?"

Gus set her own fork down carefully. If anger had come in colors, hers would have been red, and a knot of it had formed at the base of her throat. It didn't matter to her at that moment that he was probably right, that a detective was the only safe and sensible way to handle this. It was the condescension, his dismissive tone, that bridled. He was giving her an order, and Gus had never liked ultimatums. He seemed to have forgotten that she was the one being blackmailed. *She* was the public figure who would be held up to scrutiny and ridicule if their plan were exposed.

"Very clear," she said at last. She quietly gathered up her purse and black linen suit jacket and pushed back the chair. The material of her skirt had hiked up, seemingly caught on her nylons, but a touch of her hand smoothed it.

"Are you going somewhere?" he asked. "We're not done here."

"I think we are," she said.

She prided herself on her decorum as she made her excuses, telling him she had to pick up Bridget, and walked out of the restaurant, leaving Rob at the table to stare after her in shock. The old Gus would have pitched a fit and not have cared who saw it. She would have been righteously ticked and told him so, Rob be damned, Lucene's be damned, magazine be damned. There was nothing the old Gus had ever wanted so badly that she would have taken shit from people to get it, and she had loved having that kind of independence. If her toes got stepped on, she yelled, one of the traits that had quickly earned her her reputation as "difficult."

But now, suddenly, there was a great deal at stake, and she didn't want to be seen in a public fight with her manager. She was also uncertain about Rob, himself. He'd been handling the business end of the magazine, and she had allowed herself to become more dependent on him than on anyone in her life. Perhaps too dependent. She was approaching a major turning point in her life. Maybe this was the time that she needed to step back and take another look at the situation. So far it could all be chalked up to bad management, she reminded herself, which was fixable. Not to be confused with *destiny*, which wasn't.

All that and more was on Gus's mind as she pulled into the mansion's driveway and saw the police cars. They were parked everywhere, their lights flashing. One had even pulled sideways across the lawn. There must have been a half-dozen of them, and the security guard wasn't in the booth by the gate.

Alarmed, she pulled her Mercedes as close to the house

as she could and parked the car. Please God, don't let it be
Bridget, she thought. She had fibbed to Rob. One of the
other girls' mothers had promised to give several of the
children, including Bridget, a ride home from the ballet lesson.

Nearly frantic that something might have happened, she
let herself out of the car and ran all the way to the house.
The ground's maze of manicured hedges and its center-
piece, a graceful Italian fountain, blurred past her. There
was a crowd in the foyer as she burst in the door.

"There she is!" Lake's voice drew Gus's eyes to the
doorway of the main salon, where he was standing by a tall,
thin balding man in a heavily wrinkled cotton suit. Notebook and pencil in hand, the man turned to peer at Gus over
his glasses as if he were having trouble focusing his eyes.
He shambled toward her, and she realized it was his wide,
jutting jaw and Harry Truman glasses that made him look
so owlish. A plainclothes detective, she thought.

"Are you Mrs. Jack Culhane?" He enunciated the question over the noise of several milling uniformed officers.

Gus nodded, uncertain whether or not she'd just impli-
cated herself in a crime.

"Do you know where your husband is?"

Gus had left her jacket in the car, and the open doorway
created a chill that raised goosebumps on her arms. "No, I
don't. I haven't seen him since this morning. What's
wrong?"

"Her husband is right here—"

Jack's voice came from the doors behind her, and as she
turned to see him standing in the glowing archway, she experienced a moment of real fear, but not on her own behalf,
on his. Had he done something wrong?

He'd changed from that morning's jeans and jacket, but
it was still a casual look—khaki pants and a wine-red polo
shirt that emphasized the breadth of his shoulders and made
his eyes and hair look all the darker. It was his expression
that made her nervous. There was menace in his watchful-
ness.

The detective tucked his notebook and pencil in the

crumpled breast pocket of his suit coat. "Mr. Culhane, can you tell us where you were at twelve-thirty this afternoon?"

"Who wants to know? And why?"

Gus glanced around the room and realized that Lily was standing at the foot of one staircase and Frances the other. They were both being questioned by uniformed officers. The two security guards were at the far end of the foyer, talking to another policeman, and she caught glimpses of blue uniforms inside the open doors of the gallery.

The detective showed Jack his badge and repeated the question. "A valuable work of art has been stolen from the Featherstone collection, Mr. Culhane. If you would be so kind as to tell me your whereabouts?"

"Am I a suspect?" Jack asked.

"You're damn right!" Lake nearly shrieked the accusation as he crossed the room. "Someone stole my Goddard, the newest piece in my collection!"

"Blush?" Gus broke in, as startled by the intensity of Lake's reaction as she was by the theft. "The woman kissing her own reflection?"

Lake glared at Jack. "There was no sign of a break-in, so it had to be someone who had access to this house."

"Where were you, Mr. Culhane?" the detective pressed. He pulled out his notebook and pencil again.

Jack's continuing silence brought Gus around to stare at him. "W-where were you?" she asked softly.

Her stumble was indiscernible, but he seemed to have caught it, and as he glanced at her, his gaze focused piercingly on her alarmed expression. It was only for an instant, but she felt, as she often had before, that he had cut through to something vital and painful inside her, things she fought to keep hidden. *Trying to find my wife,* he seemed to be saying. *Trying to find you, Gus.*

"I was working all afternoon," Jack said, still gazing at Gus.

It struck Gus as odd that she knew he was lying. But what she realized next astonished her. *He had stolen the painting.*

"Can anyone verify that?" the detective asked. Jack's silence forced his hand. "I could always take you down to the station for questioning. It's up to you."

"Bruce Houston, the president of Houston Tire Company." Jack turned to the man, a cold smile touching his mouth. "I've been at his home since ten this morning, doing a security risk analysis. His system stinks, just like this one does."

"We'll have to contact Mr. Houston."

Jack turned his cold smile on the room then, brushing over the curious expressions and freezing everyone out, including Gus. "Tell him he's next," he said.

The chill that had burned Gus's arms seeped through to her bones. This no longer felt like bad management, she realized. It felt like destiny had just rolled the dice.

CHAPTER
17

WHEN GUS CAME DOWN TO DINNER THAT EVENING, SHE SAW immediately that the battle lines had been drawn. Lake and Lily gave small dinner parties as frequently as two or three nights a week, and though Gus rarely attended, there was no way she was going to miss this one. She had thought Lake would call it off because of the burglary, but her stepbrother assured them he would only brood if left alone, and so, despite the fact that the newest Featherstone family member, Gus's husband, was the chief suspect in the crime, dinner for nine it was.

The detective had questioned Jack extensively before he left, but hadn't had enough evidence to charge him with anything. Once the crime lab people had gone and everyone had retired to their respective rooms, the house had settled down to its more normal state, a heavy, sometimes haunting silence that prevailed as if the place were weighed down by its own solitude. But the tension still reverberated.

Even now the library resembled an armed camp as Gus entered to join the small crowd that had gathered for drinks.

Outside of her own bedroom and the atrium, it was her favorite place in the mansion, and had always had a calming
effect on her. It wasn't small and intimate as libraries so
often were, and yet the high ceiling of carved walnut, its
rich, deep burl echoed in the Edwardian furniture and the
bookshelves, gave the area an opulence that was warm and
welcoming. The outside walls boasted huge arched windows as grand and serene as a cathedral's. By contrast, the
mirrored Victorian front-and-back bar that stood across the
spacious room from the fireplace was as ornate and stylized
as a brothel's.

Gus had always thought there was an aged dignity about
the room that cast its civilizing spell on anyone who entered. Tonight a Vivaldi concerto played softly, background
music to the muted conversation, and the familiar smells of
old, leather-bound books and rich lemony furniture oil all
contrived to soothe the senses. But even those triggers
couldn't lift the present tension.

Lake and Lily were by the fireplace, sipping Manzanilla
and conversing with a cluster of guests that included Ward
McHenry and the curator of the Pasadena Art Museum and
his wife. Despite the apparent congeniality, her stepsiblings'
darting glances gave them away. The object of Lake's and
Lily's unfriendly scrutiny was her very own husband of
less than a week. Culhane was leaning against the marble-
topped bar with what looked like a Scotch in his hand, but
as usual, he wasn't drinking, he was merely staring into the
glass's fiery flames as if they represented everything he
knew of hell and its environs, which for him was clearly
right here on earth.

He hadn't even made an attempt to dress the part tonight.
He was bistro casual in a setting where the dress code was
jackets and chic dinner dresses. His white linen shirt had a
cleric's collar that flared open against the brown skin of his
throat, though the trend was to wear them buttoned up. The
only thing Jack Culhane had buttoned up were his emotions, Gus thought, and for some reason that awareness
brought a visual reminder of his sinewy torso . . . and of his

fascinating inability to have a normal sexual release. Or was it his unwillingness?

She could have watched him all night, she realized. He intrigued her that much, and she didn't honestly know why. Or maybe she didn't want to know because she was afraid of what it would say about her. It had already occurred to her that her fascination might have something to do with his criminal past. If what he'd told her was true, he'd taken lives, killed people. He had reordered the moral boundaries of normal human behavior and given himself God-like powers. That alone set him apart from anyone she'd ever known. Power, unlike evil, had both good and bad components. It attracted and repelled. Certainly it was a stimulant to the imagination, even an aphrodisiac. But was that what had captured her? His power? Or was she drawn to what drove it? He was shadowed by something, tragedy. She had seen signs of the suffering. She had responded to them.

If that's what had driven him to kill, she could almost understand it. And yet, she couldn't imagine what it would be like to do anything so extreme, and she couldn't relate to a man who had. Life was simply too precious—

A soft gasp slipped from her lips as she realized where her thoughts were going. Twice she had tricked him into situations that could easily have killed him. Afterward she'd convinced herself that however reprehensible, it was for the greater good. He threatened everything she stood for. He could crush her life, her dreams, with a word! Besides, she hadn't acted in cold blood. There were mitigating circumstances in both cases. She'd been threatened by him and had reacted defensively, but still—if she was capable of that, what else was she capable of?

There was a part of her that wanted to blame everything that was happening on him, and it was true to some extent. He posed a threat that had forced her to think the way he did, to operate outside the boundaries. He also sparked impulses so forbidden they made her wonder if the things she had always believed about herself were true.

Low laughter drifted to her, reminding her that there were other people in the room, dinner guests. A couple she knew only as architects and friends of Lily's were enjoying each other's company in a pair of Rosewood parlor chairs that faced a leather-topped library table. They were safely on the family's side, of course. Only Webb Calderon was occupying neutral territory as he perused a collection of bound first editions on the bookshelves at the far end of the room.

Gus had a moment of indecision. She couldn't hover on the threshold forever, but which way should she go, and to whom? It made no sense that she go to him, the blackmailer. This was the perfect time to join forces with her family against the interloper. They already believed he'd stolen a valuable painting; perhaps now they also believed he married her for that reason, so he could have access to the collection. If he exposed her kidnapping scheme, it shouldn't be any great trick to convince them he was lying. She could paint him as a treasure hunter whom she'd had the bad judgment to fall for, and who'd made up the kidnapping story and threatened to expose her if she didn't give him control of her trust fund. A little far-fetched perhaps, but no more so than the story he'd be telling. She would confess tearfully and allow them to feel superior, especially after what her mother had done. They'd want to believe her anyway, if only to get Culhane out of their midst.

Her decision was made as soon as Lake and Lily noticed she was there. The expression that swept both their faces when they saw her was so alike it was uncanny. They were curious, but remote. Not in any way welcoming. Foolish of her to have expected otherwise. They were not only Featherstones, they were twins, a united front that was impenetrable. She was as much an outsider to them as Culhane was, she realized. She would never be one of them, no matter what she did.

Even McHenry, who had seemed so pleased to announce the family's support of her foundation and the magazine, now had a distant, measuring air to him, as if he were trying to decide whether she might even be in league with Culhane.

It welled up inside Gus unbearably—the loneliness, the isolation and pain she'd felt over the years, all at the hands of these people, her *family*. With that fresh in her mind, she returned her stepsister's chilly smile, then had the pleasure of turning away and walking straight to Jack. He looked up as she crossed the room toward him, as if he'd known she was coming. The fires he'd been contemplating seemed to glow in his blue-black irises, bringing a strange heat to his expression.

Their gazes connected with an impact that rivaled physical force. Watching him on the sly was challenge enough, but looking directly into his eyes while she walked toward him made Gus feel as if something had been rammed down her throat. It was difficult to swallow over the obstruction. Odd, considering everything.

"The woman who flies through the air with the greatest of ease," he said when she was within hearing distance. He continued to lean against the bar, supported by one elbow as he watched her approach. He was cradling the glass of fire in both hands, and his eyes were colder now, dark with meaning.

"And the man who doesn't." She returned his measuring stare with a bold once-over. "No permanent damage, I see." Her faint smile went unacknowledged.

"It could have been very permanent," he said, setting down his drink. He rose from the bar as she reached it. "Would you like some?"

"Damage?"

"A drink." A vast array of libations were arranged on shelves that abutted the bar's mirror. He swept out a hand. "Just pretend I'm the bartender."

"Shouldn't be too difficult." She meant his shirt and let him know it, lowering her lashes as she perused the garment from stitched placard to open collar. Her eyes met his again, but only fleetingly. It was too icy and dark to stay there long, a winter night.

"What'll it be?" he asked.

Gus was aware of the background music, of violins playing out soft, extended arpeggios. He turned to the booze, and she noticed a nasty bruise where his jawbone jutted to meet his ear.

"Are you all right?" she said, aware of the husky concern in her voice. The irony didn't escape her. *What is it you want from this man, Gus? Do you want him dead? Or do you want him in bed? Make up your mind, dear.*

Culhane never got a chance to answer any of her questions, not even the one she'd voiced. A flicker of movement caught Gus's eye, and as she looked over Culhane's shoulder, she saw Webb Calderon coming their way. Another defector to the enemy? How interesting. She and Webb had spent some time together once, in a manner of speaking. They'd met two years ago at a fashion show fundraiser for one of the local art museums. She'd never been sure of him in any way, how he felt about her or what he wanted with her, because it had seemed from the beginning that he wanted something besides her sparkling company. The physical attraction hadn't been there, at least not on his part. There'd been chemistry to spare on hers. Her family had ruined it, unfortunately. They'd approved of him.

In all truth she'd never understood why. Webb had been both frightening and enigmatic. Even tonight he reminded her of a beautiful Nazi SS officer in his white mock turtleneck and severely cut black Armani suit. And though she meant beautiful only in the physical sense, perversely attractive men had always appealed to her. In Webb's case, his sun-whitened hair, bleak gray eyes, and Teutonic bone structure were the compelling features. They had the effect of quickening a woman's heart and making her wonder what cruel and unusual things such a man might do in the name of love.

She'd also decided he was a mystery better left unsolved.

If she'd had the choice, she would have made the same decision about Jack Culhane. But she was already in too deeply with him. He had taken her hostage in more ways than one with his haunting hints of desolation and desire, and somehow he had made her an integral part of his dark quest, whatever the hell it was. She still had no idea why he was here. Or what he wanted with her.

"If you're pouring drinks, I'll take one," Webb said, nodding to Jack. His smile encompassed them both, but it lingered on Gus and her flowery silk slipdress. "Apparently you're feeling great."

"I am, why?" Gus asked, laughing.

"Because you look terrific."

"She does, doesn't she?" Jack agreed. "I'm a lucky man."

He slipped a proprietary hand around Gus's waist, and the other man's eyes narrowed. Gus could almost see horns growing and hear hooves pawing the ground. It was amazing how quickly two seemingly bright adult men could be reduced to territorial posturing. Animal intelligence in action, she thought.

"Help yourself," Jack added pointedly. "To the booze. There's some champagne on ice behind the bar."

Webb conceded with the grace of a man who'd long ago learned how to prioritize. He rounded the ornate bar, and once he'd pulled the dripping bottle of Dom Ruinart rosé champagne from the ice and read the label, he poured himself a sample of the bubbling blush-pink froth. Clearly a connoisseur, he raised the flute to the light and then to his nose, breathing it in before drinking the splash he poured. The muted resonance of violins seemed the perfect accompaniment to his ritual with the sparkling wine.

"I'm told you design security systems," he said, intent on replenishing his glass. As he returned the bottle to the ice, he looked up at Jack. "I've always been curious. Are any of them fail-safe?"

"The system hasn't been designed that can't be beaten," Jack admitted. "Even one of mine."

Surrendering for the moment to Jack's claim, Gus nestled up against him and caught traces of castile soap and lanolin. The scent brought a visual of him in the shower, shampooing his hair, and then in rapid succession, several more of him in the shower, doing things that had nothing to do with shampooing and everything to do with her. He was having his way with her!

She gently extricated herself from his hold to discourage

any further flashbacks. Besides, she wanted to observe the two men. There was some kind of current running between them, transmitting signals she didn't fully understand, but she was reasonably certain they weren't just about her.

"So then any work of art could be stolen?" Webb wanted to know. "Potentially, I mean. Even one that was protected by a computerized, multisensor system?"

Jack nodded and picked up his drink, watching the chandelier light glitter and stream across its amber surface. Gus found it interesting that he never did anything more than hold the glass. He never drank from it. It was not unlike the way he had sex.

"Would you care to explain how?" Webb pressed.

"I'd be happy to. What are you planning on stealing?"

Uneasy laughter drifted from across the room. Lake, Lily, Ward McHenry, and the other couples had stopped talking, Gus realized. They were also listening to the two men.

"Since you asked, Mr. Culhane, how about a painting?" Webb held up his champagne as if he were toasting Jack. "If I were the very clever thief who'd stolen Blush, Lake's Goddard, how would I have done it?"

"There are several possible ways," Jack said, apparently more than willing to play Webb's game. "The gallery has multiple systems—a microwave intrusion system, closed circuit television cameras, plus the more valuable works have promixity sensors. All of it's computerized, so obviously the easiest way to beat it is to reprogram the software."

Webb looked intrigued. "But you'd have to be a computer hacker to do that, right?"

"Not necessarily, but you would have to be familiar enough with the technology, for example, to know how to create a time-lag between when the promixity sensor detects something and when it reports back to the computer, which is programmed to alert the guards. That's relatively easy once you have access to the software."

He set down his drink on an antique silver coaster and blotted his fingers on a cocktail napkin, taking his time, as if he were perfectly aware of the bated breath all around him. "The video cameras are a little trickier," he explained. "That requires creating a loop in the visual feed so that the same image of the undisturbed painting is seen over and over again."

Webb seemed to understand the concept, though Gus wasn't at all sure she did.

"The sequence you loop shows the gallery and the painting before the theft," Webb said. "Then while the burglary is in progress, and even after it's done, the guards are seeing the looped sequence on the screen, as if the painting were still there. Is that it?"

Jack shrugged his agreement. "As I said, it's not particularly difficult if you have access to the program."

What was he doing? Gus wondered. Knowingly incriminating himself? Now she wished she'd taken that drink. She was even tempted to pick up his.

Webb nodded, his cold gray eyes suddenly piercing. "Which means it had to have been an inside job, am I right? Someone who lived or worked here in the house?"

Jack's silence brought the tension in the room into ringing contrast. The chamber music, which had been soothing before, was verging on strident. The strings were thin, straining.

Gus wanted to intervene, but she couldn't think of a way. The others were edging closer so as not to miss a word, and she was afraid of what Jack might say. Webb's questioning seemed to be leading Jack into an admission of the crime in front of everyone, and for some reason Jack was going along with it.

"Not necessarily," he said. "With the new high-gain antennas you can pick up the electromagnetic radiation from a computer monitor or its cables at some distance. You could be sitting in a van on the street, for example."

"Sitting in a van and reading the access codes as they appear on the computer screen?"

Jack settled against the bar, a faint smile appearing at Webb's question. "That's right," he said, gazing at the other man. "You sound as if you've done this before."

Gus had clasped her hands together by this time to keep them still. It appeared that Jack had done the impossible. He'd stepped into the trap and pulled out his foot before it sprang. Was he that good? Or was there something else going on? For the first time Gus realized that Jack might be setting a trap for Webb—or someone else in the room.

"Of course," Jack went on, caressing the rim of his drink with his forefinger, "there is a much easier way to steal a work of art. It's the perfect crime in a sense."

"The perfect crime?" Lake had stepped forward, his face pale, his mouth taut with anger. "And who better to plan and pull it off than a man who designs security systems."

"Actually, you're wrong," Jack countered. "This crime would depend very little on breaching security systems. It's as simple as impersonating the customs officials who transport art to the storage areas. All you'd need is a way to divert the transport, and that could be done by interrupting their radio transmissions, telling them there's an emergency—a bomb on board, for example—and redirecting them to some way station."

Gus was astounded. *Why was he doing this?*

Webb had come around the bar by now and was standing at the end opposite Jack, facing him. "But that depends on being able to read their frequency, doesn't it?" he wanted to know. "And given the trouble they would have gone through to secure it, that would take some damn sophisticated equipment."

"Not all that sophisticated, actually. You'd need a spread-spectrum modulator to analyze the frequency and, of course, a phone with a built-in sequencer to place the call." Jack reached into his jacket and pulled out one of the tiniest cell phones Gus had ever seen. He looked up, smiled. "A phone just like this one."

The low hiss of an expletive startled Gus. It had come from somewhere behind her. She turned and saw Rob Emory standing in the doorway, wearing the same jacket and slacks he'd worn at lunch. His face was flushed and he looked as if he'd been listening for some time. He also looked angry. No, enraged, she thought.

"Fascinating scenario," Rob said, making no attempt to hide the hostility in his voice, or to join the crowd as they turned to look at him. "A valuable painting was stolen today, and you just told everyone how it was done. But you forgot the punchline, *Jack*. You forgot to tell them who did it."

"I didn't forget, Mr. Emory—"

Rob cut him off, determined to have his say. "You also forgot to tell them that you've done time, didn't you, Jack?"

He turned to Lake and the others. "This man, Jack Culhane is an ex-con. He did hard time for nearly killing a man. And as for his so-called security business, it's nothing but a front. His clients are unsavory characters looking for ways to protect the art they've acquired illegally. He consorts with thieves and smugglers and probably is one himself."

For a moment Rob's fevered breathing was the only sound in the room. Even Gus was too alarmed to speak. She wasn't as shocked by Rob's revelations as by the way he'd revealed them. Didn't he realize that cornering Jack could be dangerous? If Jack retaliated he could destroy everything she was trying to do.

"Rob, what are you doing?" Gus asked softly.

"I told you I was going to have him investigated," he countered. "Thank God I did."

He'd told her that at lunch, Gus realized. But no one could amass that much information that fast, which meant he must have had the investigator on the case for some time, probably ever since the "honeymoon" trip to Mexico.

Without warning Jack broke from the bar and walked toward the large arched window at the far end of the room.

"Stop him!" Rob shouted. "Someone call the police!"

But no one could seem to move. Massive walnut bookshelves lined the wall on either side of the window, reaching about halfway to a ceiling that was thirty feet high. They also lined a portion of the inside wall. As Jack reached the window, he began to search the molding as if he were looking for a way to open it.

"Don't be stupid, man," Lake called out. "You'll never get out that way."

Jack glanced back over his shoulder. "Don't be so sure," he said. His hand stopped on the corner piece, and as he maneuvered it ever so slightly, a section of the bookshelves lining the inside wall rolled open, revealing a passageway large enough for a man to enter.

No one spoke, not even Rob as Jack disappeared into the passageway. Everyone seemed too shocked to respond. The windowpanes sparkled and danced with light, as if the chandeliers were moving. An antique clock on the fireplace mantel counted out seconds, ticking weakly in the silence. By the time Gus and the others had begun to recover, Jack had reappeared, a framed painting in his hands.

"Jesus Christ," Rob breathed. "It *was* him. I knew it!"

Jack propped the portrait on the windowsill where everyone could see it. The young girl in Goddard's magnificent oil seemed to be blushing furiously in the warm glow of the room's light.

Webb Calderon spoke first. "Is this your idea of a joke, Culhane? What does it mean?"

Jack left the painting where it was and walked toward them. "I did it to prove a point," he said. "I told Lake his system was vulnerable, but whoever sold it to him had convinced him it was impregnable. This seemed to be the only way to get my message across."

"An odd way to pick up new business," Lake said, his voice strangely quiet.

"Believe me, I don't need new business," Jack assured him. "I subcontract out the actual installation, but I design and test the systems myself. Earlier today I checked out Bruce Houston's new system. Of course, everyone knows the president of Houston Tires is an art thief and a smuggler." He flashed a black look at Rob.

Rob colored hotly, clearly embarrassed. "That painting could be a replacement," he said, pointing at the oil. "What if it's a forgery? And even if it isn't, he stole it right out from under your nose, Lake. He was trying to make you look like a fool."

By now Gus was furious. "Speaking of fools," she told Rob, her voice hushed as she glared at him.

Lake didn't seem to be pleased with Rob's assessment of the situation, either. "I don't think we know each other well enough for you to be calling me by my first name, Mr. Emory," he said coldly.

Rob went quiet at that, much to Gus's relief. And if she'd been frightened that Lake might decide to take some kind of action against Jack, she needn't have worried. He was studying her husband in an entirely different way. There was something new in his expression, something secret and speculative. As Gus glanced from one man to the other, she wondered what was going on.

The veiled look on Calderon's face tipped her that he might be a part of it, too, and suddenly the little bits of information she'd been receiving all evening began to form a vaguely coherent whole. That's what Jack Culhane wants with me, she realized. He wants them, my stepbrother and Calderon. Whatever he's after has something to do with them, and I'm the conduit.

She glanced around the room, noting Lily's narrowed, furtive fascination, and Ward McHenry, who'd been uncharacteristically quiet and removed through it all. Now he was watching with a dark interest that told her even he might have an agenda.

Fear struck Gus then, real fear, and for the first time. Her mouth went dry and her heart unsteady. The questions forming in her mind brought with them a premonition that was all the more terrifying because it had been generated by her own psyche. Was she the only one who didn't know what was going on? Was there some conspiracy of silence here between these people and the mysterious man she married? Or did they each have their own ax to grind? Confusion overwhelmed her, coupled with a sense of helplessness. No fortune-teller could have frightened her the way she had frightened herself, and yet she still had no real sense of the threat itself. She didn't know what was wrong, she just knew something was, terribly.

*   *   *

Someone had been in his room. Jack knew it the moment he opened the door. He'd used the oldest trick in the book, a piece of thread in the doorjamb. For his purposes it was just as effective and far less trouble than a laser beam. If anyone had entered in his absence the thread would be gone, and it was. He went immediately to the computer, which he'd stashed in an intake air vent on the wall behind the bed.

He'd programmed it to record the time and date when the lid was opened, and now as he tapped out the combination and the green quartz screen materialized, he saw that the system had not been breached. The entry log indicated it hadn't been opened since he used it last. That could eliminate Gus, he reasoned, though searching his room seemed almost innocuous, considering everything else she'd done. His intuition was telling him one of the other Featherstones or their guests was even more curious.

A professional would have checked the doorjamb, which meant that whoever'd come in had probably been at the party tonight. Rob Emory had admitted to having him investigated, but Jack's money was on Lake. His erratic behavior had caught Jack's attention. He'd gone into a rage when the painting was stolen, then been strangely subdued when Jack returned it.

Jack wished now that there'd been time to inspect the painting when he had it. Something about it hadn't looked quite right. He wasn't sure what the inconsistency was, perhaps an air bubble in the canvas, but there hadn't been time to investigate. He would, first chance he got.

Moments later he'd changed into his jeans and stretched out on the bed, knowing he wouldn't sleep. He was still charged with adrenaline, and the residual sparks were flying. His mind was alive, thinking about the day's events, the woman who *was* an event. There were many things he could do tonight, including input the new data he'd picked up today into the security matrix of the Featherstone estate. He'd scoped out the house's system, using a tiny, portable, high-gain antenna to collect the data and the software he developed to analyze it. His next step was to flush out an art thief. The Van Gogh that had disappeared five years ago had never been recovered. Jack had reason to believe it was hidden somewhere here in this house, and when he found it, he would be that much closer to the criminal mastermind who'd destroyed his family.

He closed his hands, feeling their restless need for action. Yes, there was plenty he could do, but only one thing that would calm him.

The formless block of satinwood he held was going to be her. Jack knew it by the feel of the wood in his hand. It was warm in his palm, vibrant and alive beneath his clasped fingers. It wasn't the only time he'd felt as if something were waiting to be born with the virgin cut of his knife. But he was surprised at this impulse, surprised that the first human figure he'd ever carved would be her, Gus.

He sat on the braided rug in his room, resting his shoulders against the side of the bed, the block of golden wood cradled in one hand, his knife in the other. The bedroom wasn't made for a man his size. It was roughly as wide as a hospital corridor and about as inspiring. The rest of the house smelled of lemon oil and fresh-cut flowers and was sumptuously decorated with antiques, fine crystal, and damask fabrics, but this room was as spare and spartan as a monk's cell. The gleaming brass bed sported a quilted Granny Goose coverlet and had a cedar chest at the foot.

He shifted, trying to arrange himself comfortably. There'd been nowhere in the room to sit to do his carving. The rocker had been too small, the window seat too cramped, so he'd wound up here, on the floor, and discovered that it felt good, like a kid hiding out from the world, wanting to be alone with some silly, priceless thing he'd found.

The knife flashed in his hand—weapon of destruction or creation depending on who wielded it. For him it had been both.

He'd never had any kind of training in wood carving. It had been a natural pastime in prison, a harmless way to fill the hours of tedium. Weapons hadn't been allowed so he'd

used whatever he could find or fashion, mostly shivs and
sharpened rocks. At first the guards had confiscated the
crude carvings, and he'd been disciplined. Eventually
they'd come to ignore him, and he'd filled his cell with ren-
derings of more and more intricacy. Tiny cottages and castles, they'd been mysterious talismans, but he'd never
understood what they meant to him or why they held such
power. Sometimes he thought they reminded him of the
only time in his life that wasn't tainted with unbearable
pain—his childhood. Other times he wondered if they represented the future he'd been denied.

His only other preoccupation in prison had been planning
for the time when he would confront the killers of his child.
After tonight that time seemed close enough to reach out
and touch. The trap had been baited and set. All he had to
do now was wait, wait and stay laser-focused.

He worked the smooth wood with his thumb, imagining
the contours of her body in his mind, feeling them in his
flesh. She had the kind of body men dreamed about con-
quering, satin skin and sleek, firm curves. Remembering
her golden softness now made him tight, hard. Remembering her moist, pink sweetness as he fucked her—made him
ache. Christ, he should never have touched her.

In five years nothing else had taken his mind off his one
objective, to find the people who destroyed his family and
make them pay. Nothing but her, this woman hidden in the
wood. Odd that he was so close to what he'd sought all this
time, and all he could think about was her.

He didn't know what to make of her. It didn't surprise
him that she'd tried to kill him. He would have done the
same under the circumstances. What surprised him was the
way she'd taken his side tonight, against her fiancé, against
her family. What surprised him was that she'd tried to lure
him to his death and then come to his rescue all in the same
day. She'd done that twice. How the hell was he supposed
to resist a woman who couldn't decide whether she wanted
him dead or alive?

Sex with her would be like stealing fire from the gods.
Irrestible. Suicidal. She was as much a narcotic as the

booze he craved. Only unlike booze, he couldn't have her
without pain. His body wouldn't let him. He had held back
too long, and now when he wanted desperately to feel the
deep, soul-shaking pleasure of release, he was no longer capable. Maybe that was a good thing, he told himself.
Maybe it would keep him from getting so emotionally entangled that he couldn't do what he had to do. For all he
knew she might even have been involved in what happened
five years ago.

I hope you didn't have any part of it, Gus, he thought. *I
hope to God you didn't, because if you did, I'll have to take
you down with the rest of them.*

He ran the knife blade gently over the wood, stroking it
to determine the place to begin. Some energy would slow
his hand and guide his blade. She, the woman in the wood,
would tell him how to bring her to life. It was a violent and
beautiful thing he was going to do, carving a woman's
body, the very origin of life, from so basic an element of
nature as an amorphous block of wood. As he took the first
cut, the virgin cut, he thought he heard her sigh.

CHAPTER
18

"OH, YES, YES, YESSSSSSSSSSSSSSSS—"

The hissed word climbed the scale from sexual ecstasy to physical agony as Jack fought to heave two hundred and fifty pounds of barbell into the ozone. His jaw locked with the savage effort, and the tendons in his neck choked off any further sound. The sweat trickling from his brow turned to fire when it hit his eyes, forcing him to squeeze them shut. He'd been pushing it to the limit for the last two hours, and he was on the brink of muscle failure. Something was going to burst before he got through this repetition!

His hands were fused to the bar, but the wild trembling in his wrists burned down his arms and shook in his throat. This was the last set of three, and he was flat on his back, attempting to benchpress the weight for the tenth time. Fucking A! He'd done it in prison every day.

Laughter shook through him, weakening his concentration. He'd made a *rhyme*. Pain had wrung poetry from his tortured soul, and he was just demented enough to find that funny. Stupidly, asininely funny. His stomach muscles jerked with mirth. His arms wobbled and his knees knocked against the padded bench as he strained to lower the crushing weight to his chest. He was losing it and he had no one to spot for him! Two hundred and fifty pounds of steel could smash bricks into dust.

His arms swayed forward, and he snarled like a wounded animal as he fought to bring them back. He was shaking like a drunk, sweat pouring from his brow. He had to get the barbells vertical, then lower them a few agonizing inches into the power rack above him. Bracing himself with his legs, he gave it one last gut-wrenching heave and managed to bring the weight above his head. His hands ached as he released them with a tortured groan. The smell of his own sweat permeated his senses.

The cradle swayed with its burden, bowing above him.

"*Jesus,*" he breathed, jerking off the equipment. He escaped just in time to see the rack snap like a twig. The barbell thudded to the wooden bench, broke it in two and crashed to the floor. The sound was thunderous, like a cacophony of iron doors slamming shut. It rattled the other equipment and reverberated throughout the workout room as he stepped back, no longer laughing. His solo bench-pressing days were over. It was too damned dangerous.

He grabbed the towel he'd draped over the chinning station and wiped himself down, mopping his face and his hair. By the time he was done his nylon tank top and shorts were damp rather than drenched, and his vital signs had stabilized, but his arms were still vibrating. The day he'd arrived, the housekeeper had told him that there was a weight room in the basement of the mansion, but this morning was the first chance he'd had to try it out. It had seemed like a good way to work off some of last night's frustration.

"Asshole," he muttered. How many men got themselves all racked up over a wood carving? He hadn't been able to finish the damn thing. He'd become too physically aroused. His knife had found every delicate swell of flesh, every curl and crevice and sensitive hollow. He'd probed the satin-wood and discovered things he hadn't known before about her. There was a dimple near her knee, a mole beneath her left breast. He'd brought her to life in his hands, but that was as much as he could have of her. What his hands could feel, what his mind could steal. And finally it had become too painful.

More poetry, he thought. Fuck.

His clenched gut muscles told him he wasn't done exercising yet. He flipped the towel over the chinning bar, then added some weight to the leg press machine and arranged himself on the equipment, knowing it was going to hurt. Better my thighs than other less resilient places, he thought.

As he lay back and stared up at the obscene amount of weight he'd loaded, he promised himself that once he'd worked off some steam, he would begin his search of the house, which included having another look at the Goddard he'd returned to Lake. The man's behavior had made him suspicious, but he'd also noticed something odd about the painting's canvas. In one corner he'd noticed a rippling effect that could have been air bubbles. It might mean nothing, but he couldn't afford to overlook it.

He began to work the press with his legs then, forcing the massive stack of silver bars up and down. His thigh muscles rippled under the strain, and the burn rose with every thrust, forcing him to admit that he was out of shape, at least as far as weight training went.

The weights clanked against each other jarringly as he tried to focus inward, and there was something about the jangling resonance that made him uneasy. A quick visual search of the equipment above him pinpointed the source of the noise. One of the wire cables that held the weights was frayed to the point of breaking. The tremendous pressure meant it could go at any moment, and when it did, the weights would drop like bombs, some of them might even fly. He stopped pumping, trying to figure out how to get himself the hell off the machine and still keep the foot flexors depressed so the bar wouldn't fall.

A curling barbell lay on the floor within his reach.

Once he had the barbell jammed between the flexors and a chrome fixture beneath them, he swung free of the equipment and stepped back to scan it. Curious, he pulled the barbell away and quickly moved out of range, watching as the bars plummeted. Their weight snapped the frayed cable, and the broken line unleashed a barrage of silver missiles directly at the spot where he'd been lying. Nowhere to hide, he thought.

Gallows humor coaxed his mouth into a grim line. Any one of the bars could have split his skull and killed him instantly, which made him more than curious about who normally used this equipment. More to the point, who knew he was going to be using it? A cursory inspection of the broken cable told him the fraying wasn't normal wear and tear. The cable had been cut.

He caught a sound, like the shuffling of feet, and spun around. A flash of blue darted past the doorway. Someone had been watching him from the hallway. Maybe the same person who'd rigged the weight equipment.

As he reached the door of the room, he caught another glimpse of the fleeing figure rounding the corner. He took off in pursuit. It had looked like a woman in blue jeans with dark hair. Jesus, not again! Gus? His heart roared as he sprinted down the hallway. She wasn't going to give up until she had him in the grave.

"Wait!" he called out. She was heading for the stairwell as he came around the corner. He shot after her and caught her, snagging her foot before she'd scrambled to the first landing. She fell forward in a heap, and by the time she'd turned herself over, he was on top of her.

"What the hell are you up to?" he growled. It took him a moment to realize that he was staring into the astonished face of Lily Featherstone. The shadows of the hallway had made her chestnut hair appear several shades darker.

"I'm not up to anything!" Her voice was as shrill as it was shocked. "Get off me or I'll scream for the guards!"

"Was that you in the doorway?"

"I don't know what you're talking about. I was down here looking for some china I'd packed away in the store room, and you frightened me half to death, yelling at me, chasing me. Now let me up!"

Her breasts rose against his chest with every sharp breath, and her face was flushed from the run. Jack was amazed that he found Lily in any way attractive. She was too prim and fussy for him, with her small, sharp features and her penchant for white—Lily white. But her flowery perfume permeated his senses, and he was just angry enough—and God knew, horny enough—to entertain the idea of kissing this frigid witch of a stepsister-in-law.

Instead he released her and rolled away, but she must have read his intention. With a sharp little cry of relief, she crawled up to the landing and struggled to her feet. As she glared at him, her hand flew up, covering her mouth as if she were going to be sick. She sidestepped, then turned and ran.

Jack was too intrigued to be insulted. Why the hell would Lily Featherstone want him dead? he wondered, watching her flee up the steps to the first floor. Unless she knew why he was here. He doubted that she had the strength or the skill to tamper with the weight equipment, which meant she'd had help.

Easy enough to come by, Jack reasoned. The guy who hung out in the stables, Daniel, was a big, strapping twenty-something kid, probably trying to pay his way through college and happy to do handy work for extra pay. Or maybe Lily was looking for china, just like she said. At the very least it seemed that there was more than one Featherstone who considered him a threat.

Swell, he thought, that was just swell. It was beginning to look like the whole damn family wanted him dead.

Lily's hands shook as she removed the Medusa brooch from her blouse and set it in the sterling silver tray on her dressing table. She wore the heirloom religiously, but not because it had been her mother's. She'd just begun the Evelyn Meyer Randolph's school for girls when Louise Featherstone had died and she and her mother had never been close. Lily wore it because her father had pinned it on the bodice of her ivory-white organdy dress on her thirteenth birthday and told her that all of the Featherstone women before her had worn it with pride. If he had asked her to pierce her heart with the pin, she would probably have done that too.

Her eyes had been too bright that day, too hot with hope. They were glittering like that now, she realized, wishing she could avoid their green brilliance as she gazed at her own reflection in the vanity mirror. With a sudden, sharp sigh she began to undo the delicate pearl buttons of her blouse, aware that the warmth pouring through the crisp percale fabric was her own body heat.

She still felt thoroughly violated by the manhandling she'd received from Jack Culhane. The man's sweaty fingerprints were all over her, and there were soggy blotches of his perspiration on her blouse. If she could ever get the disgusting thing off, she was going to inspect herself for damage.

She tilted her chin up to get a look at her throat. Surely she'd find several bruises, at the very least. She must be black and blue after the way he'd thrown her to the floor and fallen on her. Gus had married an animal, she decided, and an adulterous animal at that. She'd seen the look in his eyes as he'd lain on top of her. It was blatantly sexual. But then why did that surprise her, considering the stock Gus came from. Her mother'd had a penchant for unsavory characters. It stood to reason Gus would be attracted to that sort of thing—danger and raw sex. What Lily would never understand was what her own father, a thoroughly cultured man, had seen in such a vulgar woman as Rita Walsh.

She drew her blouse down over her shoulders and peered at her skin in the lighted vanity mirror, turning this way and that. She didn't see any marks. Possibly they hadn't come up yet. Some bruises took shape like photographic negatives, gradually. Perhaps her hip, she thought, where she'd hit the riser of the stair when she'd fallen.

The allure of the illicit.

Lake's comment about Rita came to her as she undid the buckle of her woven leather belt. Her thumbnails clicked against the metal snap of her jeans. "There's a lecherous old goat hidden in our holier-than-thou father," he'd whis-

pered at dinner one night after Rita had shocked the small
group with an off-color joke. "She turns the sanctimonious
old bastard on."

Lake had always considered their father a puritanical,
emotionally rigid prig, though outwardly he'd never dared
to show anything but obedience and respect. Lily's wound
was that Lake, Sr., had so strongly preferred his son over
her when Lake had secretly hated him, and all she'd ever
wanted was his approval. Her father had never seemed to
have more than a passing interest in her, and she'd often
wondered if that was exactly the reason—because she had
been so much like him, and not . . . illicit.

A moment later she had her jeans around her hips and
she'd pulled her panties down by their elastic to check herself. "I knew it," she said, feeling vindicated as she examined a large red welt on her buttock. She ran a finger over
its tenderness and winced. Look what he'd done to her, the
brute! It was unfortunate for all of them that the weight
equipment hadn't crushed Mr. Culhane. That would have
made everything so much easier.

She kicked off her slip-on canvas deck shoes and began
to pin up her hair, struck by the disheveled image that
bounced back at her from the mirror. She'd left her blouse
hanging off her shoulders, her jeans and panties down
around her hips. The flush that crept up her throat made her
look all the more the sort of woman her father might have
secretly desired, a woman like Rita or Gus, an illicit creature.

By the time she had the rest of her clothes off and the
shower running, she'd found two more bruises and felt
quite pleased with herself. She wondered if Jack Culhane
abused women, and the thought gave her some small satisfaction, though she couldn't imagine any man abusing Gus.
She'd kill him first.

Lily generally preferred a soak in the vast marble
pedestal tub she'd had built into her spacious bathroom, but
the ordeal she'd just been through called for a shower, as
hot as she could get it. Lake had always accused her of harboring a moralistic streak like their father. She didn't know

if that was true, but she did seem to have a personal aversion to physical men like Culhane. All she wanted now was to get his nasty, sweaty scent off her body.

The spray was powerful. Her skin tingled as if it were being prickled by hundreds of sharp little spines when she stepped into the path of the water. It was exactly what she needed. Within seconds she was stingingly alive all over, and the inner tension was melting away like the water steaming down the drain.

She was still turning in the deluge and scrubbing feverishly moments later when she realized that someone was in her bathroom. She could see the form of a man through the steam that had condensed on the glass shower walls. Her hands dropped to her sides in a defenseless pose, and the loofah mitt slipped from her grip, battered to the floor by the force of the water. She froze as the shower door slid open.

She began to shake, an inner trembling that rang through her body like a cry of alarm. Dear God, it was him again. He had violated her privacy and now, unless she could find the will to say no, he would violate everything else that she held private and sacred—her body, her dignity. Somehow she had to find the strength. She couldn't let him take advantage of her weakness again. She couldn't let him humiliate her again.

"Turn around," he said. "Turn and pick up the mitt you dropped, you clumsy girl."

Lily barely knew what happened after that. Her heart was pounding so wildly she couldn't think. Her encounters with him had always blurred into one glaring red stream of stimulation from which she emerged gasping and ashamed. She did as he said, of course. She always did as he said.

"No, don't crouch, bend," he told her. "Bend from the waist. Show me the bruises on your buttocks."

Moments later, she was bent double like a gymnast, and the naked man who'd joined her in the shower was caressing her flared hips and driving deeply into her quaking, madly orgasming body. God, the pleasure he gave her! She knew it was wrong—very wrong—but she couldn't resist the way he took over at moments like this. His power and unyielding control of the situation were her only addictions in life. In that way he was exactly like her father.

When there's a choice between two evils, pick the one you haven't tried. Few proverbs spoke to the dark night of Webb Calderon's soul the way that one did. He was thoroughly versed in the distractions of sin and iniquity, so much so, he wouldn't have bet there were two choices left. But that was before the Featherstones. Their situation offered such an embarrassment of evils, even Webb couldn't seem to make up his mind. It was almost enough watching the very proper family reduced to a circus act by the presence of Jack Culhane.

Almost . . .

He set down the magnifying glass he'd been using to study an early seventeenth-century drawing by Guercino, pleased that the work appeared to be authentic. The artist's style had a naturalism that conveyed passion, yet nothing was sloppy or uncontrolled. It was all there in the details. Guercino was less a perfectionist than a precisionist, Webb had decided.

Interesting that all of those qualities applied to another artist as well. There were all kinds of craftsmen, and Jack Culhane had impressed Webb with his technical precision, as well as his flair for drama. He'd lived up to his legend as The Magician with that secret passageway business—Webb smiled fleetingly. That had been a nice touch. He'd thought Lake was going to have an aneurysm.

And yet there was another quality in Culhane that intrigued Webb more. Da Vinci had called it *virtu spirituale*, and the artist had tried to capture its essence in his writings and drawings. "It lives by violence and dies by liberty," he'd written. "It grows slowly from small beginnings, to terrible and marvelous energy, and by compression of itself, compels all things." Other names had been attached to this energy—life force, cosmic force, but Webb was convinced the artist had been talking about something dark, the kind of force that drove the men who kept it contained and violent within them, men like Culhane.

Suddenly restless himself, Webb rose from the drafting table where he'd been working all afternoon. Outside in the courtyard, a flock of cliff swallows had forsaken the bluffs for his dogwood trees, and they were fluttering through the leafy branches, chirruping wildly, in a frenzy over something. Their glorious greed for life—for food, territory, sex, or whatever was at risk now—echoed through the silent halls of the Spanish-style hacienda that was his southern California home.

He walked across dark wood and an old Aubusson carpet to the arched entrance of his study and gazed down the sprawling length of the house to the magnificent vista that lay beyond. He'd bought the oceanfront acreage and two-story adobe mansion as much for the tiled elegance of its breezy courtyards as for its view of the Pacific. But the sight of all that misty blue, of vast waters bleeding into an even vaster sky, never failed to hold him for a moment and remind him where he was.

The hacienda clung precariously to the cliffs of Malibu, and it had always struck Webb as ironic that the Big One, whether earthquake or mudslide, would send it—and him—into freefall. Ironic because very little of what he owned held any attachment for him, but he did feel a bond with this house and its profound contrasts. While this floor was sweeping, sunstruck and open to the elements, the level below housed a very unusual collection. Unlike the Featherstone's gallery of old masters, Webb's gallery of antiquities from the Spanish Inquisition boasted an entire *camara de tortura*.

Webb wasn't into S&M, however. He was into sensation. The crimes of his childhood had robbed him of the ability to feel except in rather extreme circumstances, and the experience of pleasure and pain was nearly the same to him now. He also understood, without modesty or ego, that what set him apart even further from the norm was his preternatural instinct for reading vulnerability in others, his restless and predatory intelligence. He had a sixth sense about people and situations.

Perhaps that was why he found the attraction between Jack Culhane and Gus Featherstone so fascinating. Whether they knew it or not, they were on a collision course. Culhane was a man driven by the darkest of forces, blood justice, and she was a woman as determined to redeem and prove herself as the sun was to rise. Like darkness and light, they could not exist together. They were doomed to extinguish each other.

She had already sensed that at the Featherstone party. He could see it in her eyes as she searched the room, and when finally she'd focused on him, he'd known it would only be a matter of time. She would be coming to see him, coming for the kind of help that only he could give her. And perhaps he would, *if* she helped him. It depended on how badly she wanted this magazine of hers, this foundation.

Webb returned to his desk and reached for the Tarot cards he kept in a carved teak box. He opened the pack, drew out the deck and began to lay out the sinister artwork, prophecy of a future that was hopelessly mired in the past. Jack Culhane had Da Vinci's force harnessed inside him, the force that drove away in fury whatever stood in the way of its ruin, according to the artist. Webb was virtually certain that he knew which way the *virtu spirituale* would take Culhane next. He wondered if the cards did.

CHAPTER
19

"PEOPLE BELIEVE THEY CAN BUY SELF-ESTEEM!" GUS AS-
serted. "I want them to know it's an inside job. *ATTI-
TUDE*'s manifesto will be freedom. I don't want women to
be slaves to fashion. I want our readers to create a look so
distinctive, so uniquely *them,* that no one can tell them
they're in or out of fashion."

Gus's words were filled with passion—there was no
doubt she believed in what she was saying. Fortunately, the
senior editorial staff of *ATTITUDE* seemed to have been in-
fected with her brio. Consigned to folding chairs in the
huge, unfinished editorial department, they laughed and ap-
plauded and razzed her as she paced the sawdust-strewn
floor and pitched her concept of the magazine. She had
done it before, with each of them individually when she offered them positions on the staff, but never with such conviction. This afternoon she was a preacher in the
wilderness, sent to save heathen souls.

Earlier in the week she had leased the twentieth and
twenty-first floors of this newly renovated bank building on

Wilshire. She'd assembled the staff for what was supposed to have been a brainstorming session, but so far it had been a one-woman show. In her excitement she'd nearly turned it into an infomercial.

"I'm sorry." Registering the amused expressions of the small group, she gave her head a slap with the heel of her hand. "I haven't given anyone else a chance to speak, have I?"

"Where'd you train?" Lisa Burns, the art director, wanted to know. "The Ross Perot school of debate?"

Applause broke out, and the young woman, a talented former *Elle* staffer, acknowledged it with a dip of her head. She then helped herself to the last piece of ham and pineapple pizza from a card table strewn with empty boxes and settled back to munch it, kicking her feet up on the table.

Dirty feet, Gus thought. The soles of her art director's feet were black everywhere that they weren't sprinkled with sawdust! It was exactly the sort of personal style statement Gus wanted for her magazine. Thirty-something and a lovely, sunstreaked blonde, Lisa had dressed unapologetically in Chinese refugee clothing and gone barefoot! Just for fun, Gus had invited her staff to come as who you *really* are, and she'd been astonished at their responses. She should have worn her boxer shorts instead of denim jeans.

The sounds of industrious hammering and drilling came from down the hallway, where a crew was still working on the building's renovations. Gus went to shut the office door, yelling at her people over the noise. "Fire away. I want to know what you think."

The racket could still be heard as she returned to the session, but she decided to take it as a good omen. Everything was under construction, she realized—the building, her magazine, and in some ways, her life. Maybe it symbolized new beginnings, which, if she were really being optimistic, could mean that Culhane wouldn't kill her with his bare hands when she got home.

ATTITUDE's editor-in-chief jumped in first. "The way I see it this magazine is about self-discovery and the courage to be what you find." A forty-five-year-old redhead, Jackie

Sanderson had washed the dye out of her hair and come with gray strands sprinkling her abundant natural curls. She'd also dressed in a silver Lycra catsuit and worn clear plastic slingbacks. Hussy-red toenails were the only touch of color offsetting the quicksilver explosion.

"It's about going boldly where no one has gone before," she told them, grinning as she stood up to show off her pear-shaped, less-than-perfect figure. "Into your own heart, to find out who lives there."

"So tell us, Jackie," the sales director quipped. "Who lives in your heart today? Heidi Fleiss?"

"Yes!" someone agreed, though it wasn't clear with which statement.

Gus agreed, too. "Brava, Jackie! But how do we put that concept in front of the masses? More important, how do we let them know this magazine is for everyone, that we *all* yearn to stop hiding and be who we really are?"

Gus thought about her stammer, which hadn't evidenced itself yet today. She'd been artfully disguising it for so many years, she wasn't honestly sure she could reveal that much of herself, even to these people, much less the world. But what a relief it would be to be free of the secret!

"We get the message across by the people we choose for our cover," Lisa announced, chewing on a piece of pineapple. "They should be mavericks who've blazed their own trails, maybe even gone up against the system. How *about* Heidi Fleiss?"

"Old news," Sammy Frye, the sales director, shot back, adjusting his Hugo Boss tie. "If we want to pull the Generation X demographics, we've gotta be *now*. We've got to be tomorrow."

An aging Generation Xer himself, he'd come dressed in a Brooks Brothers power-lunch suit that brought to mind the movie *Wall Street* and Gordon Gecko's "greed is good" statement. His only concession to the otherwise funky mood was a ponytail that hung halfway down his back. "And no dead divas, either, like Jackie O."

"I love Jackie O!" The editor-in-chief folded her arms over her chest and sank down in a mock sulk.

"Only because you were named for her," someone rifled.

As the group became embroiled in a heated discussion of "hot" cover concepts, Gus's attention was drawn to the one silent figure sitting in the back. Her former fiancé seemed determined to be the wet blanket at this planning session. Rob Emory had arrived late, and he clearly wasn't happy about anything that was going on.

Gus suspected it had more to do with their personal life than the magazine. He hadn't stayed for dinner after the embarrassment with Jack. He'd left the mansion in a huff and with considerable egg on his face for a man who hadn't eaten. Gus knew he felt betrayed, but then so did she. He hadn't told her the truth about the detective. She did have some sympathy for his situation, however. She wouldn't have liked it if some woman had dropped like a bomb into his life the way Jack Culhane had dropped into hers. He must also sense that she was having second thoughts about him and their relationship. But who wouldn't be, under the circumstances? How many relationships could take this kind of strain?

"We are going for a national launch, aren't we?" Lisa Burns wanted to know. "It would be easier to get somebody hot for the cover if we could promise them the launch issue of a national campaign."

"That's the plan," Gus assured her. "We're still crunching numbers, so don't put anything in writing. If American Naturals goes for the marketing partnership we've proposed, it's a go."

A raspy noise drew everyone's attention. It was the sound of Rob's chair scraping across the floor as he stood.

"I'm afraid it's not, Gus," he said, rising. "Not even with American Naturals. I wish I didn't have to rain on this parade of yours. I know how badly you want a big, splashy launch, but I spent the morning with the accountant going over the figures, and it's going to take another infusion of cash. There's no way to do it, otherwise."

He might as well have told them the parade had been canceled. Gus was astonished that he'd made the announcement without warning her first or giving her time to pre-

pare. Everyone had sobered and she could see the disappointment on their faces, but didn't know how to reassure
them at this point. She'd been taken off guard.

"Then we'll get more cash," she said. "We'll increase
our advertising pages. Clairol's new Natural Instincts line
would be perfect for *ATTITUDES*. I'll use my modeling
c-contacts." She'd gotten the word out, but just barely, and
now everyone was staring at her expectantly. Perspiration
broke out on her forehead and chilled the back of her neck.
She couldn't go on. The pounding in her ears was so insis-
tent it could have been the thunder coming from down the
hall. But it wasn't. It was her heart.

Rob had cast a pall over this group. She had no idea why,
and there didn't seem to be anything she could do to recap-
ture the enthusiasm. But she wasn't going to compromise
her dreams, not after having risked everything for them.
ATTITUDE would get its national launch, even if she had
to beg, borrow, or steal to make it happen.

It rocketed across the floor of the gallery and climbed the
wall like black death itself. Jack had already spotted the
shadow and taken cover, slipping into the nearest alcove
and pressing himself to the wall. He'd known for some
time that he was being followed. Now he was waiting for
the tail to get overeager and show himself.

It was one in the morning, and Jack had come down to
the gallery to have a closer look at Blush, as well as several
of the other works in Lake's collection. There were many
ways to hide a stolen painting, even in plain view. It was not
unusual to stretch one canvas over another or to paint over it
with an entirely new picture.

Jack was intimately familiar with the gallery's security.
He'd already compromised the multisensor system to get to
the Goddard, and Lake hadn't yet taken steps to upgrade
the safeguards. Tonight Jack had simply duplicated the
high-tech tinkering he'd described to Webb at dinner. But
his inspection of the gallery had immediately revealed that
someone had beaten him at his own game. Blush was gone.

The alcove wall where the Goddard painting had hung was empty.

That's when Jack had discovered he was being followed.

Now every reflex was primed for action as he waited and listened. He'd been the subject of professional surveillance for days. Someone had been following his van and undoubtedly monitoring his car phone, but several clues told him tonight's surveillance wasn't by a pro any more than the search of his room had been. Whoever was following him had taken care to hide their footsteps but not their breathing. What he'd picked up was someone's hushed and excited respiration. More important, a professional knew how to avoid throwing shadows.

As the seconds ticked by, Jack realized the tail must have been alerted, probably by Jack's disappearance. The odds were that he'd backed off, possibly even left the room. If Jack was going to catch him, he would have to act immediately.

He moved to the end of the alcove wall, ducked down, and made a quick visual search of the gallery proper. Once he was reasonably certain the cavernous room was empty, he crept silently across the hardwood floor toward the doorway. Save the ski mask, he was dressed in the same black overalls and crepe-soled commando boots he'd worn to kidnap Gus. The color absorbed light like a sponge, and the boots were virtually noiseless.

He approached the open doorway, hesitating as something white ghosted through his field of vision. It had resembled a disembodied scarf or a veil floating down the hallway outside the door. He caught another trace of it, sparkling and wispy white, as iridescent as fancy tissue paper, and then it was gone.

By the time he reached the doorway, the tissue paper had darted toward one of the staircases that arched up to the second-floor bedrooms. But it hadn't gone up the stairway; it had ducked around underneath.

Jack followed cautiously, but couldn't see where the elusive thing had gone. There were only two escape routes beyond the front entrance, a hallway running the breadth of the house that led to the kitchen on the east side and to an exit door in the west wing. The latter would take him to the parking garage, but something told him to try the kitchen first.

A hushed sound, like laughter, spun him around. In the shallow alcove created by the stairway, he spotted his tissue-paper stalker. Lurking in the gloom was a miniature person in a fluffy white tutu with a feathery tail-like object attached to her backside. Fortunately, his senses had always been acutely attuned to the darkness, and now they were telling him that she had the face of a pint-size angel and the moxie of a New York cabbie. She also smelled faintly of bubble gum and bath powder.

"Bridget?"

"I'm not Bridget," she said in a whispery voice that barely hid her exasperation. "I'm a swan maiden under the enchantment of an evil magician. By day I live as a swan, but at night I'm released to haunt this house. Haven't you ever seen a ghost?"

Her tiny features were perfectly serious, even in the darkness, and her tilted head drew his attention to the curve of her pursed lips. The baby brat, true to form, he thought. How could you not love a kid like this? Her presence also answered several questions, including the mysterious disappearance of Blush. Clearly she hadn't taken the painting, which meant that Lake had probably stashed it somewhere for safekeeping.

"Good try," Jack said. "I don't believe in ghosts."

A smile flashed unexpectedly. "Not even the one standing behind you with a huge, bloody knife?"

Humoring her, Jack glanced over his shoulder. There was nothing behind him but a shadowy hallway that led to the kitchen and a ghastly piece of nude sculpture that he'd heard someone at the Featherstone's last party call the nursing mother. "I guess it vanished," he said.

But when he turned back, she'd vanished, too. Vanished into thin air, which was the way any self-respecting magician would have described it. She couldn't have known that she was dealing with another evil magician in him, or that he was impressed by her disappearing act. His eyes had only been off her for an instant. She couldn't possibly have made a run for it without his having seen her.

He turned in a circle, visually inspecting the sculpture, the stairway, the closed gallery doors and all the other doorways on the hall. All of his senses had quickened, mobilizing to pick up any signal, but there were none to pick up. Yet, when he came back around, she was there again, beaming at him.

"Good trick, huh?"

"How'd you do that?" By now he'd figured out how she'd done it, but he didn't want to steal her thunder.

"My secret," she said.

He nodded, playing along. There was, after all, honor among magicians, and clearly she had the instincts. He'd also realized he might have in her the perfect assistant for some of the tricks he had planned. He shoved his hands in the pockets of his jumpsuit and smiled at her. "I'll bet this house is full of secrets, isn't it."

"Yeah," she said, her eyes suddenly sparkling bright, even in the dimness. In a conspiratorial whisper she added, "I think there's a hidden passageway in my room."

"What makes you think that?" Jack didn't have to pretend to be interested. His plan was to search the entire house. He'd already gone over the third-floor wing where his bedroom was located and discovered the stairway that led to the library. He assumed it had originally been intended for the servants' use. Backstairs and hallways weren't uncommon in houses as large and old as this one, but Jack hadn't been looking for secret passageways. He'd been looking for a vaultlike room, probably combination locked, temperature controlled, and otherwise outfitted for the storage of fine art and antiquities. If such a room existed, he would find it, perhaps with a little assist from the swan here.

Her tail swished in the darkness, creating that ghostly iridescent effect Jack had seen before. "Our housekeeper always shows up when I'm reading a new Sweet Valley High," she was explaining. "She and Gus don't exactly approve of them for someone my age, or anyway, that's what Frances says."

Her huge eyes rolled at the provincialism of some adults. "Trouble is she can be pretty sneaky about it when she wants to. Most of the time I don't even hear her come into the room."

"So . . . what are you saying? You think she's spying on you, like through the eyes of some picture on the wall?"

An eager nod. "I can't prove it, though." She gazed at him for several long, blinking moments. "What do you think?"

"Do you have any idea where the passage is?"

She shook her head, entranced.

"You could sprinkle powder on the floor around the perimeter of the room."

"Prim-at-her?"

"The outside edges of the room, along the molding."

"Oh, okay," she agreed instantly, then wrinkled her nose in confusion. "Why should I do that?"

"Because if there is a hidden panel, the person will have to step in the powder on the way in or out of it, and you'll see the footprints."

"Oh, cool! Like bath powder? I have lots of that."

He already knew that. She reeked sweetly of it, possibly from having doused herself after her bedtime bath. "Baking powder or flour might work better. They're not scented. And use very little, make it look like a coating of house-dust."

"I'm going to try it tonight!" Breathless, she clapped her hand over her mouth as if there were no other way to contain her excitement, and her feathery parts bobbed and sparkled with her movements.

Jack laughed softly. It was fun to see her acting like a kid instead of a tiny, imperious adult, but it had also created a strange constriction in his heart. She was a reminder of his losses, and they were unendurable. If he were smart, he would try to avoid her, no matter what secrets she might be able to tell him about this house. Emotion made you sloppy, and whatever pleasure she brought him would always be edged with pain. Which was not unlike the situation with her aunt, he reminded himself ironically. Only that wasn't an edge, that was an ax blade.

Floorboards creaked from somewhere down the hallway, and in the quiet of the night, it sounded like fingernails raking on a chalkboard.

"Someone's coming," Bridget said, yanking on his sleeve. "Come with me." She pressed the heel of her satin ballet slipper against the floor molding, stepped down, and a panel slid open. They both ducked inside as the footsteps neared.

Jack held the panel open a crack and saw a slender figure materialize in the hallway and walk toward them. She was wearing cotton boxers and a ribbed tank top, but nothing else. Her long legs gleamed in the thin light, and the tank's paper-thin material was hard-pressed to conceal anything, especially the firm bounce of her breasts. Jack's stomach dropped and so did his heart. Why the hell couldn't he control himself around this woman?

"It's Gus," he whispered. "Shall we scare her?"

Bridget's tiny gasp of laughter was all the incentive Jack needed. "We might give her a heart attack," the little girl cautioned.

Nothing less than she deserves, Jack thought. She's given me one or two. "Nah, she's tough," he said. "She'll think it's a great joke."

As Gus walked by them, Jack slid the panel open farther, snaked out a hand, and snagged her. Her startled scream forced him to move quickly. He hooked an arm around her waist, clamped a hand over her mouth, and lifted her right up off the ground.

She didn't make it easy. Apparently he'd scared the holy shit out of her, because much to his perverse satisfaction she struggled with the wrath of a hellcat. She twisted and thrashed and swung at him, not letting up for a second, even once he'd wrestled her inside the passageway. He could feel her bared teeth against his fingers and realized she was trying to bite him. "Easy!" he hissed.

It took more than a little force to subdue her, and he took

more than a little pleasure in using it. It was dead black in the hidden compartment, and he used Gus's disorientation to his full advantage, knowing that Bridget couldn't see anything he was doing. The quicker he got her under control the better, he told himself. He didn't want to frighten the kid, after all.

But Gus didn't seem to care about his noble concerns. She twisted and squirmed in his grip and those firm, bouncing breasts of hers were all over the place as he forced her to the wall, hoping to use the surface as leverage. It amazed him to think he could ever have responded to Lily with this one around. She brought several pithy *F* words to mind, and she brought them to mind all at once. *Fire* and *fear, female* and the holiest of holies, *fuck*. As in great.

If there hadn't been a little kid sharing this pitch-black space with them, Jack would have been tempted mightily by the idea of a religious experience. But maybe it was fortunate that he couldn't, because like alcohol, she'd damned near killed him when he'd succumbed before. If being with any female was painful, being with this one was agony. Besides, there *was* a little kid sharing this pitch-black space with them, and she'd suddenly gone very quiet.

"Gus, it's just me," he told her. "It's Jack. Take it easy."

"Take it easy!" she gasped as he freed her mouth. "You sonovabit—"

He muzzled her again and glanced down at Bridget, whose white feathers were the only thing that could be seen in the darkness. "I think we scared her pretty good."

Bridget's giggle was a little nervous this time.

"It's a joke, Gus," Jack said, struggling to hold her still while he spoke to her soothingly. "Bridget and I were just having some fun."

"Bridget?" she mumbled through his fingers.

"Yeah, it's me, Gus-buster," the little girl said. "I'm in here, too. Jack and I were playing a joke."

Jack lifted his hand off Gus's mouth, ready to clamp down again if he had to. She didn't scream, but he could hear the anger flaring in her breathing. He was surprised he couldn't see fire coming through her nostrils. The tiny room smelled of fear and steam heat and bath powder. It was filled with the essence of two females, both of them brats, and both of them doing their damndest to steal his heart.

"Just having some fun," he repeated.

"We were trying to scare you," Bridget explained, apparently much less certain of her plan now.

"Really?" Gus's voice was considerably strained. "Well, you did a good job. Now, if no one minds, could we get *out* of this mummy case?"

Jack was quick to acquiesce. He released her, slid the panel open, and stood back, letting the two of them pile out into the relative light of the alcove, where Gus set about to huff and puff and straighten her clothing. Bridget simply stared at her aunt thoughtfully, as if she were learning something new about women, and maybe even about life. When Gus had accomplished all she could, she crossed her arms over her breasts and glared at both of them.

"What are you two doing up at this time of night?"

"I couldn't sleep," Jack explained, perhaps not very convincingly. "I was hunting for the kitchen to fix myself a snack, some of that great lasagna Frances served for dinner. Too bad you weren't there," he added, hoping to push her guilt button and distract her. He knew she didn't like being away from Bridget, but the business meetings for her magazine had kept her away until well after the child's bedtime.

"Yeah, Gus," Bridget chimed in. "Jack and I both had two helpings."

"Really, did you?" She smiled at Bridget, but her gaze darted back to Jack quickly enough to let him know she wasn't happy with him. Not one bit.

For his part, Jack was wondering whether or not Bridget was going to play along. He had no idea how long the little girl had been stalking him tonight, but surely she'd seen some of what he'd been doing. If so, she could blow his cover with a couple of words.

He looked down at her just as she glanced up, wide-eyed.

"Did you know," she said softly, "that Gelsey fought with Misha all the time, but it was mostly because she was in love with him and was afraid he didn't love her back? Did you know that, Jack?"

"Gelsey?" Jack said, confused.

"*Bridget—*" Gus's voice held an ominous warning. "Back to bed," she said, holding out her hand to her niece. "Come on now."

The look Gus flashed him held a warning, too. Don't encourage her, it said. She's a romantic child, in love with love, the romance of the ballet, and silly childish things. *Don't encourage her.*

As she led Bridget off down the hall, Jack was aware that the little girl looked very young and not imperious at all. Like any kid, she wanted two loving parents and a stable life, he realized. She wanted her aunt Gus with a man.

"Night." Bridget glanced at Jack over her shoulder. Her feathered and sequined tail wagged good-bye to him as she trotted off, the tissue paper he'd seen flitting through the dark.

Before she turned away, he winked at her as if to say he would keep her secret if she'd keep his.

CHAPTER
20

IT WAS THE CHURCH HE'D BEEN MARRIED IN.

It was the aisle his bride had walked down, clasping her delicate bouquet of blush roses and baby's breath in one hand, her father's arm with the other. Rain had pommeled the church's roof and flooded its basement that Saturday afternoon, beating away the sunshine and enveloping St. Andrew's in pervasive gloom. But she'd lit up the chapel with her love. He'd never seen such radiance before. Gentle and eager, worshipful of him, her husband-to-be, the love must have sung through her veins with the same warm intensity as her Irish blood.

Maggie Donovan, soon to be Maggie Culhane.

Jack hadn't understood the force of her adoration, or why she'd chosen him to bestow it upon. He'd done nothing to be worthy. But that day, as he watched her take what felt like a lifetime to come and stand at his side, he vowed that he would spend the rest of his days struggling to be worthy. He would live up to all her expectations. He would be the hero she believed he was.

But that was yesterday. Today the church was flooded with sunshine. The stained-glass windows, inset with winged angels, were golden and glorious. But Jack's heart was pierced with gloom. His footsteps dragged with the raw agony of his journey.

Today *he* was the one walking down the aisle. Awaiting him at the pulpit was an open casket of rich mahogany, wreathed in the blood of dark red roses and the silence of verdant green ferns. Kidnappers had taken his only child, Haley, his six-month-old baby girl. When he wouldn't submit to their demands, they'd carried out their threats and brutally killed her.

Maggie's family turned to look at him as he walked, their eyes full of naked pain and confusion. How could you let this happen? they seemed to be asking. Why didn't you do something? But his own family's censure was the whip that flayed him. The mother and father who'd never known quite what to think of him were now unequivocal in their reproach. He had gambled with his child's life and lost. They were ashamed of him, their misbegotten issue, unwilling even to look at him.

"No!" The word resounded like a thunderbreak.

Suddenly it was a different church and a different day and Jack was bursting through the doors, running down the center aisle, frantic. There was a casket at the end, but the body lying inside was not his baby daughter . . .

It was his wife, Maggie. Maggie!

Dressed all in white, she resembled a bloodstained angel. Her wrists were brutally slashed and oozing crimson life, an atonement for the unforgivable sins of mankind, for his sins as well as her own. For he and Maggie had a terrible secret, one he had never been able to bring himself to tell anyone, a secret only the kidnappers knew. And though his wife had taken her own life, Jack knew it was more than grief at losing her baby that had killed her.

"No!" he screamed.

Jack jerked awake with such force it brought him half out of the small bed. He was soaked in sweat, one foot on the floor, and clenching a wad of sheet in his hand when he realized someone was in the room with him. He glanced up groggily. Gus stood at the end of his bed, her fingers curled around the brass bars of the footrail, her face haunted with concern. She was wearing the boxers and tank top, only now, crowded by her arms, her breasts were full and bursting. Pink flesh and ruby nipples strained the thin material, making him wish that she was a dream, that he could wake up from her, too.

"What was it, a nightmare?" she asked.

He shook his head, trying to clear the cobwebs. His skull was pounding. His heart was pounding, and she was the last thing he wanted to see right now. He was in no mood, no mood at all.

There was a light by the bed that could be turned on by a switch just inside the doorway. Apparently she'd done so when she'd entered, because the room glowed with her presence. He was also vaguely aware that he was naked beneath the sheet and that the half of him that had made contact with the floor was exposed.

"What arc you doing here?" he asked her.

"I couldn't sleep, either. Guess it's catching. I thought you might still be awake, too, and we could . . . talk. But then I heard you sh-shouting—"

He caught the hesitancy in her voice and honed in on her face, her lips, her breathy struggle. There was a vulnerability in her expression he wasn't used to seeing. Apparently she'd been frightened for him and let down her guard. Gus Featherstone to the rescue. His chest tightened at the irony.

"Go away," he said abruptly.

Her chin lifted as if she'd been tagged, and it surprised him how little he cared, what a rage of guilt and grief he was in, and how much he wanted to lash out. "Get out of here," he said again, harsher this time, glaring at her.

The stricken look in her eyes had nothing to do with him, he told himself. She carried a chip on her shoulder that dared people to reject her. When she turned on the "brat" persona, it was to test and torment people, to see how much of her shit they'd tolerate. Jack had no idea what it took to

pass her test, nor did he care. She was too fucking complicated for him. He wasn't here to forge a relationship with
her. He was here to find the bastards who destroyed his
family. He was here to wash the blood from his hands and
to cauterize the wound. Guilt had carved him up, it had torn
his heart into bloody chunks!

"You're sure?" Her voice dropped, even softer and more
hesitant than before. "I could . . . stay, we could t-talk.
Whatever it is, talking might help—"

He was amazed that she had the guts to try again. He
must look like a bloody wreck to have elicited this much
concern from her. She wasn't the type to extend herself
emotionally, except perhaps to Bridget. Down deep she expected rejection, so she rejected first. She inflicted the hurt,
thinking it would spare her from being hurt.

Not this time, he thought. Whatever he felt for her at this
moment, it wasn't empathy. Quite the opposite. There was
a part of him that wanted to hurt her. And if that's what it
took to get her out of his room, so be it. If he let her stay
she would ask questions and probe into the pain. Women
were never satisfied until they had you bleeding all over the
place.

"Talk to you?" he said contemptuously. "The magazine
mogul? The bitch-goddess of the catwalk? That would be a
little like a fly confessing to a black widow, wouldn't it?"

She stared at her hands as if determined to hang on to her
composure. He could see her cheek muscle flex and her
throat tighten as she swallowed. It took her a moment to
summon whatever it was she needed, but when she lifted
her head again, she was proud and wary. Her guard was up,
but it didn't quite hide the wounds.

His fist tightened on the wadded sheets, soaking them in
cold, angry sweat. He was pleased that he'd hit his mark.
The sharp taste of triumph sweetened his victory, because
for an instant the hurt in her eyes had distracted him from
his own.

She had looked at him as if he were a traitor, as if he had
just shattered her one last pathetic illusion and thereby vali-
dated all the rotten things she had ever believed about

mankind. That's me, he thought. Jack the Ripper. Bring me your tired, your hungry, your homeless, and I'll tear the last bit of hope from their hearts. . . .

He didn't watch her leave, but he heard the door shut, and on the heels of that sad, desolate sound came an emptiness unlike anything he'd ever experienced before. It made no sense to him that his reaction could be this profound, but he'd never felt so alone, not even after losing everything he loved. Then he'd had all those black emotions to sustain him, all that rage to fuel him. Now he had nothing. Now, in this one crazy, spinning moment, he was lost.

He swung off the bed, disgusted at himself and dragging the sheet along with him to cover himself. Lost? Christ! He barely knew the woman. What the hell was happening to him? It wasn't possible that he could feel anything real for a self-absorbed creature like Gus Featherstone. She was one of the enemy. Not only had she tried to kill him off to further her cause, but she was the exact opposite of the woman he'd been married to. Maggie was selfless and generous. It made no sense that he was obsessing over a homicidal fashion model, after someone like her. It made no sense that he was obsessing over any woman.

The satinwood carving of Gus that he'd started the night before was lying on the woven carpet where he'd left it. He gripped the sheet around him and picked up the figure gingerly, not wanting to have any contact with the parts that had felt so alive. But the breath curled tightly in his throat as he held her in his palm, and then his fingers did the same, curling over her curves as if he'd lost control of his reflexes. For several moments he couldn't do anything but watch himself touch her, and feel the desire rising in his groin like a flood.

Something hot cut into him. It stabbed low and deep, as violent as a bullet slicing through his flesh. He dropped the figure on the dresser, wondering if he was going crazy. He didn't even *like* the woman. The attraction was about sex— fucking—nothing more, and he'd long ago cut himself off from the dangers and pleasures of that distraction.

Never let personal feelings contaminate the work.

Jesus, he thought, wanting to laugh, wanting to shout. He'd gotten so caught up with Gus and the kid he'd almost forgotten what the work was. He was lying to himself. Sex was only part of the attraction. He *was* involved with her, with both of them. And now that he'd made that terrible mistake, now that he'd stolen fire, he would have to pay for it. There was no room for feelings in what he had to do. He couldn't afford to care about people who he might have to hurt, and in order not to care, he would have to hurt himself. He would have to cut the feelings out as if with a knife.

He lifted the pillow on his bed, exposing the gleaming lethal weapon he'd stashed there. He scooped it up, his hand closing over the ivory handle. The stainless steel blade glittered in the low light.

Cut clean, he thought. Cut strong.

The first sensation he felt upon awakening the next morning was paralysis. He couldn't move. Some weight was holding him down. He was still lying facedown and hungover from emotion, but as he tried to turn over, he realized the heaviness was down around his feet.

His normal reaction would have been laserlike. Had he been anywhere else he would have had a weapon at the intruder's throat by now. He wasn't sure why he was hesitating this time. Someone had had him under surveillance, and there'd been several attempts on his life, most, if not all, of them by his wife. His guard had been dangerously down ever since he'd met Gus Featherstone, yet some instinct other than self-preservation was telling him to cool it. Whatever was anchoring his ankles was too heavy for an animal and too light for a person, which made him more than a little curious.

He ducked his head around and got a glimpse of a feathery white tail. He'd been wrong. It was an animal . . . a swan.

"Did you sleep in that thing?" he asked, craning to look at the rest of her.

Bridget's slow headshake said, "Course not, silly you."

He propped himself up on his elbows and gazed at her askance. She'd straddled his ankles as if she were riding a pony; her knees were tucked beneath her and her little jaws were working furiously on what must have been a very large piece of gum.

"That would wreck the tail," she explained. "I mostly sleep in leotards. I have several pair."

"I'm relieved to hear it. Now if you'll remove yourself from my feet, I'd like to turn over."

"Oh, sorry. This bed is kind of small, and I got tired of waiting for you to wake up." She scooted off him and tucked herself, tail and all, into the corner where the brass footrail abutted the wall.

As she waited patiently for him to get his act together, she blew a huge pink bubble, then whipped it back into her mouth with a curl of her tongue. She was wearing the same white net tutu and satin slippers, but now there was an added flourish—a little headdress of white feathers to match her tail.

Sunlight poured through the window behind the bed, saturating the room with enough brightness to make him wince with pain. His neck felt as if it had been caught in a vise-grip, but he was more concerned that the sheet didn't drift off his butt and give his five-year-old niece-in-law a crash course in adult male anatomy. He made the transition gingerly—and only half successfully—but whatever she saw, it didn't seem to have done her any permanent damage.

Once he was on his back, he wrestled the rest of the sheet out from under him and propped the pillows behind his shoulders. "To what do I owe the honor?" he asked, wondering if she'd pick up on his sardonicism.

Her wrinkled nose told him she hadn't. Thank God there were still some things five-year-olds didn't "get."

"Why are you here?" he asked, rephrasing.

"Oh, I just wanted to interview you."

"For the *L.A. Times*?"

"No," she said, perfectly serious, "for my diary. I was

wondering about the spelling of your name, and . . . some other stuff."

Why wasn't he surprised? She had many things in common with her aunt, including a morbid curiosity about him. "What other stuff?"

Seeming pleased that he was going along with her plan, she snuggled into her corner and blew another bubble as if this were just what she had in mind—a long, cozy talk. "Well, I'm really curious about this one thing. It's personal but . . . ummm . . . how did you and Gus fall in love?"

The muscles in his jaw seemed to have become snarled. They ached fiercely when he spoke. "That's quite a story."

"Oh, good! My most favorite ballet in the world is *Swan Lake,* as you can probably see." She fluffed the skirt of her tutu. "Sigfried, the prince, falls madly in love with Odette, the Swan Queen, when he goes to a lake to go duck hunting, and she's there, floating on the water. She's not exactly a duck—she's a swan, because she was enchanted by a magician—so Sigfried doesn't shoot her, but he does fall in love with her. Was it anything like that with you and Gus?"

Jack had one eye closed, and he was wishing his head didn't ache so badly, that he had a cup of coffee, and that she was a tad less talkative. "Yeah," he said, wondering how anyone, even a five-year-old, could think the situation between him and Gus was remotely like some ballet about enchanted swans and duck hunting. "It was exactly like that."

She clasped her hands together, clearly excited. "I was going to change and wear my *Sleeping Beauty* outfit tomorrow, but maybe I'll wear this one again. My most favorite scene in *Swan Lake* is the pas de deux between Sigfried and Odette. Do you know what that means? Pas de deux? That's where they dance together like they're married. Anyway, I like the one where she warns him there's danger, but he takes her in his arms anyway, and she looks at him with love in her eyes. Cool, huh? I saw Gus look at you that way once, with love in her eyes."

Jack's head was throbbing by this time, but she had no mercy, this kid. Serious now, she uncurled and rearranged herself Indian powwow style. She bent forward, peering at him, hard at work on the bubble gum. "Do you and Gus do the wild thing?"

He opened his mouth, but nothing came out. His throat felt like something had rubbed it raw. The wild thing? Did they let a five-year-old watch MTV? Only belatedly did he register what she'd said in the midst of all the ballet babble. *I saw Gus look at you that way once, with love in her eyes.* Even more belatedly he realized why his throat felt like used sandpaper. He wanted that. He wanted Gus to look at him that way.

He dropped his head and a wretched groan welled in his throat. Sweet Jesus! He'd dealt with monsters in his life— thugs, thieves, assassins, *and* the government. He'd been intensively trained in the black arts of combat and intelligence, almost from the cradle. He'd lived by a rigorous code of discipline and detachment. He was a fucking killing machine by military standards, but he was helpless against this kid. He'd been brought down by one sentence from a five-year-old!

The groan in his throat became an obscenity, burning, fizzing, and finally escaping under his breath as he realized that nothing he'd done last night in the mortal battle against his own emotions had worked. *Nothing.* Even the ritual of the knife had failed. He wasn't just contaminated, he was useless.

"I guess that means you have done it?" She inquired more tentatively now, apparently aware she'd struck a nerve. "Was it that bad?"

He was saved from trying to explain by a deafening racket outside the door in the hallway. Much unintelligible shouting and footsteps preceded someone's calling out Bridget's name. It didn't sound like Frances.

"Shhhhh," Jack said, putting a finger to his lips.

"I'm in here!" Bridget yelled back. "That's Gus," she informed Jack, beaming. "I figured you'd want to see her since you guys don't share a room—How come you don't?"

The bedroom door creaked open tentatively, and Gus's head poked through. "Bridget . . . ? Are you in here?"

"Hi, Gus-buster! Jack was just telling me how you guys fell in love and why you don't sleep together."

"He was *what*?" The door rolled open and Mother Gus stood on the threshold, her eyes rotating like Robocop's. Jack was waiting for her arms to rise and guns to start blazing.

"Bridget," Gus said, clearly struggling to control herself as she entered the room. "Frances has breakfast ready, dear. Go on down and save me a bagel, okay? Make it blueberry."

"But I'm not hungry—"

"Bridget, go down to breakfast, *dear*. It's the most important meal of the day."

"Not yet! Jack was just going to tell me how you and he—"

"March, Odette!" Gus boomed, cutting her off. "I need to talk to Prince Sigfried, here."

Tears welled in the little girl's eyes. She swiped at them furiously as she knee-walked her way across the foot of the bed. She snuck a quick look at Jack and grumbled, "She ruins everything, doesn't she?"

He shrugged, coward that he was, but his sympathies were entirely with the kid. Once Bridget had trounced out the door, her tail tilting precariously, Gus turned her guns on him again.

"What were you telling her?"

Normally he would have taken his time answering for no better reason than having the pleasure of driving her nuts, but this morning he was totally legit in wanting to delay this little confrontation. He had reasons out the door, the first one being the way his pulse was pounding. The second being that his professional code of conduct had been seriously compromised and he no longer trusted himself. The third being that he couldn't take his eyes off of her stubbornly crossed arms, her ruby-tipped breasts, her flushed throat, her face.

Why the hell did she have to run around in her underwear? First chance he got he was going to steal that skimpy little outfit and burn it! But more than her outfit or her fire-cracker-hot body, he was looking for that one thing Bridget had led him to believe would be brimming in her eyes. All he could see was fury.

"I didn't tell her anything," he said, shifting around to sit up. "She wants to believe we fell in love like Sigfried and Odette, so I let her think it happened that way. You didn't want me to tell her the truth, did you?"

"Well, no, but I don't want her to think we're madly in love, either. That will only confuse her." She hesitated a moment, seemingly oblivious to the sensuality of what she was doing. She'd captured a tendril of the dark hair that had escaped from her ponytail and was absently rubbing it against her cheek. "I can't imagine where she got that idea."

The room got very quiet as Jack contemplated the wisdom of telling her. Several seconds thundered by before he spoke. "I think she got the idea from you."

"From me?"

"From the way you look at me."

She tilted her head, a startled question on her lips.

Jack tried for insouciance, but couldn't manage it. Instead his throat thickened and the words came out grainy. "With love in your eyes."

He feared for the roof. The way she gasped, he thought she was going to blow it off. Her spine stiffened and her eyes widened in horror. "That's disgusting!" she cried. "I've never looked at you that way. Never! If I were s-starving and you were my favorite food, I wouldn't look at you that w-way!"

It was all he could do not to laugh. She was so flustered she couldn't get the words out straight. Of course, she often didn't get words out straight. But she was actually blush-ing, a sight he never thought he'd see. Her cheeks were as hot pink as her nails, and her upper lip was damp with sweat. She'd embarrassed the hell out of him a few times, and he'd always wondered what it would take to make this woman blush. He'd never figured it would be the *L* word.

"What *is* your favorite food?" he asked.

"Not you! I'm going to straighten that child out immediately." She swung around to leave, and he bounded out of the bed after her, trailing sheets and blankets behind him as he overtook her.

"Let go of me!" she said, batting his hand away as he tried to grab her arm.

"What are you going to do?" He whipped around in front of her to shield the door. He was holding the sheet in front of his genitals and feeling like a bad imitation of a Greek statue. The hardwood floor was so slippery he'd had trouble getting traction, even with bare feet, and the cold doorknob was getting fresh with his bare backside.

Wisps of dark hair flew about her face. The tendril she'd been playing with was caught in her eyelashes. She swatted it away and glared at him. "I'm going to talk to Bridget. She has the wrong idea about us."

"She's just a kid, Gus, a romantic little kid."

"But I can't have her thinking—"

"Thinking what, that you're in love with me?"

She looked away, and he became aware of her breathing, the lift of her shoulders, the movement of her breasts beneath her clothing. She was angry and hurt, especially after the things he'd said last night, but something hidden in her eyes had struck him to the core. It had only flared for a moment, that naked and sweet emotion. Words defied him, but if he had to give it a name, he would have called it *yearning* . . . the yearning of an exotic creature with huge violet eyes, peeking out at the world from behind a veil . . . harem eyes.

"Why not?" he asked. "What would it hurt if she thought we were like the lovers in the ballet?"

"Because it's not true."

She was denying that there was anything between them, and he should have agreed with her, let it go. He had as much reason as she did to want to establish distance. *More.* But he couldn't. His pulse rate was telling him different. "It's not *un*true, either, is it? Bridget told me about a dance they did. She called it a pas de deux, but it sounded a whole lot like foreplay to me. Isn't that what we've been doing, Gus, a mating dance?"

She still refused to look at him. "Let me out of here," she insisted, her voice weak.

He pressed the door shut with his shoulders. The click of the latch bolt sent a shudder through her. "We need to talk," he said.

"About what?"

"About last night . . . the things I said."

That brought her head up. Now her huge violet eyes were searching his, and they were still full of hurt. She couldn't hide it. She was susceptible to him. He had hurt her. *Why did that fill him with such bittersweet pleasure? Why would knowing that he could affect her that way, that he could bring pain to her eyes, make him suddenly want her so badly?*

He swallowed back the fire that was burning his throat. This wasn't going to be an apology, he told himself, just a statement of fact. "My head was all screwed up," he admitted. "I'd had a bad dream about something that happened in the past, something I've never come to terms with, and I was pretty wasted when you came in the door."

She turned away from him and went to the small alcove where the window seat looked out on the landscaped lawn below and the hills in the distance. The streaming sunshine danced golden light over her pensive profile. "I could hear you out in the hallway," she said. "You were calling out a woman's name, Maggie."

He was glad she wasn't looking at him, glad she couldn't see the grief that raged through him. "Maggie was my wife. She's dead."

The silence seemed to stretch forever, as if both of them were coming to grips with his statement. "Is that why you're here?" she asked after a moment. "Does it have something to do with what happened to her?"

It surprised him that he almost wanted to tell her. The impulse was strong. He had shared this story with no one, and the longer he carried it alone, the heavier a burden it became. But his investigation had led him to her family, and he was reasonably sure that one or more of them was involved, possibly even her. Until he knew who it was, he couldn't trust anyone.

"Maybe I'm here because of you," he said, changing the subject. He wanted to go back to that other topic, the one where they were discussing the love in her eyes, but any mention of his past brought with it certain grim realities. "You brought me into your life when you decided to fake your own kidnapping. I'd like to know why you did that, if it's not too much trouble. And why you picked me."

"I didn't pick you."

"Someone did. Someone chose me to kidnap you. I assume it was your boyfriend, Rob."

"I have no idea how Rob chose you," she said, but the way she glanced at him and then looked away, he wondered. "He told me he'd take care of it. I assume he had some contacts who recommended you. He didn't put an ad in the paper, I can tell you that much."

"Pretty desperate, hiring a stranger to kidnap you. Pretty dangerous, too."

The quick nod of her head surprised him. Dark hair tumbled around her face and she combed the silky strands back with her fingers. "I had to do something desperate," she admitted, still staring fixedly out the window. "I'd done everything but threaten a lawsuit to get access to my trust fund. That would have been next if I hadn't thought of the kidnapping."

"McHenry wouldn't give you access to your own money?"

"The first condition of the trust was that I wasn't to have access to the principal until I was thirty-five, and the only way to override that was to fulfill the second condition, which had to do with demonstrating vision, moral fiber, and all that other good stuff that Lake, Sr., went on and on about—the old hypocrite."

Her fingers were still entangled in her hair, still trying to bring order. She seemed distressed about something, and he had the distinct feeling she was trying to avoid him. "Ward McHenry runs Featherstone Enterprises *and* this family," she said. "He thought launching a magazine was too big a risk and that I was too inexperienced and irresponsible to run one. The family agreed. I had to convince them otherwise."

And well she did, he thought.

She turned back to the room, to him, although her gaze only stayed with him a moment. She glanced around as if she were looking for something she'd lost. Her gaze fluttered about, then halted on an object propped up against the mirror of his dresser. Jack murmured a mental expletive when he saw that she'd spotted his carving of her.

She walked to the uncompleted figure, studying it. After a moment she turned to him and searched his features. A glimmer of recognition flared, brilliant as she found the answer she was looking for in his eyes. So it is me, she seemed to be saying. It is *me* you want, no matter how much you say otherwise.

"Maybe Bridget got it wrong," she whispered. "Maybe you're the one who's in love."

He didn't know how to answer that. He was just damn glad he hadn't blushed.

CHAPTER
21

GUS LET HERSELF OUT OF THE TAXI AND IMMEDIATELY glanced over her shoulder. She couldn't shake the feeling that someone was staring at her, one of those prickly sensations that comes over you suddenly when you realize you're being watched. As the cab sped off, she stepped up on the curb and took another look down the side street in the direction they'd just come.

The most alarming thing she saw was a street person relieving himself in a recessed doorway. Still, she couldn't relax until she'd taken a complete turn and made a thorough visual search of the quiet business area. No one was lurking in the shadows, spying on Gus Featherstone with binoculars, she told herself firmly. It was just one more weekday evening in the city of the angels. The worker bees had gone home, or they were celebrating their freedom in one of the crowded, popular watering holes.

Gus might liked to have joined them, but she had nothing to celebrate, at least not yet. In a few short hours she would either be euphoric or in despair, but that would all depend on tonight's mission. Everything depended on that.

A brisk walk three doors down took her to Cezanne, the restaurant she'd chosen for her campaign. One short flight of dangerously steep cement steps below street level, and she was adrift in the heyday of the French impressionist. Claret-red brocade walls were hung with prints of the artist's work and linen scrolls chronicled his life and painterly influences. The featured wine was French Tavel, a pungent vin rosé reputed to be the same vivid pink that Cezanne would have painted an onion, had he ever had the urge to paint such a vegetable.

The restaurant's reputation for discretion made it a popular haunt for business liaisons. The cavernlike quiet and lambent gold wall sconces evoked the wine cellars of elegant French turn-of-the-century chateaux. Rosewood booths lining the walls of the dining room were the equivalent of intimate conference chambers, and many a fabulous deal was rumored to have been cut within their confines.

Gus had reserved one of Cezanne's chambers in the hopes of cutting just such a deal. She'd also worn her carbon-black Donna Karan power suit and lit money-green candles to the gods of Mammon. This meeting was about the financing she needed for the launch of her magazine.

Moments later, literally on the edge of her seat in the booth, she steepled her hands and brought them to the liquid sparkle of her cherry-red lips. *Please God,* she thought, imbuing the words with all the intensity she could muster, which was considerable, *just this once, give me what I truly want. What I've always wanted. Please.*

She'd arrived alone and well ahead of her companion to be sure their booth wasn't in a heavily traveled area. She'd also insisted on a single freshly cut stalk of white orchids in the crystal bud vase and pure artesian springwater for the goblets, rather than the Perrier the restaurant usually served. And then, straining the maître d's celebrated patience even further, she'd politely declined the signature Tavel in favor of champagne. In fact, she'd ordered her favorite drink, a Bellini, a luscious mix of champagne and peach nectar.

She hadn't yet revealed the identity of the potential investor to anyone, including Rob and the magazine staff, because she didn't want to raise false hopes or compromise the investor in any way. She was also superstitious. She'd always felt too much talk about a deal could jinx it. For so many reasons, *ATTITUDE* was the most important thing she'd ever done in her life. She would never forgive herself if she lost it through some foolish blunder.

Lifting the tangy sweetness of the Bellini to her lips, she held the flute there for a moment and sighed, then set it down without drinking. Was the linen tablecloth all right? Was that a yellow spot in the corner or just a trick of the lights? It looked like a food stain, probably something with gourmet mustard. Suddenly she was searching the entire milky white cloth, looking for spots. Maybe there was time to call a waiter and have him change—

She flattened her palms on the tablecloth as if putting on the brakes. Enough, she told herself. Everything was as perfect as she could make it. There was nothing left to do now but compose herself and wait for her dinner companion. Nerves. What would people think if they knew Gus Featherstone's legendary "brat" behavior was mostly bogus? She still couldn't shake the feeling that someone was hovering, watching her, but she would have been a wreck tonight regardless. The majority of her noisier conniptions had appeared to be triggered by others' failings, but they were really about keeping her own insecurities at bay and warding off crippling attacks of nerves. Surely people would understand if they knew. They forgave Barbra Streisand, didn't they?

A shadow darted through Gus's field of vision.

She glanced up and gave out a sharp little cry, astonished as her ex-fiancé slipped into the booth opposite her without a word of explanation. Rob Emory was the last person she was expecting to see. He was wearing a dark trench coat and glaring at her with the intensity of a jealous husband who'd caught his wife red-handed.

"R-Rob?" How could he have known where she was going? She'd told no one. He must have had her followed, and perhaps even before tonight, which would explain the uneasiness she'd been feeling for the last several days. She'd written it off as stress, but had found herself scrutinizing the people on the elevator with her that morning, trying to decide if the man with the RayBan Aviators had a sinister look, or if she was imagining it.

"What's going on, Gus?" His voice was hushed, his eyes hot as he searched her face, her hairdo, her outfit.

She was not totally unsympathetic to his desperation. The mess with Jack Culhane seemed to have turned a perfectly nice man into an obsessed stalker. Rob wasn't himself lately, and she could hardly blame him, but there was too much at stake to indulge him in such crazy behavior. She'd been so upset with his bombshell at the brainstorming session, she'd confronted him afterward, and they'd argued. She hadn't spoken with him since, but this stunt was too much. He had to understand that his paranoia was damaging their relationship and possibly the magazine.

"I could ask you the same question, Rob," she said, lowering her voice. "What are you doing here?"

He reached across the table and helped himself to her drink, downing half of the flute in one gulp. "I've been trying for days to beg, borrow, or steal a goddamn minute of your time, Gus, but you haven't had *any* time for me, not even that much."

There was some truth to that, she admitted. He'd left messages on her machine at home, and when she hadn't returned them, he'd called Frances to find out where she was. He'd also come by the bank building on Wilshire, where she and the magazine staff were setting up their offices, but she'd always been involved with her people, potential advertisers or whoever else might be there. It had been chaotic. There hadn't been time, and to be fair, she hadn't been inclined to make any.

"I'm sorry, Rob, but I'm meeting someone for dinner. Maybe I could come by your place afterward, and we could talk."

"Meeting who?" He finished the rest of her drink, but didn't set the flute down. Instead he rocked it in his hand, leaning toward her aggressively, as he talked. "And since when do you make dinner appointments without telling me?"

Her backbone jutted against the brocade contours of the upholstery. "I've never cleared my dinner appointments through you."

"Cleared them, no. But we've always let each other know when we had plans with others. It's a courtesy between people who have a commitment."

"Rob, things are different now. I'm committed to Jack Culhane, or at least the rest of the world thinks so, and I have to play along."

A waiter appeared, hovering, trying to gauge whether or not it was appropriate to approach. Rob waved him away. "Why the hell aren't you taking steps to have the marriage annulled?" he asked. "Or at least to find out if it's legal? Have you even consulted an attorney?"

"I would prefer not to have Culhane act on his blackmail threat and destroy everything I've worked for. Is that so hard to understand?"

"Everything *we've* worked for, Gus. You and I, together, a team, partners. That's what we were until recently." He fell back against the seat so heavily that several locks of his dark, slicked-back hair spilled onto his face. "Where's it going from here? What's happening to us?"

"I don't know," she said honestly, aware of the powerfully spicy scent of his cologne and his dishevelment. His tie was undone and he didn't appear to have shaved, now that she could see him. She had every reason to be angry at him. He'd crashed her dinner meeting tonight, demoralized her staff with his announcement, and his reckless attempt to unmask Jack as the art thief had not only backfired, it could have been their undoing if Jack had decided to retaliate. She really didn't understand what was happening to her and Rob. He'd been a symbol of security in her life, the one person she could count on. Now he felt like her adversary, a loose cannon who was no longer thinking about the two of them. He was thinking only about himself and what he might lose. Or had he already lost it?

She didn't realize that she'd been madly tapping her nails against the table until he grasped her hand. His fingers closed around hers, gripping them too tightly. She caught her breath it was so painful.

"Is it him you're meeting?" he asked. "Is that what this private booth is all about? Gus, please, tell me you're not getting yourself emotionally involved with that bastard. He's a blackmailer. An ex-convict!"

She pulled her hand free and cupped it, massaging the blood back into her aching fingers. "This private booth is about *privacy*. I have a business dinner scheduled, and he'll be here any minute. It's for the magazine, Rob. Please, don't do this. Don't embarrass us both."

He moved quickly then, sliding to the side of the booth and flashing up from the table. His hand came up so suddenly, she flinched back, then realized he was only yanking his coat into place.

"If you think you're patting me on the head and pushing me out the door, think again," he warned. "I've already invested two years of my life in you, in your career, and in this magazine of yours. I'm not walking away from this with nothing. I want my fair share."

She felt as if he *had* struck her. "Is that what this is about then? Your fair share?"

"Yes, it is. My fair share of the magazine. And you. I want both."

What her intuition had told her was true, she realized. He was the one following her—or having her followed. And he *was* her adversary. She and Rob had made no formal plans to divide the proceeds from the magazine. Given the profitability of most new magazines, they'd assumed there would be nothing to divvy up for several years. All their energy had been focused on finding the truly staggering amount of start-up money it would take. Clearly things had changed.

"Don't worry, Rob," she told him. "I'll see that you get

whatever's coming to you. I don't want to cheat you of anything. But your 'fair share' doesn't include me."

He said nothing to that, simply turned on his heel and stormed through the restaurant toward the door. As Gus stared at the billowing darkness of his coat, she saw a figure in her peripheral vision and realized something that sent a frisson of surprise through her. The sensation was hot and sharp, like two wires touching together, sparks flying. The man she'd been waiting for, her potential investor, was sitting at the bar. His drink was half gone, and it was quite evident he'd been there for some time.

His steady gaze told her he'd seen, and perhaps heard, everything that had happened. The questions in his eyes told her that he would be factoring this new information into his decision. Somehow that didn't surprise her. She'd had enough dealings with him already to know that he missed nothing. She also knew that he was dangerous in ways that had nothing to do with their potential business arrangement, and that the price he would extract for his investment, should he make one, might be considerably more than she could afford.

It was nearly midnight when Gus returned to the mansion. She ought to have been exhausted, but she was still too much on edge. The dinner had ended without a deal in place, and as if that weren't depressing enough, she'd spent the taxi trip home looking over her shoulder and wondering why she couldn't shake the feeling of some unseen presence. Her childhood had been haunted by night terrors and shadow people, and the encounter with Rob had undoubtedly triggered those early fears, but the awareness did little to calm her.

It was to be a night of surprises, she realized as she quietly let herself into the house. A bouquet of flowers had been arranged in a crystal and silver Victorian vase, and they were sitting on the mahogany console and mirror in the foyer, several dozens of them, the fattest and most splendid rosebuds she'd ever seen. They were so perfect they didn't look real. They seemed cut of velvet-lined satin, with a nap that was rich, rouge-red, and plush.

Rob? she wondered. Had he come to his senses and realized the impossible bind she was in? Relief swept her. As angry as she was, she did care about him, perhaps even more than she'd realized. She flopped her briefcase on the console and bent to smell one of the plumpest blooms. Another possibility occurred to her as she drank in perfume so rich and deep it filled her nostrils with a pleasant burning sensation. Perhaps the dinner meeting had gone better than she'd dreamed and these roses were from her anonymous investor.

Eagerly she took the card from its holder, pulled the note from the engraved envelope and read it. Her soft gasp echoed in the marbled silence of the foyer.

There were only two typed words: BITE ME.

A postscript at the bottom said: "If you're hungry, come to the tack room."

Gus wasn't hungry in the slightest, but she was burning with curiosity. She was wary, too, as she ought to have been after the evening she'd had, but curiosity won easily. If Rob was waiting for her in the stables, he should have let her know in a less cryptic way. As it was she couldn't not respond, or he'd be spending the night with English saddles and riding crops. And if it wasn't Rob, then it had to be Jack, though she couldn't imagine such an extravagant gesture from him. *Bite me?* That was Bridget's favorite line, but Jack was the only man she'd ever bitten, so to speak. She explored the textured surface of the card with her thumb, a flush of confusion heating the softness beneath her chin. Who in the world?

The tack room had a weathered Dutch door, the top half of which was hanging open as Gus approached it moments later. The evening's balmy summer breezes had already turned unusually chilly and damp, and the patchy grass beneath her feet was soggy with moisture and sharply redolent of peat moss.

She was glad she had on a suit jacket as she picked her way through the darkness in her high-heeled pumps. If only she'd been able to find a flashlight. Even a thin beam of light would have helped to allay the gooseflesh and the shivery fears that were rising inside her.

She stepped gingerly onto the mossy stoop of broken bricks and hesitated, trying to get a look inside the room before entering. The chill made her clutch her arms, and no matter which way she angled her head, her own shadow prevented her from seeing what the open hatch might have illuminated. As she glanced around, trying not to stumble or break a heel, she realized the exterior light above the stable doors was out. It usually burned all night.

At least open the door, Gus, she told herself. *Open the door and get ready to run.*

The hatch creaked and swung free when she lifted the iron bar, which forced her to step around it. Moonlight cast a faint shadow, her own, against the far wall. Otherwise, the room appeared empty. Caution told her to shut the doors, bolt them, and go back to the house, but she never could leave a riddle unsolved. Her brain wasn't wired that way. Curiosity, she decided, might be her worst failing.

"Anyone there?" she asked, straining to make out details.

No one answered, and finally, still clutching her arms, she stepped down into the thick gloom. The place smelled strongly of old leather and saddle soap. Alfalfa, sweet and damp, mingled with the pungency of horse droppings from the stables next door.

A shadow flared against the far wall, engulfing hers.

"Who's *there?*" Panic sent her stumbling backward for the door. The high heels made her clumsy.

She barely had the words out before someone caught her by the arms, spun her around, and forced her to the wall, face-first. A brawny forearm, obviously male, anchored her shoulders. Fear rose up in her throat, gagging her. It gripped her like fists and held her even more roughly than her assailant was doing. This was the stuff of her childhood nightmares. Stupefying terror. She had to fight it off, or she wouldn't have a chance against him.

She made no attempt to resist him. Instead, she went very still, her breathing ragged. It took her a moment to get her bearings, but once she'd recovered her balance, she came to a quick and startling conclusion. She was being groped! The arm that had pinned her shoulders was her primary concern, but she was astonished and horrified to feel his other hand roving all over her, flying down her arms and snaking inside her jacket, fondling her butt, pulling up her skirt.

"Stop that!" she gasped, unable to move against him. "What are you doing?"

"Patting you down for weapons. Spread your legs."

She recognized the grainy masculine voice at once. It was the man who ground glass with his teeth. "I will not! I don't have any weapons."

"You think I'm going to take your word for that?" Jack Culhane muttered. "Somebody's trying to kill my ass! Excuse me, somebody *besides* you. My room's been searched, I'm under surveillance, and tonight I get a scribbled note that says come to the stables. So who shows up? My loving wife?"

"I got a note, too. From you! It came with roses."

"Roses? I never sent you a note *or roses.*"

"Why aren't I surprised?" She arched back against his arm, moaning with relief as he eased up on the pressure. She was still shaking from the roar of adrenaline through her system.

"Spread your legs, and I'll let you go," he said.

She had thought he was releasing her, and the shock of discovering that he wasn't filled her with mute outrage. Surely he didn't think she'd come here to kill him? That was absurd. He was just being perverse, torturing her. She kicked at him, missing repeatedly. Her aim was off. It was wild! When she finally did catch him in the shin with her high heel, she got herself shoved back up against the wall for her trouble.

"Simmer down," he said.

"Let me go!" The shrill demand backfired. He brought his knee to her backside and nudged it this way and that in a rough caress. The pressure was so suggestive it shocked her into silence for a moment. She was in a terribly vulnerable position, and the erotic quality of the attention he was applying made her all the more indignant, especially as he gently, but determinedly, tried to wedge his battering ram of a knee between her thighs and pry them open.

"You bastard," she breathed. "If you ruin my nylons I'll kill you!"

"Come on, Gus," he said, his mouth hot against the silky hair on her crown. "Spread 'em, babe. This will only take a minute. And when I'm done, you can search me if you want to."

"Only if I can take a riding crop to your naked flanks."

"No wonder horses run away with you, Ms. Lizzie Borden. I would, too, if you were riding me."

His knee was rocking against her private parts, and though she had no intention of letting him know that his show of brute force was in any way disconcerting, she was afraid of what her body might do if she let him continue. Nerve endings were fiendishly fickle things. They had a way of sparking and firing whether you wanted them to or not, and hers were already on overcharge. Her heart was kicking so hard the beat of it in her throat had begun to arouse her in perverse ways. She could feel the blood rushing from her head to destinations south, and her breasts were tingling as if they'd been exposed to the cold air. Why did he always have that damn, disgusting effect on her?

He'd frightened her so thoroughly her body didn't know which way to jump, and now he was confusing and exciting her circuits even further. They thought they were supposed to respond to what he was doing.

"All right," she said, opening her legs just enough to accommodate a hand. "Do it. Quickly."

She felt him press his entire body against her, but especially down there, his hip nudging hers, the fly of his jeans chafing at the side seam of her skirt. But it was his hand that claimed her attention as he slipped it under her ultra-slim mini.

His fingers skimmed lightly up the inside of her thighs like a spider over a web. They startled a telltale sound out of her as she braced herself for what was coming next. She closed her eyes and clenched her teeth, waiting . . . waiting for the moment of unbearable contact. That moment when he would touch her in quick, illicit, intimate ways, and she would begin to sweat through every pore. . . .

Her legs trembled and her nerves drew taut with expectation, but his hand didn't move. His fingers hovered at the apex of her legs until the tension felt as if it might pop like a tiny balloon.

"What are you doing?" she asked, her voice cracking.

"Savoring the moment . . . how about you?"

"Do it, you smartass cowboy, do it!"

"Do what?"

"You know! Get it over with . . . oh!" she cried, thinking he had touched her, thinking she'd felt the feather caress of his fingers in a tender place, and then just as quickly realizing that she hadn't. That he hadn't. Her face was burning! The exquisite tension, the heat and energy emanating from his body made it feel as if he were stroking her, and her nerves danced in anticipation. But in fact he was still tormenting her, forcing her to imagine his touch in vivid detail. Thrilling little clutches of sensation tantalized her.

"What do you want me to do?"

"N-nothing—" She got it out, but weakly.

Everything. Do everything to me. The forbidden answer flooded into her mind before she could smother it. It poured through her like steamy water, pooling in her breasts and her belly, swelling tissue and tightening the skin that lay over her flesh. She tingled deep inside. It was excitement, vibrant and alive. Excitement so vital it seemed to cry out for contact.

"Let me go," she said, fighting to keep her voice steady. "I want you to let me go."

His fingers swept from the space, grazing the silk of her pantyhose without ever really touching her, yet leaving her so sensitized it felt as if he were still there, as if he'd always been there, a dragonfly hovering between her braced legs, ready to sting.

"You're clean," he said, stepping away from her. "Too bad."

She knew one thing and one thing only. Somehow she had to get her heart steady, her legs working, and her rear end out of the place before he could think about stopping her. Without a word she yanked down her skirt and headed for the door, aware that something was wrong as she approached it. Both the top and bottom hatch were closed. She'd left them open, hadn't she?

She tried the top first, and when it wouldn't budge, she knew somehow that the bottom wouldn't either. They were trapped. Either the doors had jammed or someone had locked them in. Refusing to believe it, she summoned her strength and gave both doors a sharp push with the flat of her hands.

"What's the problem?" he asked.

She tried again, using her shoulder and shoving with all her might. She could only imagine what the moldy, slivery wood must be doing to her black suit! The doors held firm, and a sound of despair slipped out of her. "They're jammed!"

She pivoted, glaring at him, straining to make out his features in the darkness. "You did this!"

He threw up his arms. She could see that much.

"How could I have jammed the doors? I was in here with you." The floor groaned as he walked toward her, stepping over some worn cowboy boots and a saddle tree on his way.

He must have extraordinary night vision, she decided. He moved around like a cat, even though the room was rigged with hidden obstacles. "Then who did it?"

The thud of his body against old wood reverberated in the tiny room. Metal bridle bits clanged jarringly on their wall hooks as he tried the door again. "It's been barred from the outside," he said. "Somebody locked us in." He pivoted, searching the room. "There must be another way out of here."

"There is no way out," she announced with finality. "The room has no windows. We'd have to take an ax to the door."

"Isn't there an intercom in the stables?"

"Yes, but there isn't one in this room. There should be a light, though, on the wall behind you."

He found it after a bit of searching. She heard the hoarse squeak of a rusty chain being pulled and the saddles, bridles, and bits that hung on the walls suddenly materialized. The small, smoky globe didn't provide much light, and it wasn't terribly aesthetic, but at least they wouldn't be falling over each other.

"What did the note say that came with the flowers?" he asked. "That might tell us who set us up."

"My note?" She was reluctant to tell him, just as she was reluctant to mention anything that had happened that night, including the confrontation with Rob and the feeling that she was being watched. He hadn't yet convinced her that it wasn't him. Who else would go to so much trouble to trap them together? It was possible Rob had them both under surveillance, but she couldn't imagine why.

"You don't think we're being watched, do you?" she asked.

"Anything's possible." He performed an immediate search of the small room, inspecting the walls and door. When he was finished, he checked the saddles and riding gear, as if looking for bugs. "The place is clean," he pronounced at last. "What about that note? Who sent it?"

"The note was nothing, just a silly remark."

"So who sent the flowers?" he persisted.

She shrugged as if to put him off again, but the way he was staring at her made her uneasy. His gaze could quickly turn piercing, as she well knew, like diamonds drilling through rock. "I don't know who sent them."

He rested a fist on his hip. "You're not giving me much to go on here."

"Oh, all right." She sighed. "The note said 'Bite me.'"

"Come again?"

"You heard me." Unfortunately now she could see his expression better than she wanted to, and the smile that was lying in wait could only be described as wolfish. That and the hip-sprung pose made him look rather at home in this room of leather and silver, ropes and whips. His jeans were

faded out in the crotch, and they fit snug to his body, clinging to his thighs like well-worn buckskin gloves. His T-
shirt looked old and soft from many washings, and the thin
cotton material appeared fragile against the brawny curves
of his upper body.

"Who are you on 'bite me' terms with these days besides
me?" he wanted to know.

"You were the first one I thought of." That wasn't quite
true. The note's message had been playing through her
mind ever since he asked about it, and she had realized
there was someone else she was on those terms with, only
she couldn't quite believe what she was thinking. In fact,
her hunch was so preposterous she wanted to dismiss it out
of hand, especially since he seemed to have murder plots in
mind. Still, she could even imagine the person's motive.

"There is someone," she acknowledged softly, speaking
as much to herself as him. "Someone who has the words
'Bite me' immortalized in needlepoint on the wall of her
bedroom, right next to her print of Renoir's *The Young
Dancer.*

"Omigawd," she breathed. A smile startled soft laughter
out of her. She'd just realized she was right and was inordi-
nately proud of herself for figuring it out. "It's Bridget."

The hand on his hip lifted, signaling his disbelief.
"You're saying a five-year-old came up with this Machi-
avellian scheme? She sent you flowers and me a note, then
locked us in this room together?"

"Bridget does not have a five-year-old mind. This must
be her romantic idea of getting us together." The more Gus
thought about it, the more sense it made. Bridget had been
fascinated by the idea of her new stepuncle since Jack first
appeared. She'd been pestering both of them for days with
questions about their relationship. "This is probably a scene
from one of her ballets," she observed, more laughter bubbling. "Sigfried and Odette's pas de deux in the tack room."

The chuckle died in Gus's throat as she saw what Jack
was doing. He'd pulled a couple of saddles and a horse
blanket off the wall and laid them out on the floor in what

looked suspiciously like pillows on a bed. "What's that for?"

He stood back when he was done and held out a hand as if to say, "You first." The slight tilt of his mouth indicated that Mr. Quiet-but-Deadly had something other than getting a good night's rest on his mind. Apparently she wasn't the only one affected by that little pat down he'd performed.

"I'm sure Bridget's going to come to her senses," Gus said without a hint of conviction. "She'll let us out of here."

He just smiled. "After all the trouble she's gone to? Not a chance. Besides, you're right about the pas de deux. She described it to me. Let's see, I think she said it was 'a dance people do like they're *married*.' Yeah, those were her exact words as I remember. I wonder what she meant."

Gus had no idea what Bridget meant, but she knew exactly what he did. She was still pinging in places she would rather not think about and suddenly not as sure of her theory about Bridget. He seemed altogether too willing to make the most of this predicament to suit her. It was probably too far-fetched to think that he and her niece were co-conspirators, but she wouldn't have put it past either of them.

She understood Bridget's motives. He was the mystery. She'd been ejected from the shower and his bedroom, but he'd also carved her name in a tree and bandied the *L* word about. Either he was doing a masterful job of keeping her off balance, or their crazy relationship had deranged him as much as it had her. Whichever it was, she was playing it safe from here on out. He could have the deluxe accommodations all to himself. She wasn't getting anywhere near him tonight.

CHAPTER
22

GUS WOKE UP STIFF AND SHIVERING WITH COLD. SHE WAS SIT-
ting with her knees drawn up tight to her body, and her
head cradled between them. She'd fallen asleep that way,
and it had kept her warm, except for the parts of her that
were exposed. She'd kicked off her high heels, and her feet
were aching. Her arms and shoulders and the ridges of her
spine were icy, too.

Jack was lying on his back, his head resting in one of the
saddles, an arm folded back to cradle his neck. His breathing
was deep and rhythmic, and he might have been sleeping, except that his eyes were open. They were trained on her, and
Gus had never seen such a flash of unguarded hunger as when
she looked up at him. It nearly took her breath away. She
wanted to think she'd imagined it, but he tilted his head, and
in the dim light, she could see the glow of something fierce
and beautiful. It wasn't so much that he desired her. That she
could have resisted. It wasn't even the wanting. It was need in
his eyes. He needed something . . . and it was her.

"You're cold," he said. He wasn't asking. He knew.

Her nod was punctuated by a shudder.

He sat up and rocked to his feet, bringing the blanket with him. "Here take this." He knelt next to her, balanced on his toes, the blanket resting on his faded denim knees. The Good Samaritan, Gus thought, offering shelter from the storm.

"You're turning blue," he said. "I don't think that's what Bridget had in mind."

Gus accepted the gesture with another deep shudder as he tucked the coverlet around her. His hands felt warm and sheltering, much better than she wanted them to. They held promises of solace and sweetness. Or was that simply what she longed for? "If this is about what Bridget had in mind," she said softly, "the little swanlet is going to be disappointed."

He knelt there for another moment, even after she'd curled back into herself. "I can stay here," he said. "If that would help."

There was a roughness in his voice that made the underlying traces of tenderness all the more irresistible to Gus. She could feel herself responding, her heart squeezing. Yes, that would help, she wanted to tell him. More than you could possibly know.

"I'm all right." She tucked her chin into her knees and hugged herself. "Thank you . . . for the blanket."

The dim light above her was still burning when she woke a little later, only this time it was him sitting against the wall, trying to keep warm, his strong, corded arms crisscrossed against the chill. She watched him for a moment, his head tilted to one side, his eyes closed, dark lashes adrift, and for some reason she found herself wondering about that moment in the shower when he'd turned to her, his mouth taut and hungry, the stab of need in his eyes.

The sight of him had reduced her to a heartbeat, a single concussion so violent it had stormed in her ears, drowning out every other thought but him. From the first she had sensed something hidden in him, something haunted. Now, awash in the memory of that moment, she could feel it touching her from across the room. She had no idea what had triggered the awareness, except that he did look almost vulnerable with his head tilted and his arms folded.

She wanted to return the blanket to him, to share its warmth, but she knew what would happen if she did. If he woke up and their eyes met, if he looked at her that way again—needfully—she wouldn't be able to refuse him anything.

A sound rose up from somewhere inside her. The soft groan of desire was laced with despair, and she curled back into the blanket, suddenly freezing to the bone. She'd never been more aware of her frailties, of her inability to protect herself. Why was she such a sucker for dark wounded beauty in a man, for tragedy? He had *all* those qualities, despite his attempts to hide them. They were the parts of him that called to her. She was also virtually certain they would destroy her unless she could find a way to get free of him.

Rob was right. She was crazy to let herself get involved with someone like Culhane. He'd kidnapped her twice, both times at gunpoint, he was blackmailing her now, and he clearly had some sinister, ulterior motive for wanting access to her family. He was a threat to everything she wanted—

Another sound slipped out, a sigh. She'd thought it was indiscernible, but a darting glance told her that he'd opened his eyes and was watching her. He sat forward, rubbing his arms and staring at her as if he were bringing her into focus. She held her breath, waiting, waiting for the irresistible pull of his hunger. "Oh, no," she murmured as his gaze drifted to her lips. Something dark and thrilling flared in his expression.

"Gus? Are you all right?"

"Don't be tragic," she implored, refusing to look at him. "I can't deal with it."

"Okay . . ." He sounded thoughtful. "Can I be cold? It's freezing in here."

Smartass, she thought. Damn smartass cowboy. There were tears in her eyes when she looked up at him and another defeated groan on her lips. Before she could wipe the dampness away, he was there, crouching next to her, scrutinizing her with great concern, his hands poised as if to take her in his arms.

"I was only kidding," he said, searching her despairing contours. "Gus, baby, what's wrong—"

"Nothing."

"Hey . . . don't do this to me. What is it?"

"I'm not doing anything to you." She tried to push him away. "You're doing it to me!"

"What? What am I doing?"

"I don't know, I don't know." She sighed. "But just don't touch me, okay? If you touch me, I'll—"

He rested his arms on his knees. "You'll what?" His smile was slow in coming and faintly ironic. "Make another attempt on my life? Maybe this time you could try something quicker and cleaner than snakepits or runaway horses?"

"Electrocution?" she muttered, shaking her head. "Death by cattle prod?" He didn't understand. Killing him would be easy. What she would have to do if he touched her was so much worse than that. "I'll want you," she said in a tiny little voice.

A beat or two went by as he chewed on that one. "Let me see if I understand this," he said. "All I have to do is touch you, and you'll want me?"

"I'm afraid so."

"Can we establish for the record that you're talking about my body and not my mind?"

Her sigh was deep and resigned.

"So this is the *S* word . . . sex?"

She nodded and tucked herself back into the warmth of her legs, a beached vessel, waiting for the tide to take her. Her fate was no longer in her hands. She had no idea why she was feeling this way except that she was a hopeless sucker for sensitive, wounded brutes, and despite everything else that he was—killer, kidnapper, blackmailer—he was also that. Sensitive. The image that crept into her thoughts as she hugged herself was of a heart roughly carved into a tree, a heart with her name in it. That was when things had changed, she realized, that was when she'd become vulnerable.

In the space of silence that followed, she was increasingly aware of her immediate environment, of the floor's stinging hardness against her bottom, of the cold draft that blew across the back of her neck, and the gamey smell of the heavy blanket that was tucked around her. Primitive and earthy signals abounded. The pungence of horse droppings wafted from the stable next door as the animals snorted and moved restlessly in their stalls. Odd that both times she'd been on the brink of sex with him, she'd been trapped in an alien environment. If a stable was less hostile than the desert, it was no less connected to the primal cycles of life.

She shifted her weight, wanting to squirm. "You're not going to do it?" she asked, looking up at him. "You're not going to touch me?"

He gazed down at her, his facial muscles beautifully taut. He didn't answer her immediately, but the answer was there, smoldering in his features. It prowled through his eyes. It lurked in the hard, sensual lines of his mouth. He was already touching her, everywhere. The fact that his hands hadn't made contact meant nothing.

She closed her eyes, shaking inside. The sound of her own breathing was like the soft roar of a conch shell.

"Oh, yes," he said. "I'm going to do it."

She couldn't help herself. She swayed toward his voice. Its harshness was thrilling. She felt as if the most tender, sensitive parts of her were reaching out to him, unable to wait. She almost wished she were naked, so that when he touched her he could do it in more intimate, forbidden ways.

Heat burned her cheek. His fingertips? They seared her lips next as he brushed fire over that sensitive surface. Her mouth fell open, hot with yearning.

The floor groaned softly as he bent to kiss her, and the sound was reminiscent of emotions Gus couldn't put into words. It made her think of life's sweetest sorrows and its wildest joys—the searching cry of human loneliness, the sweet shock of physical contact after being alone all your life. It was the echo of inexpressible needs.

God, what that groan didn't mean.

She shuddered as his lips touched hers. The shock of it was so unexpected it made her jaw sting and her throat thicken with longing. She wanted more instantly. More than a kiss. Instantly. Not that his mouth wasn't lovely. It was. Not that she wouldn't have wanted him to go right on kissing her indefinitely. She would have. The raging softness of him was so startling that she almost forgot how hard the floor was.

But more . . . she ached for it. More.

His mouth brushed over hers like a star shower, leaving a trail of sparks in its wake. It was a glancing kiss, but the mere touch of his lips had set her mind ablaze with expectation. She needed to be touched and fondled passionately. She needed to be quenched like a deep thirst.

His hand shook as it closed over her shoulder, and the power in his grip made her remember the hunger she'd seen. There'd been pain in his eyes, such amazing, naked, lustful pain it had made her hurt, too. Unbearably. She arched up to him now, raking her nails down his face, a movement fraught with wildness and so much crazy yearning that he captured her arms and lifted her to her knees and then right up off the floor.

"Don't make me lose it, Gus," he breathed against her mouth. "I could hurt you, and I don't want to."

The blanket fell away from her shoulders and so did whatever concerns Gus might have had about consummating their union. She had no idea what legal complications making love with him would pose, how binding it might be. She didn't care. She only cared that he didn't want to do anything to hurt her. And she wanted him to do everything, *even* that, in the way that only he could. She craved the mastery of his hands and the tender crush of his mouth, the sting of his teeth against her flesh. She craved the sweet clash of sex with this man who'd kidnapped her and forced his way into her life.

His arms had begun to tremble, and she thought it was

from fatigue, that holding her had become difficult. But his hands were iron cuffs, which told her the perturbations were coming from somewhere inside him. It was something else making him shake, a passion so strong even he couldn't contain it. This was the physical need she'd seen in him, this was the soul hunger.

She wanted to touch the distended cords of his neck and smooth the knots from his jaw muscle. Her fingers curled with the urge. "Is this painful for you?" she asked, feeling foolish at the question. At least she hadn't stammered.

"Everything about you is painful for me . . . just looking at you. I can't even do that without aching."

Gus wasn't cold anymore. She couldn't feel the draft. All of her energy was consumed with the idea of making love with a man who was this beautifully, painfully savage. How would it feel to be the recipient of all that tormented power?

She could barely breathe at the desire that rose up inside her as he backed her to the wall. Her stockings snagged on the rough wooden floor. The sheer silk caught and ripped, but she was barely aware of it. He was powerful in the way he took control, and it frightened her. She had never had anyone respond to her this way, never in her life. There'd been plenty of admiration and envy, lots of men who'd made passes, but no one had ever wanted her the way he did. Even as a child she hadn't felt wanted. The people who should have loved and cherished her had been far more interested in finding ways to be rid of her.

"I love it that you're in pain," she said impulsively, her voice grainy and breathless. "In pain over me."

She jerked her arms free of his hold and tried to touch him. She didn't know quite what she intended to do, but it didn't matter anyway. He wouldn't let her. He captured her arms and spread them like wings, pinning her wrists to the wall on either side of her head and holding her there, spread-eagle and breathless, very much at his mercy. A shudder took her, and she began to tremble, shocked by what he'd done.

The pain, the hunger, all of it flared through him as he

searched her startled face. His breath was shaking, but he seemed determined to master the emotions, to prove that he didn't need anything, not sex, not love, not even her. His powerful thighs pressed her to the wall, forcing her to feel every quivering inch of the hunger that lived between his legs. He was already hard, already burgeoning, as he moved against her, grinding his hips into hers. His sex burned her soft flesh. It pressed hard against her pubic bone, searching, seeking deeper access. His eyes probed, cutting like diamonds, holding her in thrall.

There was a part of Gus that burned to resist him. Fighting back was as natural to her as breathing, but this time she couldn't summon the strength. She was too weak. This was too wonderful. Though she couldn't have thought through the reasoning or explained why if someone had asked her, she had already decided to be this man's sacrifice. It was pure impulse driving her, not reason, but the idea had taken her imagination captive. He'd kidnapped her, forced her into marriage, and now he would claim the spoils of war like a scene out of an epic medieval novel. Gus had done many things in life, but she'd never done this, never willingly surrendered herself to the enemy, even in fantasy.

He must have sensed her acquiescence. His warrior's mind must have read the signals, because he was suddenly powerful, a man who knew victory was imminent. The enemy was on her knees, but total capitulation was necessary before his triumph was complete. It was a ritual that went back to the primordial fights for territory and sex, triggered by the most basic of urges, the mating instinct.

"Be my wife," he said, his voice harsh, his breath soft.

He was nuzzling her neck, his teeth hot against her flesh, and there was a roughness about it that thrilled her. He was claiming her, physical sex the only thing on his mind now. Coupling was the ultimate destiny. And the thought of it left her breathless as his lips descended on hers. The fierce sweetness of his mouth, the sharp ache rising inside her made her want to cry out.

She broke away, needing to tell him what she'd experienced. "I feel the pain," she whispered, her voice thick with it. "My God, it's terrible. It's awful!" Her laughter was hoarse and startled. "It must be the same pain you described. It's never happened with anyone else."

His eyes were suddenly piercing as he searched her face. Even in the darkness, their blue-black radiance was unmistakable.

"This mouth of yours . . ." He caught the fullness of her lower lip between his fingers and gently pulled. "These lips that don't always get words out right . . . they're eloquent when you're kissing me. I just want you to know that. You speak perfectly."

Her throat tightened uncontrollably and tears stung at her eyes. He had touched into the part of her past she'd shown to no one, the pain she'd been guarding and hoarding for a lifetime. The speech impediment had always felt as if it were her personal stigmata, a punishment for being unwanted and the emblem of her unworthiness. Now he was telling her it was beautiful? When he cupped her breast, she felt passion so intense it was no longer pleasure, it was anguish.

If she thought she'd felt the pain before . . .

He had released her hands, but she couldn't touch him now. She couldn't do anything but sink to the floor.

He picked up the blanket and spread it out across the wooden planks for them, and then he pulled her with him onto it. There wasn't time to undress leisurely or remove their clothing, only the urgent rush to create a primal, life-sustaining bond. The hot fusion of bodies and souls. Her soul touching his. Soon all the pain would be gone and there would only be ecstasy.

He rose over her, bringing her skirt up with him and then stripping her nylons from her body with such urgent grace it felt as if he'd done it all in one unbroken wave. The stockings ended up in a heap across the room. It was ironic that she'd been worried about ruining them. They must be torn to shreds by now.

An image filled her mind as he loomed above her, his hands braced on either side of her head. She could feel the beautiful, thundering power of it all through her. She could hear the explosion of horses' hooves, the startled snorts of their breathing. She could smell the steam that came off their hot, surging bodies. The very ground seemed to shake beneath her as the magnificent herd of animals stampeded her senses.

Riding wild horses . . . the sweet, liberating power of that dream was to be hers. He would be her wild horse. He would take her on a thundering ride into the world of her senses.

She opened herself to the man braced above her and moaned softly as he fit his hardened body to hers. Throwing her arms over her head, she was aware of the pull against her shaking flesh. Her breasts were luminous. They were quivering, wanton pools, flowing with sensation, and she was offering them to him in an act of total abandon. It was one of the most thrilling things she'd ever done. Her belly tightened sweetly, and then painfully, as she imagined his mouth, the pull of his lips against her flesh.

"Jesus, you're beautiful." His jaw muscles bunched, and she could see that he was fighting the urge to drop and give her the thrill she'd imagined. He wanted to take her in his mouth, but another urge shook through him and he jerked reflexively. Muscles rippled wildly up and down his body as he tested the soft throb between her legs.

The first deep prick of his hardened flesh made Gus arch and gasp with surprise. "No, you're too big," she said, knowing he couldn't be. She'd had him before. "I'm not ready! You'll never—"

"Trust me," he grated. "You are. And I will."

He barely had the words out before he had penetrated her so deeply she could scarcely breathe. Gus's head and shoulders came off the blanket. Her muscles curled with shock and delight. She'd expected discomfort, but there was none, there was only wild, fluttering excitement and a deep, glorious fullness. The impulse to stop him had been over-whelmed by the swiftness, the utter sureness, of his possession. He'd buried himself, sword to her sheath, and now his sex was all muscle and mastery, and hers was all quivering sensation.

He began to flex slowly and she began to die with pleasure.

It was beautiful, so beautiful she could have cried. She wanted him to go on forever. He was hard and thrillingly thick. The swollen friction of his shaft, its velvet surfaces, caressed her inner walls. But the very fact that he was delving so deeply and moving so slowly made her wonder if she could possibly endure another moment.

She had never allowed herself to be dominated by anything. The thought of it terrified her, and yet, just this once in her life, she craved the thrill of abject surrender—to his rules, his pace, his male will, *whatever* that might be. She wanted to stretch out languidly, hostage to whatever wanton, terrible pleasure he could bring her. She wanted to submit to him in every way, but the pressures building up inside her were too fantastic. They wouldn't let her give up control. Sparking nerves urged her to curl around him like a cat and claw him into action.

"More," she pleaded, curving into his slow thrusts. Her fingernails racked his biceps. "Do it deeper, faster!"

His eyes flared, warning her that she was close to unleashing something dangerous in him.

"If I go any deeper," he said, "I'll be in your throat."

"I want you in my throat. I want you *every*where."

A shudder caught him, and he jerked deep inside her. "Everywhere?" he said. "You want my cock in your mouth and in the other, darker parts of your body? Are you sure?"

Gus had never been penetrated in the other, darker parts of her body that he must be talking about. Still, at this moment, in the crazed heat of sexual frenzy, she would probably have said yes to anything.

"I'm sure," she whispered, wondering what he would do. If he turned her over and began to probe in taut forbidden places, what in God's name would *she* do? "But right now . . . I need you just where you are." Deep muscles clutched involuntarily, squeezing him. "I'll die if you don't stay there."

He let out a shaking breath and lowered himself to her mouth, nipping at her lower lip, brushing it with his heated breath. "Good," he said, "because this is just where I want to be. Where I am right now."

Something was building swiftly inside her, a keening cry, and she told him so. "Make me come," she whispered. "Make me scream."

He had stopped moving altogether, and when he started again, she did scream, a sharp little gasp of pleasure that reverberated in the small room and sent him into a fabulous frenzy of coupling. He caught hold of her wrists and pinned them to the floor, arcing into her body with the grace and force of an athlete.

Gus Featherstone had wanted to ride the wild horses. She had urgently needed that liberating rampage. She had wanted him to go faster and faster and bring her the hard, thundering satisfaction her body craved. She got all of that and more. He thrust with the power of a stallion, and as their bodies came together again and again, she alternately ripped at him with sudden, urgent need and fell back to the blanket, helpless.

The pleasure he gave her penetrated her entire being, shaking her from the inside out. It moved through her in crimson waves as she felt the climb toward ecstasy begin. Within moments the first shimmering implosion had rocked her, and she knew the riotous joys of surrender in a way she never had before and might never again. In giving up control she had freed herself. She had freed feelings that were bound up in the need to protect her wounds, and her body was simply going wild with the rampageous beauty of it all.

She was spent by the time the stampede had run its course, but the moment the horses had stopped their glorious thundering and her body had sagged to the floor in exhaustion—the moment she was complete—her thoughts were of him. Had he shared her ecstasy? Was he still in pain?

Jack had felt every second of her shaking rapture, but he hadn't been able to share in it, except through his joy at her pleasure. He'd been left with the most beautiful kind of pain. The tightness that gripped and caressed him made him ache to release the pressure. He could feel the mounting, flooding heat of his semen at the base of his body, in the head of his penis. He could feel the painful smash of his heart against his ribs. Every fiber in his body was screaming for relief, but despite the force of his feelings, he couldn't let go.

Instead he watched her coil and convulse and go limp beneath him, and when she was lost to everything but her own delirium, he pulled her into his arms and held her in the low glow of the lamplight. He was still throbbing deeply inside her, but the soft comfort of her flesh might have been enough if she hadn't begun to question him, to touch and try to soothe him.

"No, don't," he whispered as she pressed her lips to the wild pulse in his throat. "It won't help."

"You haven't even let me try," she insisted.

Sighing, he watched her stroke and kiss and caress his overstimulated body, knowing that none of it would have any effect except to make him harder and more miserable. Still, he could feel a razor-sharp tension building as she worked her way down his abdomen, and when she pressed her lips to the very heart of his discomfort, he groaned aloud. His shaft jerked involuntarily under her tender attentions, nearly sending him through the roof.

"Have faith," she promised, running the tip of her tongue to the very base of him, where all the fullness had accumulated in what felt like a swollen knot.

Her mouth worked him so beautifully, he couldn't help but relax, and soon she had him taut and tingling in every fiber, yet strangely fluid. The sharp stirrings he felt told him something was happening, but it was only when she curved herself seductively over his loins and took him deeply in her mouth, it was only when she began to stroke up and down, nearly swallowing him, that the miracle occurred. He lost control. Totally and mindlessly. All decisions were taken out of his hands, and his release, when it finally came, was so agonizingly sweet, it brought tears of wonder to his eyes. Fire from the gods, he thought. Like

Prometheus, he had stolen it. And now, like Prometheus, he would die.

Lake stood in the open doorway of his sister's bedroom, watching her as she spoke in hushed tones into the receiver of her cordless telephone. He had something urgent to tell her, but her secretive manner made him hesitate. She was clearly having a private conversation with someone, and though Lake was consumed with curiosity, he was reluctant to move closer and risk giving himself away.

Lily was seated at the walnut secretary with her appointment book in front of her, making notes as she talked. Strong morning sunlight, diffused by the mullioned windows, illumined shelf after shelf of the silver knickknacks and potted pansies she loved.

As she said her good-byes, hung up, and continued writing, Lake promised himself that he would have a look at that book the first opportunity he got. It wasn't like Lily to keep things from him, and his curiosity was fueled as much by brotherly possessiveness as anything else. As he watched her delicately boned hand move across the page and saw her shoulders lift with a tense sigh, he knew. His lovely twin had a secret.

She was wearing a floaty white silk blouse and brick-colored jodphurs this morning, and she'd gathered her hair into a thick bundle at her nape. He couldn't see the front of her blouse, but he assumed it was fastened with the diamond and pearl Medusa brooch that had been their mother's, and before that, their grandmother's, and so on, going back all the way back to the daughter of the founding Featherstone, Matthew Tobias.

"You didn't come down to breakfast," he said.

She jerked around, her eyes wide and startled. "I wish you wouldn't sneak up on me like that, Lake. You know it frightens me to death." She closed the appointment book, opened the drawer of her desk, and slipped it inside.

"Did you go riding?" he asked. Ordinarily he would have entered the spacious suite of rooms and made himself at home. The Victorian settee by the terrace doors was the spot he preferred, although occasionally he sprawled on her canopy bed as he used to do when they were young. He and Lily had never observed the same rules of space and privacy that other adult siblings did. They'd been together in the womb. They would be together until the grave, or so it seemed, which was undoubtedly why he resented so deeply her keeping secrets. He was also quite sure their embryonic connection was why neither of them had ever married. Why should they when they had so much of what they needed in each other?

She had seemed distant recently, he reminded himself, although he'd assumed it had to do with Gus's situation. Having someone like Culhane skulking around was intolerable to a woman like Lily. When it came to the household, she ran a tight ship, which was undoubtedly why Frances Brightly had lasted as long as she had. The housekeeper could be a martinet, but she was also as meticulous as a surgical nurse.

"No, I didn't go riding," Lily was telling him, "but our younger sister had quite a wild time of it, apparently." She pushed back from the secretary and swung around on the chair, hooking her bootheel in one of the rungs. It made her look pensive and tomboyish, a rare pose for her, and one he found surprisingly attractive.

Lake felt a twist of nostalgia as he thought about the adventures they'd had together as children, the galloping rides through the woods on their ponies. Lily had worshipped their father, mostly from afar—he wasn't a demonstrative man—but Lake had never felt the need of anyone's company but hers. And then Gus had been thrust upon them, ruining their bucolic existence. But even her intrusion had drawn them closer. Tormenting their little stepling had been a constant source of entertainment. God, what fiendish monsters they'd been.

He regretted their cruelty now, especially when he heard Gus struggling to speak, but he was relieved to know his suspicions were true, that Gus was the source of Lily's mood. "She actually took Sapphire again? Do you want me to speak to her?"

Lily rose in a fury and started toward him as if he were the object of her wrath. "She didn't take Sapphire! She and that dumb brute husband of hers spent the night in the stables with the other dumb brutes. I'm surprised Daniel could distinguish Culhane from the horses when he discovered them."

"Were they naked?" The question slipped out uncensored. Lake had seen both Gus and Culhane naked on the security screens. Now he was trying to imagine them together. Perhaps he'd put a camera in the stables.

"Why do you ask that?"

"I thought you said they spent the night in the stables having sex."

"They were in the tack room, and yes, they were having sex. They must have been having it loud enough to wake the dead. I couldn't ride Sapphire this morning she was so skittish. Not that I wanted to, after that news."

Lake could feel himself perspiring and wished he'd worn something cooler than the white linen shirt and slacks Frances had laid out. Lily had never liked him in shorts, said his legs were too thin. "Frightening the horses? That old saw?"

The antique brooch gleamed, Medusa's frightening countenance seeming to come to life as Lily fingered the pin. "That joke is what our lives have become, Lake. I thought you were going to do something about it."

"I *am* doing something about it, Lily. I've taken steps—"

"Steps?" she said, briskly closing the remaining distance between them. "Forgive me if I take some steps myself." Her hand flashed out as she reached him, and he thought she was going to slap him. Instead, she took hold of the bedroom door as if to close it—and force him out.

That possibility stung Lake unbearably. It also brought out a rage in him that few but Lily could touch. Their father had been able to make him crazy—Lily and their father—but no one else. Lily had once betrayed him to Lake, Sr., when they were young, and Lake still considered it the only serious breach in their relationship. She had revealed that Lake had been spying on their parents' marital bed. The patriarch had been so repulsed he'd whipped Lake severely, confined him to the house, and forced him to wear a blindfold for days. He'd also been ordered to recite the commandment about honoring thy father and thy mother every time he spoke. But worst of all, Lake had always suspected Lily'd done it for the sole purpose of displacing him in their father's affections, and even though it had backfired, Lake had found that very difficult to forgive.

"What are you doing?" he asked now, harshly.

"I'd like to change my clothes. Is that all right with you? I'm meeting Ward for lunch at the club."

Lake stepped back as she swung the door shut, then braced himself and flung out a fist, slamming it open. The door crashed around violently and hit the stopper, snapping it in two. Across the room, one of Lily's collection of silver odds and ends fell off the bookshelves, adding to the clatter.

Lily's frightened gasp pleased him. The little witch needed to be brought back in line occasionally. Nothing too extreme, of course, just a reminder of who called the shots. She seemed to like it that way. And he really didn't understand why she couldn't accept that he would handle this problem. He'd always taken care of things before, hadn't he? All those problems with Jillian, all that messiness about the baby. Hadn't he handled that?

He caught the door as it rebounded and swung back at him. "The detective called me this morning with some interesting news. It seems someone is trying to kill Jack Culhane. Apparently our own sweet Gus has made several attempts on her husband's life, although it isn't clear *why* she wants him dead."

"I know why I'd like him dead," Lily muttered. She'd stepped back and was clutching herself as if Lake had hurt her, which of course, he hadn't.

Lake debated whether or not to reveal the seriousness of the situation. He had the distinct feeling that Lily was up to something, perhaps even hatching a plan of her own, and if that were the case, she would only interfere.

"Be careful, Lily," he said, softening his voice to a hush.

The house carried whispers, and he couldn't risk anyone else hearing. "Don't do anything foolish. In fact, don't do anything at all. If Jack Culhane is who I think he is, he poses a grave, grave threat to this family. We are all vulnerable, every one of us, perhaps Gus most of all."

With some satisfaction, he watched the light of recognition seep into his sister's sea-mist green eyes. On the heels of her awareness came fear. "My God, Lake, what are you saying? That he knows about Jillian? That he knows about—"

"Shhhh . . . yes, I'm afraid he might."

She began to work the clasp of her brooch. "Does Gus know about any of this? Is that why she's trying to get rid of him?"

"It's not clear what she knows and doesn't know. The detective's information has been sketchy so far. Apparently Gus and Rob Emory had a relationship that went well beyond business, and Culhane came along and upset the applecart. It was Gus and Emory who were supposed to be married. The detective hasn't been able to determine why she married Culhane instead, but he thinks Culhane may have something on her."

"Gus is being blackmailed by Culhane?" Lily's hand stilled. "Then Emory himself has a motive for wanting the man dead, doesn't he? The scorned lover?"

"Yes, possibly . . . and speaking of lovers, where is Gus now?"

She smiled tremulously. "Oh, this is rich," she said. "You're going to love this. Frances says they've all gone to the beach, the three of them! Gus, Jack Culhane, and Bridget."

"They've taken Bridget?" Lake didn't give a damn what Gus and her husband did in the stables. They could screw each other *and* the horses if they wanted, but he was genuinely unhappy to hear this news. He could wait no longer. It was time to act.

CHAPTER
23

FOR THE BORED AND THE DISAFFECTED, VENICE BEACH, CAL-
ifornia, was an oceanside carnival and fleamarket rolled
into one. The cement strand that wound along the becalmed
Pacific was thronged with the usual buff golden bodies, but
it was the fringe entertainment that had immortalized the
area—the chainsaw jugglers, the street magicians, and the
monocycling clowns.

Everyone vied for attention. Rappers jammed on
Rollerblades and acrobats walked on their hands, but the
largest crowds had congregated down by Jody Maroni's
Sausage Kingdom, where the real action was. Irresistible
smells poured from the grill of Jody's kitchen, including
the spicy sizzle of Moroccan lamb sausage and the piquant
pungency of his orange, garlic, and cumin creation. Out
front, beneath the awning, an accordionist played beer-bar-
rel polka music, but the biggest draw was several quarter-
size holes drilled in the pavement that jetted compressed air
and blew up women's skirts.

For the hungry there were pushcarts of steaming hot

dogs, billowy cotton candy and rainbow-colored Sno-Kones. One street vendor came armed with a wandlike appliance that dispensed electrical shocks, which he claimed would cure everything from migraines to inhibited sexual desire. No one in the long line for the shockmeister's services appeared to be suffering from anything worse than a sunburn.

Today Jack, Gus, and Bridget were among the curious, milling crowd. The boardwalk had been Jack's idea. It had come to him the night before, during their confinement in the tack room. "If we get out of here alive," he'd promised wryly, "I'm taking you to Venice Beach. You've got to try one of Jody Maroni's Bombay bangers."

When Daniel had found them the next morning, Jack had kept his promise. Not thirty minutes after they'd been sprung from the stable, wearing swimsuits under their jeans and T-shirts, he and Gus had piled into his Chevy Blazer. Her Mercedes wasn't a "beach" car, he'd informed her. But they hadn't driven more than a block from the house when he'd stopped the car, and they'd both murmured the same thing simultaneously.

"Bridget," they'd said, and looked at each other.

"Let's take her along!" Gus had cried.

Jack had known a moment's hesitation. He'd begun to feel like a marked man, and he was concerned about endangering the child. Whoever had him under surveillance wasn't going to take a day off to let Jack Culhane have a field trip. But his desire to spend time with Gus and Bridget doing something "normal" was profound, and Gus's enthusiasm had finally burned through his concerns.

"She'll love it," he'd said, wheeling the Blazer around in a sharp U-turn.

He'd been right. After some strenuous protesting that she should be allowed to wear her new Sleeping Beauty dance costume, Bridget had given in to Gus's imprecations that she "dress like a normal kid for once." With a sour look, she'd changed into a red-and-white polka-dot sundress, but by the time they reached the beach, her mood had brightened considerably.

"Should have let her wear that damn tutu," Jack said once they'd checked the boardwalk scene out. He pointed to a group of teenagers with spiked hair in Day-Glo colors and strange jewelry piercing even stranger places. "This is Weirdo Central. Sleeping Beauty would have fit right in."

But Gus was too busy lavishing coconut-scented sunblock on her exposed parts to give the teenagers more than a glance. She'd removed her clothes in the car and wrapped herself with a chiffon skirt that matched her tiger-striped one-piece tank suit. Now she wanted to be sure her shoulders and arms were protected from the blazing July sunshine. She'd oiled Bridget up, too, much to the child's disgust. Only Jack had refused her mother-hen ministrations. Apparently Mr. Quiet-but-Deadly was too macho for sunblock.

"Want to get zapped?" Jack whispered in Gus's ear as Bridget scampered off to check out the wares of the various booths.

"I think I already was," Gus said, laughing. She recapped the sunblock and dropped it in her shoulder bag. "Last night."

"You have a dirty mind." He pulled her close, his hand in her hair as he nibbled on the silky pink lobe of her ear and breathed a steamy appreciative sound. "I was talking about him," he said, pointing to the shockmeister.

"Oh . . ." She favored Jack with a wicked grin and ran her finger down his leg, sorry he'd decided to leave on his jeans, but glad he'd shucked his T-shirt. "I'd rather have one of those sausages you mentioned."

"Watch your language, woman, the child is nigh."

Bridget was running toward them, yelling something about wanting a souvenir. "Can I have a tattoo?" she asked, breathless and pink with excitement as she reached them. "Come look! They've got naked women and skulls and crossbones!"

"Naked women? Ouch!" Jack winced as Gus slugged his arm.

"Tattoos are permanent, darling," Gus explained to Bridget. "Madame Zola wouldn't approve of her Sleeping

Beauty looking like a biker mama, and you do want to dance that part in the recital, don't you?"

"What's a biker mama?" Bridget wanted to know.

"Cher," Jack volunteered.

"Oh . . . yeah," she agreed with a thoughtful nod. Ever resourceful, the child had a ready alternative. "Forget about the deathhead then. It wouldn't go with my costume any way. How about a live baby tarantula?"

"I've got an idea." Jack waved her with him over to a nearby stand where stuffed animals were sold. "How about this?" He held up a gray-and-white stuffed hippo with curly black eyelashes and a pink net skirt.

"What's that?" Bridget asked.

"It's a hippo in a tutu."

"I know . . . but what's the point?"

"You like ballet, don't you?"

"Yes . . ."

"Haven't you ever seen *Fantasia*?"

Apparently Bridget could see where this conversation was going. She heaved a long-suffering sigh. "I don't go to Disney movies any more," she informed him. "Haven't for years."

"How many years could it have been?" He gave her a re-proving look. "You're going to this one, Sleeping Beauty. And you're going to like it. A lot."

His firm tone said that was an order, and Bridget peered up at him, clearly startled. Traces of pink color stained her porcelain cheeks, but her blinking gaze was tinged with awe. "Okay," she said softly. "Don't get your knickers in a knot."

Gus was secretly amused at the little girl's reaction. To her credit, Bridget had already figured out that throwing a hissy fit with Jack Culhane would not be a good move. It appeared that the five-year-old had finally met her match.

Gus experienced a tiny thrill of awareness watching the chemistry between the very large man and the very little girl. They were clearly smitten with each other, and it was a wondrous thing to see. Jack's ruggedly masculine profile and powerful, scarred body was such a profound contrast to

Bridget's watchful, dimpled softness. She was the key to the future, a child of wonder and sweet, untainted promise. He was locked in the past, a man harboring profane knowledge about pain, about life and death. They seemed perfect complements, as if together they could somehow form a whole.

Gus's throat tightened and her heart wobbled. She could hardly believe she was thinking anything so impossibly sentimental. She knew the dangers of wishful thinking, of attaching romantic fantasy to real-life situations. Apparently she hadn't outgrown her childish dreams of princes and cindergirls. Nothing could come of this bizarre relationship with Jack Culhane for more reasons than she could count, but just for a second—for one stolen moment in the heedless rush of time—she wished they were a real family, all three of them.

She wished that quite desperately.

"My favorite part was the sorcerer's apprentice," Bridget enthused as the three of them came out of the movie theater the next evening. "Wasn't that great when Mickey tried to stop the broom by chopping it in splinters?"

"Magnificent," Gus agreed, "especially when all those splinters turned into more brooms."

"I saw it as a lost opportunity," Jack said, apparently determined to be the voice of reason. "If Mickey'd been smart, he could have cornered the broom market."

Bridget danced out in front of them, walking backward down the carpeted promenade of the Westpark Cinema Center, a complex of several theaters, which comprised most of the east end of the huge Westpark shopping mall.

"Could we get something to eat now?" she pleaded. Her golden pigtails bounced with each step. "I could go for a Johnny Rocket's original and some chili fries."

Gus's groan was incredulous. "After a jumbo tub of popcorn and an entire box of Jujubes? Where would you put it?" Gus, herself, had feasted on two boxes of Red Hots. Not only were they her favorite movie candy, but she'd even immortalized them on her Mercedes' personalized license plates.

Bridget pulled up the skirt of her sundress and puffed out her stomach, grinning at the potbelly she made. "Look at me, I'm one of the hippos!"

"Just like her aunt," Jack stage-whispered to Gus. "She's a flasher."

The little girl skipped back to Jack and linked her arm in his. "Wish I had that stuffed hippo now. It was way cool, just like the ones in the movie."

Pretending that she was too heavy to budge, Jack emitted a power-lifter grunt as he picked her up, hoisted her over his head, and fitted her onto the saddle of his shoulders. The skirt of her sundress billowed into his face.

"A piggyback ride!" she squealed, wrapping her arms around him and clinging so frantically to his face that she inadvertently blinded him. "I've never had one!"

"This is a first for me, too," Jack said, laughing as he struggled to get her arranged. He pried her fingers from his eyes and nose. "I've never bench-pressed a hippo."

Again, Gus was captivated by the interplay between the two of them. In the last twenty-four hours she'd glimpsed qualities of gentleness and caring in Jack she wouldn't have thought possible, especially toward Bridget. And as for Bridget's reaction to him, it was almost reverent. There didn't seem to be anything he could do that wasn't wonderful in her niece's eyes.

It was a bittersweet experience for Gus. She wanted to let herself enjoy the situation moment to moment and block everything else out, but she couldn't seem to do it. Wistful thoughts kept sneaking past her guard, thoughts of bliss that could never be. Whatever had driven him to seek her out and force his way into her life would ultimately wreak havoc for her and her family.

She and Jack Culhane were star-crossed, she reminded herself. He threatened everything she loved. She'd nearly killed him three times, saved his life once, and had sex with him twice. That should have been enough excitement to hold her, if not to warn her off, but it had only fed the obsession. He was too powerful a man to ever think you could have a taste of him like some dish at a smorgasboard and then move on. He hit too hard. He went too deep.

Bridget's giggles and Jack's horsing around brought a smile to her lips and sadly, more heartache. Why couldn't it have been Rob whom Bridget reacted to this way? Gus had some perplexing and painful decisions yet to make, one of them about Rob himself. But utmost on her mind was the crucial appointment she had set up for later that week, which might well decide everything. She was going to find out who Jack Culhane really was. Watching him now, she wondered how dangerous that knowledge might be . . . and if she really wanted to know.

If Jack was aware of Gus's intense scrutiny, he assumed it was because her niece's physical safety was momentarily in his hands. For his part he knew exactly what he was doing. He was stealing fire. He'd been running that risk ever since he met Gus Featherstone, and the thought of going up in flames only seemed to compel him more.

But this child, this sweetness he felt with her and Gus, just the three of them together . . . for that the gods would make him pay dearly. They'd already started. He couldn't look at Bridget without thinking of his own daughter, he couldn't touch her or lift her in his arms without wondering if Haley would have been that light and buoyant.

He had stopped short of allowing himself a total flight of fancy, of wondering what it would be like to be a real husband and father, part of a bonded family again, only because he knew how impossible that was. The Fates did not give new happiness to a man who had already destroyed his allotted share of it. Instead they tortured him with the prospect by offering to return every precious thing he'd lost at a time when he couldn't accept the gift.

"Oops!" Bridget said, bouncing on his shoulders as they started down a flight of stairs that led to the mezzanine. She gripped his face again, this time clamping her sticky little fingers over his mouth and nose. There was no way to un-latch her, so he succumbed to the mauling and concentrated on getting both of them down the steps.

When they got to the bottom, he lifted her over his head and somersaulted her once before he settled her on the ground. She grinned up at him dizzily, tilted and then hugged herself to his arm. God, how his heart squeezed at the sight.

"Can you perform one more miracle and find us a Johnny Rocket's?" Gus wanted to know.

She linked her arm in his and gave him a dazzling smile as they left the theater complex and entered the mall. The brightness of it made him ache almost as much as Bridget's antics had done. Gus was the impetus for all of this, he acknowledged silently. Because of her he'd felt things with a woman he hadn't experienced in years. She'd put him back together, made him feel whole again, even if only for a few moments. He didn't know how to thank her for that. He *did* know that he wanted to make love to her again. Badly.

She was waiting, her dark expressive brows arched expectantly. She wanted a miracle performed and he must look like the man to do it. Both she and the kid were gazing at him as if he were the hero they'd been waiting all their lives for. No one had looked at him that way, no one since Maggie.

He smiled ruefully, his throat tight and hot. "One burger and chili fries, coming up."

Webb Calderon glanced at his Rolex and realized he'd just checked the time five minutes ago. He rarely anticipated an appointment the way he was this one, though he would take care not to let his imminent visitor know. He'd come out to the storage room, thinking to complete some unfinished business and make use of the brief time he had to wait.

His work area was even chillier than usual this afternoon, but Webb preferred it that way, uncomfortable. Coldness made the flesh rise and ache and harden. It set the nerves exquisitely on edge, leaving the body caught somewhere in the gradations between discomfort and outright pain. But more important was its effect on the inner world. The cold that burned his flesh also made his blood hum with life and his brain buzz with energy.

He needed it, the penetrating chill, the pricking flesh. For him there was little else life had left to offer. Food, wine, and sex, the satiation of the senses—he hadn't experienced any of that as pleasure in years. Nothing stimulated him except the extremes of sensation, because nothing else could penetrate the barrier his mind had built.

Tonight he'd unpacked a crate that contained his latest acquisition, and he hadn't known whether to laugh or cry when he'd seen the work. It was a small early fifteenth-century oil of the Ferrara school, and to the extent that he could be moved by art, or by anything, he had been. He hadn't bothered with an easel. He'd simply propped it up against the crate it came in and stepped back from the worktable to study it.

Even now the thing made him want to shake his head in disbelief. Framed in intricately carved wood, the picture showed a wounded, bleeding deity. The face was gaunt with sorrow, the body starved of flesh, skin lying over bone. Webb had no religious connection at all to the figure. He wasn't a believer in any traditional way, but in the presence of such helpless suffering, he had felt something, just the tiniest bleat of pain echoing through his mind, a soul's plea for mercy.

He wanted to keep the piece for himself, but that wasn't going to be possible. And though it would have commanded a small fortune on the open market, it would never see the auction block, either. His ineffably beautiful oil was a fake, destined for the private collection of a South American drug lord, who expected to be getting a priceless Italian primitive.

No one the wiser, Webb thought. In the end it didn't matter whether art, or anything else in life, was authentic, only that people believed it was. It was all illusion. And that, if anyone cared to take the trouble to think it through, was the royal road to success. The good illusionists were the winners because people wanted so desperately to believe. Fortunately, Webb was one of the good ones. Culhane was another. They had many things in common, he and Jack Culhane. And they were about to have another.

A sudden and persistent beeping told him his appointment would arrive momentarily. He hit a button on his wristwatch, silencing the alarm as he left the workroom. Its double doors opened onto a corridor that separated the area from his office and the gallery.

He'd spread the Devil's Tarot out on his desk earlier that day, still curious about the cards' origins. The arcane images greeted him as he entered his office. The London dealer who'd found them had guessed them to be of Romanian origins and at least a century old. Webb had found that hard to believe because of their pristine condition, but they were unlike anything he'd ever seen.

He was about to gather them up when he became aware of another presence. The sweet rush of a flowery fragrance laced with female warmth pervaded his senses for a moment. "Come in," he said, glancing at the doorway. "I've been expecting you."

The woman who gazed back at him did not look warm, flowery, or sweet. She did look taut, however, as she stood lithe and tall, her dark slenderness made more striking by a severe white Chanel suit. The short skirt and stiletto elevator pumps enhanced legs well-toned by runway work.

She knew how to pose, Webb admitted, admiring her cool, watchful elegance. There was only one telltale flaw. Her fingers were too tight on the bag she was clutching. Augusta Featherstone was here to make a deal with Mephistopheles, but it was out of necessity, Webb acknowledged, not choice.

She strode toward him, moving so briskly that two of the Tarot cards floated off the desk and fell to the floor.

"Sorry." She knelt and scooped up one of them, handing it to him.

A smile flickered as he turned it over and saw which it was. "Congratulations," he told her, showing her the image—a young man in Renaissance garb holding a slender tree branch that was taller than he was. "The Page of Wands."

"What does it mean?" she asked, clearly wary, but curious.

They always were, he thought. Fatally curious.

"Good news," he assured her. "It's the signal to move ahead with a new venture. The future looks bright, Gus." He pointed to the second card still lying on the floor. "You missed one."

She bent again, and he found himself wondering what the view must have been from behind her. The twinge in his groin told him that perhaps he wasn't quite as incapable of pleasure as he thought.

She handed him the card, but he resisted smiling this time as he gazed at it. "The Ten of Swords," he said, meeting her violet eyes. He turned the card to show her the figure of a man, sprawled on his face, his body pierced by ten huge, gleaming swords. The weapons seemed to be pinning him to the ground as blood oozed from the wounds. It was a grotesque image, even to Webb.

Her eyelids dropped, creating a dark sweep of lash that extinguished whatever emotion might have been hidden in there. "I know the Tarot slightly. That means loss, doesn't it?"

"It can mean that. It can also mean advantage, profit, power. Given the first card, I think it means your gain will come through someone else's loss."

She went silent, gazing at the bag she held, at her hands, seeming transfixed by the pale grip of her own fingers.

"You're going to get everything you want." His voice harshened as he registered the tension that was rising inside her. She was trembling. "As long as you're willing to give to get. There will be a price, Gus."

It was a glorious summer evening. The sun hovered over the foothills like a stage-struck entertainer, refusing to leave the proscenium before it lit up the indigo sky with one last burst of burnt-orange glory. Warmed by the conflagration, Jack skipped up the short flight of front steps to the mansion, a stuffed hippo tucked backward under his arms. He was puffing from having jogged up the long driveway, but luck was with him as he opened the front door and entered the house. The woman he was looking for was right there in the foyer, assaulting the bric-a-brac with a bright yellow feather duster.

"Where's the brat, Mrs. Brightly?"

Frances Brightly looked him over haughtily. It was clear she didn't approve of anything about him, from his well-worn chinos and black collarless shirt to the dark, spiky-soft hair on his head. The woman who'd sold him the hippo earlier that day had flushed visibly and told him he looked like the Diet Coke guy's evil twin. It had seemed to work for her, but apparently Frances B. didn't agree.

"If you mean Gus," she said brusquely, "she hasn't come in yet. She had a full schedule today, including a doctor's appointment."

"Doctor's appointment?"

"Annual checkup. I assume that's what's held her up."

Gus Featherstone at the doctor? An unbelievably hot thought crossed Jack's mind that had to do with Gus in stirrups and him between her legs. He laughed and flushed as hotly as the Venice Beach vendor, which got another suspicious look from the housekeeper. "Actually," he explained, "I meant the kid—Bridget."

"Didn't you see her out front?" The housekeeper tucked the feather duster under her arm and slipped her hands into the pockets of her gray cardigan sweater. "She was on the front steps a moment ago. I was just going to call her for dinner."

"I'll do it." He patted the hippo's rump. "I want to give her this anyway."

Bridget wasn't on the steps or anywhere in sight as Jack descended the stairway and strode toward the fenced perimeter of the estate. As he reached the gate his uneasiness rose. It wasn't completely closed, and the night-duty guard wasn't in the booth.

"Bridget!" he yelled, spotting the little girl across the road. Somehow she'd gotten out, crossed the highway, and she was playing on the shoulder of the road.

"Hi, Jack!" She sprang up and waved. "It's a squirrel! Look, I'm feeding it peanuts!"

"Wait!" he called as she started across the road toward him. He could hear the roar of an oncoming car, but Bridget kept coming, seemingly oblivious of the wildly flashing headlights.

The car careened toward her, galvanizing Jack. He scaled the fence as if it weren't there and sprinted toward the road. But before he could get to the child, the car careened wildly and came straight at him.

"Look out!" he shouted, diving for her. He managed to shove her out of the way, but he couldn't save himself. REDHOTTT, the letters of a specialized license plate, ripped through his mind as the car ripped through his body.

He was wide awake as the car plowed into him. He was so agonizingly alert he could hear the crunch and snap of his own bones, and the shriek of the child's terror. The impact lifted him off the asphalt and flung him into the air as if he were weightless, and through it all, he was aware of everything, every bloodred streak of sunset pouring through the silhouetted trees, every gleaming white pebble on the roadside. There was a strange, joyous freedom in the flight, as if he might never come down, but as his body cartwheeled endlessly and began to plummet, he saw the ground leaping up at him like a howling black wolf.

He hit so violently he could feel his teeth shake loose from his head, his backbone snap like a bow, and his skull split wide open. He could hear every creak and crash of his terrible collision with the earth, but he could feel nothing. There was no pain, nothing but a dark, fleshy pressure.

It occurred to him as he lay there in the wetness that was seeping out of him that his own blood was rushing to warm and comfort and cushion him. It also occurred to him that he was going to die incomplete, without having kept his date with the blindfolded woman, Justice. The killers of his child would go free, they would never pay for their wanton destruction, and there was more agony in that realization than in whatever was happening to his body.

The last thing he saw before he gave in to the deadly black floodtide that was engulfing him was the red Mercedes speeding away from him. Gus's Mercedes.

CHAPTER
24

JACK COULDN'T OPEN HIS EYES THE SUNLIGHT WAS SO RAG-
ingly bright. He turned his head into the ground to block
out the blinding rays and slowly pushed himself to a sitting
position, but even when he had himself there, with his arms
fully extended, he couldn't seem to escape the white heat.
What he could see of his hands looked as if they'd been
bleached to the color of skeletal bones. What he could see
of the world looked as if nuclear winter had taken place and
left it in ashes.

There was noise. He could hear static hissing and
buzzing in his ears, but he couldn't make it out.

Bridget. Through slitted lids, he fought to bring the little
girl into focus. She was curled up in a ball across the road,
her head tucked into her knees, much like the position he'd
found her aunt Gus in when he'd crawled out of the
snakepit. The child hadn't been hit. He was reasonably sure
of that, but she was probably suffering from shock.

There was pain now, deep, tearing pain that radiated
mostly from his gut and chest area. He couldn't determine

his own injuries because he couldn't make out the details. If there was blood it had been bleached as white as everything else. He did feel a terrible piercing force as he rocked to his knees and then to his feet, but getting to Bridget was the only thing on his mind. What mattered was that his body was moving. He could walk.

His eyes were watering copiously from the glare. Light ricocheted dazzlingly off the road, and the background noise in his mind was like white noise coming through a headset. It was growing louder, harsher. Beyond the static, there were bells and pinging, melodious sounds, voices whispering.

"Bridget?" he said as he knelt down next to the little girl.

She sprang up and gaped at him. "Daddy! I thought you were dead!"

Daddy! Daddy! Daddy! The word shrieked endlessly in Jack's head. The burning lights made him squeeze his eyes shut, and his heart pounded wildly. He dropped to his knees, to his elbows, and then he toppled over.

"*Daddy!*" she shrieked.

Jack felt someone jerking at his arms, opening his clothing. There were hands all over his body and people were talking excitedly.

"His heart rate's going crazy!" someone said.

"He's lucky to have a heart rate," another countered. "Christ, he should have been dead."

"The wet grass saved him. It was soaked down from the sprinklers."

"The grass saved his ass!"

Laughter erupted around him, and Jack tried to open his eyes, but could only manage it for an instant. The light was painful. Unbearable. He was surrounded by huge, grinning figures in white—dazzling blue-white—with halos as big and bright as the moon.

Was he dead?

Were there hospitals in heaven?

Something jerked at his arm.

"Blood pressure's dropping," a voice announced. "Palpate his abdomen for internal injuries. He could have a gusher inside."

A door opened and slammed. A curtain zinged shut.

"His wife's out there, raising hell, demanding to know his condition."

"Isn't she that model? Gus Featherstone?"

"The beautiful brat? He's married to *her*?"

"That should give him something to live for."

Live for? Jack's heart surged again, wildly, as he remembered Gus's car coming straight at him, plowing into him head-on and flinging him thirty feet in the air. *She was the one trying to kill him.*

"But I must see him," Gus demanded. "He's my *husband*. I have a right to know his condition, to talk to him."

"I'm sorry." The nursing supervisor glanced at her watch and sighed, a clear indication that she was wearying of the battle to fend off Gus. "My orders are no visitors. I don't know how I can make that any more clear. Your husband doesn't want to see anyone, Mrs. Culhane, and I'm afraid that includes you. Those are the instructions he left with the attending doctor. I am sorry."

It was nearly dawn and Gus had been at the hospital all night without food, sleep, or contact with anyone who was willing to give her information. She was frustrated enough to do bodily harm to the plumpish, graying woman, but she was determined not to cause a scene and risk having the place overrun with tabloid reporters. She'd been haunting the nurses' station since she found out about Jack's accident, hoping to talk to someone with the authority to override the supervisor's "instructions."

She'd been told it was a hit-and-run, that his condition had stabilized, that he was out of recovery and resting in his room. Beyond that they would tell her nothing, not even the extent of his injuries.

"When can I talk to his doctor?" she asked, forcing a calmer tone, though she was anything but. She'd clasped her hands and nearly rubbed the skin under her thumb raw.

She simply had to see him, for so many reasons. "I was told he hasn't been here since admitting Jack last night. Doesn't he do rounds? What kind of doctor is he?"

"The doctors generally do rounds after their office hours. He'll be in this afternoon, I'm sure. Excuse me," she said as a soft bing sounded, followed by a voice echoing through the hospital paging system. "They're calling me."

She was off down the hallway before Gus could say anything else, not that it would have helped. Since no one was willing to move the hurdles out of the way, Gus was going to have to find a way over them. She'd been eavesdropping on conversations all morning, hoping to pick up something, and at one point, she'd overheard the supervisor give a candy striper instructions to replenish the water pitcher in a patient's room. His last name had sounded like Jack's. Now all Gus had to do was find the room and enter unnoticed.

The room was on the seventh floor, and to her great relief, there was no one in the corridor when she found the number. Conflict flooded her as she let herself in and saw him lying in the hospital bed, unconscious. She simply couldn't sort out her feelings for the man. She was torn between a crazy desire to run away and an even crazier need to rush to him. She wanted to pour out her heart to his silent, sleeping form and tell him everything that was welling up inside her, hoping that he could hear her, and that he would understand her plight. She had things to tell him that she knew would astound and confound him, things she didn't know how to say. Worse, she was riddled with guilt and fear, and she loathed both emotions.

She'd had no idea how badly he was hurt, but the only injuries she could see now were a bandage on his forehead and a Styrofoam-like cast on his shoulder. Other than that, he seemed to be sleeping peacefully. At least he wasn't clinging to life inside an oxygen tent. Bridget had been so hysterical, the poor kid had made it sound as if he'd been torn limb from limb.

She walked to his bedside and stood there for a moment, watching him breathe and trying to decide what to do. There were multiple cuts on his face, and the large gauze bandage on his forehead looked as if it were covering a nasty bump. She was almost glad she couldn't see the disturbing blue glints of light in his black irises. They always threw her for a loop, his eyes. For now it was enough dealing with the way he looked as he slept.

She hadn't realized his lashes were quite so long or that the width of his mouth was as sensual as it was sensitive. But it was the lacerations on his face that pulled at her, stirring an entirely new contest within her. The cuts and bruises decorating his rugged features made him look surprisingly vulnerable and tender to the touch. It was all she could do to resist the temptation.

Her hand quickened a little with the urge.

Restraint, she decided, was a greatly overrated virtue.

As she bent closer, poised to glide her fingers over the proud flesh beneath his cheekbone, she saw his lashes quiver.

"Oh!" she cried, jerking back as his eyes flicked open.

She might have run if she hadn't been so startled. He didn't move, didn't speak. He simply stared at her with the eerie calm of a man who'd been waiting for her to come that close. Lying in wait. There was no confusion in his gaze, no drowsy remnants of sleep, just cold, deadly questions.

"What are you doing in here?" he asked, his voice as glacial as his eyes. Black ice, those eyes. That's how cold they were.

She moved back, seized again with the urge to run. "They wouldn't let me in. . . . I-I had to see how you were."

He looked her up and down, taking in her Chanel suit and stiletto heels with undisguised contempt. "Who are we today? Dress-up Barbie?"

"I had meetings," she started apologetically. "I came the moment I heard."

"Really? Did you? Shame I'm not on life support, isn't it. You could have pulled the plug."

She kept backing away from the bed. "What is it?" she asked him, unable to force her voice much above the whisper-level of his own. "What's wrong with you?"

With some effort he pushed himself up to a sitting position. "Someone ran their Mercedes into me and left me for dead. Excuse me if I'm not as chipper as usual."

"They told me it was a hit-and-run, but you're all right, aren't you? Your injuries don't look that serious, I mean—"

"The doctor tells me it's a miracle I'm alive. The police report said I was thrown thirty feet into a ditch alongside the road. Fortunately it was overgrown with grass and soaked down with runoff water from the estate's sprinklers."

"Thank God for that."

"I'm not done, Gus. The report also said I was hit by a red Mercedes convertible with a personalized license plate."

"A red Mercedes . . . like mine?"

He stared at her long and hard. "Just like yours, Gus." His mouth twisted into an ugly shape as he added, "*Exactly* like yours. R-E-D-H-O-T-T-T? Ring a bell?"

"But that's not possible."

"It's not only possible, I saw it with my own eyes. I was conscious the whole time. It was your car that hit me."

"But I was at a meeting, and I *drove* my car there."

He nodded, his laughter cynical. "Someone stole it, right? Is that the story? Someone stole your car and ran me down with it to make it look like you did it?"

"No one stole my car!" She walked to the window and looked out. The parking lot seven stories below was nearly full now, but it hadn't been when she'd arrived late last night. The Mercedes was parked up front without a scratch on it, or at least nothing that could be seen from this distance.

"Come and look," she told him. "My car's where I parked it last night when I got here, and that was *after* you'd been hit. The car would be dented if I'd been in the kind of hit-and-run you're describing, wouldn't it? Badly dented. You'd be able to see the damage even from here. Look."

He struggled out of the bed, determination apparently overcoming any weakness he might have felt. He was wearing one of those embarrassing hospital gowns that fasten in the back, and this one was definitely too small for his large frame, but he didn't seem self-conscious in the slightest, even with Gus staring as she was at the considerable exposure of his strong, sinewy legs.

His grimace told her he probably had a few taped ribs in addition to his other injuries. Painful, but not serious. A sigh released inside her, all the stronger for its having been held back so long. God, how he'd frightened her.

She stepped back, giving him plenty of room as he approached the window. She didn't want to crowd him in any way. Even with his injuries, she was sure he could be dangerous given his present state of mind. She could hardly forget that he himself had once warned her that she shouldn't have made the mistake of leaving him alive in the snakepit.

He looked out the window, silent and pensive as he stared at the car. She could almost see his mind whirring, trying to make sense of what had happened. How could her car be parked outside, undamaged, if it was the same car that had run him down? He'd believed it was her and apparently steeled himself to that horrible reality, despite everything that had happened between them the last few days. She could hardly blame him, given her other attempts on his life—and what he swore he'd seen . . . her red Mercedes.

"I didn't do it," she said, barely getting the words out. "J-Jack, I didn't. How can I make you believe me?"

He turned to her, distrust still smoldering in his features. The icy contempt she'd seen was banked now, overridden by the questions in his dark eyes, but it was there. He was torn, she could tell. He didn't want to believe her. It was probably easier not to, then he could justify whatever revenge he meant to take. He could go after the Featherstones and take them all down, her included. If he wanted to brutalize her alone, he could turn her over to the law with equanimity—

She met his questioning gaze with one of her own. "If the police believe it was me, why haven't they questioned me? No one's spoken to me or looked at the car. I've been here since last night—"

"The police don't know," he said brusquely. "I told them it happened too fast, that I couldn't I.D. the car. I just wanted to see what your reaction would be."

So he'd had doubts that it *was* her; otherwise he would have reported her. "Did I pass the test?" she asked him.

"What the hell is going on, Gus?" He flared angrily and moved toward her, but stopped short of touching her. "Who's trying to kill me? If it isn't you, then who?"

Gus could think of any number of people who might want him dead, including her ex-fiancé and almost everyone else in the immediate Featherstone circle, with the single exception of Bridget. She also knew of someone outside the circle who might pose a threat to him. She'd come here to warn him about that, but she couldn't do it just yet, because he wasn't going to like her news. Of that she was certain.

"I can't imagine that you're without enemies," she said, softening her voice. "You've told me what you do for a living, and I don't mean security systems." She meant killing people. He had told her that.

He slumped back against the windowsill as if exhausted. He probably shouldn't be out of bed, she realized, and she would have offered to help him back if she thought there was any chance he'd accept. Gazing at the rather endearing spectacle he made—a big, ruggedly handsome guy in a little bitty hospital gown—she felt a sigh of despair building. Her whole body trembled inwardly as she realized what she had yet to do. This was the lousiest possible timing, but she had no choice. There was something she had to tell him, something earth-shaking that had nothing to do with his car accident, and it couldn't wait any longer.

"Shouldn't you be resting?" She pointed out the chair alongside his bed. "Can I get that for you?"

"I'm fine," he insisted.

But he quite obviously wasn't. His jaw muscles were taut with pain as he studied her, searching her nervousness and noting the way she was mangling her white leather clutch.

"You look about as innocent as a hooker in a police lineup. You're begging me to believe you didn't do it, but I'm having a real hard time with that."

He focused in on her again, his gaze hardening. "Convince me, Gus. Make me believe you."

An odd sensuality had crept into his voice, and it abraded her nerves like a wire brush. Her bright red fingernails dug creases in the satin-soft contours of her bag. She was ruining the thing, but she felt as if she would fly apart if she let go of it.

"This isn't about guilt, Jack. There are things I need to tell you, and well . . . I think it might be a good idea if you sat down."

He rose instead. "What is it?"

Gus tucked the bag under her arm and began to walk the floor. This was going to be bad, she could feel it. It was going to be worse than bad. There was no way he could possibly be receptive to her news given the situation. She could feel his eyes on her awkward gait and wished she'd had time to change. Her sky-high heels made pacing a challenge, but she was too uneasy to stand still.

"I've seen a . . . doctor, too," she said, aware of the hesitation that had snuck into her voice. This time she almost wished it would stop her, that she wouldn't be able to get the rest of it out. But no such luck. "It seems I had a little accident, too, but I didn't know anything for sure until today."

"Accident? What do you mean?"

For some reason tears welled up as she turned to him. Thank goodness he was across the room. She hoped he couldn't see the way her eyes must be glittering. There was nothing to do but say it, and yet her throat muscles grabbed frantically, and the words burned like acid as she tried to force them out.

"I'm pregnant," she told him hoarsely.

He stared at her as if she'd spoken in another language and he hadn't understood a word of it. Pain struck Gus's heart as she took in his bewildered expression. She had imagined so many different reactions. This was not one of them.

"I'm going to have a baby, Jack. I—we—"

"P-pregnant?" The word came out cold and incredulous. She nodded.

"A . . . bah . . . a baby?"

Now she could talk and he couldn't? Someone upstairs had a cruel sense of humor, she decided. His gaze was running up and down her body as if he were searching for evidence, and all the time he was shaking his head. Clearly this was not good news to him, she realized, and stupidly, she must have wanted to think it would be. But why? Because he'd carved her name in a heart on a tree? Apparently that one decidedly childish form of endearment had made her think that he cared, that he might want her enough to want her baby, too, especially if it were his child.

How perfectly absurd of her.

She drew in a deep breath, trying to calm herself. But her heart hurt so fiercely it might as well have been her flesh he'd carved instead of the tree. Too many TV commercials, Gus! Too many pregnancy test ads where the husband beams like a demented idiot and takes the little wife and mother-to-be into his arms. Too many Pampers ads, *too many ridiculously romantic, happily-ever-after fairy tales!*

"I don't see how—"

"There's no mistake." She cut him off indignantly. "I'm pregnant, and it's your child. I haven't been with anyone else."

"When did that happen? We only made love two nights ago."

"We made love in the desert, too, in the shower. Or have you forgotten?"

"Not likely, but I didn't—"

She looked at him accusingly, then added one pithy word. "Leakage."

He raised his hand, then dropped it helplessly. "Jesus, I do need to sit down." He walked stiffly to the chair that sat alongside his bed and collapsed into its creaky vinyl contours. "How long have you known?" he asked.

Gus had expected surprise, even shock, but nothing like this. All the blood had drained from his face, and he seemed totally thunderstruck, almost unable to conceive of the idea. *Conceive.* Unfortunate choice of words, she thought.

"I didn't know," she said, "not for sure. I thought there might be a chance, and it was time for a check-up anyway, so I went in—"

"A baby?" he muttered under his breath. "Christ, what a sick joke this is."

Gus stared at him in horror, unable to comprehend how he could have said such a brutal thing. She was gripped with the urge to fly at him, to slap him! But he didn't even seem to be aware of her presence. He was shaking his head as if he didn't know whether to laugh or cry.

"You bastard," she breathed. She couldn't stop herself. It spewed out of her like venom. "*You're* the sick joke."

He looked up at her, his eyes still wild and disbelieving. It was the reaction she would have expected if she'd admitted that it was she who tried to run him down. In some way that Gus couldn't understand, this seemed a worse betrayal to him. It was easier for him to deal with the possibility that she'd tried to run him over than to find out she was pregnant with his child. A bitter taste seared the lining of her mouth as she attempted to swallow. It was anger mixed with scalding hurt. Her eyes brimmed with tears, and she shook her head, realizing she'd totally misjudged the situation.

She never should have told him. She should have done something—anything!—taken care of it herself, gone to a clinic. What an idiot she'd been wanting to share it with him, thinking that they would come to a decision together. Her mistake. A terrible mistake.

"I'll handle this myself," she said, turning away from him. The door to his room might as well have been at the other end of the earth. She would never make it, it seemed so far away. She'd also come here to warn him and to confess that she'd done something stupid which might have endangered him. But none of that seemed to matter now. It was all connected to some distant, nebulous situation that had nothing to do with the acid searing its way down her windpipe when she tried to breathe. She had said all she could say. There wasn't another word left in her that her stunned heart could muster or her lips could manage.

CHAPTER
25

"SO IS HE *REEEE*ALLY ALL RIGHT? ARE YOU SURE, GUS? DID you talk to him? Wha'd he say?" Bridget was lying on her back on Gus's bedroom floor, her slippered feet propped up against the arm of the overstuffed chair. Garbed in her usual pink leotard and tights, she was exploring the mysteries of Gus's sacred Cinderella music box. Lying on its back right beside her was the hippo Jack had bought her.

"He's *fine*, Bridge. We've already established that." Gus didn't know how else to discourage the child other than to be short and sharp with her answers. Bridget had been clamoring for information all evening about the man Gus most wanted to forget. But Gus wasn't prepared to explain any of that to the child, not just yet. She couldn't. She was in far too much turmoil. She could hardly breathe for it. She could scarcely think.

If there were razor blades in her voice, it was because those same blades were cutting their way into her heart, flashing and bright as diamonds. The nicks and lacerations were as fresh and tender as those on his face. *His* face. God, the very thought of Jack Culhane brought outrage.

Curled up in the matching overstuffed chair, Gus was furiously determined to concentrate on the limited partnership agreement she would be entering into with investors in the magazine. She'd had the family lawyer draw it up, but she wanted to be totally conversant with the provisions before she sat down to any discussion. She was determined to be taken seriously, but God help her, she'd been rereading this first clause for an hour and she still didn't know what it meant. She couldn't concentrate on anything. The bitter hurt she felt kept welling up, bringing her thoughts back to him.

"Why didn't you bring him home?" Bridget pressed on, undaunted. "I mean if he was fine, he should've come home with you, right? Are you sure he was fine? That car really creamed him, Gus. I thought he was dead for sure. Did they ever find the person who did it?"

"Bridget—" Gus was struggling mightily to be patient. Her niece had been traumatized by what she'd seen, and the child needed lots of reassurance, not only about Jack's physical condition, but about whether or not he was coming back. But Gus couldn't bring herself to pretend that everything was going to be all right, not even for Bridget's sake. Her emotions had turned on her. They were cutting her to pieces. Tomorrow, she told herself. By tomorrow some of this craziness would have subsided and she and Bridget could talk. "Isn't it bedtime, kiddo?"

"Not even close. I've got another hour to go."

The bell-like chimes of the music box made Gus flinch. It was the theme from the Disney movie, and she could hardly believe that there was a time when she'd listened to it for hour upon hour, dreaming and yearning right along with Cinderella. Even a six-year-old should have known better! *Some day my prince will come?* If that wasn't the silliest piece of romantic crap she'd ever heard in her life, she didn't know what was. Whoever'd written the thing ought to be sued for putting that notion into young girls' heads! Normally she wouldn't have let Bridget play with the music box, but tonight it had seemed important to distract her.

"Could you put that away, Bridget, *please*," she implored. "I can't think straight with it jangling."

"Oh, ohhhhhkay," the little girl said, sighing. The box landed on the floor with a plunk, went blessedly silent, and was summarily forgotten as Bridget laid claim to the stuffed animal. "I just wish he'd come back so I could tell him how much I like my hippo."

"Feel free to tell me, Bridge. I'm right here."

Gus's head came up with a snap that made the room spin. She nearly lost her grip on her papers and had to squish them in her lap to keep from dropping them. Jack Culhane was standing in the doorway to her bedroom, big as life and looking infuriatingly healthy, a bemused smile on his face.

His color had returned, she noted rather cynically, taking in the deep golden tones of his skin and the flush that rose from his throat and ruddied his jaw. The cast was off his shoulder, but his forehead was still bandaged. Other than that, he didn't look like a man who'd had a recent brush with death. And was due for another one, if she had her way.

The sight of him brought Bridget's entire body off the ground. The hippo went flying. "Jack!" she squealed, jack-knifing to her feet and making a run for him.

"Hey, wait a minute!" He tried to hold her off, but couldn't. Grunting loudly, he lifted her into his arms as she flung herself at him.

Gus sprang up too, horrified. "Bridget! He has a dislocated shoulder. You're hurting him!"

"No, I'm not! Am I, Jack?"

The little girl clung to him, but Jack set her down gingerly, sweat dripping from his brow. "You're killing me, kid," he said, his laughter punctuated by genuine pain.

"Look, I saved the hippo!" She ran to get it, but by the time she'd picked it up and turned around, Jack's attention was riveted elsewhere. He was staring at Gus and the piercing intensity in his blue-black eyes told her that he'd come here for something that was going to change her life. Not that he hadn't already. God!

Bridget hesitated, looking from one of them to the other. "Jack?" she tried once more, softly. "Geez . . . what is this? Are you guys falling in love or something?"

Jack smiled. "Doesn't miss much, does she," he said to Gus, wiping the dampness from his brow with the sleeve of his black fleece workout jacket.

Still watching them both, Bridget clutched the hippo close to her cheek and nuzzled her chin in the fur. "Are we fighting?" she asked, clearly mesmerized. "Or are we making up?"

"That depends on your aunt," Jack said.

Gus tilted at him, her chin lifting rebelliously.

Bridget made a *whoops* face. "Maybe I should go?"

"Thanks, Bridge," Jack said. "It looks like your aunt and I need to talk."

"Sure does—" The little girl bit her lip, trying to hide a nervous smile, then hesitated in her dash to the door. "And while you're at it, could you please explain to her that I am *not* too young to read Sweet Valley Highs? You can't shield a child from life, you know. Better I learn in a book than on the streets, right?"

"I'll see what I can do," Jack promised. "But you've got to do me a favor, okay? Don't tell anybody I'm here."

Once Bridget was gone, and the door was closed, Gus released the breath she'd been holding. It only trembled a little, nowhere near as much as she was shaking inside. He was clearly in pain, but that didn't stop him from being one of the most irresistibly sexy men she'd ever seen, which only made her hate him more. She'd never been so reluctant and yet so frantic to see anyone in her life. Or so furious at herself for feeling that way. How could she abide the sight of him after what he'd done? How could she allow him in her room, her sanctuary, *her shrine to Cinderella?*

She knew why he was here, and it wasn't because of her. Webb Calderon had insinuated that Jack was on a single-minded quest for justice, which was just another word for vengeance. Whatever he'd gone through, Jack held the

Featherstones responsible, and he was bent on proving that. She'd hoped her news of the baby might soften him in some way, even stave him off, but she'd been wrong. It had only made things worse.

"Are you all right?" he asked.

Before she could answer, he'd begun visually searching the walls of her room. He spotted what he was looking for almost immediately, pulled a tiny can from the pocket of his sweat pants, walked to the far wall, and reached up to the wallpaper panel that abutted the ceiling.

Gus peered at his back. "What are you doing?"

"Making sure we have some privacy." He sprayed one of the wallpaper roses with what looked like water from the pressurized can. "Your stepbrother's a freak, Gus. He likes to watch people, and that includes you."

"Lake has this room monitored?" Gus's mind flashed back over all the times she'd run around naked, and her reaction was as much surprise as a sense of violation. Why hadn't it ever occurred to her? she wondered. Howard, the security guard, was the one who'd told her about Lake's roomful of monitors. Fortunately it had been well past her stepbrother's bedtime the night Rob had sneaked into her room.

Jack had turned back by then. "I asked you how you were."

"I'm fine," she snapped. "And you?"

"I'm not the one who's pregnant."

The catch of husky emotion in his voice made her hesitate on the sharp retort she had ready. He was searching her with eyes that were as dark as pitch, eyes that had narrowed with obvious concern. He almost looked as if he cared, and Gus's throat tugged as if it wanted to close off. She could have read all kinds of wonderful things into that expression, and she wanted to. She could feel a tiny shudder of rising hope, along with her fears. The thoughts running through her mind astonished her. *Don't make me believe in you, Jack Culhane. I've never believed in anyone but myself. It was safer that way with a mother like mine. I can't deal with any more heartbreak, any more disappointment. Both my parents deserted me, and no one I've loved ever kept their promises, so why should you?*

"Gus . . ."

He walked toward her as he said her name and something in the sound of it, just the sound of her name on his lips brought a stinging sensation to her jaw. The muscles constricted so sharply that her vision went blurry with tears.

By the time he reached her, he'd seen it all, the salty flood she was trying to blink away, her awkward attempt to adjust her tank top so that it didn't cling.

"Gus, I'm sorry," he said.

She ducked her head. "Sorry about what? I'm fine. Really. It's just . . . something. Suicidal hormones . . . or something, I don't know."

"Gus, what you heard was me thinking out loud—about the wretched state of my life and about how insane it is that you should be pregnant now, with my child. It had nothing to do with my feelings for you or the baby. It's the timing, the perverse irony that this is happening now. That's the sick joke. Can you understand that?"

She bit her lip hard, desperate to hold back the tears.

"It was clumsy of me, clumsy and stupid. I never should have said it, okay?" He touched one of the droplets that was clinging to her lower lash and caught it just before it fell off. "You've got to admit, you did catch me off guard. I was run down by a red Mercedes with your license plate one night, and the next morning you're in my hospital room, telling me you're pregnant."

His sigh held as much sadness as laughter. "I wasn't sure what hit me. Literally."

"Put that way it does sound pretty boggling," she admitted. "But you were so quick to believe it was me. You did, you know. You believed it was me."

"At first, yes. But you have to understand why." He was feathering her cheek now, with fingertips moist from her tears. "I wasn't in shock and I wasn't hallucinating when that car hit me. It was a red convertible with your plates. I don't know how to explain that now. I didn't want to believe it then, but nothing else made sense. You had the motive, and you'd already tried your damndest to bump me off. So here I am, thinking you're a killer, and you're trying to tell me you're pregnant."

"I had the feeling you would have preferred me as killer to mother."

His hesitation told her she might be right. "You scared the hell out of me," he admitted. "But I think I know why. Gus, I—"

"No," she said instantly, startled as she realized that she didn't want to know. She was actually afraid he'd say something that meant he did care, something that would tug at her nicked and bleeding heart and make her have to care back. And she couldn't. She just couldn't open herself to that kind of pain. It would kill her to love someone, *him*. She wouldn't survive. Everyone she'd loved had abandoned her, even Jillian.

She turned away, but he was there, his hands on her arms.

"I need to tell you this," he urged, his voice low and thrillingly harsh. "You already know that my wife died several years ago. What I didn't tell you is that I lost a child, too, a baby daughter. She was just six months old, and when I sat through her memorial service, I thought I was dying, too. I felt as if someone had doused me with gasoline and held a torch to me. I felt as if I were being burnt alive. I wished I had been."

His hands dropped away, and the hoarseness rising in his voice wouldn't let him talk for a moment. "It was my fault. Both of their deaths probably could have been prevented if I hadn't been trying to be a hero. They might be alive—"

He went silent again, and Gus sensed that he was struggling. There was so much she wanted to know—how the tragedies had happened, how he could be to blame. She also needed to understand if this had anything to do with his vendetta against her family. But more than any of that she wanted to turn into the warmth of his body and comfort him . . . only she didn't trust herself. It would take so little for her to fall apart, *to fall in love*.

"I see now why you wouldn't want more children," she said.

"Do you? Can you understand why even the thought of having another family paralyzes me?"

Yes, she did understand. She understood perfectly. He felt exactly the way she did. It meant he would have something to lose, that he would have to go through that pain again. And he didn't think he could do it. He was afraid to let himself love anything or anyone.

"Gus . . . do you want this baby?"

She didn't answer. She couldn't. Something in the way he spoke touched her on so many levels. Low and reverberant, it whispered to her dreams. This wasn't the burnt-out, toneless rasp she was used to. He was here now, emotionally involved with the question and her answer, whatever that would be. He wanted to know. Her response was important to him.

"You've got Bridget," he said, "and somehow I couldn't imagine you wanting a kid of your own, especially with the magazine." He touched her, a light brush of his hand down her arm. "Do you want it, Gus?"

She didn't know what she wanted, except the one thing that would make her life impossible . . . him. She wanted him, his arms, his mouth. It had to be the perverse side of her nature that always went after what it couldn't have, the side that set her up for failure. "I don't know," she said honestly.

She heard him sigh, felt his hand fall away, and a shock of awareness went through her. "Do you?" She spun around, unable to believe, not willing to believe that he could possibly . . . "Do you want this baby?"

His lips parted as if he wanted to say something, and there was this pained, crooked smile on his face. For a moment she thought he'd nodded his head yes, but the words that came out were achingly soft, achingly sad. "God, Gus, what would I do with a baby?"

Her heart twisted. "Yeah . . . that's what I thought."

They were silent for seconds, and finally she walked to

the window. He didn't follow her this time, and the quiet was so pervasive, she imagined that he had left.

"But if I did want . . ." He hesitated and her heart became a hammer. "If I did want it, what would you have said?"

The music box began to play softly, startling Gus as the melody from the Disney movie sang out like a choir of bells. An image of Cinderella singing wistfully shimmered in Gus's mind, and it took her a moment to realize that this wasn't a sign from the heavens. Jack was crossing the room toward her and his foot must have brushed the box.

"What would I have said?" she whispered, more to herself than him. "I'd have said that Bridget was right the first time."

"What do you mean?"

She could feel heat creeping up the back of her neck and flaring around to her throat. By the time she looked up at him, it had stormed her face clear to her hairline and her scalp was prickling with it, too—deep, rosy heat. She was blushing wildly, hotly. "That I'm falling in love . . . with you."

He touched the warmth of her cheeks as if he knew it was for him. "That's the prettiest sight I think I've ever seen," he said.

She shuddered at the contact. The caress of his fingers touched nerves that reached to her core. Lots of men had called her beautiful. She'd been described by the media with so many glowing superlatives that the words had become meaningless. She'd never believed them anyway, never believed any of the flattering things people had said about her. But pretty? That her blushing face was a pretty thing? That she believed. Because no one had ever used the word in the way he had, or meant it the way he did. He was seeing beyond the physical beauty to the miracle that was stirring in her heart.

She'd never felt so awkward in her life. Or so pretty.

Chimes filled the silence that fell between them.

"I guess Bridget left her toy," he said at last. "She is a romantic kid."

Gus glanced at the twirling figure of Cinderella and nodded, unwilling to admit who the romantic kid really was. The song was making her ache, and it had become impossible to avoid his gaze any longer. She sighed and looked up with some reluctance, not wanting him to see what she knew must be in her eyes and afraid what she might find in his.

What she feared was there, everything she feared.

She saw desire so strong and fierce it hurt her to witness it. She saw traces of rage and the unrequited need for his enemy's blood. But the tenderness and wanting that washed over her made her heart rise and tilt. The love she saw made her senses sing like the music box.

He touched her hip, his hand lingering possessively. "Yes, I want this baby," he said. "Almost as much as I want you."

A gasp of surprise welled in Gus's throat, and before she could get it under control, it shook through her like a sob. A joyous sob. Her vision misted with tears, and his eyes became diamonds, dazzling hard and bright.

"Can I make love to you?" he asked. "In your delicate condition?"

"You'd better," she whispered, unable to locate her voice in the riotous clamor of her vital signs.

They were *both* in a delicate condition as they discovered when they began to undress each other. Gus had forgotten all about his cracked ribs. "I'll be gentle," she said as she unzipped his jacket and slipped her hands inside, glorying in the feel of his hard, warm torso.

His shudder said he couldn't stand it any longer.

"You promise?" He caught his hands in her hair possessively and drew her head back, bending over her until his mouth was aligned with hers and the breath from their bodies mingled. "You promise not to hurt me?"

"I'll n-never h-hurt you." The words got terribly tangled up, but she didn't care. "I'll never leave you."

He slipped his hands inside her tank and slid them up to her breasts. She let out a sweet moan and pressed against his palms as he cupped her. They were cool against her flushed skin.

The sound of her own joyous laughter made her throw her head back. She was unable to do anything for a moment but simply feel the shaking wonder of being with him. I love you so much, she thought. So much! But she couldn't say it. That would have made her blush to her toes, and she probably never would have gotten the words out. Enough was enough. Even Gus Featherstone had some dignity . . . but not much where he was concerned.

They ended up on her frilly canopy bed, still half-dressed, Gus in her tank top, Jack in his briefs. Gus took the time to administer some first aid as she bent to kiss the bandages that wrapped his ribs, and then she addressed herself to his scars, particularly the one near his hip, where she gently pressed her lips and moaned softly. That was all it took to incite him to shed the rest of his clothes, which revealed a state of wondrous physical ardor.

He pulled up her tank, exposing her breasts. His eyes flared at the sight of her, but he didn't touch her, just drank her in for several seconds before he bent to take her in his mouth. He thrilled her with his sweet, tugging lips. He sent hot, piercing loveliness all through her, bringing her to the very brink of a spontaneous release, then pulling away. She wanted to do the same for him, but he wouldn't let her. As she tried to trail kisses down his torso to his groin, he held her at bay.

"No, you don't," he said, fending off her questing mouth and fingers. "We'll have *none* of that. I want you on your back, wife. I want to be inside you the whole time, for all of it."

Though it clearly gave him pain to do so, he lifted her bodily and arranged her beneath him on the bed. As he moved between her legs and stared into her eyes, Gus felt the need of him instantly. She didn't want to be touched or fondled or stroked, no matter how lovely that might feel. She wanted the maleness that jutted from between his thighs. She couldn't wait another second for it, and the look in her eyes must have told him so, because he opened her with his fingers and entered her with that thrilling part of him, delving into her immediately, deeply, hungrily.

Her body accepted him with a clutch of pleasure that bordered on rapture. She reached for him, crying out as he pulled her into his arms and drove into her, and though it felt as if he were touching her soul, it wasn't deep enough. She couldn't stop moaning and whimpering and gasping her astonishment at the sensations. She couldn't get enough, couldn't stop begging for more, imploring him not to stop, and finally, when he rolled her over and settled her on his hips, the depth of his penetration sent her into a swift, profound climax. She arched up and shuddered, cresting with a fury that made her shoulders sway and her head loll.

A sound locked in her throat, anguished.

His body was electric, hard-wired with virile energy. As he flexed inside her, he crushed the material of her tank in his hands and held it up, bringing her to him so that he could ravish and suckle her breasts. His wild ardor nearly sent Gus over the edge for a second time.

She was swaying with ecstasy when he began to buck and shudder, his body on a journey it had almost forgotten how to take. He caught hold of her face, searching it, gripping her at the moment of release, and she'd never seen such agony pass through a man, such dark, flaring beauty. He was being torn apart before her eyes, fighting for control, unable to contain the ravaging emotional storm. It moved through his body like a hurricane, and then his eyelids drooped and he was gone somewhere, lost in his own wondrous completion.

She saw what might have been a tear squeeze out and catch in the creases of his eye. It was gone by the time he opened them and gazed at her, but they were wet with relief and brilliant with spent passion.

Some time later, as they lay on their sides in her bed, facing each other, her head in the curve of his elbow, he let out a gust of disbelieving laughter. "What did you do to me? I lost it so totally I'm going to have to put out a missing person's report to find it again."

She laughed with him, busy exploring the nasty scar on his shoulder and wondering how he got it. Secretly she was overjoyed that he had surrendered to his feelings, but she didn't want to embarrass him in any way. "Maybe whatever it was you lost, you didn't need?" she suggested.

"Right, who needs self-control," he quipped. By now he was taking her cue and playing with her shoulder, but his fingers didn't stay there long. They drifted to the inner slope of her breast, sending a sweet shiver of anticipation through her.

"I think I may want to do that again," he said. "You've just given this kid a new toy."

She met his eyes and sighed, so full of bliss and silliness she could burst. Cinderella's got nothing on me, she thought, wanting to laugh again. If there was a lingering shadow on her horizon, she'd decided to ignore it for a bit longer. There were still things she needed to talk with him about. She hadn't yet told him what she'd done or her suspicions about who might want him out of the way. He was convinced it was her family, but she had reason to believe otherwise. She couldn't do that now, however, not quite yet. She couldn't bear to break the mood.

If only he wasn't touching her so beautifully, if only he wasn't gazing at her as if she were the woman of his dreams. Morning, she thought. It will keep until then.

She was asleep when Jack woke up, deeply asleep and curled up beside him like a kitten. His need for her was immediate and intense. The stitch of pain he felt with each breath barely registered. He wanted to do it again, like some kind of fourteen-year-old kid, who'd just had sex for the first time; he wanted the amazing beauty of it again.

He curled his hand to the softness of her butt and kissed her shoulder. He wanted to revel in the control he'd lost with her. He wanted to come inside her again and again, until he couldn't any more, but something about her concerned him. Despite all of her blushing last night, she looked oddly fragile this morning, pale and thin, too thin for a pregnant woman, and her breathing seemed a little labored. Had he hurt her last night?

"Gus? Wake up, baby. Are you okay?"

Before he could rouse her, a noise distracted him. The melodious chimes of the front doorbell drifted up from downstairs. They were followed by a pounding that alerted him something was wrong. He glanced at his watch and saw that it was nearly ten A.M. Quietly he slipped on his sweatpants and went to investigate.

He hesitated in the hallway that led to the stairway, and confirmed his suspicions that someone had come to the front door. He heard voices, the only one of which he recognized was Lake's. As he neared he was able to pick up enough of the conversation to know that there were at least two men, they were from the Treasury Department, and they were looking for him.

"What relation is Jack Culhane to you, Mr. Featherstone? And how long has he been residing at this address?" one of them asked.

"He's my brother-in-law," Lake answered. "He's been here a week, maybe, I'm not sure. Is something wrong?"

"A valuable painting's been stolen, and we'd like to ask Mr. Culhane some questions. Is he here now?"

"Yes, he's upstairs with his wife, my sister, Augusta."

Jack crept forward, totally alert. Lake must have seen Jack enter Gus's room before Jack covered the aperture. That was the only way he could have known Jack spent the night, unless Bridget told him, which was unlikely.

"Where upstairs?" one of the men asked.

"You're sure he's in there?" the other questioned.

Jack didn't need to hear any more to know that he was a suspect in an art theft. The two men claimed to be Treasury, which he had no reason to doubt, except that he doubted everything in circumstances like these. It was easy enough to come up with phony ID. Still, it didn't matter what their story was, or who they were, they'd come after him. That was enough reason to perform a vanishing act.

"Shall I get him for you?" Lake was asking.

Yeah, you asshole, Jack thought. Hand me over to the Feds.

"Why don't you take us upstairs," one of them said. "We'll talk to him there."

"If you'll come with me," Lake was telling the men.

Jack began to ease back down the hallway, his mind zeroing in on a mental floorplan of the huge house and all the various exit strategies. Getting out was only part of the problem. He didn't know what he'd be facing once he was out. It was unlikely they'd staked the place out, but if they had, there could be a guard posted at every exit.

Lake had been much too eager to accommodate the visitors, now that Jack thought about it. They hadn't mentioned a warrant, so Lake must have okayed them at the guard gate, which meant he'd had plenty of time to call Gus on the intercom and warn her that they were there.

The footsteps coming Jack's way told him to move out. Hiding in the house was a trap. With Lake running interference for them, they wouldn't need a warrant to search the place. He'd probably escort them room-by-room, the deluxe tour, including back stairways and hidden passageways. There wasn't going to be time to tell Gus, Jack realized. He couldn't even leave her a note. He had to get out now.

Torn by his need to escape and his need to protect her, especially now that she was pregnant, he hesitated in the hallway. If he lost his freedom, he would never catch the monsters responsible for his wife and child's deaths. He couldn't let that happen. He'd followed the demons into hell and become one of them in order to get to this place. He was close, too close. He could smell the bastard who had masterminded it all. He could almost reach out and grab him by the balls he was so close. All he needed was the proof. If his hunch was right, all he needed was that painting, Blush.

He turned and sprinted down the hallway toward the same secret stairway he'd used the night he'd pulled off his vanishing act in the library. He was about to do an encore.

CHAPTER
26

JACK PUSHED THE SCAN BUTTON ON THE CAR RADIO, LETTING the stations stutter by until a news bulletin about the art theft came up. He jabbed the button again to stop the scanner, knowing the news wasn't going to be good. He'd been listening to essentially the same bulletin for the last hour.

"Investigators from the Treasury Department have joined forces with the FBI and the LAPD," the reporter was saying, "and they are currently seeking the prime suspect, a former security expert from the U.S. Customs Office who goes by the alias Jack Culhane. Culhane was relieved of his Customs duties five years ago after a job-related blackmail attempt resulted in the kidnapping and death of his baby daughter. He later served time in prison for the felony assault of a man he mistakenly believed to be one of the kidnappers—"

A twist of the Power knob killed the radio.

Jack needed the silence to think. Someone had pulled off the heist he'd described at dinner and framed him for it. They'd stolen a thirty-million-dollar Picasso. He'd known his strategy was a risky way to up the ante, but he'd had to show enough of his hand to let the other players know he wasn't bluffing. The old adage about it taking a thief to catch a thief was true. The one about honor among thieves was bullshit.

Besides Lake, Lily, and Gus, there had been four others there that night—Ward McHenry, Rob Emory, Webb Calderon, and the housekeeper. When none of them had taken the bait and approached Jack to inquire about his unique services, Jack had suspected something was wrong. Now he understood what it was. His cover had been blown. Jack's nemesis had discovered who he was dealing with. Someone had found The Magician's bag of tricks, reached in, and pulled out a Picasso.

It was fucking brilliant, Jack thought, aware of the car's temperature gauge as he headed into the crematorium heat of the Mojave. His admiration was almost as great as his need to nail the bastard, because he was virtually certain that once he'd done that, he would have the one who had set him up five years ago.

The gauge's climbing needle warned him that the Blazer's engine was laboring under the load of the air-conditioning. He switched the unit off and rolled down the window, grimacing at the haymaker punch the desert heat packed, even at this hour of the morning.

The Mojave was as hot and silent as a tomb in hell by the time he pulled the car to a stop in the same deserted stretch of road where he'd brought Gus when he'd kidnapped her. Remembering her antics coaxed a fleeting smile from his lips, but the memory was bittersweet now. It held far more pain than amusement, especially since he couldn't be with her or do anything to ensure that she and the baby would be safe.

It astonished him how much he wanted that—to protect her in every way possible, with his life, if necessary. He would have done almost anything. The way his heart fisted told him he wanted that perhaps even more than he wanted to reconcile the errors of his past. But as he sat in the Blazer's cab and stared at the bleached and deadly landscape awaiting him, he understood that he couldn't allow that to happen. He couldn't want anything more than he wanted justice for his family and retribution for the killers. If he did, his soul was lost.

The car door slammed shut with a resounding crack as he let himself out and went around to the hatch for his duffel bag.

Moments later as he trekked through the desert toward the shack, he forced his thoughts back to the mental grid on which he had always mapped his strategies. At least where the Feds were concerned, he knew what he was up against. His background gave him that advantage. Specialized units would be mobilized like the LAPD Art Bunco Squad and the U.S. Customs & Excise Investigative Unit. A manhunt would be organized and an APB issued, which meant his mug shot, rap sheet, and other vital information would be flashed coast-to-coast on the television news, as well as the vast computer network of law enforcement agencies.

But none of that was the reason he'd headed for the desert. He was playing out a hunch by going to the miner's shack. It was a hellishly risky one, but he had to follow his instincts. They'd failed him five years ago, probably because he'd been in such a rage to catch the killers, he'd nearly annihilated the decoy they'd thrown his way. The game was bloodsport, and he'd made too many errors. He couldn't afford to make any now, and even if he played it expertly, *perfectly*, he could still come out the loser because he'd been forced into a counterplot that was fraught with pitfalls. Normally he would have gone into hiding, but he couldn't do that now. He had to hide in plain sight. This time he had to *be* the decoy.

A chill floated up Jack's arm, prickling the skin. He grew instantly still, aware of another presence in the mining shack. He'd repositioned the cot against the far wall, and he was lying there now, waiting. The door had fallen open, though he hadn't heard a sound, and a silent white form was standing on the threshold. It seemed to have materialized out of the phosphorescence, and Jack couldn't tell if it was human or moonlight. He touched the gun at his side as the brightness slowly skated toward him.

Moonlight could move, but it didn't bleed.

The gun's safety was off, and his trigger finger was poised and ready to fire. The greatest challenge was knowing exactly when. If he miscalculated, it was all over. His plan went up. In the meantime he couldn't do anything to signal the apparition that he was awake and watching. He couldn't allow the rhythm of his breathing to change. If the thing got suspicious, if it stopped to investigate, he might as well shoot himself.

Come on, he urged silently as the silvery form approached. *Five more feet and we'll see whether you're a ghost or not.*

Jack had been holed up in the shack for three days, seventy-two hours of waiting for this moment. It was all he could do to keep breathing as the thing hesitated near the tarp that lay on the floor. To avoid the tarp it had to move left, which would be the last step it took.

Wood crackled and split. Jack sprang up, gun in hand, as the phantom broke through the loose boards and vanished from sight. The fleshy swish and thump of muscle and bone told him it had hit the bottom of the pit. A snarled obscenity told him it was human.

Jack had stashed a wall lantern and some matches under the cot. Once he had the lantern lit, he left it near the cot and approached the pit from another angle, weapon ready, in case the intruder was armed.

"Christ," he breathed as he saw who it was. Webb Calderon was brushing the loose dirt from his long dun-colored coat, and when he looked up the barrel of Jack's cocked gun, the ice crystals in his winter-gray eyes glittered and froze.

"A deadfall?" he said with a cold smile. "Interesting idea, Jack. I was expecting some kind of ambush, but not this."

"And I was expecting someone to come after me, but not you. How'd you find me, Calderon? *Why* did you find me?"

"Your wife told me you might be here."

"My wife?" *Rage*. It flared so violently Jack felt as if he were lunging forward, though he hadn't moved. He knew men like Calderon. They baited and switched until they'd tricked you into something stupid. "What the fuck does that mean?"

"I spoke with her, Culhane. I didn't sleep with her . . . and if I had, I wouldn't have been so careless as to get her pregnant."

The gun jerked in Jack's grip. He yanked his hand still and took deadly aim, imagining the blood that would gush from Calderon's shattered skull, relishing it.

"I'm not the enemy." Webb stepped back as if to prove that. "I had something your wife wanted, so she gave me something I wanted. Information. It was all very civilized."

"Killing you quickly is about as civilized as I'm going to get tonight." Jack imagined squeezing one off and feeling the wild satisfaction of the gun's kick in the back of his neck. He vividly imagined it. And then he did it. He pulled the trigger.

To Calderon's credit he never moved, not even when the bullet dug into the mud wall behind him with a liquid *whommp*.

The soft, profane word he uttered sounded more like a prayer of thanks than a curse. "What's the rush, Jack?" he wanted to know. "I came here with news about Gus. You may want to hear it."

Jack moved in, gripping the gun in both hands. He wanted to be sure he was close enough to blow the bastard's head off if he said the wrong thing. "What about her?"

"She's in trouble."

"What kind of trouble?"

"You're not going to like this, Jack."

The rage was still simmering, and Jack knew it would take very little to push it to flashpoint. For five years it had been the demon driving him, but more often than not, he'd managed to keep it leashed. Now it was going to snap the rein. He could feel it. *He wanted it to*. He wanted the violence. He wanted the blood. He wanted the justice.

"You better hope I like it, Calderon," he warned.

They stared at each other, the two of them, deadlocked.

Jack remained silent and finally Calderon spoke. "She lost the baby . . . and she's taking it badly."

Jack felt a cold fist in his gut. He nearly dropped to his knees, and then he was swept with a sense of disbelief. "Lost the baby? She just found out she was pregnant."

"A woman can lose a baby at any time. That's not the point. Apparently Gus wanted this baby badly. She's devastated by the loss. She hasn't been out of her room. She won't see a doctor."

If Jack had had any doubt how much Gus meant to him, he didn't now. His other losses had cut him to ribbons. He'd thought there was nothing left of him alive, but some tiny spark of hope was still there, a starving ember in need of oxygen. The agony he felt told him that.

Calderon kept talking, his voice oddly soothing, yet at the same time, disturbing. "She's not going to make it without you, Jack," he said. "She's in danger, both she and Bridget are, but they don't know it."

The scars on Jack's body burned, as if he'd just been shot, just that second, as if the wounds were bleeding. "What kind of danger?"

The art dealer lifted his head. "I've said all I can."

"You sick bastard!"

"Pull the trigger if you think that will help anything. Go ahead, all you can do is kill me." The cold smile surfaced again, turning Calderon's eyes to icy pools. "It wouldn't be anything new."

Jack had no idea what the man was talking about. He could hardly believe the pain that had gripped him. *She'd lost the baby? Christ, he wanted to tear the place apart. He wanted to drop to his knees and sob.*

The impulse that shook through him was as powerful as anything he'd ever felt. He had to get the hell out of the shack and go to her. He had to help her get through this.

He could take Calderon's car, leave the bastard in the pit for snake food, and *go*. But something was holding him back. It wasn't that easy, he realized. Beneath the pain, he sensed the desperation again, felt it rising up like a flood. This could be a trap and Gus could be the bait. Calderon might be setting him up for whoever was waiting for him back at the Featherstone mansion.

"Why are you telling me this?" he asked the art dealer. "What's in it for you?"

"Let's just say I have a stake in the outcome and leave it at that."

Jack hesitated, wanting to voice the questions he'd been waiting five years to ask. *Were you the one behind the theft of the Van Gogh? Did you have my child kidnapped and brutally murdered? Were you the monster, Calderon? Are you still?*

Rage flared, a cauterizing white laser. Jack could feel it burning through his heart and out his eyes, etching the questions in flames on the other man's soul.

Calderon went quiet, but his eyes were piercingly focused.

There was a moment, a connection, and though Jack didn't believe in such things, had ceased to believe in anything years ago, his breath stung in his nostrils. He felt as if he knew Webb Calderon from somewhere, as if they'd shared something. Christ, he did know this man. He *was* this man. He also knew that Calderon had given him an answer, but the meaning wasn't available to him.

"We humans do what we have to," Calderon said. "The rest we leave to the gods. Go do what you have to do, Jack," he urged. "It will eat you alive if you don't."

"I don't know what the fuck you're talking about."

"I'm talking about you, a man who lost everything. Energy lives only to destroy itself. That's its sole purpose, and you're overflowing with it. *Virtu spirituale.* Use the energy. Don't let it destroy you."

Jack found it painful to breathe. "What do you know about the theft of the Van Gogh still life? The one that was stolen from the warehouse vault in El Segundo five years ago? *What do you know about it, Calderon?*"

Webb shook his head. "Nothing that will help you now.

You couldn't save Maggie, but you can save Gus. Go to her. Save your wife, Jack. Save yourself."

"Calderon!"

"You'll have to kill me. I've told you everything I can."

"You fucking bastard!"

"Pull the trigger," he challenged. "Blow my head off. Do it! I'd welcome it."

Jack stepped away from the pit. "If you're lying—"

The art dealer cut him off. "If I'm sending you into a trap, the odds are you won't come out alive. And even if you beat the odds, don't bother making the trip back. I won't be here."

Jack took Webb Calderon's car and sped south on highway 395, heading back to Los Angeles, barely aware of what he was doing or where he was going until he hit the sinuous curves of the 14 freeway and began to ascend into the hills of the Angeles National Forest. His emotions had been locked up in solitary for so long there were times when he couldn't remember what it was like to feel anything but a kind of deadened self-hatred, and even that barely felt real. He was the man without a heart who carved hearts on trees.

Only now he was a man with so much pain he couldn't breathe without feeling it. Emotion made you sloppy? He wanted to laugh. The thundering claw-hammer in his chest had taken over his will. It was ripping his heart from its bearings. It was taking him home and to hell with the consequences, to hell with anything but getting to Gus.

Calderon's black Jaguar XJS clung to the road as Jack roared through the eerie hills, blue with moonlight. The curves rushed at him at ninety miles an hour, and the image that exploded in his mind was an incendiary car crash, a woman dead, and a baby murdered.

He began to shake and his hands closed on the wheel.

Emotion made you sloppy. Emotion killed.

He couldn't do this. He had to stop. He had to think it through.

*   *   *

He had no idea how long he sat parked on the shoulder of an isolated access road, contemplating his next step, the one that would plunge him off the cliff. It felt like hours. It felt like days he was so cold. Something had locked off inside him, some instinct that was so fundamentally indoctrinated in guerrilla survival, nothing could block it. The risk in going after Gus was incalculable. He'd already realized that, but it wasn't a question of his own safety. It wasn't about redemption, either. There was so little left of him to save it was laughable.

This was about lost hope and shattered lives. It was his chance to give meaning to mindless destruction and make the tragedies count for something. He'd been waiting five long years, his whole life it seemed, and now he was about to forfeit everything on a reckless attempt to rescue a woman who'd wanted him dead from the first moment she saw him and a little girl he barely knew. The fact that the rescue attempt was almost surely a setup didn't concern him nearly as much as the possibility that Gus was in on it. Enveloped in the strange blue glow of the moon, he had even begun to question her claim of pregnancy. What a perfect way to ensnare him. What a sublime trap.

He glanced into the rearview mirror, saw the cold heat burning in his eyes. Was she capable of betraying him that way? He didn't know. He didn't want to know, but he wasn't sure he had a choice. Gus was his wife, Bridget the child of her heart. They were virtual strangers to him compared to the memories he carried, but both had become a part of his life, and undeniably, his heart. . . .

The first golden light of dawn was coming over the hills when he made his decision. He keyed the XJS to life, pulled it around, and floored the gas pedal, leaving a flying wake of sand and dirt behind him. It took him another forty minutes to get back to the Featherstone estate, and when he did, he spotted the stakeout car immediately.

He had to assume the back driveway that led to the guest cottages was under surveillance as well, so he put the luxury car to the test on a rugged horse trail that took him behind the property. He abandoned the Jaguar in a dry creek bed, hoping it wasn't one of the riding paths Lily normally took, and headed for the house on foot. He'd already accessed and disabled the external security with his software, and he'd assembled the equipment he would need once he got inside the mansion. The one trick that was beyond even The Magician was invisibility. Somehow he had to get into the house unseen.

Fortunately, he had a distraction planned.

CHAPTER
27

THE BACK STAIRWAY TOOK HIM UP TO THE THIRD FLOOR AND Gus's bedroom. He'd half expected someone to be watching her room, but the hallway was deserted, and what he saw when he eased the door open was a magnificently flounced canopy bed and a silent, supine form, covered only by a sheet.

Sleeping Beauty, he thought. She was straight out of one of Bridget's ballets. The claw-hammer twisted in his chest, defying his attempt to keep the pain at bay. He'd bought some time. The guards and the cops would be busy with the horses he'd let loose from the stables and stampeded toward the guard gate. What he had to do next might be the hardest thing of all. He had to wake Gus and talk to her. He would know if she was lying the moment he looked in her eyes.

As he approached the bed and got a closer look at her, his heart wrenched. She was frighteningly still and gaunt. Her breasts swelled against the ribbed tank top that had driven him crazy a time or two, and his eyes flicked there involuntarily, but the thought that struck him was that she was barely breathing.

He wanted to gather her up in his arms and get her out of there. Instead, he sat down beside her and touched her pale face. She felt feverish and cold at the same time, clearly in need of medical attention. She began to stir under his touch, and as her lashes fluttered and lifted, he shushed her gently and told her that everything was all right. But it wasn't.

Her grief-stricken expression answered all his questions, even the ones he'd barely allowed himself to ask. If this was a setup, she had nothing to do with it.

"The baby," she said, her voice breaking. "I'm sorry."

Tears welled in her eyes and something closed off in Jack's throat, a constriction he knew would be with him as long as he lived. Part of the price of loving her would be remembering this moment. "It's all right," he promised. "There will be lots of babies if that's what you want, Gus, as many as you want."

She reached out to him, and he gathered her into his arms, needing to hold her, afraid he would hurt her. He would wait to let her tell him how it had happened. This wasn't the time. She was still grieving, and his heart felt as if it were cracking open, rupturing from its center, as he rocked her in his arms. He was sure he was dying, and yet somehow he knew that this was the opposite of dying. He was coming alive, perhaps for the first time ever.

"Those agents from the Treasury Department—" She struggled to explain. "They were going to take me in for questioning, but I couldn't go, I was too ill . . . and then the bleeding started."

"Shhh," he said quickly, wishing he could stop her. "Don't talk now, rest."

"I thought you'd run away." She buried her face in his fleece jacket. "When I woke up, and you were gone, I wasn't even surprised. Everyone I love runs away. I know it's my fault. I push people away, I won't let them love me, but you—" Her voice caught on a heartbroken sob, and her body shook. "You, I wanted to stay."

There was nothing he could do to ease her misery. It was

too close to the surface. It was a thorn in her flesh, and she had to get it out. But she wasn't lashing out as she'd always done before. Instead she seemed driven by the impulse to reach out to another human heart, to heal herself, the way blood rushes to a new wound. And God, he wanted desperately to help her heal.

"Look at me," she said, clinging fast to his shoulders. "Look at what you've done to me."

His heart went cold and still. Did she hold him responsible for losing the baby? What was she saying? That this was the second child he'd caused to be sacrificed through some well-intentioned blunder?

"You made me believe," she croaked.

"Made you believe?"

"In Cinderella, in that stupid fairy tale. You made me believe in love when I knew—when I've always known—that love hurts, it destroys."

"No—" Much as he wanted to deny her assertion, he knew that love did hurt, it could destroy.

"Yes," she insisted, "you pried me open like a shell and forced me to feel everything I was terrified of. I felt it all, Jack. I felt it all with you, even the pain. I thought I was going to break in two when I found you gone."

"I came back, Gus. I'm here."

She shuddered and clung to him. "You made me believe," she whispered. "You made me believe in love."

He didn't know if holding her tight would stave off the agony that was welling in his chest, but he couldn't help himself. Gently he kissed her temple. "Don't stop believing now," he said. "You have to believe, Gus . . . because I do love you."

Her chin trembled and the lips that had so much trouble forming words failed her. She looked up at him, tears glittering like stars. Their brightness ripped through him.

Nothing she said could have touched him the way her forlorn, searching gaze did. The physical beauty people talked about was insignificant compared to this. There was real beauty in her now, the kind that came from courage and burned bright and hot. She was risking everything to trust him. She did believe. And he couldn't let her down. He would die first.

Her mouth worked to speak, or perhaps to smile, but she couldn't manage either. He felt as if he were watching her be born, a brittle shell crumbling away, a naked, wondrous thing emerging. Her face was suffused with color. Her eyes quivered with life. But a moment later those beautiful violet eyes had clouded over with fear.

"What is it?" he asked.

The energy seemed to drain out of her. "I went to Webb Calderon for money."

"I know, Gus. It's all right."

"No, it isn't. He knew about the kidnapping, and he asked me questions about you. He wanted to know where you took me, where your hideout was. He said you were someone called The Magician—"

Her voice cracked and gave out. Jack tried to quiet her, but her agitation was too great.

"It's not safe here," she told him. "There are police everywhere. They're looking for you—"

Jack's senses picked up a soft but deadly click. It had come from behind, from the doorway. "Quiet," he whispered to Gus. "Don't move or scream. Don't do anything."

The sense of separation was almost a physical thing as he settled her in the ruffled chintz pillows. It was like ripping off an arm, but he had no choice. If he was right, their lives were at stake. In order to protect her, he had to cut himself off from her, from the tenderness he felt for her.

He touched her mouth, signaling her to be silent, and then he rose from the bed and turned. "What took you so long?" he asked the woman who had entered the room.

Lily Featherstone was standing in the bedroom doorway, a small revolver in her hand. Jack recognized it as a .38 Special, a gun made especially for women. He wasn't in any way surprised to see it. Or her. During their one brief encounter in the stairway, he'd sensed an explosive quality to Lily, something roiling beneath the surface ice. She'd impressed him as the type who would be capable of almost anything under the right circumstances, including this.

"She was waiting for me."

Ward McHenry materialized in the doorway, and Jack found himself searching the man's craggy features and lofty demeanor in mild disbelief. This time he *was* surprised. He'd been expecting Lake, not the Featherstone chairman. Perhaps this family drama was not going to play out quite the way he'd anticipated.

Jack raised his hands in the traditional gesture of surrender and prayed Gus wouldn't do anything foolish. She'd seemed too emotionally and physically spent for heroics. He hoped that was true. "Just for the record," he said, asking the question of Lily. "Who framed me for the theft of the Picasso? Because if it was the two of you, I'd like to extend my compliments."

Lily smiled faintly. "Frame you? Why would we do that? It's Gus we intend to frame, for your murder."

The bed creaked softly behind him, and Jack realized that Gus was reacting to Lily's pronouncement. It had rocked him, too, particularly the eerie calm with which she'd said it. "So it was you who rigged the weight room? And the hit-and-run?"

Neither Lily nor McHenry answered him, but the glittery quiver of triumph in Lily's eyes told him that she was instrumental in all of it, perhaps even the instigator. The woman was anything but calm. She was dangerously wired, probably from the rush of her newfound power, Jack realized. It might as well have been a drug she was so high.

"Isn't that a pretty extreme way to reassume control of Gus's trust money?" he asked, hazarding a guess at their motives.

"It would be," McHenry said, "if that's what we wanted. Gus's trust is only a small part of the prize. Her voting stock, combined with mine and Lily's, will give us the majority share."

And kick Lake totally out of the picture, Jack thought. Apparently Lily's twin wasn't in on this. "And my death is going to help you accomplish that?" he asked. It was more than curiosity on Jack's part. He needed to keep them talking.

"Precisely." Lily's tone was soft, scathing.

McHenry gave her a quelling look, and she quieted, but for a moment Jack had thought she was going to turn the gun on him. Lily Featherstone had been surrounded by powerful men all her life, Jack realized, and quite possibly she had let them control her. Now she was grabbing some power for herself. Jack guessed before she was through, she would have total control. She would be running everything, even McHenry.

"You're going to shoot me?" Jack pressed, again to Lily. He was hoping to provoke an argument, but McHenry seemed more than willing to clear up his confusion.

"It won't be Lily who pulls the trigger as far as the police are concerned," the older man explained. "It will be your wife. Gus has been trying to kill you off since the day you coerced her into marrying you. Today she's going to succeed with a gun she took from Lily's drawer."

Jack knew it wouldn't be difficult to establish that Gus had shot and killed him, especially after the car accident. He hadn't reported that it was a car with her plates, but Lily could easily come forward during the investigation with information that would implicate Gus.

Jack curled his fingers into the strip of tape that was stuck to his palm, just one of the surprises he had planned for this family get-together. He'd wired a remote that was hidden in the lining of his workout jacket. "I still don't see how my death will give you control of anything."

"Not your death," McHenry said, "*hers*. Sadly, Gus is going to crack under the emotional strain and have an accident. As trust officer, I'll be required to reassume control of the trust, as well as her voting shares. The board isn't likely to object, especially when Lily and I present a united front."

"Ward," Lily warned. "He's up to something!"

Every good magician has something up his sleeve, Jack thought as he stabbed the trigger. An explosion rocked the grounds outside. It lit up the room like a signal flare. Windows rattled and shook with the concussion.

Startled, Lily reared backward. Her hand flew up, and

McHenry shouted at her to give him the gun. When she wouldn't, he tried to wrestle it away from her. A shot rang out, blasting a hole in the ceiling. Fortunately, Jack was on top of the man before either he or Lily could do any more damage.

Jack made quick work of subduing and disposing of both of them. Gus was sitting up by now, and though her wan features still concerned him, he tossed her the .38 with instructions to keep them at gunpoint while he bound, gagged and stashed the "united front" in the bathroom for safekeeping. Once he had that accomplished, he gave Gus a crash course on the gun's use, cautioning her at length about being careful.

"Stay here," he told her, gently but emphatically. He wanted to say a great deal more, but the constriction in his throat made that impossible as he bent to kiss her lips. Tenderness flowed through him. "I'll come back for you," he promised. "I'm going to get Bridget."

"Please," she whispered as he slipped out the door. "Don't d-die."

Jack found Bridget hiding in her closet, frightened by the explosion. The noise had drawn the housekeeper outside with everyone else, so he took a moment to calm the child. She was hidden amidst a profusion of toys and ballet gear, and as he coaxed her out, he noticed the trail of white footprints she left on the shiny hardwood floor.

"It's flour," she explained, obviously pleased with herself. "Remember how you told me that I should powder around the outside of the room to see if Frances was sneaking in through some hidden passage? Well, I did? Look, I powdered the whole room! I used Frances's sifter from the kitchen."

The evidence of her handiwork was everywhere. There was a path of pale dust decorating the perimeter of the entire place, except for the doorways. She'd done it exactly the way he'd described, too, sprinkling a thin film that resembled house dust more than flour. Unless you were looking for it, you'd never notice it. "Did you catch her?" he asked.

She scratched her nose with her knuckle as if she were about to sneeze. "Not exactly. But I powdered the linen closet and then I did the storage room in the basement, too, because she uses those rooms alot, and guess what?" She scrunched her face, then beamed at him.

"You found something?" Jack remembered telling her that footprints leading to a solid wall could indicate a secret passageway, but his only thought had been to entertain her.

"In the storage room! Cool, huh? I spotted footprints in the flour by the back wall, so that proves it. She *is* spying on me. She's coming up from the basement. I just haven't figured out how she gets in here yet."

A surge of adrenaline nearly took off the top of Jack's head. "Bridge, can you keep a promise?" At her eager nod, he knelt and caught hold of her arm. "Promise me you'll stay right here until I get back. Can you do that? If you get scared, go back in the closet, and I'll find you, but stay here, all right?"

"Are you going to find the passageway for me?" Her eyes bugged with excitement as he nodded.

"I'm going to try," he said.

The storage room did have a secret panel, but it didn't lead to the passageway that Bridget had hoped for. The panel opened onto a vaultlike room with a door that Jack scanned with a metal detector from his bag of tricks. A pinging noise told him there was a magnetic device within the door. From his experience that kind of device kept a metal lever from depressing the alarm switch until the door was opened. It was a relatively simple concept as intrusion detectors went, and he quickly defeated it with a powerful magnet of his own.

The small room he found himself in was a storage area for fine art, and the first painting that caught his eye was the one he'd recently been searching for. Blush looked as if she'd been hastily propped against the shelves and abandoned. Jack felt another slam-dunk of adrenaline. His heart jerked hard, and his skull throbbed with it as he crouched beside her and picked her up, cradling the frame in his palms.

He didn't have time to admire her. He had to find what she was concealing, if anything. A damp finger rubbed over a corner of her skirt revealed no signs of another artist's work painted underneath, but the loose grips on the back of the frame made him think that she might have been stretched over another canvas. If that was the case, the other painting had already been removed, he realized. He was too late.

Despair washed over him, sapping him of strength for a moment. His skull was still throbbing hotly, but now it was the pain of an incipient headache. It was even an effort to push to his feet. Christ, was this *never* to end? He felt as if he'd had the sealed book of Fate in his hands, and it had been snatched away from him again.

A faint scuffing behind him alerted him that he wasn't alone. The sound was so slight it registered on his nerves more than his conscious mind, but when he turned, it was to one of the most confounding sights he'd ever seen.

Lake and Bridget had entered the room behind him, and the child looked as if she were about to cry. It took Jack another moment to register that Lake was holding a gun to the child's head. He had a Walther .380 pressed to her temple.

"Bridget told me you might be down here," Lake explained. "I found her in her closet. She said the explosion had frightened her, and you'd told her to stay there."

The little girl hadn't realized what she was doing by telling Lake, Jack knew. She had simply responded to her uncle's questions. His heart went out to her now. She was terrified and bewildered, perhaps even thinking she'd caused this nightmare. He tried to reassure her with a silent nod, and then his gaze flicked to her captor, murderously. If he could have gotten his hands on the man without endangering Bridget, Lake would have had the gun rammed down his sick throat.

Jack no longer needed to find the Van Gogh. "It was you, wasn't it," he said, searching Lake's fine-boned features for the signs of depravity he knew must be hidden there. "You sent the thugs who terrorized my family. You had my child kidnapped and killed."

"Your child wasn't killed." Lake's thumb dragged down the hammer, forcing a sharp click out of the gun. It echoed like a rifle blast in the small room. "But this time she *will* be."

Bridget whimpered with fear, and Jack stared at the five-year-old, his heart freezing. His brain could barely make sense of what was happening, but some instinctive part of him knew the moment he began to search her imploring blue eyes and her round, tear-stained features. In that one life-turning moment he understood that she was the infant who'd been taken five years ago. His child.

He said her name. "Haley . . . ?"

"I had nothing to do with the kidnapping—"

It was Lake who spoke, but Jack barely heard the man other than to register that he was apparently making a feeble attempt to disassociate himself from the crime.

"The men who approached you did work for me," Lake went on, seemingly determined to explain. "But I had no idea they would resort to anything as desperate as kidnapping. Their instructions were to persuade you to cooperate, nothing more. I was horrified when I found out what they'd done. And when I learned that they were planning to sell the baby on the black market, I had to intervene—"

Jack tore his gaze from Bridget, enraged as he thought about the devastation that Lake's "instructions" had brought about. "Horrified? If your conscience was bothering you that badly, why didn't you give her back to me?"

"I couldn't," Lake averred softly. "My younger sister, Jillian, was dying of anorexia. We'd done everything we could—doctors, clinics, but nothing helped. She admitted to me once that she'd always wanted a baby and regretted terribly that the anorexia had made her sterile. I urged her to get well so that she could have a child of her own, but by that time it was too late. Her sterility couldn't be reversed."

Jack stared at him, disbelieving. "And you thought that gave you the right to steal someone else's child?"

Lake's shoulders lifted. An expiration seemed to weaken his voice. "Jillian believed it would save her life. She actually believed she couldn't die if she had something important to live for, something as precious as a baby. So I had some adoption papers falsified, and I gave her Bridget."

Jack's hand formed a fist. Unfortunately he didn't have another trick up his sleeve, nothing taped to his palm. It was just him against this demented man, who clearly thought that his name and his privileged existence put him at the front of the line where human needs were concerned.

"She was my sister." Lake's voice dropped to a softness that asked, even begged, Jack to understand. "She was *dying*. Bridget was her last chance. I had to give her that."

"My *wife* died. She killed herself because of what you did. Or they killed her, I don't know which. It hardly matters now."

Lake seized upon that. "But it does matter! It's all that matters, don't you see? They were the ones who came up with the plan and executed it. They were—they *are*—the kidnappers, the murderers, not me. I can supply you with their names," he offered. "I can tell you how to find them."

Rage shook through Jack—black, blinding rage that he had to strangle off before it could find its way into his reflexes. He wanted to kill the bastard, crush him where he stood. It would be easy enough to do. Lake had no resources but a gun that he might not have the courage to use, and the odds were that Jack could take him down before he got a shot off.

But the five-year-old child who was watching Jack's every move had terror rising in her eyes, and Jack would not let himself contribute to that. He'd already lost her once trying to be a hero. Now he was sworn to protect her no matter what that required him to do, even if it meant bargaining with a moral monster like Lake Featherstone.

He pulled a breath, aware that he had to have some answers before he could do anything else. "How much did Gus know about this? Did she know Bridget was mine?"

Lake used the question to further justify what he'd done. "She knew Bridget was adopted and that it wasn't done through the normal channels, but that was all. She didn't speak of it, none of us did. We were a family, trying to save one of our own. Can't you understand that?"

Gus didn't know. That brought Jack a moment of relief, the first he'd had in days. Now he was free to believe, just as she was, except there was a man holding a gun on him, a man holding his heart hostage. "What about Calderon?" he asked. "How is he involved?"

"Calderon?" Lake seemed genuinely startled at the question. "Calderon is involved in *everything*, but don't ask me how. The man is a total enigma. The art world calls him a dealer and a buying agent, but he's a great deal more than that. He wields enormous power, frightening power. It wouldn't surprise me if he were running the black market in art—"

It was all Jack could do not to spin and kick the bastard's head off. "Save the tribute," he bit out. "I want to know whether he was behind any of this."

Lake's crooked smile turned into laughter—weak, cracked laughter. "I couldn't possibly tell you. I imagine he's in on everything in one way or another. He came to my aid once years ago when I found myself in possession of stolen artifacts and was in danger of being prosecuted. He took the merchandise off my hands. He handled everything."

"Did he take the Van Gogh off your hands?"

"No! Oh, no, I wouldn't part with the still life, not for any price. My father wanted it, you see. All his life he coveted that painting. He actually told me once that nothing he'd accomplished mattered because he'd never been able to acquire the Van Gogh for his collection. He'd had his chance, too. He was in the bidding at Christie's, but he lost his nerve. I didn't—"

Lake indicated a hastily rolled canvas lying on a storage shelf near him. The Van Gogh, Jack realized.

Lake's mouth shook as he spoke. "*I didn't lose my nerve.*"

Jack could see the signs. The man was on the edge. It

wouldn't take much to push him over, but Jack would have to be careful. Push too hard and Bridget went with him.

He softened his voice. "Your sister's been trying her damndest to kill me, but I guess you know all about that, don't you, Lake. I guess you know about her and McHenry."

Lake's head lifted. His eyes narrowed, glinting. "What do you mean? Lily? McHenry? What are you saying?"

Jack merely smiled.

"Tell me, godammit!" Lake lurched forward, jerking the child with him. "What *about* Lily and Ward?"

"They didn't share their grand plan with you?"

"What grand plan?"

"They were going to get rid of me and Gus, assume control of Gus's voting stock, and take over the company. Interesting that they didn't tell you, Lake. I wonder why? Maybe because you were going to be next?"

"Lily?" he breathed his sister's name as if it were part of a religious litany, something mystical. His expression took on a desperate, bewildered quality, as if he couldn't possibly assimilate what Jack had told him. "Lily with Ward McHenry? I don't believe you."

The twins both harbored a fatal flaw, Jack realized, but that was where the similarity ended. Lily coveted power, while her brother coveted Lily. He was obsessed with her.

"You don't believe me?" Jack said softly. "Go upstairs and check Gus's bathroom. Your sister and Ward McHenry are tied up there. *Together*."

Fury shook Lake's body. The gun jerked in his hand.

Bridget made a strange sound and shrank away, and as Lake yanked her back, Jack knew terror beyond his darkest nightmares, terror beyond all reason. Lake was losing it. He was even crazy enough to pull a trigger without even realizing it. The man holding his daughter hostage was having a nervous breakdown, and there was nothing Jack could do. Nothing he dared do.

"Let her go," Jack said.

Rage flared, and with it came Webb Calderon's voice. *Virtu spirituale*. It stormed Jack's senses with deafening chaos, but in the eerie silence at the back of his mind, he heard a dream-like sound—the scrape of footsteps in the hallway.

Lake heard them, too, and whirled. "You?" he cried softly. He stumbled back, revealing the figure who'd crept up behind him. It was Gus and she had the gun. Jack doubted she had the strength to use it, but her presence alone gave him what he needed, an opening.

"Gus, watch out!" Bridget cried. She twisted out of Lake's hold and ducked down, scrambling toward her aunt.

In the confusion Jack lunged for Lake and caught him by the head and shoulders. The two men crashed to the ground and rolled, the Walther firing repeatedly, wildly, as if Lake's finger was convulsing on the trigger.

The gun was frozen in Lake's fist, and Jack knew he had a madman on his hands. Gus or Bridget could have been hit by a stray bullet! Fury made him violent. He slammed Lake's arm to the ground with a force that shook the small room. The weapon flew free, but Lake reared up in a frenzy, swinging and slashing with the strength of the possessed.

Jack blocked the wild blows and connected with a single savage uppercut that knocked Lake cold and sprawled him out on the floor. Half-hoping he'd killed him, Jack sprang up and searched the room.

Gus and Bridget were in a heap by the door. Something near terror gripped him, but by the time he got to them, Jack realized they weren't hit, just badly frightened. He scooped Gus into his arms, then reached out for Bridget, and the three of them clung to each other, heads bowed, hearts flooding out their fear and relief. It was probably only moments, but it seemed a very long time before Jack began to feel himself calming. Still, he didn't know if he could ever let go of them, either one of them.

"Thank you," Gus whispered.

"For what?" he asked.

"For not dying."

He wanted to laugh, but all he could do was shake his head.

Finally Bridget roused and peered at him searchingly. Her eyes were full of fear and wonder. "Who's Haley?" she asked.

Jack's throat seized painfully. Now he had to laugh or he would have cried. "Haley is someone I loved very much," he told her. "Someone I thought I'd lost."

He drew her back, melded by the sudden, fierce love that flooded him. It *was* love, Jack realized, pure and undiluted, and he had never known anything its equal in his life. The kiss he pressed to his wife's tear-soaked face whispered of feelings that were shouting to the heavens. The staggering relief he felt trembled in his soul. But as he gave up thanks, he was aware of the profound silence all around them, as if the gods were listening, as if the gods were pleased.

A mere mortal had stolen their fire and used it well.